Dear Reader,

Welcome to *Big Sky Mountain*, near the town of Parable, Montana.

Hutch Carmody is as much a part of the land as his favorite hideout, the mountain overlooking Whisper Creek Ranch, his home since birth. With both parents gone, he's the sole owner, and he's determined to keep it that way. After ditching one bride at the altar, he's not in the market for another, but his feelings for former flame Kendra Shepherd aren't so easy to shake off. She's beautiful, she's sexy and she's smart—everything Hutch wants and admires in a woman—but she's already burned him once, running off to England to marry a title and a lot of money. Now that she's back in Parable, with a small daughter in tow, he's as jumpy as cold water on a hot griddle.

Kendra, determined to raise her little girl with all the emotional security she *didn't* have as a child, sees Parable, with its down-home values and salt-of-the-earth folks, as the perfect place to do that. She's not about to complicate matters with a husband, having learned the hard way that she's better off on her own than married. Even if she wanted a man in her life, though, she certainly wouldn't be stupid enough to choose a renegade rancher-cowboy like Hutch.

So what if he makes her heart race like a runaway Thoroughbred?

My very best,

Linda Lael Miller

LINDA LAEL MILLER

BIG SKY
Mountain

HARLEQUIN®
entertain, enrich, inspire™

Recycling programs
for this product may
not exist in your area.

ISBN-13: 978-0-373-77661-0

BIG SKY MOUNTAIN

In loving memory of my cherished beagle-dog, Sadie.
I'm grateful for every second of our eleven years together.

CHAPTER ONE

A FINE SWEAT broke out between Hutch Carmody's shoulders and his gut warned that he was fixing to stumble straight into the teeth of a screeching buzz saw. The rented tux itched against his hide and his collar seemed to be getting tighter with every flower-scented breath he drew.

The air was dense, weighted, cloying. The small church was overheated, especially for a sunny day in mid-June, and the pews were crammed with eager guests, a few weeping women and a fair number of skeptics.

Hutch's best man, Boone Taylor, fidgeted beside him.

The organist sounded a jarring chord and then launched into a perky tune Hutch didn't recognize. The first of three bridesmaids, all clad in silly-looking pink dresses more suited to little girls than grown women—in his opinion anyhow—drag-stepped her way up the aisle to stand beside the altar, across from him and Boone.

Hutch's head reeled, but he quickly reminded himself, silently of course, that he had to live in this town—his ranch was just a few miles outside of it. If he passed out cold at his own wedding, he'd still be getting ribbed about it when he was ninety.

While the next bridesmaid started forward, he did his distracted best to avoid so much as glancing toward Brylee Parrish, his wife to be, who was standing at the back of the church beside her brother, Walker. He knew all too well how good she looked in that heirloom wedding gown of hers, with its billowing veil and dazzling sprinkle of rhinestones.

Brylee was beautiful, with cascades of red-brown hair that tumbled to her waist when she let it down. Her wide-set hazel eyes revealed passion, as well as formidable intelligence, humor and a country girl's in-born practicality.

He was a lucky man.

Brylee, on the other hand, was not so fortunate, having hooked up with the likes of him. She deserved a husband who loved her.

Suddenly, Hutch's gaze connected with that of his half brother, Slade Barlow. Seated near the front, next to his very pregnant wife, Joslyn, Slade slowly shook his head from side to side, his expression so solemn that a person would have thought somebody was about to be buried instead of hitched to one of the choicest women Parable County had ever produced.

Hutch's insides churned, then coalesced into a quivering gob and did a slow, backward roll.

The last bridesmaid had arrived.

The minister was in place.

The smell of the flowers intensified, nearly overwhelming Hutch.

And then the first notes of "Here Comes the Bride" rang out.

Hutch felt the room—hell, the whole planet—sway again.

Brylee, beaming behind the thin fabric of her veil, nodded in response to something her brother whispered to her and they stepped forward.

"Hold it," Hutch heard himself say loudly enough to be heard over the thundering joy of the organ. He held up both hands, like a referee about to call a foul in some fast-paced game. "Stop."

Everything halted—with a sickening lurch.

The music died.

The bride and her brother seemed frozen in mid-stride.

Hutch would have sworn the universe itself had stopped expanding.

"This is all wrong," he went on miserably, but with his back straight and his head up. It wasn't as if he hadn't broached the subject with Brylee before—he'd been trying to get out of this fix for weeks. Just the night before, in fact, he'd sat Brylee down in a vinyl upholstered booth at the Silver Lanes snack bar and told her straight out that he had serious misgivings about getting married and needed some breathing space.

Brylee had cried, her mascara smudging, her nose reddening at the tip.

"You don't mean it," she'd said, which was her standard response to any attempt he made to put on the brakes before they both plummeted over a matrimonial cliff. "You're just nervous, that's all. It's entirely normal. But once the wedding is over and we're on our honeymoon—"

Hutch couldn't stand it when a woman cried, especially when he was the cause of her tears. Like every other time, he'd backed down, tried to convince himself that Brylee was right—he just had cold feet, that was all.

Now, though, "push" had run smack up against "shove."

It was now or never.

He faced Brylee squarely.

The universe unfroze itself, like some big machine with rusted gears, and all hell broke loose.

Brylee threw down her bouquet, stomped on it once, whirled on one heel and rushed out of the church. Walker flung a beleaguered and not entirely friendly look in Hutch's direction, then turned to go after his sister.

The guests, already on their feet in honor of the bride, all started talking at once, abuzz with shock and speculation.

Things like this might happen in books or movies, but they *didn't* happen in Parable, Montana.

Until now, Hutch reflected dismally.

He started to follow Brylee out of the church, not an easy proposition with folks crowding the aisle. He didn't have the first clue what he could say to her, but he figured he had to say *something*.

Before he'd taken two strides, though, Slade and Boone closed in on him from either side, each taking a firm grip on one of his arms.

"Let her go," Boone said quietly.

"There's nothing you can do," Slade confirmed.

With that, they hustled him quickly out of the main chapel and into the small side room where the choir robes, hymnals and Communion gear were stored.

Hutch wondered if a lynch mob was forming back there in the sanctuary.

"You picked a fine time to change your mind about getting married," Boone remarked, but his tone was light and his eyes twinkled with something that looked a lot like relief.

Hutch unfastened his fancy tie and shoved it into one coat pocket. Then he opened his collar halfway to his breastbone and sucked in a breath. "I tried to tell her," he muttered. He knew it sounded lame, but the truth was the truth.

Although he and Slade shared a father, they had been at bloody-knuckled odds most of their lives. They'd made some progress toward getting along since the old man's death and the upheaval that followed, but neither of them related to the other as a buddy, let alone a brother.

"Come on out to our place," Slade said, surprising him. "You'd best lay low for a few hours. Give Brylee— and Walker—a little time to cool off."

Hutch stiffened slightly, though he found the invitation oddly welcome. Home, being Whisper Creek Ranch, was a lonely outpost these days—which was probably why he'd talked himself into proposing to Brylee in the first place.

"I have to talk to Brylee," he repeated.

"There'll be time for that later on," Slade reasoned.

"Slade's right," Boone agreed. Boone, being violently allergic to marriage himself, probably thought Hutch had just dodged a figurative bullet.

Or maybe he was remembering that Brylee was a crack shot with a pistol, a rifle, or a Civil War cannon.

Given what had just happened, she was probably leaning toward the cannon right about now.

Hutch sighed. "All right," he said to Slade. "I'll kick

back at your place for a while—but I've got to stop off at home first, so I can change out of this monkey suit."

"Fine," Slade agreed. "I'll round up the women and meet you at the Windfall in an hour or two."

By "the women," Slade meant his lovely wife, Joslyn, his teenage stepdaughter, Shea, and Opal Dennison, the force-of-nature who kept house for the Barlow outfit. Slade's mother, Callie, had had the good grace to skip the ceremony—old scandals die hard in a town the size of Parable and recollections of her long-ago affair with Carmody Senior, from which Slade had famously resulted, were as sharp as ever.

Today's escapade would put all that in the shade, of course. Tongues were wagging and jaws were flapping for sure—by now, various up-to-the-minute accounts were probably popping up on all the major social media sites. Before Slade and Boone had dragged Hutch out of the sanctuary, he'd seen several people whip out their cell phones and start texting. A few pictures had been taken, too, with those same ubiquitous devices.

The thought of all that amateur reporting made Hutch close his eyes for a moment. "Shit," he murmured.

"Knee-deep and rising," Slade confirmed, sounding resigned.

KENDRA SAT AT the antique table in her best friend Joslyn's kitchen, with Callie Barlow in the chair directly across from hers. The ranch house was unusually quiet, with its usual occupants gone to town.

A glance over one shoulder assured Kendra that her recently adopted four-year-old daughter, Madison, was still napping on a padded window seat, her stuffed purple kangaroo, Rupert, clenched in her arms. The little girl's gleaming hair, the color of a newly minted penny, lay in tousled curls around her cherubic face and Kendra felt the usual pang of hopeless devotion just looking at her.

This long-sought, hard-won, much-wanted child.

This miracle.

Not that every woman would have seen the situation from the same perspective as Kendra did—Madison was, after all, living proof that Jeffrey had been unfaithful, a constant reminder that it was dangerous to love, treacherous to trust, foolish to believe in another person too much. But none of that had mattered to Kendra in the end—she'd essentially been abandoned herself as a small child, left to grow up with a disinterested grandmother, and that gave her a special affinity for Madison. Besides, Jeffrey, having returned to his native England after summarily ending their marriage, had been dying.

Some men might have turned to family for help in such a situation—Jeffrey Chamberlain came from a very wealthy and influential one—but in this case, that wasn't possible. Jeffrey's aging parents were landed gentry with a string of titles, several sprawling estates and a fortune that dated back to the heyday of the East India Company, and were no more inclined toward child-rearing than they had been when their own two sons were small. They'd left Jeffrey and his brother in the care of nannies and housekeepers from infancy, and shipped them off to boarding school as soon as they turned six.

Understandably, Jeffrey hadn't wanted that kind of cold and isolated childhood for his daughter.

So he'd sent word to Kendra that he had to see her, in person. He had something important to tell her.

She'd made that first of several trips to the U.K., keeping protracted vigils at her ex-husband's hospital bedside while he drifted in and out of consciousness.

Eventually, he'd managed to get his message across: he told her about Madison, living somewhere in the U.S., and begged Kendra to find his daughter, adopt her and bring her up in love and safety. She was, he told her, the only person on earth he could or would trust with the child.

Kendra wanted nothing so much as a child and, during their brief marriage, Jeffrey had denied her repeated requests to start a family. It was a bitter pill to swallow, learning that he'd refused her a baby and then fathered one with someone else, someone he'd met on a business trip.

She'd done what Jeffrey asked, not so much for his sake—though she'd loved him once, or believed she did—as for Madison's. And her own.

The search hadn't been an easy one, even with the funds Jeffrey had set aside for the purpose, involving a great deal of web-surfing, phone calls and emails, travel and so many highs and lows that she nearly gave up several times.

Then it happened. She found Madison.

Kendra hadn't known what she'd feel upon actually meeting her former husband's child, but any doubts she might have had had been dispelled the moment—the *moment*—she'd met this cautious, winsome little girl.

The first encounter had taken place in a social worker's dingy office, in a dusty desert town in California, and for Kendra, it was love at first sight.

The forever kind of love.

Months of legal hassles had followed, but now, at long last, Kendra and Madison were officially mother and daughter, in the eyes of God and government, and Kendra knew she couldn't have loved her baby girl any more if she'd carried her in her own body for nine months.

Callie brought Kendra back to the present moment by reaching for the teapot in the center of the table and refilling Kendra's cup, then her own.

"Do you think it's over yet?" Kendra asked, instantly regretting the question but unable to hold back still another. "The wedding, I mean?"

Callie's smile was gentle as she glanced at the clock on the stove top and met Kendra's gaze again. "Probably," she said quietly. Then, without another word, she reached out to give Kendra's hand a light squeeze.

Madison, meanwhile, stirred on the window seat. "Mommy?"

Kendra turned again. "I'm here, honey," she said.

Although Madison was adjusting rapidly, in the resilient way of young children, she still had bad dreams sometimes and she tended to panic if she lost sight of Kendra for more than a moment.

"Are you hungry, sweetie?" Callie asked the little girl. Slade's mom would make a wonderful grandmother; she had a way with children, easy and forthright.

Madison shook her head as she moved toward Kendra and then scrambled up onto her lap.

"It's been a while since lunch," Kendra suggested, kissing the top of Madison's head and holding her close.

"Maybe you'd like a glass of milk and one of Opal's oatmeal raisin cookies?"

Again, Madison shook her head, snuggling closer still. "No, thank you," she said clearly, sounding, as she often did, more like a small adult than a four-year-old.

They'd arrived by car the night before and spent the night in the Barlows' guest room, at Joslyn's insistence.

The old house, the very heart of Windfall Ranch, was undergoing considerable renovation, which only added to the exuberant chaos of the place—and Madison was wary of everyone but Opal, the family housekeeper.

Just then, Slade and Joslyn's dog, Jasper, heretofore snoozing on his bed in front of the newly installed kitchen fireplace, sat bolt upright and gave a questioning little whine. His floppy ears were pitched slightly forward, though he seemed to be listening with his entire body. Joslyn's cat, Lucy-Maude, remained singularly unconcerned.

Madison looked at the animal with shy interest, still unsure whether to make friends with him or keep her distance.

"Well," Callie remarked, getting to her feet and heading for the nearest window, the one over the steel sink, and peering out as the sound of a car's engine reached them, "*they're* back early. They must have decided to skip the reception."

Jasper barked happily and hurried to the door. Joslyn had long since dubbed him the one-dog welcoming committee and at the moment he was spilling over with a wild desire to greet whoever happened to show up.

With a little chuckle, Callie opened the back door so Jasper could shoot through it like a fur-covered bullet, positively beside himself with joy. There was a little frown nestled between the older woman's eyebrows, though, as she looked toward Kendra again. "This is odd," she reiterated. "I hope Joslyn is feeling all right."

Shea, Slade's lovely dark-haired stepdaughter, just turned seventeen, burst into the house first, her violet eyes huge with excitement. "You're not going to *believe* this, Grands," she told Callie breathlessly. "The music was playing. The bridesmaids were all lined up and the preacher had his book open, ready to start. And what do you suppose happened?"

Kendra's heart fluttered in her chest, but she didn't speak.

A number of drastic scenarios flashed through her mind—a wedding guest toppling over from a heart attack, then a cattle truck crashing through a wall, followed by lightning boring its way right through the roof of the church and striking the bridegroom dead where he stood.

She shook the images off. Waited with her breath snagged painfully in the back of her throat.

"What?" Callie prodded good-naturedly, studying her step-granddaughter. She and Shea were close— the girl worked part-time at Callie's Curly Burly Hair Salon in town, and during the school year, Shea went to Callie's place after the last bell rang, spending hours tweaking the website she'd built for the shop.

"Hutch called the whole thing off," Shea blurted. "He stopped the wedding!"

"Oh, my," Callie said. The door was still open, and Kendra heard Joslyn's voice, then Opal's, as they came toward the house. Slade must have been with them, but he was keeping quiet, as usual.

Kendra realized she was squeezing Madison too tightly and relaxed her arms a little. Her mouth had dropped open at some point and she closed it, hoping no one had noticed. Just then, she couldn't have uttered a word if the place caught fire.

Opal, tall and dressed to the nines in one of her home-sewn and brightly patterned jersey dresses, crossed the threshold next, shaking her head as she unpinned her old-fashioned hat, with its tiny stuffed bird and inch-wide veiling.

Slade and Joslyn came in behind her, Joslyn's huge belly preceding her "by half an hour," as her adoring husband liked to say.

By then, the bomb dropped, Shea had shifted her focus to Madison. She'd been trying to win the little girl over from the beginning, and her smile dazzled, like sunlight on still waters. "Hey, kiddo," she said. "Since we missed out on the wedding cake, I'm up for a major cookie binge. Want to join me?"

Somewhat to Kendra's surprise, Madison slid down off her lap, Rupert the kangaroo dangling from one small hand, and approached the older girl, albeit slowly. "Okay," she said, her voice tentative.

Joslyn, meanwhile, lumbered over to the table, pulled back a chair and sank into it. She looked incandescent in her summery maternity dress, a blue confection with white polka dots, and she fanned her flushed face with her thin white clutch for a few moments before plunking it down on the tabletop.

"Do you need to lie down?" Callie asked her daughter-in-law worriedly, one hand resting on Joslyn's shoulder.

Madison and Shea, meanwhile, were plundering the cookie jar.

"No," Joslyn told her. "I'm fine. Really."

Opal tied on an apron and instructed firmly, "Now don't you girls stuff yourselves on those cookies with me fixing to put a meal on the table in a little while."

A swift tenderness came over Kendra as she took it all in—including Opal's bluster. As Kendra was growing up, the woman had been like a mother to her, if not a patron saint.

Slade, his blue gaze resting softly on Joslyn, hung up his hat and bent to ruffle the dog's ears.

"Poor Brylee," Opal said as she opened the refrigerator door and began rummaging about inside it for the makings of one of her legendary meals.

"Sounded to me like it was her own fault," Slade observed, leaving the dog in order to wash his hands at the sink. He was clad in a suit, but Kendra knew he'd be back in his customary jeans, beat-up boots and lightweight shirt at the first opportunity. "Hutch said he told Brylee he didn't want to get married, more than once, and she wouldn't listen."

For Slade, this was a virtual torrent of words. He was a quiet, deliberate man, and he normally liked to mull things over before he offered an opinion—in contrast to his half brother, Hutch, who tended to go barreling in where angels feared to tread and consider the wisdom of his words and actions later. Or not at all.

Joslyn, meanwhile, tuned in on Kendra's face and read her expression, however guarded it was, with perfect accuracy. They'd been friends since they were barely older than Madison was now, and for the past year, they'd been business partners, too—Joslyn taking over the reins at Shepherd Real Estate, in nearby

Parable, while Kendra scoured the countryside for Jeffrey's daughter.

"Thank heaven he came to his senses," Joslyn said, with her usual certainty. "Brylee is a wonderful person, but she's all wrong for Hutch and he's all wrong for her. They wouldn't have lasted a year."

The crowd in the kitchen began to thin out a little then—Shea, the dog and Madison headed into the family room with their cookies, and Callie followed, Shea regaling her "Grands" with an account of who did what and who wore what and who said what.

Slade ascended the back stairway, chuckling, no doubt on his way to the master bedroom to change clothes. Except for bankers and lawyers, few men in rural Montana wore suits on a regular basis—such get-ups were reserved for Sunday services, funerals and… weddings, ill-fated or otherwise.

Opal, for her part, kept murmuring to herself and shaking her head as she began measuring out flour and lard for a batch of her world-class biscuits. "Land sakes," she muttered repeatedly, along with, "Well, I never, in all my live-long days—"

Joslyn laid her hands on her bulging stomach and sighed. "I swear this baby is practicing to be a rodeo star. It feels as though he's riding a bull in there."

Kendra laughed softly, partly at the image her friend had painted and partly as a way to relieve the dizzying tension brought on by Shea's breathless announcement. *Hutch called the whole thing off. He stopped the wedding.*

"The least you could do," she teased Joslyn, trying to get a grip on her crazy emotions, "is go into labor already and let the little guy get a start on his cowboy career."

As serene as a Botticelli Madonna, Joslyn grinned. "He's taking his time, all right," she agreed. The briefest frown flickered in her shining eyes as she regarded Kendra more closely than before. "It's only fair to warn you," she went on, quietly resolute, "that Slade invited Hutch to come to supper with us tonight—"

Joslyn continued to talk, saying she expected both Slade and Hutch would saddle up and ride the range for a while, but Kendra barely heard her. She flat-out wasn't ready to encounter Hutch Carmody, even at her closest friend's table. Why, the last time she'd seen him, after that stupid, macho horse race of his and Slade's, she'd kicked him, hard, in the shins.

Because he'd just kissed her.

Because he'd risked his life for no good reason.

Because hers was just one of the many hearts he'd broken along his merry way.

Plus she was a mess. She'd been on the road for three days, and even after a good night's sleep in Joslyn's guest room and two showers, she felt rumpled and grungy.

She stood up. She'd get Madison and head for town, she decided, hurry to her own place, where she should have gone in the beginning.

Not that she planned to live there very long.

The mega-mansion was too big for her and Madison, too full of memories.

"Kendra," Joslyn ordered kindly, "sit down."

Opal could be heard poking around in the pantry, still talking to herself.

Slade came down the back stairway, looking like himself in worn jeans, a faded flannel shirt and boots.

Passing Joslyn, he paused and leaned down to plant a kiss on top of her head. Kendra sank slowly back into her own chair.

"Don't start without me," Slade said, spreading one big hand on Joslyn's baby-bulge and grinning down into her upturned face.

It was almost enough to make a person believe in love again, Kendra thought glumly, watching these two.

"Not a chance, cowboy," Joslyn replied, almost purring the words. "We made this baby together and we're having it together."

Kendra was really starting to feel like some kind of voyeuristic intruder when Opal came out of the pantry, looked Slade over from behind the thick lenses of her glasses, and demanded, "Just where do you think you're going, Slade Barlow? Didn't I just say I'm starting supper?"

Slade straightened, smiled at Opal. "Now don't get all riled up," he cajoled. "I'm just going out to check on the horses, not driving a herd to Texas."

"Do I look like I was born yesterday?" Opal challenged, with gruff good humor. "You mean to saddle up and ride. I can tell by looking at you."

Slade laughed, shook his head, shoved a hand through his dark hair before crossing the room to take his everyday hat from a peg beside the back door and plop it on his head. "I promise you," he told Opal, "that the minute that dinner bell rings, I'll be here."

Opal huffed, cheerfully unappeased, then waved Slade off with one hand and went back to making supper.

"You might as well stay here and face Hutch," Joslyn told Kendra, as though there had been no interruption in their conversation. "After all, Parable is a small town, and you're bound to run into him sooner rather than later. Why not get it over with?"

The twinkle in Joslyn's eyes might have annoyed Kendra if she hadn't been so fond of her. Like many happily married people, Joslyn wanted all her friends to see the light and get hitched, pronto.

An image of Brylee Parrish bloomed in Kendra's mind and she felt a stab of sorrow for the woman. Loving Hutch Carmody was asking for trouble—she could have told Brylee that.

Not that Brylee would have listened, any more than *she* had long ago, when various friends had warned her that she was marrying Jeffrey on the rebound, had urged her to take time to think before leaping feetfirst into a whole different world.

"I need to get Madison settled," Kendra fretted. "There are groceries to buy and I've been away from the business way too long as it is—"

"The business is just fine," Joslyn said reasonably. "And so is Madison."

As if on cue, the little girl gave a delighted laugh in the next room.

It was a sweet sound, all too rare, and it made the backs of Kendra's eyes scald. "I don't know if I can handle it," she confessed, very softly. "Seeing Hutch again right away, I mean. I was counting on having some time to adjust to being back—"

Joslyn reached out, took her hand. Squeezed. "You can handle it," she said with quiet certainty. "Trust yourself, Kendra. Nothing is going to happen between you and Hutch unless you want it to."

"That's just the trouble," Kendra reflected miserably, careful to keep her voice down so Madison wouldn't overhear. "Wanting a man—wanting *Hutch*—and knowing better the whole time—well, you know—"

"I do know," Joslyn said, smiling.

"I have a daughter now," Kendra reminded her friend. "I want Madison to grow up in Parable, go to the same schools from kindergarten through high school. I want to give her security, a real sense of community, the whole works. And getting sucked into Hutch's orbit would be the stupidest thing I could possibly do."

"Would it?" Joslyn asked, raising one delicate eyebrow as she waited for a reply.

"Of course it would," Kendra whispered fiercely. "The man broke my heart into a gazillion pieces, remember? And now he's dumped some poor woman virtually at the altar, which only goes to prove he hasn't changed!"

"Did it ever occur to you," Joslyn inquired, unruffled, "that Hutch might have 'dumped' Brylee for the simple reason that she's not you?"

"No," Kendra said firmly, shaken by the mere possibility, "that did *not* occur to me. He did it because he can't commit to anything or anyone long-term, because Whisper Creek Ranch is all he really cares about in this world—*because* he's a heartless, womanizing *bastard*."

Before Joslyn could offer a response to that, Madison, Shea, Callie and the dog trailed back in the kitchen, making further discussion of Hutch Carmody impossible.

Kendra was still flustered, though. Her heart pounded

and her throat and sinuses felt strangely thick—was she coming down with something? Every instinct urged her to get the heck out of there, *now,* but the idea seemed cowardly and, besides, Madison was just starting to let herself be part of the group.

If they rushed off to town, the little girl would be understandably confused.

So Kendra decided to stay, at least until after supper.

She was a grown woman, a mother. Joslyn had been right—it was time she started trusting herself. Hutch had always held an infuriating attraction for her, but she was older now, and wiser, and she had more self-control.

The next hour was taken up with getting ready, coming and going, table-setting and a lot of companionable, lighthearted chatter. Slade returned from the barn as he'd promised and, after washing up in a downstairs bathroom, made the whole crew promise not to pester Hutch with questions about the interrupted wedding.

As if, Kendra thought. She probably wouldn't say more than a few polite words to the man. If she spoke to him at all.

She felt strong, confident, ready for anything.

Until he actually walked into the ranch house kitchen, that is.

Seeing her, he tightened his jaw and shot an accusatory glance in his half brother's direction.

"Didn't I mention that Kendra's here?" Slade asked, breaking the brief, pulsing silence. There was a smile in his voice, though his blue eyes conveyed nothing but innocent concern.

Hutch, his dark blond hair sun-kissed with gold,

recovered his normal affable manner within the space of a heartbeat.

He even smiled, flashing those perfect white teeth and setting Kendra back on her figurative heels.

"Hello, Kendra," he said with a nod, after taking off his hat. Like Slade, he was dressed "cowboy" and the look suited him.

Kendra replied with a nod of her own. "Hutch," she said, turning from the chopping board, where she'd been preparing a salad, and wished she'd cleared her throat first, because the name came out like a croak.

His gaze moved straight to Madison, and Kendra read the questions in his eyes even before he hid them behind a smile. Madison, meanwhile, raised Rupert, as if presenting him to this stranger for inspection.

"Howdy, there," he said, all charm. "Do my eyes deceive me or is that critter a kangaroo?"

CHAPTER TWO

THE WAY HUTCH figured it, a solid week should have
been plenty long enough for the fuss over the wedding-
that-never-was to die down, but when Saturday afternoon rolled around again and he sat down at his
computer to get a quick read on the gossip situation,
tired from rounding up strays with the ranch hands
since just after dawn, he was promptly disabused of
the notion.

This jabber-fest was getting worse by the moment.

Apparently he'd made every "jerk" list in cyber-
space, not just locally, but worldwide. Indignant females
from as far away as the Philippines thought he ought to
be tarred and feathered, and a couple of Brylee's girlfriends, bless their vengeful little hearts, had set up a
page on one of the major networking sites solely for the
purpose of warning every woman with a pulse to steer
clear of Hutch Carmody.

The reverse version, he supposed, grimly amused,
of an old West "Wanted" poster.

Of course, this being the digital age, there were pictures up the wazoo—Bride-Doll Brylee, flushed and
furious in her over-the-top dress, stomping on her bouquet in the church aisle. Brylee, outside in the bright
June sunshine, probably only moments after the first
shot was taken, wrenching the taped-on "Just Married"

sign from the back of the limo that would have carried the two of them over to the Community Center for the reception, ripping the cardboard in two and flinging the pieces into the gutter. Brylee, later still, hair pulled back and caught up in a long, messy ponytail, face puffy and scrubbed clean of makeup, her gown swapped out for jeans and a T-shirt bearing the motto Men Suck. She was surrounded by a dozen or so of her friends, at a table in the center of the Boot Scoot Tavern, the jukebox lit up behind her. No doubt, it was playing a somebody-done-me-wrong song.

Hutch sighed. He hadn't escaped the amateur paparazzi himself—these days, every yahoo and his Aunt Bessie had a smart phone, and they were mighty quick on the draw with them.

One memorable image showed him standing in the center of the sanctuary, clearly uncomfortable in the penguin get-up he'd rented from Wally's Wedding World, over in Three Trees, the neighboring town, looking pale and bleakly determined not to get married no matter what he had to do to avoid it. And those were just the stills—there were videos, too. In one thirty-second wonder, he could be seen climbing into his rusted-out pickup truck, right there in the Presbyterians' gravel parking lot, and in the next, he was heading for the horizon, a dust plume spiraling behind his rig.

Yep, that was him all right, beating a hasty retreat, like a yellow-bellied coward on the run.

That impression rested sour on the back of his tongue.

Someday, he suspected, when Brylee met up with her own personal Mr. Right, got hitched for real, and had herself a houseful of kids, she'd thank him for stopping the wedding and thereby preventing certain catastrophe.

At present, though, that particular "someday" seemed a long way off.

Weary to the aching marrow of his bones, Hutch logged off the internet, pushed back from the rolltop desk that had been in his family since the Lincoln administration, and stood up, stretching luxuriously before retrieving his coffee mug and ambling out of the little office behind the ranch house kitchen.

Taking Slade's advice, he'd kept a low profile since the day that, like the bombing of Pearl Harbor and the 9/11 attacks, would forever live in infamy. Against his own better judgment, he hadn't gone to see Brylee in person, called her on the phone, or even sent her an email.

He hadn't done much guilt-wallowing, either, which might be proof that he really *was* a "selfish, heartless, narcissistic bastard," as members of Team Brylee universally agreed, at least online. By now, the group probably had its own secret handshake.

Hutch regretted hurting Brylee, of course, and he certainly wished he could have spared her the humiliation of that very public breakup, but his overriding emotion was a sense of relief so profound that it still made his head reel even after a week.

Train wreck, averted.

Apocalypse, canceled.

Check and check.

Running into Kendra Shepherd at Slade and Joslyn's place after the debacle had *definitely* thrown him, however—slammed the wind out of him as surely as if he'd been hurled off the back of a bad bull or a sun-fishing bronco and landed on hard ground.

He'd loved Kendra once and he'd believed she loved him.

He'd expected to spend the rest of his life with the woman, happy to make babies, run Whisper Creek Ranch with Kendra at his side, a full partner in every way.

Instead, enter Jeffrey Chamberlain, he of the nominal titles and English estates, practically a prince to a woman like Kendra, brought up in a small Montana town by a grandmother who resented the responsibility of raising her errant daughter's child. Chamberlain had been visiting friends at the time—Hollywood types with delusions of living the ranching life in grand style—and damned if Sir Jeffrey hadn't struck up a conversation with Kendra at the post office one fine day and parlayed that, over the coming weeks, into a romance so epic that it could only have ended badly.

Not that Kendra had fallen for Chamberlain right away—at the get-go, she'd insisted he was just a friend, interesting and funny. Hutch, though nettled, had reluctantly—okay, *grudgingly*—accepted the explanation.

Down deep, he'd been out-of-his-gourd jealous, though, and soon enough the bickering commenced.

Chamberlain, knowing full well what he'd set in motion, had found excuses to stay on in Parable and he just bided his time while things got worse and worse between Hutch and Kendra.

Inevitably, the bickering escalated to fiery yelling matches and, worse, single words, terse and biting, punctuated by long, achy silences.

Eventually, Kendra had given Hutch an ultimatum—trust her or leave her.

He'd chosen the latter option, being a stubborn, hard-headed cowboy from a long line of stubborn, hard-headed cowboys, never really thinking she'd go at all, let alone stay gone; everybody knew they belonged to-gether, he and Kendra. After a semidecent interval, though, she'd hauled off and eloped with Jeffrey.

There were still days—moments, really—when Hutch couldn't believe it had come to that, and this was one of them.

Now, standing in his kitchen, he closed his eyes, remembering.

Kendra had called him three days after tying the knot down in Vegas.

Even then he'd wanted to say, "This isn't right. Come home."

But he'd been too cussed proud to take the high road.

He'd wished "Lady Chamberlain" well and hung up in her ear. Hard. They'd seen each other numerous times afterward, the way things shook out, especially after Chamberlain bought his way out of the marriage and crossed the pond to resume his Lord-of-the-manor lifestyle while Kendra remained in Parable, rattling around in that hotel-sized mansion on Rodeo Road.

Small as Parable was, he and Kendra had come close to patching things up a few times, making another start, but something always went wrong, probably because neither one of them trusted the other any further than they could have thrown them.

They'd been civil last Saturday night at Slade and Joslyn's noisy supper table, but Kendra had looked ready to jump out of her skin at any moment, and as soon as the meal was over and the dishes were in the machine, she'd grabbed up her little girl and boogied for town in her boxy mom-car.

What had happened to that little BMW convertible she used to drive?

"She wasn't expecting to see you tonight," Joslyn had explained, touching his hand once Kendra and the child were out of the house.

Hutch had slanted an evil look at his half brother. "I know the feeling," he'd said.

Slade had merely looked smug.

Now with another long, dirty workday behind him and lunch a distant memory, Hutch stood there in his stupidly big kitchen and tried to shift his focus to rustling up some kind of a supper, but the few budding science experiments hunkered down in the fridge held no appeal. Neither did the resoundingly empty house—by rights, the place should have been bursting with noisy ranch kids and rescued dogs by now. Instead it was neat, cold and stone silent.

Hutch sighed, shoved a hand through his hair. Stepped back from the refrigerator and shut the door.

Upstairs he took a quick shower and donned fresh jeans, a white shirt and go-to-town boots.

He'd hidden out long enough, damn it.

By God, he was through keeping a low profile—he meant to fire up one of the ranch trucks, drive into Parable to the Butter Biscuit Café, claim one of the stools at the counter and order up his usual cheeseburger, shake and fries. As for the joshing and the questions and the speculative glances he was bound to run into?

Bring it, he thought.

KENDRA HAD HAD a week to put that off-the-wall encounter with Hutch the previous Saturday night behind her
and she was mostly over it.

Mostly.

She'd been busy, after all, overseeing the move of
her real estate company from the mansion on Rodeo
Road to the little storefront, catty-corner from the Butter Biscuit Café, enrolling Madison at the year-round
preschool/day-care center and scanning the multiple-
listings for cozy two-bedroom houses within a reasonable radius of Parable.

In a town like that one, smaller properties were
always hard to find—people didn't necessarily sell their
houses when they retired to Florida or Arizona or entered a nursing home. They often passed them down
to the next generation.

At present, Kendra's choices were a double-wide
trailer in the very court where she'd grown up so un-
happily with her grandmother—no possible way—what
resembled a converted chicken coop on the far side
of Three Trees, which was thirty miles away, or the
cramped apartment over old Mrs. Lund's garage on
Cinch Buckle Street, which rented for a tidy sum and
didn't even have its own entrance.

With her fifteen-thousand-square-foot mega-mansion
on the market, already swarming with cleaning people
and painters these days in preparation for showing—
she and Madison had taken up temporary residence in
the estate's small guesthouse.

Given that two different potential buyers, both
highly qualified, had already expressed interest in the
main residence, Kendra had no intention of getting too
settled in the cottage, cheery and convenient though

the place was. Upscale homes were much easier to sell than regular houses, at least in that part of Montana, because so many jet-setters liked to buy them up and visit them once in a blue moon.

For now, though, the guesthouse was sufficient for their needs. Madison loved the big yard, the thriving flower gardens and the swing on the mansion's screened-in sun porch. The four-year-old was content to share the cottage's one bedroom with Kendra, take meals in the tiny, sun-splashed kitchen, and ease, an hour or two at a time, into the preschool program, where there were plenty of playmates around her own age.

Already Madison's fair skin was golden, having absorbed so much country sunshine, and she didn't cry at the prospect of even the shortest separation from Kendra.

Tara Kendall stopped by the real estate office just as Kendra was about to close up for the day. She and Madison planned on picking up a takeout meal over at the Butter Biscuit, then eating at the small white wrought-iron table at the edge of the rose garden on Rodeo Road.

"Can we get a dog now?" Madison was asking for the umpteenth time, when Tara breezed in, pretty with her shoulder-length brown hair expertly layered and her perfect makeup that looked like no makeup at all.

"Do I have an offer for you," Tara said, with a broad grin. She wore a sleek yellow sundress that flattered her slight but womanly figure, and her legs were so tanned she didn't need panty hose. "My golden retriever, Lucy, just happens to have a sister who still needs a home."

"Gee," Kendra drawled, feeling self-conscious in her jeans and T-shirt. "Thanks so much for that suggestion, Tara."

Madison was already jumping up and down in anticipation. "My very own dog!" she crowed.

Tara chuckled and reached out a manicured hand to ruffle Madison's bright copper curls. "Oops," she said, addressing Kendra in a singsong voice that sounded warmly insincere. "Did I just put my foot in my mouth?"

"More like your entire leg," Kendra replied sweetly. Tara, a relative newcomer to Parable, had fit right in with her and Joslyn, turning a duet into a trio—the three of them had been fast friends from the beginning. "We're not ready for a dog yet, since we don't really have a place to—" She paused, looked down at Madison, who was glowing like a firefly on a moonless night, and reconsidered the word she'd intended to use, which was "live," diverting to "permanently reside."

"We have the cottage," Madison pointed out. "There's a yard and Lucy's sister could sleep with us."

"Says you," Kendra said, but with affection. She remembered how badly she'd wanted a pet as a little girl, but her grandmother had always refused, saying she had enough on her hands looking after a kid. She wasn't about to clean up after a dog or a cat, too.

"You promised," Madison reminded her sagely. She was so like Jeffrey—she had his eyes, his red hair, his insouciant certainty that everything good would come to him as a matter of course—including golden retriever puppies with sisters named Lucy.

"I said we could get a pet when we were settled," Kendra clarified patiently after shooting a see-what-you've-done glance at a singularly unrepentant Tara. "We'll be moving soon."

"So will the dog," Tara put in lightly. "Martie Wren

can only keep her at the shelter for so long, then it's off to—well—wherever."

"Thanks *again,* Tara," Kendra said. She knew her friend meant well, but the woman wasn't known for her good judgment. Hadn't she given up a great job in New York, heading up a world-class cosmetics company, to buy, of all things, a dilapidated chicken ranch on the outskirts of Parable, Montana?

Huge tears welled in Madison's eyes. "Nobody *wants* Lucy's sister?"

At last, Tara looked shamefaced. "She's a beautiful dog," she told the little girl gently. "Somebody will adopt her for sure."

"You, for instance?" Kendra said.

"I guess she could live with Lucy and me for a while," Tara decided, shifting her expensive hobo bag from her right shoulder to her left.

Madison grabbed Kendra's hand, squeezed. "We could just *look* at Emma, couldn't we?"

"Emma?" Kendra echoed, dancing on ice now, Bambi with all four limbs scrabbling for traction.

"That's what we'd call Lucy's sister," Madison said matter-of-factly, her little face shining more brightly than the sunset gathering in shades of pink and orange at the rims of the mountains to the east. "Emma."

Emma. It was Madison's birth mother's name. Did she know that?

How could she? She'd been only a year old when Emma gave her up.

"Why 'Emma'?" Kendra asked carefully, hoping to hide her dismayed surprise from the child.

Tara, she instantly noted, had already read her face,

though she couldn't have known the significance of the name, and she looked way beyond apologetic.

"It's a pretty name," Madison said. "Don't you think so, Mommy?"

"It's lovely," Kendra conceded. "Now, shouldn't we pick up our supper and head for home?" She glanced at Tara. "Join us? Nothing fancy—we're getting takeout—but we'd love to share."

Tara blinked, clearly uncertain what response she ought to give. "Well—"

"And it would be fun to meet Lucy," Madison went on. "Is she with you?"

"As a matter of fact," Tara said, "yes. She's in the car. We just came from the vet's office and—"

"You're both welcome," Kendra insisted. Firstly because Tara *was* a dear friend and secondly, because she was enjoying the other woman's obvious discomfort. "You *and* Lucy."

"Well," Tara murmured, with a weak little smile, "okay."

Kendra smiled. "Let's go, then," she said, jingling the ring of keys she'd just plucked from her purse.

She shut off the inside lights, stepped out onto the sidewalk and locked up behind them. Leaving Kendra's Volvo in the parking lot out back, they crossed the street to the Butter Biscuit Café. Tara's flashy red sports car was parked on the street in front of the restaurant, the yellow dandelion-fluff dog, Lucy, pressing her muzzle against the driver's-side window, steaming up the glass.

Kendra's heart softened at the very sight of that dog, while Madison rushed over to stand on tiptoe and press the palms of both hands against the window.

"Hello, Lucy!" Madison cried gleefully.

Lucy barked joyously, her brown eyes luminous with impromptu adoration. She tongued the window where Madison's right palm rested.

Tara laughed. "See?" she said, giving Kendra a light elbow to the ribs. "It's fate."

"I'll get you for this," Kendra told her friend with an undertone.

"No, you'll thank me." Tara beamed, all confidence again. "I'm counting on Emma to win you over." She whispered that last part.

They practically had to drag Madison away from the car, and the dog, each adult gripping one of her small hands as they approached the entrance to the Butter Biscuit Café.

The place was rocking, as always, with dishes clinking and waitresses rushing back and forth and the jukebox blaring an old Randy Travis song.

All the noise and busyness subsided though, at least for Kendra, when her gaze found and landed unerringly on Hutch Carmody.

He sat alone at the counter, ridiculously handsome in ordinary jeans, a white shirt and black boots. A plate sat in front of him, containing half a cheeseburger, a few French fries and some pickles.

It wouldn't have been so awkward if he hadn't noticed Kendra—or at least, if he'd *pretended* not to notice her—but he turned toward her immediately, as though equipped with Kendra-detecting radar.

A slow smile lifted his mouth at one corner and his greenish-blue eyes sparked with amused interest.

Madison rushed straight toward him, as if they were old friends. "We're getting a dog!" she piped. "Well, *maybe.*"

Hutch grinned down at the child, his expression softening a little, full of a kindness Kendra had never seen in him before, not even in their most private and tender moments. The man definitely had a way with kids.

"Is that so?" he asked companionably. "Is this dog purple, like your kangaroo?"

Madison giggled at this question. "No, silly," she said. "Dogs are *never* purple!"

Hutch chuckled. "Neither are kangaroos, in my experience. Not that we have a whole lot of them hopping around the great state of Montana."

"They mostly live in Australia," Madison told him solemnly. "Rupert is only purple because he's a *toy.*"

"I guess that explains it," Hutch replied, his gaze rising slowly to reconnect with Kendra's. Electricity arced, potent, between them. "I'm glad to have the purple kangaroo question settled. It's been troubling me a lot."

And that wasn't the only thing he'd been wondering about, Kendra suddenly realized. He wanted to know how she'd managed to produce a child without ever being pregnant.

As if that were any of his business.

"Hello, Hutch," Kendra said, her voice strangely wooden.

He merely nodded.

Tara spoke up. "How have you been?" she asked him nervously.

Something flickered in Hutch's eyes; it was obvious that he'd figured out what Tara really wanted to know. "I've been just fine, Tara," he replied evenly and without rancor. "Except, of course, for that whole non-wedding thing."

Tara blushed.

So did Kendra.

"G-good," Tara said.

"We'd better place our order," Kendra added, and immediately felt like a complete fool. A well-spoken person otherwise, she never seemed to know what to say around Hutch. "B-before the café gets any busier, I mean—"

"Plus Lucy's locked up in the red car outside," Madison put in.

"Plus that," Kendra said lamely.

"Lucy?" Hutch asked, raising one eyebrow.

"My dog," Tara explained.

"Right," Hutch answered. His gaze remained on Kendra, stirring up all sorts of totally unwanted memories, like the way his hands felt on her bare thighs or the touch of his lips gliding softly over the tops of her breasts. "Nice to see you again," he added casually.

When he looked at her that way, Kendra always felt as though her clothes were made of cellophane, and that got her hackles up. Not to mention her nipples, which, thankfully, were well hidden under the loose fabric of her T-shirt.

Even though she turned away quickly and began studying the big menu board on the wall behind the cash register, Kendra was still acutely aware of Hutch, of little Madison, who so clearly adored him, and of Tara, who was trying to pick up the dangling conversational thread.

"Rodeo Days are almost upon us," Tara said brightly. Every Independence Day weekend since the beginning of time, Parable had hosted the county rodeo, fireworks and carnival. People came from miles around to eat barbecued pork and beef in the park, root for their favorite cowboys and barrel-racing cowgirls, and ride the Ferris wheel and the Whirly-Gig. "The cleanup committee is looking for volunteers. Shall I put your name down to help out, Hutch?"

The woman was wasted as a chicken rancher, Kendra thought, pretending to puzzle between the café's famous corn-bread casserole and deep-fried catfish. Tara should have been selling ice to penguins.

"Sure," she heard Hutch say.

Kendra settled on the corn-bread casserole, preferring to avoid deep-fried *anything,* slanted a glance at Tara and raised her voice a little to place the order with a waitress. "To go, please," she added, perhaps a touch pointedly.

She heard Hutch chuckle, low and gruff.

What was funny?

Tara edged over to Kendra's side, digging in her purse for money.

"My treat," Kendra said, watching out of the corner of her eye as Madison tore herself out of Hutch's orbit and joined the women in front of the cash register.

The food was packed for transport, handed over and paid for, all in due course. As they were leaving, Madison turned back to wave at Hutch.

"I like that cowboy man," she announced, to all and sundry, her little voice ringing like a silver bell at Christmas.

An affectionate group chuckle rippled through the café and Kendra hid a sigh behind the smile she turned on her daughter. "Let's go," she said, taking Madison's small and somewhat grubby hand in hers before they crossed the street to get to Kendra's Volvo.

"Meet you at your place," Tara called, unlocking her

car door and then laughing as she wrestled the eager puppy back so she could slide into the driver's seat and take the wheel.

Kendra nodded and, when the Walk sign flashed, she and Madison started across the street.

"Don't you like the cowboy man, Mommy?" Madison asked, wrinkling her face against the bright dazzle of afternoon sunshine.

The question surprised Kendra so much that she nearly stopped right there in the middle of the road. "Now why on earth would you ask such a thing, Madison Rose Shepherd?" she asked, keeping her tone light, almost teasing.

"If he looks at you," Madison observed, as they stepped up onto the sidewalk and started toward the Volvo, "you look away."

Thinking it was uncanny, the things children not only noticed but could verbalize, Kendra turned up her inner-smile dial a notch and squeezed Madison's hand gently. "Do I?" she countered, knowing full well that she did.

Madison nodded. "He looks at you a lot, too," she added.

Mercifully they'd reached the car, and the next few minutes were taken up with settling Madison in her booster seat and placing the take-out bag carefully on the floor, so the food inside wouldn't spill.

A four-year-old's attention span being what it was, Kendra had reason to hope the subject would have changed by the time she'd buckled herself in behind the wheel and started the car with an unintended roar of the motor.

"Do you know if the cowboy man likes dogs?" Madison ventured, from her perch in the backseat.

Kendra calmly took her foot off the gas pedal, shifted into Drive and steered carefully into the nonexistent traffic. "Yes, I think so," she replied, as matter-of-factly as she could.

"That's good," Madison said happily.

Kendra wasn't about to pursue that observation. "Have you ever been to a rodeo?" she asked, a way of deflecting the topic away from dogs and Hutch Carmody.

"What's a rodeo?" Madison asked.

Kendra took the short drive home to describe the phenomenon in words her small daughter might be expected to understand.

"Oh," Madison said when Kendra was finished. "Will the cowboy man be there?"

LUCY THE GOLDEN retriever turned out to be a real charmer, with her butter-colored fur and those saintly brown eyes dancing with intermittent mischief.

After supper, served as planned at the metal table beside the rose garden, Madison and the pup ran madly around the yard, celebrating green grass and vivid colors and the cool breeze of a summer evening.

Watching them, Tara smiled. "I'm sorry if I put you on the spot before," she said to Kendra, after taking a sip from her glass of iced tea. "About Lucy's sister, I mean."

"That was her birth mother's name," Kendra reflected, watching the child and the dog as they played in the gathering twilight.

Tara set the glass down. "What? Lucy?"

Kendra shook her head. "No," she said, very softly. "Emma. Do you suppose Madison remembers her mother?"

"*You* are Madison's mother," Tara replied.

"Tara," Kendra said wearily.

"From what you've told Joslyn and me, Madison's been in foster care since she was a year old. How could she remember?"

Kendra lifted one shoulder slightly, then let it fall. "It seems like a pretty big coincidence that Madison would choose that particular name. She must have overheard it somewhere."

"Probably," Tara allowed. Then she added, "Kendra, look at me."

Kendra shifted her gaze from drinking in the sight of Madison and Lucy, frolicking against a backdrop of blooming flowers of every hue, to Tara's concerned face.

"You're not afraid she'll come back, are you?" Tara prompted, almost in a whisper. "This Emma person, I mean, and try to take Madison away?"

Kendra shook her head. She was at once comforted and saddened by the knowledge that Madison's biological mother hadn't wanted her baby enough to fight for her.

The woman had demanded money, naturally, but she'd signed off readily enough once Jeffrey's American lawyers got the point across that the buying and selling of babies was illegal.

"She's relinquished all rights to Madison," she finally answered.

Tara sighed. "It's hard to understand some people," she said.

"Impossible," Kendra agreed. Oddly, though, she wasn't thinking of Madison's birth mom anymore, but of Hutch.

The man was a mystery, an enigma.

He fractured women's hearts with apparent impunity—there always seemed to be another hopeful waiting in the wings, certain she'd be the exception to the rule—and yet kids, dogs and horses saw nothing in him to fear and everything to love.

Was he actually a good man, underneath all that bad-boy mojo and easy charm?

"Still planning to sell this place, then?" Tara asked with a gesture of one hand that took in the mansion as well as the grounds.

Kendra nodded. "I'll be putting the proceeds in trust for Madison," she said. She hadn't told Joslyn and Tara everything, but they both knew Jeffrey had fathered the little girl. "It's rightfully hers."

Tara absorbed that quietly and took another sip from her iced tea. "You won't miss it? The money, I mean? Living in the biggest and fanciest house in town?"

Kendra's smile was rueful. "I'm not broke, Tara," she said. "I've racked up a lot of commissions since I started Shepherd Real Estate." She looked back over one shoulder at the looming structure behind them. "As for missing this house, no, I won't, not for a moment. It's a showplace, not a home."

Tara didn't answer. She seemed to be musing, mulling something over.

"So," Kendra said, "how's the chicken ranch coming along?"

At that, Tara rolled her beautiful eyes. "It's a disaster," she answered with honest good humor. "The

nesting-house roof is sagging, the hens aren't laying—
I suspect that's because the roosters are secretly gay—
and Boone Taylor still refuses to plant shrubbery to
hide that eyesore of a trailer he lives in so it won't be
the first thing I see when I look out my kitchen window every morning."

"Regrets?" Kendra asked gently. Madison and Lucy
seemed to be winding down; moving in slow motion as
the shadows thickened. After a bath and a story, Madison would sleep soundly.

Tara immediately shook her head. "No," she said.
"It's hard, but I'm a long way from giving up."

"Good," Kendra said with a smile. "Because I'd feel
guilty if you were having second thoughts, considering
I was the one who sold you the place."

"You might have warned me about the neighbors,"
Tara joked.

"Boone isn't so bad," Kendra felt honor-bound to say.
She'd known him since childhood, known his late wife,
Corrie, too. He'd lost interest in life for a long time after
Corrie's death from breast cancer a few years back, but
last November he'd up and run for sheriff and gotten
himself elected by a country mile. "He's just stubborn,
like most of the men around here. That's what gets them
through the hard times."

Tara's eyes widened a little. "Does that apply to
Hutch, too?"

Kendra stood up, beckoned to her tired daughter.
"Time to get ready for bed," she called to Madison,
who meandered slowly toward her—proof in itself that
she was exhausted. Like most small children, she normally resisted sleep with all her might, lest she miss
something.

The puppy trotted over to Tara, nuzzling her knee, and she laughed as she bent to ruffle her ears.

"If you think Lucy's perfect," she said, instead of goodbye, "just wait till you meet her sister."

CHAPTER THREE

THE NEXT MORNING after church, Kendra gave in to the pressures of fate—and her very persistent daughter—and drove across town to Paws for Reflection, the private animal shelter run by a woman named Martie Wren.

Martie, an institution in Parable, oversaw the operation out of an office in her small living room, surviving entirely on donations and the help of numerous volunteers. She'd converted the two large greenhouses in back to dog-and-cat housing, though she also took in birds and rabbits and even the occasional pygmy goat. The place was never officially closed, even on Sundays and holidays.

A sturdy woman with kindly eyes and a shock of unruly gray hair, Martie was watering the flower beds in her front yard when Kendra and Madison arrived, parking on the street.

"Tara said you might be stopping by," Martie sang out happily, waving and then hurrying over to shut off the faucet and wind the garden hose around its plastic spool.

Kendra, busy helping Madison out of her safety rigging in the backseat, smiled wryly back at the other woman. "Of course she did," she replied cheerfully.

"We're here to see Lucy's sister," Madison remarked.

Martie, at the front gate by then, pushing it wide open in welcome, chuckled. "Well, come on inside then, and have a look at her. She's been waiting for you. Got her all dolled up just in case the two of you happened to take a shine to each other."

Kendra stifled a sigh. She wanted a dog as much as Madison did—there had been a canine-shaped hole in her heart for as long as she could remember—but she'd hoped to find a permanent place to live before acquiring a pet. Get settled in.

Alas, the universe did not seem concerned with her personal plans.

She and Madison passed through the gate, closing it behind them, and Martie led the way onto the neatly painted front porch and up to the door.

The retriever puppy did indeed seem to be waiting—she was sitting primly on the hooked rug in the tiny entryway, with a bright red ribbon tied to her collar and her chocolate-brown eyes practically liquid with hope.

Kendra immediately melted.

Madison, meanwhile, placed her hands on her hips and tilted her head to one side, studying the yellow fluff-ball intently.

The puppy rose from its haunches and approached the little girl, looking for all the world as though it were smiling at her. *Where have you been?* the animal's expression seemed to say. *We're supposed to be having fun together.*

Madison turned her eyes to Kendra. "She's so pretty," she said, sounding awed, as though there had never been and never would be another dog like this one.

"Very pretty," Kendra agreed, choking up a little.

She saw so much of her childhood self in Madison and that realization made her cautious. Madison was Madison, and trying to soothe her own childhood hurts through her daughter would be wrong on so many levels.

Martie, an old hand at finding good homes for otherwise unwanted critters, simply waited, benignly silent. She believed in letting things unfold at their own pace—not a bad philosophy in Kendra's opinion, though she'd yet to master it herself.

As a little girl she'd had to fight for every scrap of her grandmother's attention. In her career she'd been virtually *driven* to succeed, believing with all her heart that nothing good would happen unless she *made* it happen.

Now that Madison had entered her life, though, it was time to make some changes. Shifting her type-A personality down a few gears, so she could appreciate what she had, rather than always striving for something more, was at the top of the list.

Madison was still gazing at Kendra's face. "Can we take her home with us, Mommy?" she asked, clearly living for a "yes." "Please? Can we name her Daisy?"

Kendra's eyes burned as she crouched beside her daughter, putting herself at eye level with the child. "I thought you wanted to call her Emma," she said.

Madison shook her head. "Daisy's not an Emma. She's a Daisy."

Kendra put an arm around Madison, but loosely. "Okay," she said, very gently. "Daisy it is."

"She can come home with us, then?" Madison asked, wide-eyed, a small, pulsing bundle of barely contained energy.

"Well, there's a procedure that has to be followed," Kendra replied, looking over at Martie as she stood up straight again, leaving one hand resting on the top of Madison's head.

"Daisy's had her shots," Martie said, "and I've known you since you were the size of a bean sprout, Kendra Shepherd. You'll give this dog a good home and lots of love, and that's all that matters."

Something unspoken passed between the two women. Martie was probably remembering other visits to the shelter, when Kendra was small. She'd been the youngest volunteer at the shelter, cleaning kennels, filling water bowls and making sure every critter in the place got a gentle pat and a few kind words.

"You get a free vet visit, too," Martie said, as though further persuasion might be required.

Madison's face shone with delight. "Let's take Daisy home right now," she said.

Kendra and Martie both laughed.

"There are a few papers to be signed," Martie said to the child. "Why don't you and Daisy come on into the office with your mom and me, and keep each other company while we grown-ups take care of a few things?"

Madison, though obviously eager to take Daisy and run before one of the adults changed their mind, nodded dutifully. "All right," she said, her hand nestled into the golden fur at Daisy's nape. "But we're in a hurry."

Martie chuckled again.

Kendra hid a smile and said, *"Madison Rose."*

"We'll be very quick," Martie promised over one shoulder.

They all trailed into Martie's office, Daisy sticking close to Madison's side.

"It isn't polite to rush people, Madison," Kendra told her daughter.

"You *said*," Madison reminded her, "that the church man took too long to stop talking, and everybody wanted to get out of there and have lunch. You wanted him to hurry up and finish."

Kendra blushed slightly. She *had* said something along those lines as they were driving away from the church, but that was different from standing up when the sermon seemed never-ending and saying something like, "Wrap it up, will you? We're in a hurry."

Explaining that to a four-year-old, obviously, would take some doing.

Martie chuckled again. "Lloyd's a dear, but he does tend to run on when he's got a captive audience on a Sunday morning," she remarked with kindly tolerance. "Bless his heart."

The Reverend Lloyd Atherton, like Martie, was a fixture in Parable. Long-winded though he was, everybody loved him.

Kendra made a donation, in lieu of a fee, listened to a brief and heartrending explanation of Daisy's background—she'd literally been left on Martie's doorstep in a cardboard box along with six of her brothers and sisters—and signed a simple document promising to return Daisy to Paws for Reflection if things didn't work out.

"Is Daisy hungry?" Madison wanted to know. It was a subtle nudge. *We're in a hurry.*

Martie smiled. "Puppies always seem to *think* they are, but Daisy had a bowl of kibble less than half an hour ago. She'll be just fine until supper time."

Madison nodded, apparently satisfied. She was staring raptly at the little dog, stroking its soft coat as she waited for the adoption to be finalized.

Soon enough, the details had been handled and Madison was in the back of the Volvo again, buckled into her booster seat, with Daisy sitting alertly beside her, panting in happy anticipation of whatever.

They made a quick stop at the big discount store out on the highway, leaving Daisy waiting patiently in the car with a window partly rolled down for air while they rushed inside to buy assorted gear—a collar and leash, a package of poop bags, a fleecy bed large enough for a golden retriever puppy to grow into, grooming supplies, a few toys and the brand of kibble Martie had recommended.

Daisy was thrilled at their return and when Kendra tossed the bed into the backseat, the animal frolicked back and forth across the expanse of it, unable to contain her delight, causing Madison to laugh in a way Kendra had never heard her laugh before— rambunctiously and without self-consciousness or restraint.

It was a beautiful thing to hear and Kendra was glad there were so many small tasks to be performed before she could put the car in motion, because her vision was a little blurred.

Back at the guesthouse, Kendra put away the dog's belongings while Madison and Daisy ran frenetically around the backyard, both of them bursting with pent-up energy and pure celebration of each other.

"We need a poop bag, please," Madison announced presently, appearing in the cottage doorway, a vision in her little blue Sunday-school dress.

Smiling, Kendra opened the pertinent package, followed Madison outside to the evidence and proceeded to demonstrate the proper collection and disposal of dog doo-doo.

Afterward, she insisted they both wash their hands at the bathroom sink.

Daisy looked on from the doorway, wagging her tail and looking pleased to be in the midst of so much interesting activity.

Lunch, long overdue by then, was next on the agenda. Madison and Kendra made peanut butter and jelly sandwiches in the impossibly small kitchen, and Kendra poured a glass of milk for both of them.

Daisy settled herself near Madison's chair, ears perked forward, nose raised to sniff the air, probably hoping that manna, in the form of scraps of a PB and J, might fall from heaven.

Martie had been adamant on that point, though. No people food and very few treats. The treat a dog needed most, she'd said, was plenty of love and affection.

When the meal was over and the table had been cleared, Madison announced, yawning, that Daisy had had a big morning and therefore needed a nap.

Amused—Madison normally napped only under protest—Kendra suggested that they ought to change out of their church clothes first.

Madison put on pink cotton shorts and a blue short-sleeved shirt, and Kendra opted for jeans and a lightweight green pullover. When she came out of the bedroom, Madison and Daisy were already curled up together on the new fleece dog bed, and Kendra didn't have the heart to raise an objection.

Lie down with dogs, get up with fleas, she heard her grandmother say.

Shut up, Gramma, was her silent response.

"Sleep tight," she said aloud, taking a book from the shelf and stepping outside, planning to sit in the shade of the maple trees and read for a while.

The scene was idyllic—bees buzzing, flowers nodding their many-colored heads in the light breeze, the big Montana sky sweeping blue and cloudless and eternal overhead.

Kendra relaxed as she read, and at some point, she must have dozed off, because she opened her eyes suddenly and found Hutch Carmody standing a few feet away, big as life.

She blinked a couple of times, but he didn't disappear.

Not a dream, then. Crap.

"Sorry," he said without a smidgeon of regret. "Didn't mean to wake you."

Kendra straightened and glanced toward the open doorway of the cottage, looking for Madison. There was no sign of either the child or the dog, but Kendra went inside to check on them anyway. They were both sleeping, curled up together on Daisy's cloud-soft bed.

Quietly, Kendra went back outside to face Hutch.

How could she not have heard him arrive? His truck was parked right there in the driveway, a stone's throw from where she'd been sitting. At the very least, she should have heard the tires in the gravel or the closing of the driver's door.

"What are you doing here?" she whispered, too rattled to be polite.

Hutch spread his hands wide, grinning. "I'm unarmed," he said, sidestepping the question. He was, she recalled, a master at sidestepping any topic he didn't want to discuss. "Don't shoot."

Kendra huffed out a sigh, picked up her book, which she'd dropped in the grass when she'd woken up to an eyeful of Hutch, and held it tightly against her side. "What. Are. You. Doing. Here?" she repeated.

He gestured for her to sit down, and since her knees were weak, she dropped back into her lawn chair. He drew another one up alongside hers and sat. They were both gazing straight ahead, like two strangers in the same row on an airplane, intent on the seat belt/oxygen mask lecture from an invisible flight attendant.

"Tell me about your little girl," Hutch finally said.

"Why should I?" Kendra asked reasonably, proud of her calm tone.

"I guess because she could have been ours," he replied.

For a moment, Kendra felt as if he'd elbowed her, hard, or even punched her in the stomach. Once the adrenaline rush subsided, though, she knew there was no point in withholding the information.

A person could practically throw a rock from one end of Parable to the other and juicy stories got around fast.

"You'll hear about it soon enough," she conceded, though ungraciously, keeping her voice down in case Madison woke up and somehow homed in on the conversation, "so I might as well tell you."

Hutch gave a long-suffering sigh and she felt him looking in her direction now, though she was careful not to meet his gaze. "Might as well," he agreed quietly.

"Not that it's any of your business," Kendra pointed out.

He simply waited.

Distractedly, Kendra wondered if the man thought she'd given birth to Madison herself and kept her existence hidden from everyone in Parable all this time.

"Madison is adopted," she said. It was a simple statement, but it left her feeling as though she'd spilled her guts on some ludicrous tell-all TV show.

"Why do I think there's more to the story?" Hutch asked after a pause. His very patience galled Kendra— what right did he have to be *patient?* This was a courtesy explanation—she didn't owe it to him. She didn't owe him *anything* except maybe a broken heart.

"Madison's father was my ex-husband," Kendra said. Suddenly, she wanted to cry and it had nothing to do with her previous hesitation to talk about something so bruising and private. Why couldn't Madison have been born to *her,* as she should have been?

"And her mother?"

Once again, Kendra looked to make sure Madison hadn't turned up in the cottage doorway, all ears. "She was one of Jeffrey's girlfriends."

Hutch swore under his breath. "That rat bastard," he added a moment later.

Kendra stiffened her spine, squared her shoulders, jutted out her chin a little way. "I beg your pardon?" she said in a tone meant to point out the sheer irony, not to mention the audacity, of the pot calling the kettle black.

"Could we not argue, just this once?" Hutch asked hoarsely.

"Just this once," Kendra said, and one corner of her mouth twitched with a strange urge to smile. Probably some form of hysteria, she decided.

"I'm sorry I called your ex-husband a rat bastard," Hutch offered.

"You are not," Kendra challenged, still without looking at him. Except out of the corner of one eye, that is.

"All right," Hutch ground out, *"fine."* He sighed and shoved a hand through his hair. "Let me rephrase that. I'm sorry I didn't keep my opinion to myself."

A brief, sputtering laugh escaped Kendra then. "Since when have you ever been known to keep your opinion to yourself?"

"You're determined to turn this into a shouting match, aren't you?"

"No," Kendra said pointedly, bristling. "I am *not* planning on arguing with you, Hutch Carmody. *Not ever again.*"

"Kendra," Hutch said, "you can hedge and stall all you want, but eventually we're going to have this conversation, so we might as well just go ahead and get it done."

She made a swatting motion in his general direction, as though trying to chase away a fly. Now she was digging in her heels again and she couldn't seem to help it. "Madison is *my* daughter now, and that's all that matters."

"You're an amazing woman, Kendra," Hutch told her, and he sounded so serious that she swiveled on the seat of her lawn chair to look at him with narrowed, suspicious eyes.

"I mean it," he said with a gruff chuckle, the sound gentle and yet innately masculine. "Some people couldn't handle raising another woman's child—under those circumstances, anyhow."

"It isn't Madison's fault that Jeffrey Chamberlain was a—"

Hutch's mouth crooked up at one corner and sad

mischief danced in his eyes. "Rat bastard?" he finished for her.

"Yes," she said. "That's about the size of it."

He grinned full-out, which put him at an unfair advantage because when he did that, her bones turned to jelly and her IQ plummeted at least twenty points. "Well now," he said. "We finally agree on something."

"Go figure," Kendra remarked, going for a snippy tone but not quite getting there.

"We're on a roll."

"Or not."

He laughed, shook his head. "I'm about to say something you'll have to agree with, whether you want to or not," he warned.

She felt a weird little thrill and could have shaken herself for it. "Is that so?"

Hutch nodded toward the cottage doorway, where Madison finally stood, rubbing her eyes and yawning, Daisy at her side. "You're lucky to have that little girl in your life, however it came about, and the reverse is true, too. You were born to be a mother, Kendra—and a good one."

"Damn it," Kendra muttered, at a loss for a comeback.

Hutch grinned as Madison's eyes widened—she was slowly waking up—and a glorious smile lit her face. She scrambled toward them.

"Hello, cowboy man!" she whooped, feet still bare, curls rumpled, cheeks flushed.

Hutch laughed again. "I guess you might as well call me that as anything else," he said. He exuded the kind of quiet, wholesome approval little girls crave from daddy-types.

Not that Hutch was any such thing.

"Do you like dogs?" Madison asked earnestly.

As if she'd already made her own decision on that score, Daisy suddenly leaped into Hutch's lap in a single bound, bracing her forepaws on his shoulders and licking his face.

"Yep," he said from behind all that squirming dog. "And, as you can see, they're inclined to like me, too."

"Good," Madison said.

Kendra felt unaccountably nervous, though she couldn't have said why. "Madison—" she began, but her voice fell away.

"Do you like kids, too?" Madison pressed.

Kendra groaned inwardly.

Hutch set Daisy carefully on the ground, patting her still-bouncing head. "I like kids just fine," he said.

"Do you have any?"

Hutch shook his head. "Nope."

"Madison," Kendra repeated, with no more effect than before.

"Do you like my Mommy, too?"

Kendra squeezed her eyes shut.

"As a matter of fact," Hutch replied easily, "I do. Your mother and I are old friends."

Kendra squirmed again and forced herself to open her eyes.

Even rummaged up a smile that wouldn't quite stick.

Before she could think of anything to say, however, Hutch unfolded himself from his lawn chair with Madison standing nearby, still basking in his presence. "I guess I'd better head on home before I wear out my welcome," he drawled, and there was a twinkle in his eyes when he snagged Kendra's gaze. "See you around," he added.

Madison caught hold of his hand. "Wait," she said, in a near whisper.

He leaned down, resting his hands on his knees. "What?" he asked, with a smile in his voice.

"Will you be at the rodeo thing?" Madison continued.

"Sure enough," Hutch said, his tone and manner so void of condescension that he might have been addressing another adult. Maybe that was his gift, that he treated children like people, not some lesser species. "Never miss it. After all, I'm a cowboy man."

Madison beamed, evidently satisfied, and when Daisy bounded off in pursuit of a passing butterfly, her small mistress gamboled after her, arms wheeling as if she might take flight.

"Cowboy man," Kendra reflected thoughtfully.

"I've been called worse," Hutch joked.

"That's a fact," Kendra said brightly. She could have listed half a dozen names she'd called him over the years, to his face and in the privacy of her own head.

Whistling some ditty under his breath, and still grinning, Hutch turned and headed for his truck, lifting a hand in farewell as he went.

He got behind the wheel and drove away, and Kendra didn't watch him go.

"YOU'RE WAY TOO pregnant to be at work," Kendra told Joslyn the next day, stepping into the storefront office after dropping Madison off for the morning preschool session and leaving Daisy at Tara's for a doggy playdate with Lucy, only to find her business partner already there, tapping away at the keyboard of her computer.

Joslyn flashed her a smile as she looked up from the monitor. "So I hear," she said. She sighed good-naturedly. "From Slade. From Opal. From Callie."

"And now, from me," Kendra replied, setting her handbag on the edge of the desk since she'd be going out again as soon as she'd checked her messages. She was due at her lawyer's office at ten-thirty, which was why she hadn't brought Daisy to work with her.

Madison had been beside herself at the thought of Daisy being left at home alone because, as she'd explained it, "Daisy is a puppy and a puppy is the same as a baby and a baby needs somebody with it at all times."

Kendra had given in, at least temporarily.

"You're supposed to be on maternity leave, remember?" she prompted, happy to see her friend for whatever reason, all protests aside.

"Ouch," Joslyn said out of nowhere, spreading a hand over her zeppelin of a belly and making a wincey face.

"Is the little guy practicing his rodeo moves again?" Kendra asked, smiling. If only every baby could be born into a union as loving and warm as Joslyn and Slade's—it would be a different world.

"It would seem he's switched to pole vaulting," Joslyn said in a tone of cheerful acceptance. After a few slow, deep breaths, she focused on the computer monitor again. "Come over here and check out this listing, Kendra. It's a rental, but I think it might be exactly what you've been looking for."

Immediately interested, Kendra rounded her friend's desk to stand behind her and peer at the small white house on the screen. She recognized it, of course; she had at least a passing knowledge of every piece of property in Parable County, be it residential or commercial.

This charming little one-story colonial, with its white clapboard walls and green shutters and wrap-around porch, was situated across the street from the town park, just two blocks from the public library. Both Madison's preschool and the new real estate office were within easy walking distance.

"Why didn't I know about this?" Kendra mused, studying the enticing image on the monitor.

Joslyn raised and lowered one shoulder, very slightly. "You've been out of town," she replied. "Plus we only *sell* real estate, we don't manage rentals."

Kendra's brain sifted through the facts she already knew: the colonial had belonged to attorney Maggie Landers's late aunt, Billie. Upon Billie's death, at least a decade before, Maggie had inherited the property. She'd had some much-needed renovations done, Kendra recalled, but never actually lived in the house herself. She'd rented it out to a schoolteacher, long-term. Now, apparently, it was empty—or about to be.

She practically dived for the telephone. Sure she already had an appointment with Maggie about Madison's trust fund, but she didn't want someone else snapping up the house.

Maggie's front office assistant put Kendra through to the boss right away.

"Tell me you're not canceling our appointment," Maggie said without preamble. "If you do, you'll be the third one today."

Kendra's heart had begun to pound. "No," she said quickly, smiling. Hoping. "No, it isn't that—I'll be there at ten-thirty, like we agreed—"

"Kendra," Maggie broke in, sounding concerned now. "What on earth is the matter? You sound as though you've just completed a triathlon."

"Your house—the rental—Joslyn just showed me the listing on the internet—"

Maggie gave a nervous little laugh and Kendra could see her in her mind's eye, fiddling with that strand of priceless pearls she always wore. "Yes? What about it?"

"Is it still available?"

Maggie sounded relieved when she answered, "Of course. The ad just went up today."

"I'll take it," Kendra burst out. Her own recklessness left her gasping for breath—she never did reckless things. Well, not reckless things that didn't involve Hutch Carmody, anyway.

"Sight unseen?" Maggie echoed.

"It's perfect for Madison and me," Kendra said, relaxing a little.

"Don't you even want to know how much the rent will be?"

Kendra strained to see Joslyn's monitor again and scanned quickly for the price. "That won't be a problem," she nearly chimed.

Maggie was quiet for a few moments, taking it all in. "All right," she said finally. "Come early and we'll go over the details of the trust fund, then run over to the house so you can have a look inside before you commit yourself to a year's lease—"

Kendra bit back a very un-Kendra-like response, which would have gone something like this: *I'm committing right now. Do you hear me? Right now!*

"Fine," she said moderately. "But please don't show it to anyone else in the meantime."

"In the meantime?" Maggie echoed, with a friendly little laugh. "As in, say, the next half hour? Relax, Kendra—if you want the house, it's yours."

Joslyn was grinning throughout the whole conversation.

"Thank you," Kendra said, near tears, she was so excited. She said goodbye, hung up and grabbed her purse from the corner of her desk.

"Kendra," Joslyn said, "take a breath. It's meant to be."

"That," Kendra retorted lightly, already on her way to the door, car keys in hand, "is what you said about Hutch and me. Remember?"

"Oh," Joslyn answered breezily, "I haven't changed my mind on that score. Sooner or later, I'm sure you'll both come around."

Kendra shook her head, gave a rueful chuckle. "Don't work too hard," she said, opening the office door. "If you're still here when I get back, I'll buy you lunch at the Butter Biscuit."

"One more lunch at the Butter Biscuit," Joslyn said, "and I'll be a butter*ball*. Anyway, I promised to meet Shea at the Curly Burly at one—we're going shopping."

Kendra nodded and rushed out.

Five minutes later, she was seated in Maggie's office, on the very edge of her chair.

Maggie had already warned her that building a legal structure that would protect Madison's considerable financial interests would require a series of meetings, if only because of the complexity of the task.

Kendra listened to Maggie's explanations and suggestions as patiently as she could, but her mind was on the one-story colonial with the fenced backyard. This, too, was unlike her—she usually focused keenly on whatever she was doing at the time, but today, it was impossible.

Maggie, a pretty woman with short hair, gamine eyes and very nice clothes, finally chuckled and laid down her expensive fountain pen.

"You're not getting a word of this, are you, Kendra?" she asked.

Kendra smiled and shook her head. "I'm sorry. From the moment I realized the house might be available, I've been fidgety."

Maggie collected her handbag from a drawer of her desk. "Then let's go and do the walk-through," she said. "Then we'll come back here and take another shot at running the numbers for Madison's fund."

"I'd like that," Kendra said, feeling almost giddy.

"Follow me, then," Maggie said, jangling her car keys.

The cottage had been freshly painted, Kendra noticed with a pang of sweet avarice, and so had the picket fence out front. The flower beds were in full bloom and the lawn, newly mown, smelled sweetly of cut grass.

It was so easy to imagine herself and Madison living here.

"I knew you were selling the mansion, of course," Maggie said when they got out of their cars and met on the sidewalk in front of the colonial. "But I guess I thought you'd be in the market to buy a place, rather than rent."

"I did plan on buying," Kendra answered, letting her gaze wander over the sleeping-in-the-sunshine face of that perfect little house, "but I'm learning that it's wise to be open to surprises."

Maggie smiled and opened the creaky gate. "Isn't that the truth?" she responded.

CHAPTER FOUR

WHEN HUTCH FINALLY caught up with Brylee, she was in her small but well-organized warehouse on the outskirts of Three Trees, helping to stack boxes as they were unloaded from the back of a delivery truck.

Clad in jeans, sneakers and a blue U of M pullover, she looked more like a teenager than a thirty-year-old woman with a successful business and a bad-luck wedding day to her credit. Her russet-brown hair hung down her back in a long, fairly tidy braid, and she hadn't bothered with makeup.

She didn't notice Hutch right away and he used those moments to gather his resolve, all the while wishing he *felt* something for Brylee—God knew, she was beautiful and she was sweet and she was smart. She was definitely wife and mother material—but she didn't stir him down deep where it counted and that was a deal-breaker.

At last Brylee stilled, like a doe catching the scent of some threat on the wind, she turned her head his way and saw him standing just a few feet inside the roll-up doorway of the warehouse,

Her large eyes, bluish today because of the color of the shirt she was wearing, looked hollow as she took him in and he knew she was weighing her options— seriously considering walking away without deigning to speak, if not shooting him down where he stood or running him over with the first handy forklift.

Brylee had a temper and she could be as hardheaded as any statue, but she was no coward. She spoke sotto voce to the other workers, all female, all of whom were staring now, as though Hannibal Lector had just appeared in their midst, wearing the leather mask and holding a plate of fava beans, and then came slowly toward him.

Brylee ran a small but thriving party-planning company that sold home decor items and various gifts. She had a network of sales people that covered a five-state area, holding lucrative little gatherings in people's homes, and operated a thriving online store, as well.

"Hello, Hutch," she said, indicating her nearby office with a nod and leading the way.

He fell into step with her after muttering a gruff "hello" of his own.

The office was small and furnished in early army surplus. Brylee evidently reserved her creative capacities for choosing and photographing products, training her "independent home decor consultants" and coming up with innovative marketing strategies. Here, in this little room off the warehouse, she handled the practical end of things.

"I wondered when you'd show up," she said once they were inside her enclave with the door closed against listening ears.

"I wanted to come and see you right after the—well, after—but I was persuaded that it wouldn't be a good idea," Hutch replied. He stood with his back to the door, while Brylee perched on the edge of her beat-up steel desk, with her arms folded and her head tipped to one side in skeptical anticipation.

"I could have spared you the trouble of paying a visit," Brylee replied quietly. She looked strained, exhausted, a little pale, but pride flashed in her changeable hazel eyes and stiffened her generous mouth. "I don't have anything to say to you, Hutch. Nothing I'd want written in the Book of Life, anyway."

"Well," he drawled, after stifling a wry chuckle, "it just so happens that I have something to say to you."

Brylee arched one eyebrow and waited. She looked bored now, but wary, too. What, she might have been wondering, was this yahoo going to spring on her now?

Hutch shoved a hand through his hair. He'd left his hat in the truck, but otherwise he was dressed as usual in work clothes and boots. Whisper Creek Ranch practically ran itself these days, well-staffed and well-organized as it was, but he still felt the need to get up every morning before the sun rose and tend to the business of herding cattle, mending fences and all the rest.

Today he hadn't been able to keep his mind on the routine, though, and it was a damn confusing situation, too. He thought about Kendra 24/7, but he'd been drawn to Brylee ever since that broken-road wedding that didn't quite come off.

"I can't say I'm sorry for what I did," he said straightforwardly. "Going through with that ceremony would have been the mistake of a lifetime—for both of us."

"Yes, you made that pretty clear," Brylee answered, her tone terse. "Is that what you drove all the way from Whisper Creek to tell me?"

"No," Hutch said, standing his ground. "I came to say that you'll find the right man, no matter what you think now, and when you do, you'll be damn glad you didn't marry me and wreck your chances to be happy."

"Maybe I'm *already* 'damn glad I didn't marry you,'" Brylee reasoned tartly. "Did you ever consider *that* possibility?"

He grinned. "That one did occur to me, believe it or not," he said. "I should have made you listen to me, Brylee, before things went as far as they did."

"That was my grandmother's dress I was wearing," she said, after a short pause. "It had to be restored and altered and specially cleaned. I spent a fortune on the cake and the invitations and the flowers and all the rest. It's going to take *weeks,* even with help from my friends, to send back all those wedding gifts." Her shoulders moved in the ghost of a shrug. "But, hey, what the heck? You win some, you lose some. And besides, who needs six toaster ovens anyhow?"

Tears brimmed in her eyes and she looked away, fiercely dignified.

"Brylee," Hutch said, not daring to touch her or even take a step in her direction. "I know you're hurt. I'm sorry about that—sorrier than I've ever been about anything in my life. And I'm more than ready to reimburse you for any of the costs—"

"I don't want your *money!*" she flared suddenly, looking straight at him now, with fire flashing behind the pride and sorrow in her eyes. "This was never about money—I have plenty of my own, in case you haven't noticed."

"I know that, Brylee," he said gently.

"Then what did you expect to accomplish by coming here?" She held up an index finger. "Wait, let me answer for you," she added. "Your conscience is bothering you—what *passes* for a conscience with you—and you want me to say all is forgiven and we can be *friends* and go on as if nothing happened." With that, Brylee slipped past him and jerked the office door open wide. "Well, you can just go to hell, Hutch Carmody, and take your lame apologies with you." A sharp, indrawn breath. *"Get out."*

"You might want to try *listening* to what's really being said to you, Brylee, instead of just the parts you want to hear," he told her calmly, not moving. "It would save a lot of wear and tear on you and everybody else."

"Get. Out." Brylee parsed the words out. *"Now."*

He spread his hands in an "I give up" gesture and ambled past her, across the warehouse, which was as still as a mausoleum, and out through the doorway into the sunshine.

Walker Parrish, Brylee's brother, had just driven up in a big, extended-cab pickup with his stock company logo painted on the doors. He raised rodeo stock on his ranch outside of Three Trees, where he and Brylee had grown up.

Hutch stopped. He frankly wasn't in the mood for any more yammer and recrimination, but he wouldn't have it said that he'd tucked his tail and run from Walker or anybody else.

"We-e-e-l-ll," Walker said, dragging out the word. "If it isn't the runaway bridegroom."

Hutch wasn't about to give an inch. "No autographs, please," he retorted dryly. He wasn't looking for a fight, but if Walker wanted one, he'd come to the right man.

Walker chuckled and shook his head. Hutch knew women found Brylee's big brother attractive, with his lean but wide-shouldered build and his rugged features, but so far he'd managed to steer clear of marriage, which should have made him at least a little sympathetic to Hutch's side of the story, and clearly hadn't.

"I can't imagine what you're doing on my sister's property right now," Walker observed, his water-gray eyes narrowed as he studied Hutch.

Hutch took his time shaping a reply. "I felt a need to offer an apology," he finally said, his tone level, even affable. "She wasn't in the frame of mind to accept it."

"I don't reckon she would be," Walker said. "Far as I'm concerned, Brylee always was half again too good for you, and in the long run you probably did her a favor by calling off the wedding. None of which means I wouldn't like to smash your face in for putting her through all that."

While Hutch privately agreed with much of what Walker had just said, he wasn't inclined to explain his repeated attempts to put the brakes on before he and Brylee and half the town ended up in the church on that fateful Saturday afternoon. And he'd come to Three Trees to apologize to Brylee, not her brother.

"If you want a fight, Walker," he said, "I'll give you one."

Walker appeared to consider the pros and cons of getting it on right there in the warehouse parking lot. In the end, though, he shook his head. "What goes around, comes around," he finally said. "You'll get what's coming to you." Then, as an apparent afterthought, he added, "You planning on entering the rodeo this year?"

"Don't I always?" Hutch answered, mindful that Walker provided the bulls and broncos for such events all over the West, including the one in Parable. He was well-known for breeding almost unrideable critters.

Walker grinned. "Here's hoping you draw the bull I have in mind for you," he said. "He's a real rib-stomper."

"Bring him on," Hutch replied, grinning back.

With that, the two men, having said their pieces, went their separate ways—Hutch heading for his truck, Walker going on into the warehouse.

Behind the wheel of his pickup, Hutch ground the key into the ignition.

He didn't know what he'd expected of this first post-disaster encounter with Brylee, but he'd *hoped* they could at least begin the process of burying the hatchet.

After all, neither of them were going anywhere.

Parable and Three Trees were only thirty miles apart, and the two communities were closely linked. In other words, they'd see each other all the time.

He sighed and drove away. Maybe there was something to Brylee's accusation that, in coming on this fool's errand, he'd been more interested in soothing his own conscience than making any kind of amends, but at least he'd tried—again—to set things right, so they could at least be civil to each other.

He figured it was probably too soon and wondered if the anti-Hutch internet campaign would ramp up a notch or two, since several of the key players—Brylee's friends and employees—had basically witnessed the confrontation.

These days everybody was an ace reporter.

"Well, cowboy man," he muttered to himself, "you're batting a thousand. Might as well go for broke."

Reaching the highway, he rolled on toward Parable. And Kendra.

MADISON WAS THRILLED with the new house when Kendra sprang the surprise on the little girl after picking her up at preschool that afternoon, and Daisy was thrilled with the spacious backyard.

The small colonial boasted two quite spacious bedrooms, plus a little cubicle Kendra planned to use as a home office, and two full baths. The kitchen was sunny, with plenty of cupboard space and a small pantry, and there was a large, old-fashioned brick fireplace in the living room. Closer inspection revealed small hooks in the wooden mantel for hanging Christmas stockings.

All in all, the place was perfect—except, of course, for being a rental and therefore impermanent. Kendra had asked Maggie about buying the house, but Maggie was understandably reluctant to sell. She said it would be like putting a price on her childhood, and she couldn't do that.

"This is my room!" Madison exulted now, standing in the center of the space with window seats and built-in bookshelves and shiny plank floors worn to a warmly aged patina. The folding closet doors were louvered, and the overhead light fixture was small but ornate.

Daisy gave a single joyous bark, as though seconding Madison's motion and making a claim of her own.

Kendra laughed. "Yes," she said to both of them. "This is your room."

"Am I going to have a bed?" Madison inquired matter-of-factly.

"Of course," Kendra replied. "We'll visit the furniture store over in Three Trees and you can pick it out yourself."

The town of Three Trees was actually smaller than Parable by a couple of thousand people, but it boasted a large outlet mall that drew customers from all over that part of the state, along with a movie house, a large bookstore and a Main Street lined with shops.

"Can we go *now?*" Madison asked.

"I don't see why not," Kendra replied. Her gaze fell on Daisy. Shopping for furniture with a puppy in tow didn't mesh.

The next question was inevitable, not to be forestalled. "Can Daisy come with us?" Madison wanted to know.

Sadly, Kendra shook her head. "That won't work, sweetie. But she'll be fine at the guesthouse, I promise."

Madison mulled that over, then her face brightened again. "All right," she said. "Daisy must be tired from playing with Lucy all day. She can take a nap while we're gone."

"Good thinking," Kendra said, holding out a hand to her daughter. "Let's get going."

Daisy was remarkably cooperative when they got back to the guest cottage. She lapped up half the water in her bowl, munched on some kibble, went outside with Madison to take care of dog business and returned to settle on her soft bed in the kitchen, yawning big.

Kendra's heart swelled into her throat as Madison crouched next to the puppy, patting its head gently and whispering, "Don't be scared, okay? Because Mommy and I will be back before it gets dark."

For the thousandth—if not millionth—time, Kendra wondered what life in that series of foster homes had been like for Madison. Had she felt safe, secure, loved?

According to the social workers, Madison's care had been exceptional—most foster parents were decent, dedicated people, generous enough to make room in their homes and their hearts for children in crisis.

Still, Madison had been passed around a lot, shuffled from one stand-in family to another. How could she *not* have been affected by so many changes in her short life?

Kendra was pondering all these things as she fastened the child into her booster seat in the backseat of the Volvo, and then as she slipped behind the wheel and started the engine. "I'm not going anywhere, you know," she felt compelled to say, making an effort to keep her voice light as they pulled out onto Rodeo Road.

She didn't so much as glance at the mansion either as they passed it or in the rearview mirror; it might have been rendered invisible.

Maybe, as some scientists claimed, things didn't actually exist until someone looked at them.

"Yes, you are *too* going somewhere," Madison responded, after a few moments of thought. "You're going to Three Trees so we can buy a bed!"

Kendra laughed, blinked a couple of times and focused her attention on the road, where it belonged. "That isn't what I meant, silly."

"My first mommy left," Madison said, perhaps sensing that Kendra's conversation was leading somewhere.

"Yes," Kendra said gently. "I know."

"But you won't leave," Madison said with reassuring conviction. "Because you *like* being a mommy."

Kendra sniffled. Blinked again, hard. "I love being *your* mommy," she replied. "You're the best thing that's ever happened to me, kiddo. Remember that, okay?"

"Okay," Madison said, her tone almost breezy. "Some of the kids at preschool have daddies, not just mommies."

The ache of emotion slipped from Kendra's throat to settle into her heart. Part of the child's remark echoed to the very center of her soul. *Not* just *mommies*.

"My daddy died," Madison went on. It was an exchange they'd had before, but repeating the facts seemed to comfort the little girl somehow, to anchor her in a new and better present. "He's in heaven."

"Yes," Kendra said, thick-voiced. She considered pulling over for a few moments, in order to pull herself together. "But he loved you very much. That's why he sent me to find you."

Thank you for that, Jeffrey. In spite of everything else, thank you for bringing Madison into my life.

The topic ricocheted with the speed of a bullet. "Is the cowboy man somebody's daddy?"

The question pierced Kendra's heart like an arrow. They were near the park, and she pulled over in the shade of a row of hundred-year-old maples, all dressed up in leafy green for summer, to regain her composure.

"I don't think so," she managed, after swallowing hard.

"I like the cowboy man," Madison said. A short pause followed and when she spoke again she sounded puzzled. "Why are we stopping, Mommy?"

Kendra touched the back of her right hand to one cheek, then the other. "I just needed a moment," she said.

"Are you crying?" Madison sounded worried now.

"Yes," Kendra answered, because it was her policy never to lie to the child, if it could be avoided.

"Why?"

"Because I'm happy," Kendra said. And that was

the truth. She *was* happy and she was grateful. She had a great life.

Still, there was the daddy thing.

As a little girl, lonely and adrift, tolerated by her grandmother rather than loved, Kendra had longed for a father even more than she had for a dog or a kitten. She could still feel the ache of that singular yearning to be carried, laughing, on strong shoulders, to feel protected and cherished and totally safe.

She was all grown up now, perfectly capable of protecting and cherishing her daughter as well as looking after herself and a certain golden retriever puppy in the bargain. But could she be both mother and father to her little girl?

Was she, and the love she offered, enough?

"I don't cry when I'm happy," Madison said as Kendra pulled the car back out onto the road. "I *laugh* when I'm happy."

"Makes sense," Kendra conceded, laughing herself.

They drove on to Three Trees, parked in front of the furniture store and hastened inside, hand in hand.

And they found the perfect bed almost immediately— it was twin-size, made of gleaming brass, with four high posts and a canopy frame on top. A dresser, a bureau and two night tables, all French provincial in style, completed the ensemble.

Kendra paid for their purchases—the pieces were to be delivered the next day, bright and early—and before they knew it, they were almost home again.

Madison, seemingly deep in thought for most of the drive, piped up as they pulled into the driveway. "Mommy, we forgot to buy a bed for *you*."

"I already have one, honey," Kendra responded, stopping the car alongside the guesthouse. She'd selected a few modest pieces from the mansion to take along to the new place. Most of the furniture in the main house was too big and too fancy for the simple colonial. There was a queen-size bed in one of the guest rooms that would work, a floral couch in the study, and they could use the table and chairs from Opal's old apartment.

Kendra wanted to leave room for some new things, too.

She parked the car and turned Madison loose, and they raced each other to the guest cottage, where Daisy met them at the door, barking a happy greeting.

Kendra set aside her purse, washed her hands, and searched the cottage fridge for the makings of an evening meal. She was chopping the vegetables for a salad, to which she would add leftover chicken breasts, also chopped, when she heard a vehicle coming up the driveway.

Peering out the kitchen window, she saw Hutch Carmody getting out of his truck.

Her stomach lurched and her heartbeat quickened as she hurriedly wiped her hands on a dish towel and went outside. Daisy and Madison, who had been playing in the kitchen moments before, rushed out to greet him.

Soon they were all over him.

He laughed at their antics and swung Madison off the ground and up onto his shoulders, where she clung, laughing, too.

The last of the afternoon sunlight caught in their hair—Hutch's a butternut color, Madison's like copper flames—and the dog circled them, barking her excitement.

Kendra couldn't help being struck by the sight of the

man and the little girl and the dog, looking so happy, so *right*.

She went outside.

"I was here earlier," Hutch told her, easing Madison off his back and setting her on her feet, where she jumped, reaching up, wanting to be lifted up again. "You weren't home."

Kendra couldn't speak for a moment, knowing, as she somehow did, that she might never get the image of the three of them together out of her head. It had been unspeakably beautiful, like some otherworldly vision of what family life *could* be.

"Hello?" Hutch teased, when she didn't say anything, standing close to her now, his head tipped a little to one side, like his grin. All the while, Madison was trying to climb him like a bean pole and he finally swung her back onto his shoulders.

"Come in," Kendra heard herself say, her voice all croaky and strange.

He nodded and followed her into the guest cottage, ducking so Madison wouldn't bump her head on the door frame. This time when he put the child down, she seemed content just to hover nearby.

He accepted the chair Kendra offered him at the small dining table and the coffee she brought him— black, the way he liked it.

Funny, the things you didn't forget about a person— mostly small and ordinary stuff, like coffee preferences and the way they always smelled of sun-dried cloth, even after a day spent hauling cattle out of mud holes or digging postholes.

Kendra gave herself a mental shake, sent a protesting Madison off to wash her hands and face before supper. Daisy, of course, tagged along with her small mistress, though she cast a few glances back at Hutch as she went.

"Join us for supper?" Kendra asked, hoping she sounded—well—neighborly.

Hutch shook his head. "No, thanks," he said, offering no further explanation, which was like him.

Kendra could hear Madison in the bathroom, running water in the sink, splashing around, talking nonstop to Daisy about the new house and the new bed and whether or not they'd be allowed to watch a DVD that night before they had to go to bed.

"Why are you here?" she finally asked very quietly. And this time, it wasn't a challenge. She was too tired for challenges, too wrung-out emotionally from the things Madison had said in the car.

Hutch sighed.

The distant splashing continued, as did the child-to-dog chatter.

"I'm not entirely sure," he said at some length, taking Kendra aback a little.

She couldn't remember one single instance in all the time she'd known Hutch Carmody when he hadn't been completely sure of everything and everybody, especially himself.

"That's helpful," she said mildly.

Any moment now Madison would be back in the room, thereby curtailing anything but the most mundane conversation.

"Joslyn tells me there's a cleanup day over at Pioneer Cemetery on Saturday," he finally said, after casting about visibly for something to say. "There'll be a town picnic afterward, like always, and, well, I was just wondering if you and Madison and Daisy might be interested in going along." He paused, cleared his throat. "With me."

Kendra was astounded, not so much by the invitation as by Hutch's apparent nervousness. Was he afraid she'd say no?

Or was he afraid she'd say yes?

"Okay," she agreed, as a compromise between the two extremes. She wanted, she realized, to see how he'd react.

Would he backpedal?

Instead he favored her with a dazzling grin, rose from his chair and passed her to set his coffee cup, still mostly full, in the sink. Their arms brushed and his nearness, the hard heat of his very masculine body, sent a jolt of sweet fire through her.

"Okay," he said with affable finality.

Madison was back by then, holding up her clean hands for Kendra to see but obviously more interested in Hutch than in her mother.

"Very good," Kendra said approvingly, and began moving briskly around the infinitesimal kitchen, setting out plates and silverware and glasses—which Madison promptly counted.

"Aren't you hungry, cowboy man?" she asked Hutch when the tally was two places at the table, rather than three.

He looked down at Madison with such fondness that Kendra felt another pang of—*something*. "Can't stay," he said. "I have horses to look after and they like their supper served on time, just like people do."

Madison's eyes widened. "You have *horses?*" From

her tone she might have asked, "You can walk on water?"

"Couldn't very well call myself a cowboy if I didn't have horses," Hutch said reasonably.

Madison pondered that, then nodded in agreement. Her eyes widened. "Can I ride one of your horses sometime? Please?"

"That would definitely be your mother's call," Hutch told her. It was grown-up vernacular, but Madison understood and immediately turned an imploring face to Kendra.

"Maybe sometime," Kendra said, because she couldn't quite get to a flat-out no. Not with all that ingenuous hope beaming up at her.

Remarkably, that noncommittal answer seemed to satisfy Madison. She scrambled into her chair at the table and waited for supper to start.

"See you on Saturday," Hutch said lightly.

And then he tousled Madison's hair, nodded to Kendra and the dog, and left the house.

"*Are* we going to see the cowboy man on Saturday?" Madison asked eagerly. Once again, it struck Kendra that, for a four-year-old, the child didn't miss much.

"Yes," Kendra said, setting the salad bowl in the center of the table and then pouring milk for herself and Madison. Daisy curled up on her dog bed in the corner, rested her muzzle on her forepaws, and rolled her lively brown eyes from Madison to Kendra and back again. "The whole town gets together every year to spruce the place up for the rodeo and the carnival. Lots of people like to visit the Pioneer Cemetery while they're here, and we like it to look presentable, so you and I and Hutch will be helping out there. After the work is done, there's always a picnic, and games for the kids to play."

"Games?" Madison was intrigued. "What kind of games?"

"Sack races." Kendra smiled, remembering happy times. "Things like that. There are even prizes."

"What's a sack race?" Madison pursued, a little frown creasing the alabaster skin between her eyebrows.

Kendra explained about stepping into a feed sack, holding it at waist level and hopping toward the finish line. She didn't mention the three-legged race, not wanting to describe that, too, but she smiled at the memory of herself and Joslyn tied together at the ankles and laughing hysterically when they lost their balance and tumbled into the venerable cemetery grass.

"And there are prizes?" Madison prompted.

Kendra nodded. "I won a doll once. She had a real camera hanging around her neck by a plastic strap. I still have her, somewhere."

Madison's eyes were huge. "Wow," she said. "There were cameras when you were a little girl?"

Kendra laughed. "Yes," she replied, "there were cameras. There were cars, too, and airplanes and even TVs."

Madison pondered all this, the turning gears in her little brain practically visible behind her forehead. "Wow," she repeated in awe.

After supper, Madison had her bath and put on her pajamas, and Kendra popped a favorite DVD of an animated movie into the player attached to the living room TV.

Madison snuggled on the floor with Daisy, one arm

flung companionably across the small dog's gleaming back, and the two of them were quickly absorbed in the on-screen story.

Kendra, relieved that she wouldn't have to sit through the movie for what must have been the seventy-second time, set up her laptop on the freshly cleared kitchen table and booted it up.

She'd surf the web for a while, she decided, and see if there were any for-sale-by-owner listings posted for the Parable/Three Trees area. She was, after all, a working real estate broker, and sometimes a well-placed phone call to said owners would produce a new client. Most folks didn't realize all that was entailed in selling a property themselves—title searches and tax liens were only *some* of the snags they might run into.

Alas, despite her good intentions, Kendra ended up running a search on Hutch Carmody instead, using the key word *wedding*.

The page that came up might as well have been called "We Hate Hutch."

Kendra found herself in the odd position of wanting to defend him—and furiously—as she looked at the pictures.

Brylee, the discarded bride, heartbroken and furious in her grandmother's wedding gown.

Hutch, standing straight and tall and obviously miserable midway down the aisle, guests gawking on either side as he held up both hands in a gesture that plainly said, "Hold everything."

The condolence party over at the Boot Scoot Tavern, Brylee wearing a sad expression and a T-shirt that said Men Suck.

Beware, murmured a voice in the back of Kendra's mind.

But even then she knew she wouldn't heed her own warning.

After all, what could happen in broad daylight, in a cemetery, with Madison and half the county right there?

CHAPTER FIVE

"DOES THIS SEEM a little weird to you?" Kendra asked Joslyn on Saturday morning as they helped Opal and a dozen other women set out tons of home-prepared food on the picnic tables at Pioneer Cemetery. "Holding what amounts to a party in a graveyard, I mean?"

Joslyn, who looked as though she might be having trouble keeping her center of gravity balanced, smiled and plunked herself down on one of the benches while the cheerful work went on around her. "I think it's one of the best things about small towns," she replied. "The way life and death are integrated—after all, they're part of the same cycle, aren't they? You can't have one without the other."

Thoughtful, Kendra scanned the surrounding area for Madison, something that came automatically to her now, and found her and Daisy industriously "helping" Hutch, Shea and several of the older girl's friends from school pull weeds around a nearby scattering of very old graves. The water tower loomed in the distance, with its six-foot stenciled letters reading "Parable," its rickety ladders and its silent challenge to every new generation of teenagers: *Climb me.*

"I guess you're right," Kendra said very quietly, though by then the actual substance of her friend's remark had essentially slipped her mind. An instant

later, though, at some small sound—a gasp, maybe—
she turned to look straight at Joslyn.

Joslyn sat with one hand splayed against either side
of her copiously distended stomach, her eyes huge with
delighted alarm. "I think it's time," she said in a joyous whisper.

"Oh, my God," Kendra replied, instantly panicked,
stopping herself just short of putting a hand to her
mouth.

Opal stepped up, exuding a take-charge attitude.
"Now everybody, just stay calm," she commanded.
"Babies are born every second of every day in every
part of the world, and this is going to turn out just fine."

"G-get Slade," Joslyn managed, smiling and winc-
ing at the same time. "Please."

No one had to go in search of Joslyn's husband; he
seemed to have sonar where his wife was concerned.

Kendra watched with relief as he came toward them,
his strides long and purposeful, but calm and measured,
too. He was grinning from ear to ear when he reached
Joslyn and crouched in front of her, taking both her
hands in his.

"Breathe," he told her.

Joslyn laughed, nodded and breathed.

"It's time, then?" he asked her, gruffly gentle. His
strength was quiet and unshakable.

"Definitely," Joslyn replied.

"Then let's get this thing done," Slade replied,
straightening to his full height and easing Joslyn to
her feet, supporting her in the curve of one steel-strong
arm as they headed for the parking lot.

Opal took off her apron, thrust it into the hands of

a woman standing nearby and hurried after them, taking her big patent leather purse with her.

Shea materialized at Kendra's side with Madison and Daisy and leaned into her a little, her expression worried and faintly lost.

Kendra wrapped an arm around the teenage girl's slender shoulders and squeezed. "Everything's going to be all right," she said softly. "Just like Opal said."

"They forgot all about me," Shea murmured, staring after her stepparents and Opal as they retreated.

"No, sweetheart," Kendra said quickly. "They're just excited because the baby's coming and maybe a little scared, that's all."

Shea bit her lower lip, swallowed visibly, and rummaged up a small, tremulous smile. "A baby brother will be hard to compete with," she reflected. "Especially since he really belongs to them and I don't."

Kendra knew Shea adored Slade—her mother, his ex-wife, was remarried and living in L.A.—and she also knew that Slade loved this girl as much as if he'd fathered her himself. And Joslyn loved her, too.

"You belong to them, too, Shea," Kendra assured the girl. "Don't forget that."

Madison, perhaps sobered by Shea's mood—the two had been hanging out together since Madison and Kendra had arrived with Hutch—slipped her hand into Kendra's and looked up at her with wide, solemn eyes.

"Are babies better than big kids?" she asked very seriously.

Kendra's heart turned over. "Babies are very special," she answered carefully, "and so are the big kids they turn into."

As she spoke, Hutch stepped into her line of sight,

and something happened inside Kendra as she watched him watching Slade and Joslyn's departing vehicle. Opal sat tall and stalwart in the backseat.

What *was* that look in his eyes? Worry, perhaps? Envy?

Back in high school, Kendra recalled, Joslyn had been Hutch's first love and he hers. Most people had expected them to marry at some point, perhaps after college, but they'd grown apart instead, from a romantic standpoint at least. They had remained close friends.

She, Kendra, had been his *second* love.

Maybe that was why he hadn't stepped in when she threw herself into an ill-fated relationship with Jeffrey Chamberlain, way back when. Possibly, letting her go had been easy because he hadn't really been over Joslyn at that point.

In fact it could well be that he *still* wasn't over her, even though she was happily married to his half brother and about to give birth to their first child.

Now you're just being silly, Kendra scolded herself silently, straightening her spine and raising her chin. Besides, what did it matter who Hutch Carmody did or did not love? He'd hurt every woman he'd ever cared about—except Joslyn.

"Do you want me to drive you to the hospital?"

The question had come from Hutch and he was looking at Shea as he spoke. Although he and Slade were still working on being brothers, he was already an uncle to Shea and she was a niece to him.

Shea shook her head, slipped away from Kendra's side and held out a hand to Madison. "The three-legged race is starting soon," she said to the little girl. "Want to be my partner?"

Madison nodded eagerly and crowed, "Yes!" for good measure, in case there might be any ambiguity in the matter.

"Let's go check out the prize table then," Shea said. And just like that, they were off, racing through the grass, Daisy and Jasper, the Barlows' dog, bounding after them.

"Slade and Joslyn do realize," Kendra began, without really meaning to say anything at all, "that Shea is worried that they won't love her as much once the baby is here?"

Hutch, standing nearer than she'd thought, replied quietly, "Slade and I may have our differences," he said, "but the man is rock-solid when it comes to loving his family." A pause followed, then a wistful, "Not a trait he learned from our dad."

Picking up on the pain in his words, she looked at him directly.

They were essentially alone together, under those leafy, breeze-rustled trees, because everyone else had gone back to what they were doing before Joslyn had gone into labor—setting out food, pulling weeds, mowing grass, generally getting ready for the festivities that would follow on the heels of the cleanup effort.

Hutch, meanwhile, looked as though he regretted the remark about John Carmody, not because he hadn't meant it, but because it revealed more than he wanted her or anyone else to know.

"Tell me about your dad," Kendra said, pushing the envelope a little. She remembered the elder Carmody clearly, of course, but she hadn't really known him. He'd been a grown-up, after all, and a reserved one at that, handsome like Slade and almost religious about minding his own business.

Hutch took her hand, and she let him, and they drifted away from the others to sit on rocks overlooking the town of Parable, nestled into the shallow valley below. "Not much to tell," he said in belated reply to her earlier request. "The old man and I didn't see eye to eye on most things, and he made it pretty plain that I didn't measure up to his expectations."

"But you loved him?"

"I loved him," Hutch confirmed, staring out over the town, past the church steeples and the courthouse roof. "And I guess, in his own way, he probably loved me. Do you remember your dad, Kendra?"

She shook her head. "He was long gone by the time I was born," she said.

Remarkably, as close as they'd been, she and Hutch hadn't talked much about their childhoods. They'd been totally, passionately engrossed in the present.

Now Kendra thought about her mother, Sherry, beautiful and flaky and too footloose to raise a little girl on her own. In a moment, Kendra was right back there, like a time traveler, standing in the overgrown yard in front of her grandmother's trailer, clutching Sherry's fingers with one hand and gripping the handle of a toy suitcase in the other.

She'd been five years old at the time, only a few months older than Madison was now.

"I'll be back soon, I promise," she heard Sherry say as clearly as if a quarter of a century hadn't passed since that summer day. "You just sit there on the porch like a good girl and wait for your grandma to get home from work. She'll take care of you until I can come and get you."

Maybe the suitcase, hastily purchased in a thrift store, should have been a clue about what was to come, but Kendra was, after all, a child and a trusting one at that. She hadn't known she was being lied to, not consciously at least.

Most likely Sherry hadn't known she was lying, either. Never mean, Sherry had always meant well. She just had trouble following through on her better intentions.

In the end, she'd leaned down, kissed Kendra on the top of her head, promised they'd be together again soon, this time for good. They'd get a house of their own and a dog and a nice car.

With that, Sherry waggled her fingers in farewell, climbed into her ancient, smoke-belching station wagon and drove away.

Kendra simply sat and waited—it wouldn't have occurred to her to wander off or run after Sherry's car.

When her grandmother arrived home a couple hours later, she got out of her car, lit up a cigarette and drew deeply on the smoke. Then she crossed the overgrown yard to stand there frowning down at Kendra.

With her bent and buckled plastic suitcase beside her, Kendra looked up into her grandmother's lined and sorrow-hardened face, and saw no welcome there.

"Just what I need," the old woman had said bitterly. "A kid to take care of."

But Alva Shepherd *had* given Kendra a home, however reluctantly.

She'd put food on the table and kept a roof over their heads and if love and laughter had been lacking from the relationship, well, nobody had everything. If Sherry hadn't dropped her off that day, she probably would have been killed in the car accident that took her mom's life six months later.

After that, her grandma had been a little nicer to her, not out of compassion—she didn't seem to grieve over losing a daughter or Kendra's loss of her mother, apparently regarding it as a fitting end to a misspent life—but because Kendra became eligible for a small monthly check from the government. That made things easier all around.

"Kendra?" Hutch tugged her back into the here and now, still holding her hand.

"There are too many broken people in this world," she said, thinking aloud.

Hutch simply gazed at her for a long, unreadable moment. "True enough," he agreed finally, almost hoarsely. "But there are plenty of good ones, too, built to stay the course."

Happy noises in the distance indicated that the games were about to start and picnic food was being served. Hutch was right, of course—these sturdy people all around them were the proof, teaming up to tend the grounds of a decrepit old cemetery, to serve potato salad and hot dogs and the like to old friends and new, to hold races for children who would remember sunny, communal days like this one well into their own old age.

In that moment, Kendra felt a wistful sort of hope that places like Parable would always exist, so babies could be born and grow up and get married and live on into their golden years, always in touch with their own histories and those of the people around them, always a part of something, always belonging somewhere.

It was what Kendra had wanted for Madison, that kind of stability, and what she wanted for herself, too— because her story hadn't ended with her overwhelmed grandmother on the rickety porch of a double-wide that had, even then, seen better days. Because Opal had taken her into her heart and Joslyn had been the sister she'd never had, and the generous souls who called Parable home had taken her into their midst without hesitation, made her one of them.

Tears brimmed in her eyes.

Hutch, seeing them, stopped and cupped a hand under her chin. "What?" he asked with a tenderness that made Kendra's breath catch.

"I was just thinking how perfect life is," Kendra admitted, "even when it's *im*perfect."

He grinned. "It's worth the trouble, all right," he agreed. "Want to enter the three-legged race? I can't think of anybody I'd rather be tied to at the ankle."

She laughed and said yes, and threw herself head-first into the celebration.

PARABLE COUNTY HOSPITAL was small, with brightly painted white walls, and most of the staff had been born and raised within fifty miles of the place, so folks felt safe when they were sick or hurt, knowing they'd be cared for by friends, or friends of friends, or even kinfolk.

Hutch hadn't been there since his dad died, but now there was the baby boy, born a few hours before, ratcheting up the population by one. The numbers on the sign at the edge of town were magnetic, so they could be altered when somebody drew their first breath, sighed out their last one or simply moved to or from the community.

Slade, standing beside him, rested a hand briefly on his shoulder. After the races and the picnic and the prizes, he'd dropped Kendra and Madison and that goofy dog of theirs off at their new digs before heading home to shower, shave, put on clean clothes and make the drive back to town.

"You done good, brother," Hutch said without looking at Slade.

Slade chuckled. He hadn't taken his eyes off that little blue-bundled yahoo in the plastic baby bed since they'd stepped up to the window. "Thanks," he replied, "but Joslyn deserves at least some of the credit. She handled the tough part."

Hutch smiled, nodded. The kid hadn't even been in the world for a full day and he was already looking more like John Carmody, as did Slade, by the second. He guessed it was the old man's way of keeping one foot in the world, even though he was six feet under. "What are you going to call him?" he asked.

"Trace," Slade answered, with a touch of quiet awe in his voice, as though he didn't quite believe his own good fortune. "Trace Carmody Barlow."

Hutch wasn't prepared for the "Carmody" part. While Slade was technically as much a Carmody as Hutch himself was, their dad hadn't raised him, hadn't even claimed him until his will was read.

Slade interpreted his half brother's silence accurately. "It's a way of telling the truth," he said. "About who Trace is and who I am."

Hutch swallowed. Nodded. "How's Joslyn?" he managed to ask.

"She's ready to take the boy and head home to Windfall," Slade said with another chuckle. "Opal and I overruled her, insisting that she spend the night here in the hospital, just to make sure she and the baby don't run into any hitches."

Windfall was the aptly chosen name of Slade and Joslyn's ranch, which bordered Hutch's land on one side. Slade had bought the spread with the proceeds from selling his share of Whisper Creek to Hutch and, as convoluted as the situation had been, Hutch would always be grateful. He was a part of that ranch and it was a part of him, and losing half of it would have been like being chopped into two pieces himself.

"I see you brought Kendra and her little girl to the cleanup today," Slade remarked lightly.

Hutch looked straight at him. "Some first date, huh?" he joked, not that it actually *was* a first date, considering that he and Kendra had once been a couple. "A picnic at a cemetery."

Slade grinned. "I took Joslyn to a horse auction the first time we went out," he reminded Hutch. "Maybe chivalry runs in the family."

"Or maybe not," Hutch said, and they both laughed. Shook hands.

"Thanks for showing up to have a look at the boy," Slade said.

Hutch nodded, said a quiet goodbye and turned to go while Slade stayed behind to admire his son for a little while longer.

Shea and Opal were standing in the corridor when Hutch got there, talking quietly with a beaming Callie Barlow.

"That's one fine little brother you've got there," he told Shea.

Apparently over her earlier angst at no longer being the only bird in the nest, Shea smiled brightly and nodded in happy agreement. Callie hugged her step-granddaughter, her own eyes full of tears.

"He's the best," Shea murmured.

"Congratulations," Hutch said to Callie. It was, if he recalled correctly, the first word he'd ever said to the woman, even though he'd always known her. It wasn't that he'd judged her—he supposed she'd loved the old man once upon a time, since she'd had a child with him—but Hutch's mother's heartache and rage over the affair was still fresh in his mind. Until Trace, acknowledging Callie would have seemed like an act of disloyalty to his mom, as crazy as that sounded. After all, she'd died when he was twelve.

"Thank you, Hutch," Callie said, dashing at her wet eyes with the back of one hand.

"You look skinnier every time I see you," Opal put in, giving Hutch the once-over and frowning with devoted disapproval. To Opal, everybody in Parable was her concern, one way or the other. "You need me to come out to Whisper Creek and cook for you for a couple of weeks. Put some meat on those bones. And who ironed that shirt—a chimpanzee?"

Hutch grinned, though he felt a thousand years old all of a sudden and bone-weary in the bargain. "Nobody ironed it," he said, even as he wondered why he'd risen to the bait. "It's permanent press." He'd taken the garment out of the dryer and pulled it on just before leaving the house to drive back to town.

"There's no such thing as 'permanent press.'" Opal sniffed. "A shirt ought to be *ironed*."

That seemed like a good time to steer the conversation in another direction. "I appreciate your offer, Opal," he said honestly, "but Joslyn's going to need you to help take care of Trace."

"Joslyn's mama is on her way to Parable as we speak," Opal replied succinctly. "She'll provide all the lookin' after that family needs, at least for a week or two. I'll be at your place first thing tomorrow morning with my suitcase, so be ready for me."

Hutch opened his mouth, closed it again.

There was no point in arguing with Opal Dennison once she'd made up her mind, which she obviously had. If she meant to take over his house—or his whole life, for that matter—she'd do it. She was about as stoppable as a tornado gobbling up flat ground.

Best to just get out of the way and wait for the dust to settle.

"See you tomorrow," he finally said.

"Pick up some spray starch on your way home," Opal ordered. "And a decent iron, too, if you don't have one."

He pretended not to hear and walked off toward the elevator.

THE ELEVATOR DOORS opened, and Kendra came face-to-face with Hutch when she stepped out.

Even after spending much of the day in his company over at the Pioneer Cemetery, she felt startled by the encounter. Unprepared and very nervous.

"Where's Madison?" he asked, his gaze drifting lightly over Kendra's cotton print sundress, which she changed into after the picnic, and then back to her face.

Kendra found her voice. Stepping past him, she remembered that she'd come to the hospital on a mission—to see her best friend's brand-new baby for the first time. "Downstairs," she answered automatically. "The receptionist is looking after her."

"I'll say howdy to her on my way out," Hutch replied.

He entered the elevator. The doors whispered shut between them and Kendra was left with the odd sensation that she'd imagined the whole exchange, if not the whole crazy *day*.

Had she really entered—and lost—a three-legged race at a cemetery picnic?

Seeing Callie and Shea and Opal in a happy huddle, she joined them.

"How's the new mama?" she asked.

Shea rolled her eyes. She was flushed and twinkly with excitement, like a girl-shaped topiary draped in fairy lights. "Would you believe Joss wants to go home—*right now?* Dad and Opal are making her stay the night, though—just to be on the safe side."

"So I guess that means Joslyn's doing just fine," Kendra said, smiling.

"She's amazing," Callie put in. "And so is little Trace. Lordy, he looks just like his daddy. Slade Barlow in miniature, that's him."

"Dad's walking about a foot off the ground," Shea said, pleased.

"Hutch's mama would roll over in her grave if she saw him wearing that wrinkled shirt out in public," Opal fretted, her gaze focused on the closed elevator doors. "She took pride in things like that."

Kendra blinked, confused.

"Don't mind Opal," Shea said in a conspiratorial

whisper, slipping an arm through Kendra's. "She's suffering from a laundry fixation at the moment—it'll pass."

"Oh," Kendra said, no less confused than before but allowing herself to be swept into Joslyn's room.

Her friend was sitting up in bed, hair brushed, face scrubbed and glowing, eyes lively with joy. "Did you see him yet?" she asked, her tone happy and urgent.

Kendra laughed. "Not yet," she admitted. "I just got here a minute ago."

That dazed feeling, as if she couldn't quite catch up with herself, was still with her.

There were flowers everywhere, making the small quarters look and feel more like a garden than a hospital room.

Joslyn beamed. "I can't wait to have another one," she said.

"Whoa," protested Slade, from the doorway, grinning. "We just got out of the delivery room a couple of hours ago, woman."

"Come here and kiss me," Joslyn told him.

Shea laughed and made a face. "Gross," she said fondly.

By that time, Slade had crossed the room, bent over Joslyn, and touched his mouth to hers. The air crackled with electricity.

Kendra, still befuddled, remembered the bouquet of yellow carnations she was carrying and found a place for it among the tangle of color filling the room nearly to overflowing.

A nurse brought little Trace in then and placed him gently in Joslyn's waiting arms. The sight of the three of them—father, mother and child—was a poignant one to Kendra and she felt a warm twinge of affection—along with a touch of envy. The latter was followed by a swift plunge into guilt, because she loved Madison so fiercely, and wanting to bear a child of her own seemed almost greedy.

Joslyn's gaze over the baby's downy head rested warmly on Kendra for a moment and the kind of understanding only close friends can share passed between them.

Shea took a cautious step forward. "Could—could I hold him?" she asked.

Joslyn smiled at the girl. "Of course," she replied easily. "Here—let me show you how to support his head…."

As simply, as beautifully, as that, Shea took her place in this newly expanded family—and then there were four.

Kendra was so choked up she nearly fled the room, fearing she'd cry and Joslyn would misunderstand.

"I'll pay you a visit when you get home," she told her friend, aware of Callie and Opal entering the room behind her. The walls were starting to close in; she needed fresh air and space to recover her equilibrium.

What was wrong with her, anyway?

"Wait," Joslyn said when Kendra would have made her exit. "There's something I want to ask you before you go and it's important."

Kendra, mystified and strangely hopeful, approached the bedside. Shea, holding the baby expertly, made room for her in the small, cozy circle, and Slade looked at her with a smile in his eyes.

Up close, Trace was so beautiful that he claimed a piece of Kendra's heart, right then and there, and she knew she'd never get it back, never even *want* to get it back.

"Will you be Trace's godmother?" Joslyn asked softly, reaching out to cover Kendra's cool and somewhat unsteady hand with her own warm one. Her grasp was firm.

The request was a simple one and yet it touched Kendra to the center of her soul, an unexpected grace. "I'd be proud," she managed in a ragged voice.

Joslyn squeezed her hand. "Good," she said, tearing up herself. "That's good."

Overcome, Kendra touched Trace's tiny head, turned and hurried out of Joslyn's hospital room. The instant she crossed the threshold, the tears came in rivers and she ducked into the women's restroom to pull herself together.

At one of the sinks, she splashed cold water on her face, not caring that she'd ruined her mascara. She used a moist paper towel to wipe away the dark trails on her cheeks, drew a deep breath and squared her shoulders, ready to face the world.

For the most part, anyway.

Downstairs Madison was ensconced at the main desk, coloring importantly and enjoying being the center of attention.

It threw Kendra a little when she realized that Hutch was there, too, chatting amicably with the receptionist. Barely out of her teens, the young woman, whose name tag read Darcy, looked up at him with an expression that resembled wonder, hanging on his every word.

Kendra found herself withdrawing slightly—she might have been able to hide her puffy eyes from Madison, but Hutch was another matter. He noticed right away and she knew he probably wouldn't ignore the only-too-obvious fact that she'd been crying, very recently and a lot.

He might even deduce that, while she was very happy for Slade and Joslyn, she was feeling oddly hopeless at the moment, and that would make her too vulnerable to all that cowboy charm.

"Maybe I ought to drive you and Madison home in my truck," he said, straightening and stepping back from the tall reception counter. "I can call one of the ranch hands to bring your car back over to your place."

Hutch's attention had fully shifted by then, entirely focused on Kendra, and the receptionist seemed not just miffed but crestfallen, as though the sun had suddenly stopped shining for good.

"Mommy cries when she's happy," Madison announced. "She told me so, when we went to buy my bed at the store in Three Trees."

Hutch's mouth quirked upward at one side. "Crying and driving don't mix very well," he said easily, huskily. "Especially when there's precious cargo aboard."

"What's precipitous car-blow?" Madison asked.

"It's what you are," Hutch told the child, though his eyes hadn't left Kendra's face.

There was no question of refusing to accept his offer of a ride home; that would make her look like a careless mother, willing to risk her daughter's safety in order to protect her pride, which, of course, she wasn't. And never mind that she was perfectly capable of operating a motor vehicle; it wasn't as if she'd been drinking, for Pete's sake.

For these reasons, and others not so easy to recognize, she gave in.

She even said, "Thank you."

Outside Hutch sprinted over to the Volvo to fetch Madison's car seat from the back, and within a few moments he was installing the gear inside his extended cab truck. His hands moved with a deftness Kendra well remembered as he hoisted Madison into the seat—he, the bachelor rancher and local heartthrob, might have performed the task a million times before.

Madison loved being fussed over by a daddy type— what little girl didn't?—and if she'd been wearing a dress instead of those little jeans and a T-shirt, she probably would have stood right there in the hospital parking lot and twirled her skirt.

A softness settled over Kendra's heart as she looked on, but it was soon replaced by a flicker of dread. She could certainly prevent herself from falling in love with Hutch Carmody, but could she prevent *Madison* from buying into the illusion?

Hutch, despite his wild ways, was decent through and through. He genuinely liked people, particularly children, and he talked to them with a rare, enfolding ease that naturally made them feel special, even entirely unique.

It wasn't a deception, Kendra concluded sadly, not really. The problem was that, to Hutch, *every* child was special and every woman. Every dog and horse, too.

She tried to shake off these thoughts as she climbed into the front passenger seat, once Madison was settled, and buckled herself in for the short ride home.

If she didn't allow herself to care too much for this man, she reasoned fitfully, as Hutch took the wheel and started the truck's engine, maybe Madison wouldn't care too much for him, either.

CHAPTER SIX

MADISON, AFTER GREETING a wildly joyful Daisy the moment they entered the new house, where there were still boxes all around, accumulated over several days of moving, took Hutch by one hand and practically dragged him from one room to another, showing the place off. Of course the dog followed them, occasionally putting in her two-bits with a happy little bark.

Kendra, emotionally winded from a long and eventful day, remained in the kitchen doing busywork, washing her hands at the sink, debating whether or not she ought to brew some coffee. The stuff could keep her up half the night, but as she remembered only too well, Hutch could drink the strongest java at midnight and still enjoy the sleep of the innocent and the just.

Talk about ironic.

Still Hutch had brought her and Madison safely home from the hospital visit to see the newest member of the Barlow clan—she was going to be Trace's godmother and the honor humbled her—and she owed the man the courtesy of a cup of coffee if he wanted one.

He'd pretty well gone to the wall that day, Hutch had, and he'd been a big part of some very memorable experiences for both her and Madison. At his suggestion, she'd left the keys to her Volvo at the hospital reception desk, and a couple of his ranch hands were already en route from Whisper Creek to pick up the vehicle and bring it to her.

Yes, the least she could do was offer the man coffee.

She didn't dare think about the *most* she could have done.

In the distance she heard Madison's ringing laugh, the dog's excitement at having the family intact and a visitor thrown in as a bonus, and Hutch's now-and-again comment, all along the lines of, "Well, isn't *that* something."

By the time the three wayfarers got back to the kitchen, Kendra had brewed a coffee for Hutch and an herbal tea for herself, using the one-cup wonder machine brought over from the big house. The device looked massive in this much smaller room, and way too fancy, but it served its purpose and for now that was enough.

"This is quite a change from the mansion," Hutch observed quietly as Madison hurried for the back door, calling over one shoulder that Daisy needed to go outside, and quick!

Kendra merely smiled and held out the cup of black coffee.

"Don't mind if I do," Hutch said, taking the mug. It looked fragile as a china teacup in his strong rancher's hands. "Thanks."

She inclined her head toward the table and he drew back a chair, but waited until she sat down with her tea before he took a seat himself.

His manners were yet another of Hutch's contradictions: he would leave a woman practically at the altar, wearing her heirloom wedding dress, break her heart right there in the presence of all her friends and family, but he opened doors for anyone of the female persuasion, whatever her age, and his male elders, too.

Through the open screen door, with its creaky hinges, Madison could be heard encouraging Daisy to hurry up and be a good girl so they could go back inside and be with the cowboy man.

Hutch grinned across the expanse of the tabletop and Kendra grinned back.

"This has been quite a day," she said, wondering if Hutch had the same odd mixture of feelings as she had where Slade and Joslyn's new baby was concerned. He was clearly happy for the Barlows, but she knew he wanted kids, too—it had been a favorite topic between them, back in the day, how many children they'd have, the ideal ratio of boys to girls, and even what their names would be.

A weary sort of sorrow overtook Kendra, just for that moment, and nearly brought tears to her eyes.

She shook it off. No sense getting all moody and nostalgic.

"That it has," Hutch agreed in his own good time, which was the way he did everything. The habit could be exasperating, Kendra reflected, except in bed.

Whoa, she thought. *Don't go down that road.*

A warm flush pulsed in her cheeks, though, and he noticed, of course. He always noticed what she'd rather have hidden, and overlooked things that should have caught his attention.

She looked away for a moment, recovering from the sexual flashback.

Madison and the dog came back inside, which helped Kendra calm down, and Madison sort of hovered around Hutch like a moth around a lightbulb.

Kendra finally sent Madison into the living room to watch the cartoon channel for the allowed half-hour before bath and bed, not because she wanted to get rid of her, but because the child's obvious adoration for Hutch was so unnerving.

Only cartoons could have distracted Madison from this admittedly fascinating man and even then she was reluctant to leave the room.

As soon as they were alone, Kendra opened her mouth and stuck her foot in it. "Don't let her get too attached to you, Hutch," she heard herself almost plead, in a sort of fractured whisper. "Madison's already lost so much."

Hutch looked stunned; he even paled a little, under his year-round tan, but in a nanosecond, he'd gone from stunned to quietly furious.

"What the hell is *that* supposed to mean?" he demanded, and though he kept his voice low, it rumbled like thunder gathering beyond the nearby hills.

Kendra let out a long breath, closed her eyes briefly, and rubbed her temples with the fingertips of both hands. "I wasn't saying—"

He leaned slightly forward in his chair, his bluish-green eyes fierce on her face. "What *were* you saying, then?" he pressed. She knew that look—he wasn't going to let this one go, would sit there all night if he had to, until he got an answer he could accept as the unvarnished truth.

"Madison is only four years old," she said weakly. Carefully. "She doesn't understand that your charm, like sunshine and rain, pretty much falls on everybody." She tried for more clarity and spoke with more strength now. "I don't want her getting too fond of you, Hutch.

You're so nice to her and she might read things into that that aren't there."

Hutch shoved a hand through his hair in a gesture of pure annoyance. His jawline went a bloodless white, he was clenching his back molars together so tightly. "You think I play *games* with people—with kids?" he finally asked, as though the concept had come out of left field and mowed him down. "You think I get some kind of kick out of making them believe I care so I can kick their feelings around later, just for the fun of it?"

Kendra hiked up her chin and met his gaze straight on. "Maybe not with children," she allowed evenly, "but do you 'play games' with women? That's a definite yes, Hutch. And I'm sure Brylee Parrish isn't the only person who'd be willing to back me up on the theory."

"You believe all that—" he paused, looked back over one shoulder, probably to make sure Madison hadn't wandered back into earshot and, seeing that she hadn't, finished with "—*crap* on the internet?"

Kendra's chuckle was light, but edged with a degree of bitterness that surprised even her. "Pictures don't lie," she said. "Besides, this goes back a lot further than your infamy on the web. Maybe you've forgotten that one of those broken hearts was mine?"

He looked as though he couldn't believe what he was hearing. "And maybe *you've* forgotten that we had something good going for us before you decided to kick off the traces and become Lady Chamberlain."

"It wasn't like that at all!" Kendra whispered.

"Go ahead and rewrite history to suit yourself," Hutch rasped, pushing back his chair and standing up, his half-finished coffee forgotten. He made the move so quietly that his chair didn't so much as scrape the floor, but rage was hardwired into every lean, power-ful line of him. He set his hands on his hips and looked down at her for a long moment, then added, "The fact is, sweetheart, *you* walked out on *me*."

A knock sounded at the screen door just then, and a man's face appeared on the other side of the mesh. "Brought the car," he said, jangling the keys.

Hutch crossed the room, yanked the screen door open, and stormed right past the guy without even glancing at him.

The ranch hand looked at him curiously and ex-tended the Volvo keys to Kendra, who had followed Hutch as far as the threshold, even though she had no intention of pursuing him. All the things she wanted to say to Hutch—okay, *scream* at him—were lodged painfully in the back of her throat, where she'd barely managed to stop them.

"Thank you," Kendra said mildly, taking the keys from the visitor's hand.

"You're mighty welcome," the weathered cowboy replied with a practiced tug at his hat brim. A mischie-vous twinkle lit his eyes. "Seems like this wouldn't be a good time to hit the boss up for a raise."

Kendra smiled at the joke. "You're probably right," she replied.

Hutch's truck started up with a roar, and both Ken-dra and the ranch hand winced a little when the tires screeched as he pulled away from the curb.

The cowboy shook his head, smiled ruefully and turned toward the other Whisper Creek truck waiting in the short driveway alongside the house, a second man at the wheel.

Kendra waved, closed the screen door, then its inside counterpart, hung the keys on a nearby hook and turned to find herself facing her daughter.

Madison and Daisy stood side by side, in the middle of the kitchen, their heads tilted at exactly the same angle, their gazes questioning and worried.

Kendra had to smile at the picture they made, even though she was still so irritated with Hutch that she felt like tearing out hanks of her own hair.

"The cowboy man didn't say goodbye," Madison said, and her lower lip wobbled slightly.

It was one of those rare times when only a lie would do, Kendra decided ruefully. "Actually, Mr. Carmody was in a big hurry, and he asked me to tell you goodbye and say he was sorry he had to rush off."

Madison, being an intelligent child, looked skeptical and unappeased, but she accepted the fib—to a degree. "I heard mad voices," she challenged Kendra after a few beats.

They'd been so careful not to yell, she and Hutch, though she'd *wanted* to and it was probably safe to assume Hutch had, as well. Madison had picked up on the energy of the exchange, rather than the actual words.

"It's time for your bath and a story," Kendra said moderately, striving for normalcy. How could Hutch claim, for one *moment,* that she'd been the one to break them up? He'd virtually *handed her over* to Jeffrey and walked away whistling.

"You should be nice to people," Madison lectured. "That's what you always tell me."

Kendra placed splayed fingers gently between her daughter's shoulders and started her in the direction of the main bathroom. "Let's have this discussion another time, please," she said.

Daisy's toenails clicked on the hardwood floor behind them as she and Madison headed down the hall, Madison resisting ever so slightly as they went.

"But you forgot *supper*," the child reasoned.

Sure enough, Kendra realized, the evening meal had completely slipped her mind. "You're right," she replied, at once chagrined and glad to find common ground, even if it was a little shaky. "Tell you what— we'll feed Daisy and then, after you've had your bath, I'll whip up a couple of grilled cheese sandwiches for us. How would that be?"

Madison looked up at her and something in her small, obstinate face relented. "I like grilled cheese sandwiches," she admitted.

Kendra smiled. "Me, too," she said.

With Madison stripping and Daisy supervising the whole enterprise, Kendra managed to prepare the little girl's bath—a few inches of warm water with bubbles.

Madison climbed in and Daisy rested her muzzle on the edge of the bathtub, watching her small mistress, brown eyes shining with love.

"Can Daisy get into the tub, too?" Madison asked, reaching for her pink sponge and the duck-shaped bar of soap she favored.

"Not this time, sweetie," Kendra said, since that seemed better than a flat no.

Madison huffed out a sigh and began her ablutions, perfectly capable of bathing herself.

A few minutes later, she announced, "I'm clean now, Mommy!"

Smiling, despite the quiet but persistent ache in the

region of her heart Hutch still claimed, Kendra gave her a kiss and reached for a towel.

HUTCH HAD ALWAYS been good at letting stuff roll off his back—he'd had to be—but that tangle with Kendra back at her place made him want to fight.

With anybody, about anything.

When the lights of Boone's cop car flashed behind him, just before the turn-in at Whisper Creek, it almost pleased him to pull over.

"What?" he snapped, rolling down the window on the passenger side of the truck so Boone could peer in at him.

"You headed for a fire?" Boone countered. "I clocked you at fifty in a thirty-five back there."

Hutch swore under his breath, tightened his grip on the steering wheel. "Sorry," he lied, glaring through the windshield at the dirt road ahead. It did some twisting and turning, that old road, before it joined the highway and rolled right on into Idaho and Washington.

At the moment, he sure felt like following it till it ended at the Pacific Ocean.

"Look at me, Hutch," the sheriff said, and he sounded dead serious.

Hutch turned his head, met Boone's gaze. "Write the ticket and be done with it," he growled.

"Well, who spit in *your* oatmeal this morning?" Boone asked, folding his arms against the base of the window and studying Hutch intently.

"I've got a lot on my mind right now," Hutch snapped. "All right?"

Boone sighed, shoved a hand through his dark hair. "I know that," he said, "but I can't let you go speeding around my county, now can I? Pretty soon, folks will be saying I turn a blind eye when my friends break the law and I can't have that, Hutch. You know I can't."

"So *write the ticket*," Hutch reiterated. He just wanted to be gone, to be moving, to be riding hard across darkening ground on a horse or climbing Big Sky Mountain on foot—*anything* but sitting still.

"Have it your way," Boone said. He took his ticket book from his belt, scrawled on a piece of paper, ripped it free, and held it out to Hutch, who snatched it from his hand and barely managed to keep from chucking it out his own window out of sheer cussedness.

"Thanks," Hutch told him, glaring.

Boone laughed. "I'd say 'you're welcome,' but that would add up to one too many smart-asses per square yard." He wouldn't unpin Hutch from that penetrating gaze of his. "I'm off duty and I was headed for home until you went shooting by me like a bat out of hell," he said companionably. "Why don't you follow me back over to my place? We'll have a couple of beers and feel sorry for ourselves for a while."

Hutch had to chuckle at that, though it was against his will and he resented it. "All right," he agreed at last, and grudgingly. "Long as you promise not to run me in for drunk driving after plying me with liquor."

"You have my word," Boone said with a grin. "See you over there."

With that, he backed away from the window and strolled back to his cruiser where the lights were still swirling, blue and white, causing the few passersby to slow down to gawk.

Boone's land, situated on the far side of Parable from where they started, was prime, fronting the river and sloping gently up toward the foothills, but it had the look of a place bogged down in hard times. The double-wide trailer was ugly as sin, and there were a couple of junked-out cars parked in the tall grass that surrounded it.

The double-wide had rust around its skirting, the makeshift porch dipped in the middle, and there was an honest-to-God toilet out front, with a bunch of dead flowers poking out of the bowl. Boone and his wife, Corrie—she'd never have stood for a john in the yard— had planned to live in the trailer only until they'd built their modest dream house, but when Corrie died of breast cancer a few years back, everything else in Boone's life seemed to stall.

If he'd had a dog, folks said, he'd have given it away. He *had* sent his two young sons, Griffin and Fletcher, off to live with his sister and her family in Missoula, where he probably figured they were better off.

Running for sheriff, after Slade announced that he wouldn't be seeking reelection, had been the first real sign of life in Boone since Corrie was laid to rest and for a while optimistic locals had hoped he'd get his act together, bring his kids home to Parable where they belonged, and just generally get on with things.

Parking behind the cruiser, Hutch felt an ache of sorrow on his friend's behalf—Boone had loved Corrie with all he had, from first grade on through college and in some ways, it was as if he'd just given up and crawled right into that grave with her.

"I swear this place looks worse every time I see it," Hutch remarked after getting out of the truck. There should have been two little boys running to greet their dad after a day at work, he thought, and a dog barking in celebration of his return, if not a woman smiling on the porch of the new house.

Instead it was dead quiet, like a graveyard with rusted headstones.

"You sound like the chicken rancher," Boone responded dryly, cocking a thumb in the direction of the neighboring place where Tara Kendall had set up housekeeping the year before. "She says this place is an eyesore."

Hutch had to grin. "She has a point," he said. Then, aware that he was pushing it, he added, "How are the boys?"

Boone, starting toward the sagging porch, tossed him a look. "They're just fine with their aunt and uncle and their brood," he said. "So don't start in on me, Hutch."

Hutch pretended to brace himself for a blow from his oldest and best friend. "You won't hear any relationship advice from me, old buddy," he said. "These days, I'm on America's Ten Most Unwanted list, which hardly makes me an authority."

"Damn straight," Boone grumbled. "And that's where you belong, too. On a master shit-list, I mean. I knew all that womanizing was bound to catch up with you someday."

Hutch laughed and followed his friend into the trailer. Boone always said what he thought; nobody was required to like it.

The inside of the double-wide was clean enough, but it was dismal, too. Full of shadows and smelling of the bachelor life—musty clothes left in the washing machine too long, garbage in need of taking out, the remains of last night's lonely pizza.

Boone opened the refrigerator and took out two cans of beer, handing one to Hutch and popping the top on another, taking a long drink before starting back outside again to sit in one of the rickety lawn chairs on that sorry excuse for a porch.

Hutch joined him.

"Old friend," Hutch ventured, looking out over what passed for a yard, "you need a woman. And that's just the start."

Boone grinned ruefully. "So do you," he said. "But you keep running them off."

Hutch sipped his beer. It was icy cold and it hit a dry spot, way down deep, unknotting him a little. "Slade's a dad now," he remarked, letting the gibe pass. "Can you believe it?"

"Hell, yes, I can believe it," Boone responded. They had a three-cornered alliance, Slade and Hutch and Boone. Slade and Hutch, being half brothers, hadn't gotten along until after the old man died, but Boone was close friends with both of them and always had been. "One look at Joslyn and Slade was a goner. Mark my words, they'll have a houseful of little Barlows before too long."

Hutch chuckled, but his thoughts had taken a somber turn just the same. "I reckon they enjoy the process of making them, all right," he said. A pause followed and another slow sip of cold beer. "What do you suppose it is about Slade, that's missing in you and me?" he asked.

Boone didn't pretend not to understand the question, but he took his time answering. "I hate to admit it," he finally replied, "but I think it's just plain-old backbone. Slade's not afraid to throw his heart in the ring and risk getting it stomped on. You and me, now, we're a couple of cowards."

Hutch absorbed that for a while. It was a tough truth to acknowledge—he wasn't afraid of anything besides climbing the water tower in town and giving up a chunk of his ranch to some vindictive ex-wife—but he couldn't deny that Boone had a point. Therefore, he didn't take offense. "What scares you the most, Boone?" he asked quietly.

Boone studied the horizon for a few moments, weighing his reply. "Loving a woman the way I loved Corrie," he said at long last. "And then losing her in the same way I lost Corrie. I don't honestly think I could take that, Hutch."

They were quiet for a long time, beers in hand, gazes fixed on things that were long ago and faraway.

"Your boys are growing up, Boone," Hutch ventured, after a decent interval. "They need you."

"They *need* what they have," Boone said, his voice taut now, his grip on his beer threatening to crush the can between his fingers, "which is a normal life with a normal family." He paused, swore, shook his head. "Hell, Hutch, you know I can't take care of them the way Molly does."

Hutch bit back the obvious response—that if Boone would just get his act together, he could make a home for himself and his boys, like millions of other single parents did. But who was he to talk about having it together, after all?

He didn't have kids and a wife waiting at home, either.

Didn't even have a dog, for God's sake, since Jasper had moved in with Slade.

For whatever reason, Boone didn't point out the holes in Hutch's own story, but that didn't mean he'd let him off the conversational hook, either.

Fair was fair and Hutch had been the one to set this particular ball rolling.

"That's quite a hubbub Brylee's friends are stirring up on the web," Boone said.

Hutch swallowed a sigh—and a couple more gulps of beer. "I am," he replied gravely, "a casualty of the digital age."

Boone laughed outright at that. "And innocent as the driven snow on top of it all," he added, before swilling more beer. As Slade had done when he held the office, Boone rarely wore a uniform—he dressed like any other Montana rancher, in jeans, boots and shirts cut Western-style. Now he unfastened the top two buttons of his shirt and breathed in as if he'd been smothering until then. "You and me," he said, "we're destined to be crusty old bachelors, it seems."

Kendra filled Hutch's mind just then. He saw her in the kitchen at his place, starting supper. He saw Madison, too, and even the dog, Daisy, hurrying out of the house to greet him when he got out of his truck or climbed down off his horse.

"I guess there are worse fates," Hutch allowed, but his throat felt tight all of a sudden and a little on the raw side.

"Like what?" Boone asked, gruffly companionable, still reflective. He was probably remembering happier days and hurting over the contrast between then and now.

"Being married to the wrong woman," Hutch said with grim certainty.

Boone sighed, finished his beer and stared solemnly at the can. "I wouldn't know about that," he answered, and though his voice didn't actually break, there was a crack in it. He'd been hitched to the *right* woman, was what he meant.

Finished with his own beer, Hutch stood up. He had work to do at home and besides, the emptiness would be there waiting, no matter how long he delayed his return, so he might as well get it over with. "We're a pair to draw to," he said, tossing the can into a wheelbar-row overflowing with them in roughly the place where Corrie used to set flowers in big pots.

Boone stood, too. Tried for a grin and fell short.

"You signed up for the bull-riding again this year?" he asked, referring to the upcoming rodeo. The Fourth fell on a Saturday this year, a convenient thing for most folks if not for Boone, who would surely have to bring a few former deputies out of retirement to make sure Parable County remained peaceable.

"Course I am," Hutch retorted, feeling a mite touchy again. "Walker Parrish promised me the worst bull that ever drew breath."

"I'll just bet he did," Boone said with another chuckle, throwing his own beer can in the general di-rection of the wheelbarrow and missing by a couple of feet. "When it's your turn to ride, I reckon a few of the spectators will be rooting for the bull."

Hutch started toward his truck. Twilight was gath-ering at the edges of the land, pulling inward like the top of a drawstring bag, and his horses would be won-dering when he planned on showing up with their hay and grain rations. "No different than any other year," he said. "Somebody's *always* on the bull's side."

"You might want to think about that," Boone answered, and damn if he didn't sound serious as a heart attack. *Him,* with his sons farmed out to kinfolk, however loving, and the weeds taking over, threatening to swallow up the trailer itself.

Hutch stopped in his tracks. "Think about *what?*" he demanded.

"Life. People. How time gets away from a man and, before he knows it, he's sitting in some nursing home without a tooth in his head or a hope in his heart that anybody's going to trouble themselves to visit."

"Damned if you aren't dumber than the average post," Hutch said, moving again, jerking open the door of his truck and climbing inside.

"At least I know my limitations," Boone said affably.

"Thanks for the beer," Hutch replied ungraciously, and slammed the truck's door.

He drove away at a slower pace than he would have liked, though. Boone had already written him up for speeding once and he wasn't above doing it again.

By the time he got back to Whisper Creek, he'd simmered down quite a bit, though what Boone had said about the pair of them being cowards still stuck in him like barbed wire.

A familiar station wagon, three years older than dirt, was parked next to the house when he pulled in.

Opal, he realized, had arrived early.

He muttered something under his breath, got out of the pickup and went directly into the barn, where he spent the better part of an hour attending to horses.

It was almost dark by the time he'd finished, and the lights were on in the kitchen, spilling a golden glow of welcome into the yard.

Stepping inside, he nodded a howdy to Opal, refusing to give her the satisfaction of demanding to know what the hell she was doing in his house. For one thing, he already knew—she was frying up chicken, country-style, and it smelled like three levels of heaven.

"Wash up before you eat," Opal ordered, tightening her apron strings and eyeing him through the big lenses of her glasses.

"I generally do," Hutch said mildly, running water at the sink and picking up the bar of harsh orange soap he kept handy.

"Look at those boots," Opal scolded with that strange, gruff tenderness she reserved for people in need of her guidance and correction. "Bet the soles are caked with manure."

Hutch sighed. He'd scraped them clean outside, on the porch, as he'd been taught to do around the time he started *wearing* boots.

"With you over here," he quipped, "who's going to nag Slade Barlow?"

"Shea's mama got in early," Opal replied, spearing pieces of chicken onto a platter with a meat fork. "So I figured I might as well get started setting things to rights around here."

Hutch dried his hands on a towel and grinned at her. "You're off to a good start with supper," he conceded.

She chuckled. "I made mashed potatoes and gravy, too, and boiled up some green beans with bacon and onion to boot. Sit yourself down, Hutch Carmody, and eat the first balanced meal you've probably had in a month of Sundays."

He waited until all the food was on the table and Opal was seated before taking a chair, wryly amused to recall that this was just the scenario he'd imagined for himself earlier.

Only the woman was different.

CHAPTER SEVEN

THE MANSION ON Rodeo Road seemed strangely hollow the next morning when Kendra stepped through the front door, even though most of the original furniture remained and there were painters and other workers in various rooms throughout.

Standing in the enormous entryway, she tipped her head back and looked up at the exquisite ceiling, waited for a pang of regret—some kind of sadness was to be expected, she supposed, given that she'd spent part of her life here. She'd wanted so much to live in this house, long before she'd met and married Jeffrey Chamberlain, and after her marriage a number of dreams had lived—and died—right here in these rooms.

Somewhat surprisingly, what Kendra actually felt was a swell of relief, a healthy sense of letting go, of moving on, even of becoming some more complete and authentic version of herself.

There was comfort in that, even exhilaration.

When she'd first set foot in the place, as an awestruck little girl recently dumped on the porch of a rundown double-wide on the wrong side of the railroad tracks, Joslyn had been the one who lived here, along with her mom, Dana, and stepfather, Elliott, and, of course, Opal.

To Kendra the place had seemed like a castle, especially at Christmas, with Joslyn as resident princess.

During her childhood and her teens, the mere scope of that house had amazed Kendra—there were rooms not just for sleeping or eating or bathing, like in most homes, but ones set aside just for plants to grow in, or for playing cards and watching TV, or for reading books and doing homework or simply for *sitting*. Her grandmother's trailer had closets, of course, but here there were *dressing* rooms, too, with glass cubicles for shoes and handbags, and what seemed like a million bathrooms. There had even been a nook—several times larger than the living room in the double-wide—set aside for wrapping gifts, tying them up with elaborate bows, decorating them with small ornaments or glittery artificial flowers.

To a child who was handed money and told to buy her own birthday and Christmas presents, the mere concept of such finery had been magical.

Alas Kendra had been quick enough to realize, once she became the mistress of this monstrosity of a place, that it was never the structure itself, or any of its fancy trappings, that she'd wanted.

Instead it was the family, the sense of fitting in and belonging somewhere, of being a valued part of something larger.

Seen from the outside, Joslyn's life had certainly *seemed* happy in those early days, even enchanted, although a shattering scandal would eventually erupt, leaving everything in ruins.

Before her stepfather's financial fall from grace, when he'd ripped off friends and strangers alike, Joslyn had had it all—and while some people had been jealous of her and thought of her as spoiled and self-centered, Kendra had seen a different side of Joslyn. She'd shown empathy for Kendra's very different situation, but never pity, and she'd been willing to share her toys and her skates and, later on, her beautiful clothes.

More importantly, Joslyn had shared her mom and Opal and the little cocker spaniel, Spunky. Elliott Rossiter, the stepfather, had come and gone, funny and affable and generous, but always busy doing something important.

Stealing, as it turned out.

As an adult, Kendra had hoped to fulfill at least a part of her own dream with Jeffrey—the formation of a family—and in a roundabout way, she'd succeeded, because she had Madison now.

"Hello?" The voice startled Kendra out of her musings, even though she'd known she wasn't alone, having seen the painters' and cleaning service's vans in the driveway.

Charlie Duke, who ran Duke's Painting and Construction, stepped into view, clad in splotched overalls and wiping his hands on a shop rag. He grinned, showing the wide gap between his front teeth.

"Mornin', Ms. Shepherd," he said. "Here to see how the place is comin' along, are you?"

Kendra smiled. "Something like that," she replied. She'd known Charlie and his wife, Tina, for years and in the post office or the grocery store or over at the Butter Biscuit Café, either one of them would have addressed her simply as "Kendra," but the Dukes were old-fashioned people. When Charlie was on the job, all exchanges were formal, and Kendra was "Ms. Shepherd."

"We've about finished up in the main parlor," Charlie told her, with quiet pride, leading the way along the corridor. He wore paper booties over his work boots, and his T-shirt had a hole in the right shoulder, only partially covered by one of his overall straps.

Kendra followed, like someone taking a tour of some grand residence in an unfamiliar country.

It was almost as though she'd never been inside the place before, which was crazy of course, but such was her mood—reflective, calmly detached.

The parlor had been her office, as well as the main reception area for Shepherd Real Estate, and what furniture she hadn't moved over to the storefront was still in place, though covered by huge canvas tarps. The walls, formerly a soft shade of dusty rose, were now eggshell, neutral colors allegedly being the way to go when a house was on the market, in the hope of appealing to a broader spectrum of potential buyers.

Kendra did a quick walk-through—no small undertaking in a house the size of the average high school gymnasium—greeted Charlie's two sons, who were busy painting the kitchen a very pale yellow, and various members of the cleaning team, perched stoutly on high ladders, polishing window glass, and then went back to her car, where Daisy waited patiently in the passenger seat. They'd dropped Madison off at preschool first thing, the two of them, and the next stop was Kendra's office.

Upon arriving there, she took Daisy for a quick turn around the parking lot and then they both entered through the back way.

While Daisy explored the space—she'd been there before but, in her canine brain, there was always the exciting possibility that something had changed since the last visit—sniffing at silk plants and file cabinets and windowsills, Kendra booted up her computer, unlocked the front door and turned the Closed sign around to read Open.

She was in the tiny, closed-off kitchenette/storage room, starting a pot of coffee brewing, when she heard someone come in from the street. Daisy's low, almost inquisitive growl made her hurry back to the main part of the office.

The man standing just inside the door was strikingly handsome, wearing the regulation jeans, boots, Western-cut shirt and hat, as most men in Parable did.

He removed the hat, acknowledging Kendra with a cordial nod, and grinned down at Daisy, who by then must have decided he didn't represent a threat after all. Far from growling at him, she was nuzzling the hand he lowered for her to inspect.

It was a moment or two before Kendra placed the man—not a stranger, but not a resident of Parable proper, either. Of course, some new people could have moved into town while she was traveling, somehow managing to escape her notice, but that didn't seem very likely. After all, it was her business to know what was going on in the community, who was moving in and who was moving out, and she'd kept pretty close tabs on such local doings, through Joslyn, even while she was away.

The visitor smiled and recognition finally clicked. His name was Walker Parrish, and he was a wealthy rancher with a place over near Three Trees. Besides raising prize beef, he bred bulls and broncos for rodeos, as well.

And he was brother of the almost-bride, Brylee Parrish, Hutch's latest casualty-of-the-heart.

Surely, Kendra thought, a little desperately, he didn't think *she'd* been a factor in the wedding-day breakup? Everyone knew she'd been involved with Hutch at one time, but that had been over for years.

Still, what other business could Parrish have with her? He already owned a major chunk of the county, so he probably wasn't looking to acquire property, and since his place had been in his family for several generations, she couldn't imagine him selling out, either.

She finally gathered enough presence of mind to smile back at him and ask, "What can I help you with today, Mr. Parrish?"

"Well," he said with a grin that cocked up at one side, "you could start by calling me by my given name, Walker."

Daisy, by that time, had dropped to her belly in what looked like a dog-swoon, her long nose resting atop Walker's right boot, as though to pin him in place so she could stare up at him forever in uninterrupted adoration.

"All right," Kendra said. "Walker it is, then." As a somewhat flustered afterthought, she added, "I'm Kendra."

Again, the grin flashed. "Yes," he said. "I know who you are." He cleared his throat. "I came by to ask you about the house on Rodeo Road. I understand you're getting ready to sell it."

Kendra nodded, surprised and hoping it didn't show. Maybe she'd been wrong earlier, deciding that Walker hadn't come to buy or sell real estate. "Yes," she said, at last summoning up her manners and offering him one of the chairs reserved for customers while she moved behind her desk and sat down. "What would you like to know?"

Daisy sighed and lifted her head when Walker moved away, then wandered off to curl up in a corner of the office for a snooze.

Once Kendra was seated, Walker took a seat, too, letting his hat rest, crown to the cushion, on the chair nearest his. There was an attractive crease in his brown hair where the hatband had been, and it struck her, once again, how handsome he was—and how, oddly, his good looks didn't move her at all.

She reviewed what she knew about him—which was almost nothing. She didn't think he had a wife or even a girlfriend, but since the impression was mainly intuitive, she couldn't be sure.

Wishful thinking? Perhaps. If he *was* single, the question was, why? Why was a man like Walker Parrish still running around loose? Evidently the good ones *weren't* already taken.

"I guess I'd be interested in the price, to start," Walker replied with a slight twinkle in his eyes. Had he guessed what she was thinking in regard to his marital status? The idea mortified her instantly.

Her tone was normal when she recited the astronomical numbers.

Walker didn't flinch. "Reasonable," he said.

The curiosity was just too much for Kendra. "You're thinking of moving to Parable?" she asked.

He chuckled at that, shook his head. "No," he said. "I'm here on behalf of a friend of mine. She's—in show business, divorced, and she has a couple of kids she'd like to raise in a small town. Wants a big place because she plans to set up her own recording studio, and between the band and the road crew and her household and office staff, she needs a lot of elbow room."

Kendra couldn't help being intrigued—and a little wary. It wasn't uncommon for famous people to buy land around Parable, build houses even bigger than her own and landing strips for their private jets, and proceed to set up "sanctuaries" for exotic animals that didn't mix all that well with the cattle, horses, sheep and chickens ordinary mortals tended to raise, among other visibly noble and charitable efforts. Generally these out-of-towners were friendly enough, and the locals were willing to give them the benefit of the doubt, but in time the newcomers always seemed to stir up trouble over water rights or bounties on wolves and coyotes or some such, alienate all their neighbors, and then simply move on to the next place, the next adventure.

It was as though their lives were movies and Parable was just another set, instead of a real place populated by real people.

"Anybody I might have heard of?" Kendra asked carefully.

Something in Walker's heretofore open face closed up just slightly. "You'd know her name," he replied. "She's asked me not to mention it right away, that's all. In case the whole thing comes to nothing."

Kendra nodded; she'd had plenty of practice with this sort of thing. Most celebrities were private nearly to the point of paranoia, and not without reason. Besides the paparazzi, they had to worry about stalkers and kidnappers and worse. Safety—or the illusion of it—lay in secrecy, and safety was usually what made places like Parable and Three Trees attractive to them.

"Fair enough," she said easily. "There are always a few upscale properties available in the county...." She could think of two that had been standing empty for a while; one had an Olympic-size indoor pool, and the other boasted a home theater with a rotating screen and plush seats for almost a hundred. The asking prices were in the mid-to-high seven-figure range, not surprisingly, but it didn't sound as though that would strain Walker's mysterious friend's budget.

But Walker was already shaking his head. Being a local, he knew as well as anybody which properties were for sale, what kind of shape they were in, and approximately what they'd cost to buy, restore and maintain—and he'd asked specifically about the house on Rodeo Road. "She wants to be in town," he said. Then a frown creased his tanned forehead. "Is there some reason why you don't want to show your house just yet?"

"No, no," Kendra said, "it's nothing like that. We can head over there right now if you want. It's just that—" She stopped in the middle of the sentence because she couldn't think of a diplomatic way to go on.

"Show business people are sometimes unreliable," Walker finished for her. The frown had smoothed away and he was grinning again. "I remember that rock band a few years back—the ones who built a pseudo haunted house, trashed the Grange Hall in Three Trees one night when they were partying and then nearly burned down a state forest, conducting some kind of crazy ritual. But it wouldn't be fair to hold that against everybody who sings and plays a guitar to earn a paycheck, would it?"

Kendra let out a long breath, shook her head no. Walker was right—that *wouldn't* be fair—and besides, hadn't he *said* this woman wanted to raise her children in a small town? That gave her at least one thing in common with Kendra herself, and with most of her friends, too.

Parable had its problems, like any community, but the crime rate was low, people knew each other and down-to-earth values were still important there. In a very real sense, Parable was a *family*. And it was cousin to Three Trees.

The two towns were rivals in many ways, but when trouble came to one or the other, they stood up to it shoulder to shoulder.

"If you have time," she reiterated, "I can show you through the house right now."

"That would be great," Walker said, rising from his chair. "I was there a few times when I was a kid, for parties and the like, but I don't remember too many of the details."

Kendra stood, too, simultaneously reaching for her purse and Daisy's leash. She blushed a little, imagining the state of the Volvo's interior. Pre-Madison and pre-dog, she'd kept her vehicles immaculate, as a courtesy to her clients, but now...

"I'm afraid my car needs vacuuming. The dog..."

Walker laughed. "Given my line of work," he said, "I'm not squeamish about a little dog hair. Matter of fact, I have three of the motley critters myself. But I'll take my own rig because I've got some other places to go to this morning, after we're through at your place."

Kendra nodded, clipped on Daisy's leash and indicated that she'd be leaving by the back way, so she'd need to lock up behind Walker after he stepped outside.

"Meet you over there," he said, and went out.

She nodded and locked the door between them.

Daisy paused for a pee break in the parking lot, and then Kendra and the retriever climbed into the Volvo and headed for Rodeo Road for the second time that morning.

"AT THIS RATE," Hutch grumbled good-naturedly, surveying the meal Opal had just set before him—a late lunch or an early supper, depending on your perspective, "I'll be too fat to ride in the rodeo, even though it's only a few days away."

Opal laughed. "Oh, stop your fussing and sit down and eat," she ordered.

She'd been busy—had the ironing board set up in the middle of the kitchen, and she must have washed and pressed every shirt he owned because she'd evidently been hard at it all day. Except, of course, for when she took time out to build the meat loaf she'd just set down in front of him. The main dish was accompanied by creamed peas and mashed potatoes drowning in gravy; and just looking at all that food, woman-cooked and from scratch, too, made his mouth water and his stomach growl.

But he didn't sit, because Opal was still standing.

With a little sigh and a sparkle of flattered comprehension in her eyes, she took the chair indicated and nodded for him to follow suit.

He did, but he was still uncomfortable. "Aren't you going to join me?" he asked, troubled to notice that she hadn't set a place for herself.

Opal's chuckle was warm and vibrant, vaguely reminiscent of the gospel music she loved to belt out when she thought she was alone. "I can't eat like a cowboy," she answered. "Be the size of a house in no time if I do."

Hutch was fresh out of self-restraint. He was simply too hungry, and the food looked and smelled too good. He took up his knife and fork and dug in. After complimenting Opal on her cooking—by comparison to years of eating his own burnt sacrifices or his dad's similar efforts, it seemed miraculous they survived—he asked about Joslyn and the baby.

"They're doing just fine," Opal said with satisfaction. Her gaze followed his fork from his plate to his mouth and she smiled like she might be enjoying the meal vicariously. "Dana—that's Joslyn's mother, you remember—is a born grandma, and so is Callie Barlow. Between the two of them, Slade, Shea and of course the little mama herself, I was purely in the way."

"I doubt that," Hutch observed. Opal, it seemed to him, was more than an ordinary human being, she was a living archetype, a wise woman, an earth mother.

And damned if he wasn't going all greeting-card philosophical in his old age.

"I like to go where I'm needed," she said lightly.

Hutch chuckled. "So now I'm some kind of—case?" he asked, figuring he was probably that and a lot more.

Opal's gaze softened. "Your mama was a good friend to me when I first came to Parable to work for old Mrs. Rossiter," she said, very quietly. "Least I can do to return the favor is make sure her only boy doesn't go around half-starved and looking like a homeless person."

That time, he laughed. "I look like a homeless person?" he countered, at once amused and mildly indignant. Living on this same land all his life, like several generations of Carmodys before him, letting the dirt soak up his blood and sweat and tears, he figured he was about as *un*homeless as it was possible to be.

"Not exactly," Opal said thoughtfully, and in all seriousness, going by her expression and her tone. "A *wifeless* person would be a better way of putting it."

Hutch sobered. Opal hadn't said much about the near-miss wedding, but he knew it was on her mind. Hell, it was on *everybody's* mind, and he wished something big would happen so people would have something else to obsess about.

An earthquake, maybe.

Possibly the Second Coming.

Or at least a local lottery winner.

"You figure a wife is the answer to all my problems?" he asked moderately, setting down his fork.

"Just most of them," Opal clarified with a mischievous grin. "But here's what I'm *not* saying, Hutch— I'm not saying that you should have gone ahead and married Brylee Parrish. Marriage is hard enough when both partners want it with all their hearts. When one doesn't, there's no making it work. So by my reckoning, you definitely did the right thing by putting a stop to things, although your timing could have been better."

Hutch relaxed, picked up his fork again. "I tried to tell Brylee beforehand," he said. He'd long since stopped explaining this to most people, but Opal wasn't "most people." "She wouldn't listen."

Opal sighed. "She's headstrong, that girl," she reflected. "Her and Walker's mama was like that, you know. Folks used to say you could tell a Parrish, but you couldn't tell them much."

Hutch went right on eating. "Is there anybody within

fifty miles of here whose mama you *didn't* know?" he teased between bites. He was ravenous, he realized, and slowing down was an effort. *Keep one foot on the floor, son,* he remembered his dad saying, whenever he'd shown a little too much eagerness at the table.

"I don't know a lot of the new people," she said, "nor their kinfolks, neither. But I knew *your* mother, sure enough, and she certainly did love her boy. It broke her heart when she got sick, knowing she'd have to leave you to grow up with just your daddy."

Hutch's throat tightened slightly, making the next swallow an effort. He'd been just twelve years old when his mother died of cancer, and although he'd definitely grieved her loss, he'd also learned fairly quickly that the old man believed in letting the dead bury the dead. John Carmody had rarely spoken of his late wife after the funeral, and he hadn't encouraged Hutch to talk about her, either. In fact, he'd put away all the pictures of her and given away her personal possessions almost before she was cold in the grave.

So Hutch had set her on a shelf in a dusty corner of his mind and tried not to think about the hole she'd left in his life when she was torn away.

"Dad wasn't the best when it came to parenting," Hutch commented belatedly, thinking back. "But he wasn't the worst, either."

Opal's usually gentle face seemed to tighten a little, around her mouth especially. "John Carmody was just plain selfish," she decreed with absolute conviction but no particular rancor. To her, the remark amounted to an observation, not a judgment. "Long as he got what he wanted, he didn't reckon anything else mattered."

Hutch was a little surprised by the bluntness of

Opal's statement, though he couldn't think why he should have been. She was one of the most direct people he'd ever known—and he considered the trait a positive one, at least in her. There were those, of course, who used what they liked to call "honesty" as an excuse to be mean, but Opal wasn't like that.

He opened his mouth to reply, couldn't think what to say, and closed it again.

Opal smiled and reached across the table to lay a hand briefly on his right forearm. "I had no business saying that, Hutch," she told him, "and I'm sorry."

Hutch found his voice, but it came out gruff. "Don't be," he said. "I like a reminder every once in a while that I'm not the only one who thought my father was an asshole."

This time it was Opal who was taken aback. "Hutch Carmody," she finally managed to sputter, "I'll thank you not to use that kind of language in my presence again, particularly in reference to the departed."

"Sorry," he said, and the word was still a little rough around the edges.

"We can either talk about your daddy and your mama," Opal said presently, "or we can drop the whole subject. It's up to you."

His hunger—for food, at least—assuaged, Hutch pushed his mostly empty plate away and met Opal's gaze. "Obviously," he said mildly, "you've got something to say. So go ahead and say it."

"I'm not sure what kind of father Mr. Carmody was," she began, "but I know he wasn't up for any awards as a husband."

Offering no response, Hutch rested his forearms on the tabletop and settled in for some serious listening.

When she went on, Opal seemed to be picking up in the middle of some rambling thought. "Oh, I know he wasn't actually married to your mother when he got involved with Callie Barlow, but she had his engagement ring on her finger, all right, and the date had been set."

Hutch guessed the apple didn't fall far from the tree, as the old saying went. He hadn't cheated on Brylee, but he'd done the next worst thing by breaking up with her at their wedding with half the county looking on.

"That was hard for Mom," he said. "She never really got over it, as far as I could tell."

Opal nodded. "She was fragile in some ways," she replied.

Hutch felt the sting of chagrin. He'd loved his mother, but he'd always thought of her as weak, too, and maybe even a mite on the foolish side. She'd gone right ahead and married the old man, after all, knowing that he'd not only betrayed her trust, but fathered a child by another woman.

A child—Slade Barlow—who would grow up practically under her nose and bear such a resemblance to John Carmody that there could be no doubt of his paternity.

"I guess she liked to think the whole thing was Callie's fault," Hutch reasoned, "and Dad was just an innocent victim."

"Some victim," Opal scoffed, but sadly. "He wanted Callie and he went after her. She was young and naive, and he was good-looking and a real smooth talker when he wanted to be. I think Callie really believed he loved her—and it was a brave thing she did, barely grown herself and raising Slade all by herself in a place the size of Parable."

Hutch recalled his encounter with Callie at the hospital, how happy she was about the new baby, her grandson. And his heart, long-since hardened against the woman, softened a little more. "I reckon most people are doing the best they can with whatever cards they were dealt," he said. "Callie included."

"It's a shame," Opal said after a long and thoughtful pause, "that you and Slade grew up at odds. Why your daddy never acknowledged him as his son is more than I can fathom. It just doesn't make any sense, the two of them looking so much alike and all."

Hutch considered what he was about to say for a long moment before he actually came out with it. Opal knew everybody's business, but she didn't carry tales, so he could trust her. And he didn't want to sound as if he felt sorry for himself, because he knew that, for all of it, he was one of the lucky ones. "When it was just Dad and me," he finally replied, "nobody else around, he used to tell me he wished I'd been the one born on the wrong side of the blanket instead of Slade. I guess by Dad's reckoning, Callie got the better end of the deal."

Opal didn't respond immediately, not verbally anyway, but her eyes flashed with temper and then narrowed. "Slade is a fine man—Callie did a good job bringing him up and no sensible person would claim otherwise—but he's no better and no worse than you are, Hutch."

Hutch just smiled at that, albeit a bit sadly. Sure, he wished his dad had shown some pride in him, just once, but there was no point in dwelling on things that couldn't be changed. To his mind, the only way to set the matter right was to be a different kind of father himself, when the time came.

He pushed back his chair, stood up and slowly carried his plate and silverware to the sink.

Opal was right there beside him, in a heartbeat, elbowing him aside even as she took the utensils out of his hand. "I'll do that," she said. "You go on and do whatever it is you do in the evenings."

Hutch smiled. "I was thinking I might head into town," he said. "See what's happening at the Boot Scoot."

"I'll *tell* you what's happening at that run-down old bar," Opal said, with mock disapproval. "Folks are wasting good time and good money, swilling liquor and listening to songs about being in prison and their mama's bad luck and how their old dog got run over when their wife left them in a hurry."

"Why, Opal," Hutch teased cheerfully, "does that mean you don't want to go along as my date?"

"You just hush," Opal scolded, snapping at him with a dish towel and then giving a laugh. "And mind you don't drink too much beer."

CHAPTER EIGHT

AFTER TAKING A quick shower and putting on clean clothes, Hutch traveled a round-about road to get to the Boot Scoot Tavern that night—a place he had no real interest in going to—and the meandering trail led him right past Kendra Shepherd's brightly lit rental house.

In simpler times, he wouldn't have needed a reason to knock on Kendra's door at pretty much any hour of the day or night, but things had certainly changed between them, and not just because she had a daughter now. Not even because he'd almost married Brylee Parrish and Kendra *had* married Sir Jeffrey, as Hutch privately thought of the man—when he was in a charitable frame of mind, that is.

No, there was more to it.

The whole time he'd known Kendra, she'd coveted that monster of a house over on Rodeo Road. As a kid, she'd haunted it like a small and wistful ghost, Joslyn's pale shadow. As a grown-up, she'd found herself a prince with the means to buy the place for her and after the divorce she'd held on to it, rattling around in it all alone for several years, like a lone plug of buckshot in the bottom of a fifty-gallon drum.

Now all of a sudden, she'd moved into modest digs, rented from Maggie Landers, opened a storefront office to sell real estate out of and switched rides from a swanky sports car to a *Volvo,* for God's sake.

What did all of that mean—beyond, of course, the fact that she was now a mother? Did it, in fact, mean *anything?* Women were strange and magnificent creatures, in Hutch's opinion, their workings mysterious, often even to themselves, never mind some hapless man like him.

Kendra had, except for staying put in Parable, turned her entire life upside down, changed practically everything.

Was that a good omen—or a bad one?

Hutch wanted an answer to that question far more than he wanted a draft beer, but since he could get the latter for a couple of bucks and the former might just cost him a chunk of his pride, he kept going until he pulled into the gravel-and-dirt parking lot next to the Boot Scoot.

The front doors of that never-painted Quonset hut, a relic of World War II, stood open to the evening breeze, and light and sound spilled and tumbled out into the thickening twilight—he heard laughter, twangy music rocking from the jukebox, the distinctive click of pool balls at the break.

With a smile and a shake of his head, Hutch shut off the headlights, cranked off the truck's trusty engine, pushed open the door and got out. The soles of his boots crunched in the gravel when he landed, and he shut the truck door behind him, then headed for the entrance.

Once the place would have been blue with shifting billows of cigarette smoke, hazy and acrid, but now it was illegal to light up in a public building, though the smell of burning tobacco—and occasionally something else—was still noticeable even out in the open air. He caught the down-at-the-heels Montana-tavern scent of the sawdust covering the floor as he entered, stale sweat overridden by colognes of both the male and female persuasions, and he felt that peculiar brand of personal loneliness that drove folks to the Boot Scoot when they had better things to be doing elsewhere.

Hutch nodded to a few friends as he approached the bar and then ordered a beer.

Two or three couples were dancing to the wails of the jukebox—he thought of Opal's description of the tavern and smiled at its accuracy—but most of the action seemed to center around the two pool tables at the far end of the long room.

Hutch's beer was drawn from a spigot and brought to him; he paid for it, picked up the mug in one hand and made his way toward the pool tables. By the weekend, when the rodeo and other Independence Day celebrations would be in full swing, the crowds would be so thick in here, at least at night, that just getting from one side of the tavern to the other would be like swimming through chest-deep mud of the variety Montanans call "gumbo."

Finding a place to stand without bumping elbows with anybody, Hutch watched the proceedings. Deputy Treat McQuillan, off duty and out of uniform but still clearly marked as a cop by his old-fashioned buzz haircut, watched sourly, pool cue in hand, while another player basically ran the table, plunking ball after ball into the appropriate pocket.

Never a gracious loser, McQuillan reddened steadily throughout, and when the bloodbath was over, he turned on one heel, rammed his cue stick back into the wall-rack with a sharp motion of one scrawny arm and stormed off.

A few of the good old boys, mostly farmers and ranchers Hutch had known since the last Ice Age, shook their heads in tolerant disgust and then ignored McQuillan, as most people tended to do. Getting along with him was just too damn much work and consequently the number of friends he could claim usually hovered somewhere around zero.

For some reason Hutch couldn't put his finger on— beyond a prickle at the nape of his neck—he was strangely uneasy and getting more so by the moment. He watched the deputy shoulder his way toward the bar, evidently impervious to the good-natured joshing of the people he passed.

Hutch had never liked McQuillan, and he certainly wasn't in the minority on that score, but in that moment he found himself feeling a little sorry for the man, if no less watchful. The very air had a zip in it, a sure sign that something was about to go down, and it probably wasn't good.

Halfway across the sawdust-covered floor, McQuillan stopped at a table encircled by women, put out his hand and jerked one of them to her feet, hard against his torso and into a slow dance. At first, Hutch couldn't make out who she was, with folks milling in between.

A scuffle ensued—the lady evidently preferred not to participate, at least not with Treat McQuillan for a dancing partner—and the other females at the table rose as one, so fast that a few of their chairs tipped over backward.

"Stop it, Treat," one of them said.

And then, as people shifted and pressed in on the

scene, Hutch recognized the woman who didn't want to dance. It was Brylee.

He plunked down his mug on another table and instinctively headed in that direction, ready to take McQuillan apart at the joints like a Sunday-supper chicken just out of the stewpot. But right when he would have reached the couple, an arm shot out in front of his chest and stopped him as surely as if a steel barricade had slammed down from the ceiling.

"My sister," Walker Parrish said evenly, "my fight."

Hutch hadn't spotted either Walker *or* Brylee when he came in, so he hadn't had a chance to square away their presence in his mind. He felt a little off-balance.

In the next instant, Parrish shoved McQuillan away from Brylee, hard, hauled back one fist and clocked the deputy square in the beak.

That was it. The whole fight. Though in the days to come it would grow with every retelling, eventually becoming almost unrecognizable.

McQuillan's eyes rolled back, his knees buckled and he went down.

Walker, meanwhile, gripped Brylee firmly by one arm, barely giving her a chance to retrieve her purse from the floor next to her chair, and propelled her toward the exit.

"We're going home now," he was heard to say in a tone that left no room for negotiation.

"Damn it, Walker," Brylee yelled in response, struggling in vain to yank free from her brother's grasp. "Let me go! I can take care of *myself!*"

In spite of everything, Hutch had to smile a little, because what Brylee said was true—she *could* take care of herself and in the long run she'd be just fine.

Oh, the woman had spirit, all right. Life would have been so much simpler all around, Hutch thought, if only he could have loved her.

Moments later, the Parrishes were gone and somebody was helping McQuillan back to his feet. He was rubbing his jaw and had one hell of a nosebleed going, but he looked all right, otherwise—no obvious need for any wires, stitches or casts, anyhow.

"I'm pressing charges!" McQuillan raged. "You're all witnesses! You all saw what Walker Parrish did to me!"

"Ah, Treat," one man drawled, "let it go. You put your hands on the man's *sister,* and after she told you straight out she didn't care to dance—"

McQuillan's small, beady eyes flashed fire. He was trying to staunch the nosebleed with the sleeve of his shirt, but not having much luck. Some of the sawdust on the floor would definitely have to be shoveled out and replaced.

"I mean it," he insisted furiously. "Parrish assaulted an officer of the law and he's going to face the consequences!"

Hutch, standing nearby, flexed his fist slowly and waited for the urge to drop McQuillan right back to the floor again to pass.

Presently, it did.

The show was over and Hutch turned, meaning to go back for the beer he'd set aside minutes earlier. He nearly collided with Brylee's best friend, Amy Jo DuPree in the process.

"You have your nerve coming in here, Hutch Carmody!" Amy Jo seethed, standing practically toe-to-toe with him and craning her neck back so she could look up at him. Five-foot-nothing and weighing a hundred pounds soaking wet, Frank and Marge DuPree's baby girl was a pretty thing, but feisty, afraid of nothing and no one.

Montana seemed to breed women like that.

Hutch arched an eyebrow. "Excuse me?" he countered, raising his voice a little as the jukebox cranked up and Carrie Underwood took to extolling the virtues of baseball bats and kerosene-fueled revenge.

Maybe that was what was making the whole female sex seem more impossible to deal with by the day, Hutch speculated fleetingly. Maybe it was the inflammatory nature of the music they listened to on their iPods and other such devices.

"You heard me," Amy Jo all but snarled through her little white teeth, and gave him a light but solid punch to the solar plexus.

Intrigued and, okay, a little pissed off at the injustice of it all, Hutch took Amy Jo by the arm and squired her outside.

The parking lot was hardly quieter than the interior of the bar, what with Walker and Brylee yelling at each other and then peeling away in Walker's truck, and then Boone arriving with his lights flashing and his siren giving a single mournful whoop in case the blinding strobe left any doubt he was there.

"Hell," Hutch breathed, watching as the sheriff climbed, somewhat wearily, out of his cruiser and came toward the doors of the Boot Scoot. "McQuillan's really going to do it—he's going to press charges against Walker."

"Somebody ought to press charges against *you*," Amy Jo huffed out, but she wasn't quite as steam-powered as before. "How could you, Hutch? How could you let things go so far and then humiliate Brylee in public the way you did? Do you even know how much a wedding *means* to a woman? She looks forward to it her whole life, from the time she's a little bit of a thing, and then—"

Boone passed them, nodded in grim acknowledgment as he went inside the tavern to investigate the scene of the crime, as McQuillan, who must have gotten right on his cell phone to report the event, would no doubt term it.

By now the damn idiot had probably taped off a body-shape in the sawdust, to mark the place where he'd fallen.

Hutch turned his attention back to Amy Jo. "Just exactly what is it," he asked, exasperated, "that you people want me to do, here?"

Amy Jo jutted out her spunky little chin. "'You people'? You mean Brylee's friends?"

"I *mean*," Hutch bit out tersely, "that all this Team Brylee crap is getting old. I've always lived here and I always will, and I will be *damned* if I'll stay away from the Boot Scoot or anyplace else I want to go, just because you and the rest of Brylee's bunch think I ought to be ashamed of what I did." He leaned in, and Amy Jo's eyes widened. "Here's a flash for you—pass it on. Post it on that stupid website. Print up T-shirts, put fliers on windshields, whatever. *I'm not going anywhere. Deal with it.*"

Amy Jo blinked. She wasn't a bad sort, really. It was just that she and Brylee had grown up as close friends, the way Kendra and Joslyn had. The way he and Slade might have, if it hadn't been for the old man's cussed determination to ignore one of them and browbeat the other.

Loyalty was an important quality in a friend, even when it was the bullheaded kind like Amy Jo's.

"Nobody expects you to move away or anything," Amy Jo said belatedly and in a lame tone.

"Good," Hutch sputtered, as another ruckus of some kind erupted inside the Boot Scoot. "Because when hell freezes over, I'll still be right here in Parable."

Amy Jo swallowed, nodded and went back into the tavern to find her friends.

Although Hutch's better angels urged him to get in his truck and go home, where he should have stayed in the first place, he figured Boone might need some help settling things down, so he followed Amy Jo inside.

McQuillan was out of control, waving his free arm and guarding his gushing nose with the other, yelling in Boone's face.

Boone, for his part, calmly stood his ground. "Now, Treat," he reasoned, amiable but serious, "I would hate to have to run one of my own deputies in for drunk-and-disorderly and creating a public nuisance, but I'll do it, by God, I'll throw you straight into the hoosegow if you keep this up."

At the periphery of his vision, Hutch saw Amy Jo and the rest of the Brylee contingent quietly gather their purses and other assorted gear and trail out of the tavern. Probably a wise decision, given the incendiary mood McQuillan was creating.

"Arrest *me?*" the deputy bellowed. Treat never had known when to keep his mouth shut, which was part of his problem. "I'm the *victim* here! I was *assaulted!*"

"We'll discuss that," Boone assured him, "but not until you calm down."

"I'd have knocked you on your ass, too, McQuillan," a male voice contributed from somewhere in the dwindling crowd. "You can't expect any different when you grab on to a woman in a goddamn cowboy bar!"

"Harley," Boone said, recognizing the speaker immediately, and without looking away from McQuillan's bloody, temper-twisted face, "shut up."

Hutch, looking on, privately agreed with Harley. Manhandling a lady was asking for trouble pretty much anywhere, but square in the middle of cowboy-central, it was close to suicidal.

Just the same, he positioned himself at Boone's left side, not quite in his space but close enough to jump in if the shit hit the fan.

Boone slanted a brief glance in his direction. "You involved in this?" he asked.

Hutch folded his arms, rocked back slightly on his heels. "Now Boone, I am downright *insulted* by that question. I just happened to be here, that's all."

Boone's expression remained skeptical, but only mildly so. He sighed heavily. "Come on, Treat," he said to his disgruntled deputy. "I'll give you a lift over to the hospital, get them to check you out, and take you home. No way you're in any condition to drive."

Treat was all bristled up, like a little rooster with his feathers brushed in the wrong direction. "I'd rather walk," he replied coldly. Boone might have been McQuillan's boss, but he was also the man who'd trounced him at the polls last Election Day and he clearly wasn't over the disappointment. McQuillan had wanted to be sheriff from the time he was little, never mind that he was constitutionally unsuited for the job.

"Whatever you say, Treat," Boone responded. "But leave your rig right where it's parked until morning."

"I'll be filing charges against Walker Parrish as soon as the courthouse opens," McQuillan maintained, but he was on the move as he spoke, headed for the doors.

The onlookers finally lost all interest and dispersed, going back to their pool playing and their beer drinking and their armchair quarterbacking.

Boone turned to Hutch. "What happened here?" he asked.

The incident, though it had already drifted into the annals of history, still chapped Hutch's hide a little. He wasn't in love with Brylee Parrish, but standing around watching while some drunken bastard strong-armed her into something she didn't want to do went against his grain in about a million ways.

Hutch told Boone the story, leaving out the part about how he'd meant to go after McQuillan himself but Walker had stepped in and thrown a punch of his own.

"Well," Boone said on a long breath, "that's fine. That's just *fine*. Because if McQuillan doesn't cool off overnight—and experience tells me that won't happen— I'll probably have to charge Walker with assault."

"Come on," Hutch protested. "I told you what happened—McQuillan brought that haymaker on himself."

Boone was on his way toward the exit and Hutch, tired of the bar, tired of just about everything, followed. "Walker had the right to defend his sister," the sheriff allowed quietly, over one shoulder, "but he took it too far. He's half again McQuillan's size and whatever my personal opinion of old Treat might be, he *is* a sworn officer of the court. Landing a punch in the middle of his face, though a sore temptation at times, I admit, is a little worse in the eyes of the law than if Walker had decked, say, for instance—*you.*"

They were in the parking lot by then. The lights on top of Boone's squad car still splashed blue and white over everything around them in dizzying swirls.

"He's welcome to try," Hutch said, hackles rising again. Did *everybody,* even his best friend, think he had a fat lip and a shiner coming to him just because he hadn't gone through with the wedding?

Boone opened his cruiser door, leaned in and shut off the lights, which was a relief to Hutch, who was starting to get a headache. "Go home, Hutch," Boone said. "I've got one loose cannon on my hands in Treat McQuillan and I don't need another one."

"I'm not breaking any laws," Hutch pointed out, putting an edge to the words. There it was again, somebody telling him where to go, what to do. Damn it, the last time he looked, he'd still lived in a free country.

"True," Boone agreed. "But if Walker hadn't gotten to McQuillan first, you'd have clocked him yourself, and don't try to claim otherwise, because I *know* you, Hutch. You've got *pissed-off* written all over you, and if you hang around town on the lookout for trouble, you're bound to find some." The sheriff sighed again. "It's my job to keep the peace and I mean to do it."

Hutch's strongest instinct was to dig in his heels and stand up for his rights, even if Boone *was* making a convoluted kind of sense. And it still stung a little, remembering how Walker had gotten in his way back there when McQuillan crossed the line with Brylee. He felt thwarted and primed for action at the same time—not a promising combination.

Before he could say anything more, though, Boone changed the subject in midstream by announcing, "My boys are coming for a visit. Spending the Fourth of July weekend with me."

Hutch went still. Grinned. "That's good," he said, pleased. Then, after a pause, "Isn't it?"

"Hell, no, it isn't good," Boone answered, looking distracted and miserable. "That trailer of mine isn't fit for human habitation. I wouldn't know what to feed them, or what time they ought to go to bed, or how much television they should be allowed to watch—"

Hutch laughed, and it was a welcome tension-breaker. The muscles in his neck and shoulders relaxed with a swiftness that almost made him feel as though he'd just downed a double-shot of straight whiskey.

"Then maybe you ought to clean the place up a little," he suggested. "As for bedtime and TV, well, it shouldn't take a rocket scientist to figure those things out. These are kids we're talking about here, Boone, not some alien species nobody knows anything about."

Boone ground some gravel under the toe of his right boot. "That's easy enough for you to say, old buddy, since you don't have to do a damn thing except share your infinite wisdom with regard to parenting."

Hutch slapped Boone's shoulder. "What if I told you, *old buddy,* that if you can take a day or two off from sheriffing, I'll come over and help you dig out?"

Boone narrowed his eyes. "You'd do that?"

Hutch pretended injury. "You doubt me? You, who was almost the best man at my almost wedding?"

Boone eased up a little himself, even chuckled, albeit

hoarsely. "I'll have to deal with McQuillan, one way or the other, but I can take tomorrow off and part of the next day, too."

"Fine," Hutch said. "Give me a call when you're ready to start and I'll be at your place with a couple of machetes and some dynamite."

Boone laughed, this time for real. "Machetes and dynamite?" he echoed, taking mock offense. "No flame gun?"

"Fresh out of flame guns," Hutch answered, walking away, getting into his truck and starting up the engine.

He honked the horn once and headed for home.

KENDRA, HAVING JUST dropped Madison off at preschool and Daisy at Tara's for a doggy playdate with Lucy, stopped by the Butter Biscuit Café to buy a chocolate croissant and a double-tall nonfat latte before heading to the office the next morning. She was in a buoyant mood, since Walker Parrish had shown definite interest in the mansion the day before when she'd taken him through it. He hadn't come right out and said the place was exactly what his mystery friend was looking for, but Kendra's well-honed sales instincts had struck up an immediate *ka-ching* chorus.

No offer had been made, she reminded herself dutifully, as she waited at the counter to place her take-out order. And a deal was only a deal, at least in the real estate business, when the escrow check cleared the bank.

Thus focused on her internal dialogue, Kendra didn't notice Deputy McQuillan right away. When she did, she saw that he sat nearby at the long counter with open spaces on both sides of him, crowded as the Butter Biscuit always was during the breakfast rush, his nose not only bandaged, but splinted and both his eyes blackened.

"I'm pressing charges," he said to everyone in general, his tone as stiff as a wire brush. He had the air of a man just winding up a long and volatile oration.

The café patrons politely ignored him.

"Don't mind Treat," the aging waitress whispered to Kendra when she reached the counter, order pad in hand. "He's just running off at the mouth because he made a move on Brylee Parrish last night, over at the Boot Scoot Tavern, and Walker let him have it, right in the teeth."

Kendra winced at the violent image. "Ouch," she said, keeping her voice down.

"Broke his nose for him," the waitress added unnecessarily and with a note of satisfaction.

McQuillan must have overheard because his gaze swung in their direction, and Kendra felt scalded by it, as though he'd splashed her with acid.

"Go ahead, Millie," he growled at the still recalcitrant waitress. "Tell the whole world *Walker's* side of the story."

"It's everybody's side of the story," Millie said, undaunted. "You made a damn fool of yourself at the Boot Scoot and that's a fact. Ask me, you're just lucky Walker got to you before Hutch Carmody did."

Hutch's name, at least in connection with an apparent bar brawl over one Brylee Parrish, caught in Kendra's throat like rusty barbed wire snagging in flesh.

McQuillan's face flamed, and his full attention shifted, for whatever reason, to Kendra. "You'd do well to think twice before you take up with Carmody again," he informed her. "He's no good."

Kendra couldn't speak, she was so galled by Mc-Quillan's presumption. Who the *hell* did the man think he was, talking to her like that?

"Shut up, Treat," Millie said dismissively. "All these good people are trying to enjoy their morning coffee or catch a quick breakfast. Why don't you let them?"

A terrible tension stretched taut across the whole café, like massive rubber bands. The snap-back, if it happened, would be terrible.

Chair legs scraped against the floor as men in various parts of the room pushed back from tables, ready to intercede if the situation went any further south.

"All I wanted to do," McQuillan went on, as an ominous, anticipatory silence settled over the place, "was help Brylee forget about her broken heart. Dance with her a little, maybe buy her a drink." He pointed to his battered face with one index finger. "And *this* is what I got for my trouble."

Just then, Essie, the long-time owner of the Butter Biscuit and a no-nonsense type to the crepe soles of her sensible shoes, trundled out of the kitchen, wiping her hands on her apron and advancing until she stood opposite Treat McQuillan with only the counter between them. Her eyes, with their Cleopatra-style liner and shadow, were hot with temper.

"I've had just about enough out of you, Treat," she said, her voice ringing off every window and wall. "You behave yourself, or I'll call Boone and have you hauled out of here!"

McQuillan flushed a dangerous crimson. "You'll have to call Slade instead," he retorted bitterly, apropos of who-knew-what, "because he's filling in for Boone.

Guess he didn't quite get being sheriff out of his system, old Slade."

"I'll call the damn *President,* if I have to," Essie answered back, "and don't you sass me again, Treat McQuillan. I knew your mama."

I knew your mama.

Kendra almost smiled at the familiar phrase, in spite of the tinderbox climate in the Butter Biscuit Café that sunny and otherwise beautiful late June morning. In Parable, the bonds of friendship and enmity both ran deep, intertwining like tree roots under an old-growth forest until they were hopelessly tangled.

"I knew your mama" was enough to shut most anybody up.

Sure enough, McQuillan subsided, spun around on his stool, stepped down and strode out of the cafe, looking neither to the right nor the left.

The chuckles and comments commenced as soon as the door closed behind him.

"I'm not sure that man is entirely sane," Essie observed, watching him go.

Nobody disagreed.

Kendra ordered her latte and croissant, waited, paid for her purchase and left the restaurant, still feeling strangely shaken by the episode.

Walking back to the office, she got out her cell phone and speed-dialed Joslyn's number, hoping she wouldn't wake her friend up from a post-partum nap or something equally vital.

Joslyn answered on the first ring, though, sounding too chipper to have delivered a baby so recently or to be contemplating a nap. "Hi, Kendra," she said. "What's up?"

"I'm not sure," Kendra answered honestly. Why *was* she calling Joslyn?

Joslyn simply waited.

"I hear Slade is standing in for Boone," Kendra finally said, reaching her storefront and fumbling with her keys. "As sheriff, I mean." She was used to juggling purses and briefcases, cell phones and coffee, but her fingers seemed slippery this morning.

Joslyn replied cheerfully. "Boone's sons are coming for a visit, so he needed some time off to get his place ready. Slade offered to take over the job for a few days."

"Oh," Kendra said, opening the office door and practically fleeing inside. What was she going to say if Joslyn wanted to know why she'd bother to ask about something so clearly not her concern in the first place?

"Why do you ask?" Joslyn said, right on cue.

Kendra sighed, dropping her purse onto her desk, then setting down the coffee and the bag with the croissant inside, too. Even with those few extra seconds to think, she didn't come up with a plausible excuse for the inquiry.

The truth was going to have to do. "Deputy McQuillan was making a big fuss when I stopped in at the Butter Biscuit a little while ago. Going on about how Walker Parrish assaulted him last night and he's going to see that he's charged."

Joslyn sighed. "There was a little scuffle at the Boot Scoot last night, as I understand it," she said with just a touch of hesitation.

"And Hutch was involved," Kendra said.

"Indirectly," Joslyn confirmed.

"Not that it's any business of mine, what Hutch Carmody does." Kendra was speaking to herself then, more than Joslyn.

Joslyn gave a delighted little chuckle. "Except that you do seem a little worried," she observed. "Why don't you just admit, if only to me, your main BFF, that you still have a thing for the guy?"

"Because I *don't* 'have a thing for the guy.'"

"Right," Joslyn replied.

"I'm a mother now," Kendra prattled on, unable, for some weird reason, to stop herself. "I have a dog and a Volvo, and I need to make a life."

This time, Joslyn actually laughed. "All of which means—*what,* exactly? That you don't need a little romance in this life you're making? A little sex, maybe?"

"Sex?" The word came out high-pitched, like a squeak. "Who said anything about sex?"

"You did," Joslyn replied with good-humored certainty. "Oh, not in so many words. But you're feeling a little jealous, aren't you? Because you have some scenario in your head of Hutch defending Brylee's honor at the Boot Scoot Tavern?"

"I wouldn't call it…jealousy," Kendra finally replied, her tone tentative.

"Okay," Joslyn agreed sunnily. "What *would* you call it?"

"You're no help at all," Kendra accused, further deflated, but smiling now. Talking to Joslyn always made her feel better, even when nothing was really resolved.

"Let's do lunch in a couple of days," Joslyn said, "after Mom goes back to Santa Fe and things return to normal around here. Maybe Tara can join us."

Still feeling like an idiot, Kendra replied that she'd enjoy a girlfriend lunch, said goodbye and hung up.

She spent the morning noodling around on her computer, carefully avoiding the "Down With Hutch Carmody" webpage, along with the temptation to add a thing or two, and answered a grand total of two inquiries by phone.

By ten forty-five, she felt so restless that she set the business phone to forward any calls to her cell, locked up the office and drove out to Tara's chicken ranch, intending to pick up Daisy and go home. Madison still had a couple of hours to go at preschool, which she was starting to enjoy, and Kendra didn't want to disrupt the flow by taking her out early.

Tara was outside when Kendra pulled into her rutted dirt driveway, wearing red coveralls and wielding a shovel. Daisy and Lucy frolicked happily nearby, playing catch-tumble-roll with each other.

"Don't tell me," Tara chimed mischievously, approaching Kendra's car on the driver's side. "You're here to help me clean out the chicken coop! What a true friend you are, Kendra Shepherd."

Kendra laughed. "You wish," she said. It was a relief to stop thinking about Hutch Carmody and sex for a while. They were two separate subjects, of course, but she hadn't been able untangle one from the other since her phone conversation with Joslyn.

"Then what *are* you doing here?" Tara asked, looking like half of "American Gothic," except young and pretty instead of severe.

"Can't I visit a friend?" Kendra bantered back, pushing open the door and stepping somewhat gingerly into the muck of the barnyard. She wished she'd swapped out her Manolos for a pair of gum boots before leaving town.

Not that she actually *owned* gum boots.

Tara laughed at Kendra's mincing steps, pointed out a relatively clean pathway nearby and paused to lean her shovel against the wall of the chicken coop before following Kendra toward the old farmhouse she'd been refurbishing over the past year.

The woman was the very personification of incongruity, to Kendra's mind, with her model's face and figure and those ridiculous coveralls.

They settled in chairs on Tara's porch, since the weather was so nice and the dogs seemed to be having such a fine time dashing around in the grass, two flashes of happy gold, busy being puppies.

Once seated, Tara nodded in the direction of Boone Taylor's place, which neighbored hers. "He's finally cleaning up over there," she said in a tone that struck Kendra as oddly pensive. "I wonder why."

CHAPTER NINE

WHEN HUTCH ARRIVED at Boone's place that morning, he brought along plenty of tools, a truck with a hydraulic winch for heavy lifting and half a dozen ranch hands to help with the work. Opal followed in her tank of a station wagon, bucket-loads of potato salad and fried chicken and homemade biscuits stashed in the backseat.

Boone, standing bare-chested in his overgrown yard, plucked his T-shirt from the handle of a wheelbarrow where he'd left it earlier, now that he was in the presence of a lady.

Hutch grinned at the sight, and backed the truck up to a pile of old tires and got out.

Boone walked over to greet him, taking in the other trucks, the ranch hands and Opal's behemoth vehicle with a nod of his head. "You always were something of a show off, Carmody," he said.

"Go big or go home," Hutch answered lightly. "That's my motto."

"Along with 'make trouble wherever possible' and 'ride bulls at rodeos till you get your teeth knocked out'?" Boone gibed.

"Is there a law, Sheriff Andy Taylor, that says I can only have one motto?" Hutch retorted. The Maybury reference had been a running joke between them since the election results came in last November.

"Reckon not," Boone conceded, looking around at the unholy mess that was his property and turning serious. "I appreciate your help, old buddy," he said.

"Don't mention it," Hutch replied easily. "It's what friends do, that's all."

Boone nodded, looked away for a moment, cleared his throat. "What if Griff and Fletch get here and want to turn right around and head back to Missoula?" he asked, keeping his voice down so the ranch hands and Opal wouldn't overhear.

"One step at a time, Boone," Hutch reminded him. "Seems like the first thing on our agenda ought to be making sure the little guys don't get lost in all this tall grass."

Boone's chuckle was gruff. "I laid in plenty of beer," he said.

"Well," Hutch replied, heading around to the back of his pickup to haul out shovels and electric Weedwackers, "don't bring it out while Opal's around or we'll get a rousing sermon on the evils of alcohol, instead of all that good grub she was up half the night making."

Boone's chuckle was replaced by a gruff burst of laughter. "If she's brought any of her famous potato salad, she can preach all the sermons she wants," he answered, and went to greet the woman as she climbed out of her car and stood with her feet planted like she was putting down roots right there on the spot.

Out of the corner of his eye, Hutch watched as Boone leaned down to place a smacking kiss on Opal's forehead.

Pleased, she flushed a color she would have described as "plum" and pretended to look stern. "It's about time you got your act together, Boone Taylor," she scolded. Right away, her gaze found the toilet with the flowers growing out of the bowl and her eyes widened in horrified disapproval. "That commode," she announced, "has *got* to go."

She summoned two of the ranch hands and ordered them to remove the offending lawn ornament immediately. Two others were dispatched to carry the food and cleaning supplies she'd brought into Boone's disreputable trailer.

"If it isn't just like a man to put a *toilet* in his front yard," she muttered, shaking her head as she followed her willing lackeys toward the sagging front porch. "What's wrong with one of those cute little gnomes, for pity's sake, or a big flower that turns when the wind blows?"

"Does she always talk to herself like that?" Boone asked, helping himself to a Weedwacker from the back of Hutch's pickup.

"In my limited experience," Hutch responded, reaching for a plastic gas can to fill the tank on the lawnmower, "yes."

The next few hours were spent whacking weeds, and the result was to reveal a lot more rusty junk, numerous broken bottles and the carcass of a gopher that must have died of old age around the time Montana achieved statehood.

Opal occasionally appeared on the stooped porch, shaking out her apron, resting her hands on her hips and demanding to know how any reasonable person could live in a place like that.

"She thinks you're reasonable," Hutch commented to Boone, who was working beside him, hefting debris into the backs of the several trucks to be hauled away.

"Imagine that." Boone frowned, shaking his head in puzzlement. He'd worked up a sweat, like the rest of them, and his T-shirt stuck to his chest and back in big wet splotches.

"And don't think I didn't notice all that beer in the fridge!" Opal called out, to all and sundry, before turning and grumbling her way back inside that sorry old trailer to fight on in her private war against dust, dirt and disarray of all kinds.

"Beer," one of the ranch hands groaned, his voice full of comical longing. "I could sure use one—or ten— right about now."

Later on, when the sun was high and all their bellies were rumbling, Opal appeared on the porch again and announced that the kitchen was finally fit to serve food in, and the thought of her cooking rallied the troops to trail inside, take turns washing up at the sink and fill plates, buffet style, at the table.

The ranch hands each sneaked a can of beer from the fridge—Opal turned a blind eye to those particular proceedings—and wandered outside to eat in the shade of the trees.

Opal sat at the table in the middle of Boone's freshly scrubbed kitchen, and Boone and Hutch joined her.

"You're a miracle worker," Boone told her, looking around. The place was still scuffed and worn, just this side of being condemned by some government agency, but all the surfaces appeared to be clean.

"And you've been without a woman for way too long," Opal retorted, with her trademark combination of gruffness and relentless affection.

Boone loaded up on potato salad—he probably hadn't had the homemade version since before Corrie got sick—and helped himself to a couple of crunchy-coated chicken breasts. "I'm surprised at you, Opal," he teased. "To hear you tell it, women are made to clean up after men. If *that* gets out, militant females will burn you in effigy."

She expelled a huffy breath and waved off the remark for the foolishness it was. After a moment or two, her expression turned solemn and she studied Boone as though she'd never seen him before, peering at him through the lenses of her out-of-style eyeglasses.

"This isn't what Corrie would want, Boone," she said quietly. "Not for you and certainly not for those two little boys of yours."

Boone put down his fork, still heaping with potato salad, and stared down into his plate in silence. He looked so stricken that Hutch felt a crazy need to come to his friend's rescue somehow, but he quelled it. Intellectually, he knew Opal was right; maybe she could get through to Boone where he and Slade and a lot of other people had failed.

"We weren't planning to live in this trailer for more than a year," Boone said without looking up. "It was just a place to hang our hats while we built the new house."

"I know," Opal said gently. "But don't you think it's time you moved on—built that house, brought your boys home where they belong and maybe even found yourself a wife?"

At last, Boone looked up. The misery in his eyes made the backs of Hutch's sting a little.

"I can't marry a woman I don't love," he said hoarsely, "and I'm never going to love anybody but Corrie."

A silence fell.

Boone took up his fork again, making a resolute effort to go on eating, but his appetite was clearly on the wane.

"It was a hard thing, what happened to you," Opal allowed after some moments, her voice quiet and gentle to the point of tenderness, "but Corrie's gone for good, Boone, and you're still alive, and so are your sons. They need their daddy."

"My sister—"

"I know Molly loves them," Opal said, when Boone fell silent after just those two words. "But they're *yours*, those precious boys, flesh of your flesh, bone of your bone, blood of your blood. *They belong with you.*"

Boone pushed his chair back, looking as though he might bolt to his feet, but in the end stayed put. "I truly appreciate your hard work, Opal," he said, without looking at her *or* at Hutch, "and I mean no disrespect, but you don't know what you're talking about. You don't know how good Griff and Fletch have it with their aunt and uncle and all those cousins."

"I'm sorry, Boone," Opal said. "You didn't ask for my opinion and I should have kept it to myself."

Boone left the table then, left the kitchen, without a backward glance or a word of parting. The screen door, half off its hinges, crashed shut behind him.

"It's progress, Opal," Hutch told the woman quietly, painfully aware of the tears gathering in her wise old eyes. "That Boone will let the boys come back to Parable even for a holiday weekend—it's a big thing. Last Christmas, he went to Missoula, rather than bring them here. Now he's cleaning up the place and he's letting us help, and that's something he's resisted for a long, long time, believe me."

Opal sniffled, swatted at Hutch, and stood up to clear away her plate and Boone's. "When did you get so smart?" she countered. "I'd have sworn you didn't have a lick of sense yourself, entering rodeos, stopping weddings, living all by yourself like some fusty old codger twice your age."

"Why sugarcoat anything, Opal?" Hutch joked, and commenced eating again. "Tell me how you really feel."

The food was good, after all, and there wasn't a damn thing wrong with *his* appetite, whatever might be going on with Boone's.

"The man's depressed," Opal fretted, scraping the plates clean and setting them in the newly unearthed sink. "He puts on a fine show, as far as being sheriff, but he's got to be feeling pretty darn low to let things come to this."

"Try not to worry," Hutch said. "Corrie's death threw Boone for a loop and that's for sure, but he's coming around, Opal. He's finally coming around."

"I hope you're right," Opal fussed, sounding unconvinced.

"You'll see," Hutch answered, wondering where he was getting all this confidence in his best friend's future all of a sudden. He and Slade and plenty of other people had been worried about Boone for years.

Running for sheriff was the first sign of life he'd shown since losing Corrie, and there had been precious little reason to be encouraged since then.

Boone knew his job—even as Slade's deputy, he'd been a standout, steady, dependable, honest to the bone. His clothes were pressed, his boots polished and he got his hair trimmed over at the Curly Burly salon once a month like clockwork.

But then he came home to a hellhole of a trailer and did God knows what with his free time.

"He'd be a good match for Tara Kendall, you know," Opal speculated aloud, her tone wistful. "Both of them lonely, with their places bordering each other the way they do—"

"They hate each other," Hutch said.

"Same way you and Kendra do, I reckon," Opal shot back, smiling.

Hutch felt a slow flush climb his neck to pulse hard under his ears, which were probably red by then. "I don't hate Kendra," he informed his friend gravely. He couldn't say whether or not Kendra hated *him,* but he sure hoped not, because that was just too desolate a thing to consider.

"And Boone doesn't hate Tara, either," Opal went on, self-assured to the max. "She makes him feel some things he'd rather not feel, and that scares the heck out of him, and the reverse is true, too. Tara's as scared of Boone Taylor as he is of her." She paused, probably for dramatic effect, then delivered the final salvo. "Just like you and Kendra."

Hutch was suddenly too exasperated to eat, even though he was still a little hungry after working like a field hand all morning. Ranching involved some effort, but these days he spent more and more of his time supervising the men who worked for him, driving around in his pickup, riding horseback for the fun of it instead of rounding up strays or driving cattle from one feeding ground to another, or checking fence lines.

If he didn't watch out, his own prediction would prove true and he'd be too fat to compete in the rodeo by the end of the week.

He excused himself, rose stiffly from the table and carried his dishes and silverware toward the sink. He scraped his plate into the trash, set it in the hot, soapy water Opal had ready, and left the kitchen.

"Go over there?" Kendra repeated, peering through the pair of binoculars Tara had brought out onto the porch so they could spy on the doings over at Boone's place. Heat surged through her as she watched Hutch haul his shirt off over his head, revealing that lean, rock-hard chest—the one she'd loved to nestle against once upon a time. "Are you crazy?"

"It would the neighborly thing to do," Tara replied, appropriating the binoculars and raising them to her face. Lucy and Daisy, having run off all that energy chasing each other around Tara's yard and trying to catch grasshoppers, were asleep in the shade of a gnarl-trunked old apple tree nearby.

"Since when are you and Boone on 'neighborly' terms?" Kendra countered. Damned if she didn't want to get a look at Hutch Carmody, up close and shirtless, but damned if she'd indulge the whim, either.

"We're not," Tara admitted. "But after all the verbal potshots I've taken at the man for maintaining an eyesore, the least I can do is encourage him to stick with the cleanup campaign." She handed the binoculars back to Kendra, who immediately used them. "Besides, Opal is over there, working her fingers to nubs. Maybe she could use some help from us."

"Right," Kendra said, thinking of her business suit and high-heeled shoes. "I'm certainly dressed for it." She watched, heartbeat quickening, as Hutch used the T-shirt to wipe his forehead and the back of his neck.

Muscles flexed in his arms and shoulders, making her mouth water. "You, on the other hand, look like a fugitive from a rerun of *Green Acres,* so you might as well go right on over there with your bad self."

"Not without backup," Tara said.

"Opal is backup enough for anybody," Kendra replied. It was almost as though Hutch knew she was watching him from afar; he seemed to be overdoing the whole manly thing on purpose just to rile her up.

Take the way he walked, for instance, with the slow, rolling gait of an old-time gunslinger, like his hips were greased, like he owned whatever ground he set his foot down on. And the way he threw back his head and laughed at something Opal called to him from the porch of Boone's trailer.

"Scared?" Tara challenged.

"No," Kendra lied, lowering the binoculars with some reluctance. She needed a few moments to process the sight of Hutch Carmody walking around half-naked. "I'm supposed to pick Madison up at preschool. And there's supper to think about, and—"

"You're supposed to pick Madison up in *two hours,*" Tara pointed out.

"Why do you want to do this?" Kendra asked, almost pitifully. She felt cornered by Tara's calm logic. "You can't *stand* Boone Taylor."

"Like I said," Tara replied with a self-righteous air, "good behavior should be encouraged. Besides, I'm dying to know why he's suddenly so interested in all this DIY stuff."

Kendra sighed, recalling her phone conversation with Joslyn earlier that day. "Well, *I* can tell you that," she said importantly. "Boone's boys are coming to stay with him for the weekend. He's getting the place ready for them."

"Boone has *children?*" Tara looked honestly surprised.

"Two," Kendra replied, wondering how Tara could have lived around Parable for so long without knowing a detail like that. "They've been living with his sister and her family in Missoula since his wife died."

"I knew he was a widower," Tara mused sadly. "But *kids?* The man just packed his own children off to his sister's place after they lost their mother?"

"Well, I don't think it was as cut and dried as that...." Kendra began, but her voice fell away. She liked Boone, and felt a need to take his side, if sides were being taken, though like just about everyone else he knew, she could have shaken him for turning his back on a pair of small, motherless boys the way he had.

"He's even more selfish than I thought," Tara said decisively. She got out of her chair, still holding the binoculars, and went into the house, returning without them a few moments later. Evidently their spy careers were over. "Who *does* a thing like that?" she ranted on under her breath as she plunked back into her chair.

Compassion for Boone welled up in Kendra's chest. "You weren't here when his wife died," she said quietly. "It was *terrible,* Tara. Corrie was in so much pain toward the end and Boone couldn't do a thing to help her. That would be hard for anybody, but especially for a man who's been strong all his life."

"You can bet it was hard for those little boys, too," Tara pointed out, but her tone had softened somewhat by then. "How old are they?"

Kendra made some calculations, "Probably five and

six," she said. "Something like that. Cute as can be—both of them look just like their dad."

A deep sadness moved in Tara's lovely eyes.

Kendra considered the possibility that her own mother might have abandoned her not because she didn't love her, but because she was overwhelmed by life in general. Maybe she'd suffered from depression, like Boone, and become trapped in it.

Maybe, maybe, maybe.

"Don't be too hard on Boone," she said, deciding it was time she and Daisy headed back to town. "He and Corrie married young, and they loved each other so desperately."

Tara nodded slowly. She was looking in the direction of Boone's trailer, although at that distance, with no binoculars to bring them closer, the people appeared tiny and it was hard to tell one from the other.

"Hey," Kendra said to her distracted friend, preparing to descend the porch steps, call for Daisy and head for her car. "Why don't you and Lucy come into town later and have supper with us?"

Tara smiled, rose from her chair, came to stand at the porch railing, resting her hands on top of it. "Thanks," she said, with a little shake of her head. "Maybe some other time."

Kendra nodded, and moments later she and Daisy were in the Volvo, heading down the driveway toward the main road.

Her thoughts and emotions were jumbled—visions of Hutch, bare-chested in the afternoon sunlight, predominated, but there were images of Boone at Corrie's funeral, too. It had rained that gloomy late-winter day, and a bitterly cold wind had driven all the mourners from the graveside the moment the last "Amen" had been said—except for Boone. He'd simply stood there, all alone, with his head down, his hands folded and his suit drenched, gazing downward at his wife's coffin.

Finally Hutch and Slade and a few others had gone out there to collect him, and he'd swung at them, shouting that he wasn't going to leave Corrie alone in the rain. They'd finally prevailed, but it was a struggle, Boone saw to that.

Since then, he'd never been the same.

He worked hard—it was common knowledge that he sent a lot of his paycheck to his sister for the boys' support—and then he went back to that sad piece of land he'd once had such great plans for, and that was all.

It grieved the whole town, because Parable was, after all, a family, and Boone, like Hutch and Slade, was a favorite son.

When Boone ran for sheriff, everyone's hopes rose—maybe things were finally turning around for him—but until today, when the cleanup effort had apparently begun, there had been no further indication that anything much had changed.

At home, Kendra changed into khaki walking shorts, a green tank top and sandals. Then she brushed her shoulder-length hair, caught it up in a ponytail and checked the contents of her refrigerator, considering various supper possibilities.

She'd stopped thinking about Boone's situation, which was a relief, but Hutch refused to budge from her mind no matter how she tried to distract herself.

And she definitely tried.

She tossed an old tennis ball for Daisy in the backyard for at least fifteen minutes, then collected the day's mail from the box attached to her front gate. Nothing but sales fliers and missives addressed to "occupant"— everything had to be forwarded from her old address on Rodeo Road.

Not that she received a lot of mail in this day of instant electronic communication.

She chucked everything into the recycle bin and booted up her computer, a streamlined desktop set up in her home office. Nothing there, either.

Finally it was time—or close enough to it—to drive over to the preschool and collect Madison. Daisy rode shotgun in the Volvo's front seat, panting and taking in everything they passed with those gentle brown eyes, as if there might be a quiz later on what she'd seen and she wanted to be ready for any question.

The preschool occupied a corner of the community center, a long, rambling building that also housed the Chamber of Commerce, along with several conference rooms and a performance area with a stage. The local amateur theater group used the latter, as did the art and garden clubs, and dances, wedding receptions and other events were held there, too. Outside, there was a pool, a tennis court and a baseball field.

The town was justifiably proud of the whole setup, and maintaining the place was a labor of love, done mostly by volunteers.

Kendra parked near the baseball field, her usual place, and walked Daisy around on a leash, poop bag at the ready, while they waited for Madison's "class" to be dismissed for the day.

The bell rang and children catapulted through the open doors of the preschool, releasing pent-up energy as they laughed and jostled each other, celebrating their freedom.

Kendra, standing beside the car with Daisy, smiled as she watched Madison's head turn in her direction, watched her smile broaden as she raced over, waving a paper over her head.

"Look what I drew!" she crowed, shoving the sheet of paper at Kendra and then dropping to her knees in the grass to cover Daisy's muzzle with kisses and ruffle her silken ears.

Kendra looked down at her daughter's artwork and felt a wrench in the center of her heart. Madison had drawn a house with green crayon, recognizable as the one they lived in, with four distinct figures standing in the front yard—a little girl with bright red hair, a yellow dog, a stick-figure rendition of Kendra herself, notable for an enormous necklace of what seemed to be blue beads, and a tall man wearing jeans, a purple shirt, brown boots and an outsize cowboy hat.

Hutch.

"It's a *family!*" Madison said excitedly. "One with a cowboy daddy in it."

Kendra swallowed. "I can see that," she said quietly, before handing the paper back to Madison. "That's a very nice picture," she added, afraid to say more, lest the sudden tears pressing behind her eyes break free.

"Can we tape it to the 'frigerator?" Madison asked, her huge gray eyes solemn now, as though she expected a refusal and was already bracing to argue the point.

"Sure," Kendra said with a smile after clearing her throat.

She spent the next five minutes getting Madison, the dog and herself squared away in the Volvo.

"My friend Brooke has a daddy," Madison announced, once they were in motion. "So do lots of the other kids."

Give me strength, Kendra thought prayerfully. "Yes," she said.

"They put daddies in their pictures, so I did, too," Madison explained. "I made mine a cowboy."

"Does this cowboy have a name?" Kendra ventured. She couldn't just shut the child down, after all, and there was no use trying to change the subject before Madison was ready because she'd pursue it.

"Cowboy man," Madison said in a cheery, who-else tone of voice. "He has lots of horses, and I get to ride one of them sometime."

"That will be exciting," Kendra agreed, smiling.

"He said that," Madison chimed from her place in the backseat, Daisy beside her. "You heard him say that, didn't you, Mommy? That I could ride one of his horses if you said it was okay?"

"I heard," Kendra said. Did Hutch even remember making the offer? Or had he simply been making conversation, telling the child what he thought she wanted to hear at that particular moment?

To him, it was probably just small talk.

To Madison it was a promise, sacred and precious.

Kendra bit her lower lip, thinking. She could play the heavy, of course, say she'd rather Madison didn't get on a horse until she was a little older—conveniently, that was the truth—but one, she didn't want to raise a fearful child and, two, why should *she* be the one to disappoint Madison, while Hutch came off as the good guy, the one who'd tried to make the dream happen and would have succeeded, if not for her?

No.

This time, for once in his life, he was going to follow through.

Madison would have her horseback ride; Kendra would make sure of that, for her little girl's sake.

As soon as they got home, Madison fetched a roll of cellophane tape from Kendra's office, climbed onto a chair and proudly affixed her "family" drawing to the refrigerator door.

"There," she said, getting down and standing back to admire the installation.

Kendra admired it, too. "You'd better make some more pictures," she said thoughtfully. "That one looks a little lonely all by itself."

Madison readily agreed and ran off, Daisy on her heels, to find her crayons.

Kendra returned the chair to its place at the table, got out her cell phone and bravely keyed through stored numbers until she found Hutch's. When was the last time she'd dialed *that* one?

"Hello?" he said after the second ring.

"We need to talk," Kendra answered, employing a clandestine whisper. "When can we get together?"

CHAPTER TEN

WE NEED TO TALK. When can we get together?

To say Kendra's words had caught Hutch off guard would be the understatement of the century, but he hoped his tone sounded casual when he replied, "Okay, sure. I'm just leaving Boone's place—I've got some chores to do at home, and I could really use a shower."

TMI, he thought ruefully. *Too much information.* The woman hadn't asked for a personal hygiene report, after all.

Because he disapproved of other people talking on their cell phones while they drove, Hutch pulled over to one side of Boone's weed-shorn yard and let the men he'd brought over from Whisper Creek pass on by him in their trucks, and Opal, too.

Probably thinking there might be trouble, Opal stopped her big station wagon and started to roll down her window to ask if everything was all right, but Hutch grinned and waved her on.

Kendra sounded a little flustered when she answered, as though she might be wishing not only that she hadn't phrased the invite the way she had, but that she'd never called him at all. "Tonight, tomorrow—whenever," she stumbled.

Hutch felt better, aching muscles and ravenous hunger notwithstanding. Obviously, he wasn't the only one feeling a little out of their depth at the moment and he had to admit, the "we need to talk" part intrigued him in a big way.

"So this is nothing urgent," he concluded with a smile in his voice. He didn't need to see Kendra to know she was blushing to the roots of her pale gold hair; practically every emotion showed plainly on the landscape of her face and usually her inner climate did, too.

Kendra Shepherd might look like a Nordic ice queen, but Hutch knew she was capable of tropical heat.

Meanwhile, Kendra struggled bravely on, determined to make her point, whatever the heck *that* was. "No—I mean—well, I suppose we could discuss it now—"

"That's fine, too," Hutch said amiably, relishing the exchange.

"Yes, Madison," she said to her daughter, who could be heard asking questions in the background, "you *do* have to wash your hands before supper. You've been petting the dog, for Pete's sake."

Hutch chuckled at that. "I'll stop by later tonight," he offered. "What time does Madison go to bed?"

"Eight," Kendra said weakly.

"Then I'll be there around eight-thirty."

There was a pause, during which Hutch half expected Kendra to change her mind, tell him there was no need to come over in person because she could just say what she had to say right there on the phone.

Except that, for whatever reason, Kendra didn't seem to want Madison to be privy to what was said.

"Eight-thirty," Kendra confirmed, sighing the words.

Hutch agreed on the time, set his phone aside and hurried home, where he fed the horses, took a shower, wolfed down cold chicken and potato salad, leftovers from the meal Opal had served over at Boone's earlier in the day, and checked the clock about every five minutes.

It wasn't even six yet.

He'd done everything that needed doing at warp-speed, it seemed. What the hell was he supposed to do with the two and a half hours still to go before he could show up on Kendra's doorstep?

"You've sure got a burr under your hide about something," Opal commented, putting away the remains of the feast. She'd left some of the overflow with Boone and given shares to the ranch hands who'd helped out with the work, too. Nobody turned down Opal's potato salad, ever. "Jumpy as a cat on a griddle, that's what you are."

Good-naturedly, Hutch elbowed her aside and took over the job she'd been doing, shoving chicken and potato salad every which way into the fridge. "Why don't you take the night off?" he asked companionably, when he thought enough time had elapsed so the question wouldn't sound contrived.

"Given that I don't work for you in the first place," Opal informed him, "that's an interesting suggestion. What are you up to, Hutch Carmody? You planning on heading back to the Boot Scoot Tavern again tonight, looking to drum up some more trouble?"

He laughed. "No," he said. "I'm *not* going to the Boot Scoot, and never mind that, it's none of your business if I do."

Opal's eyes were sly, even suspicious. "There's Bingo tonight," she said. "I never miss a game, especially when I'm on a lucky streak. Since I'm headed into town anyway, I could drop you someplace, pick you up later on."

"I do my own driving these days," he reminded her dryly. "Have been since the day I got my license."

"Fine," Opal said with a sniff, untying her apron and heading for her part of the house, presumably to get dolled up for a big night wielding Bingo daubers in the basement of the Elks' Club. "*Don't* tell me what's going on. It isn't as if I won't find out sooner or later. All I've got to do is keep my ear to the ground and sure enough, somebody will mention seeing you tonight, and they'll have the details, too."

Hutch laughed again, shook his head. He'd have sworn he'd never miss being nagged by a woman, but he surely had. Having Opal around was like having a mom again—a good feeling, even if it was a bit on the constricting side. "I'm going to see Kendra," he admitted. "And don't ask me why, because the whole thing was her idea and I don't have the first clue what she wants."

Opal's eyes were suddenly alight with mischievous supposition. "Well, now," she said. "Kendra wants to see you. As for what she wants, anybody but a big dumb cowboy like you would know that from the get-go." She paused to reflect for a few moments, and at the tail end of the thought process, she was looking a little less delighted than before. "You get on the wrong side of her again? Is that it?"

"I'm always on the wrong side of Kendra," Hutch said lightly. *But the view is good from any direction.*

Opal shuffled past him, yanked open the refrigerator, and neatly rearranged everything he'd just shoved in there. "Make sure you pick up some flowers on your way over," she instructed, dusting her hands together as she turned to face him again. "That way if you *are* in the doghouse, which wouldn't surprise me, Kendra might forgive you quicker."

"Forgive me?" Hutch echoed, pretending to be offended. "I haven't done anything she needs to forgive me *for*."

"Maybe not recently," Opal conceded, with another sniff and a glance that begrudged him all grace. "But you did enough damage to last a lifetime back in the day. Get the flowers. There were some nice Gerbera daisies at the supermarket when I was there yesterday."

Hutch executed a deep bow of acquiescence.

Opal gave a scoffing laugh, waved a hand at him and went off to get ready for a wild night of Bingo.

KENDRA PEERED INTO the yellow glow of the porch light and caught her breath.

She'd been expecting Hutch, of course, but for some reason, every encounter with the man, planned as well as unplanned, made her feel as though she'd just taken hold of the wrong end of a cattle prod.

He wore newish jeans, a crisply pressed and possibly even starched cotton shirt in a pale shade of yellow, polished boots and a good hat instead of the usual one that looked as though it had just been trampled in a stampede or retrieved from the bed of a pickup truck.

And he was holding a colorful bouquet of flowers in his left hand.

He must have misunderstood her phone call, she thought, with a sort of delicious desperation. Her heart hammered against her breastbone, and her breathing was so shallow that she was afraid she might hyperventilate if she didn't get a grip.

After drawing a very deep breath, Kendra opened the front door; he'd seen her through the frosted oval window, so it was too late to pretend she wasn't home.

He took off the hat with a deftness that reminded her instantly of other subtle moves he'd made, under much more intimate circumstances, way back in those thrilling days—and nights—of yesteryear.

"The flowers were Opal's idea," he said first thing.

Kendra's mouth twitched with amusement. Hutch was doing a good job of hiding the fact, but he was as nervous as she was, maybe even more so.

"No wine?" she quipped. "You're slipping, cowboy."

He let his gaze range over her, just briefly, as she stepped back so he could come inside. "I figured that would be pushing my luck," he said, and she couldn't tell if he was kidding or serious.

Kendra led the way through the house to the kitchen and offered him a seat at the table. She'd long since cleared away all evidence of supper, supervised Madison's bath, read her a story and heard her prayers, and she'd checked on the child a couple of times over the past half hour, as well.

Both Madison and Daisy had been sound asleep each time she looked in.

Kendra accepted the flowers, found a vase and arranged them quickly. The colors, reds and maroons, oranges and deep pinks and purples, thrilled her senses, a riot of beauty.

When she turned around with the bouquet in hand, she nearly collided with Hutch.

Color climbed her cheeks and she stepped around him to set the flowers in the middle of the kitchen table.

"There's coffee, if you'd like some," she told him, feeling as shy as if he were a stranger and not a man who'd made love to her in all sorts of scandalous places and positions.

Stop it, she scolded herself.

Hutch's eyes twinkled as he watched her—he was seeing too much. Although he could be infuriatingly obtuse, he had a perceptive side, too. One that generally worked to his advantage. "Thanks," he said, "but I've had plenty of java already. One more cup and I'll be up all night putting a new roof on the barn or something."

Kendra smiled at the image, calming down a little on the inside. "I'll just look in on Madison once more," she said, and beat a hasty retreat for the hallway. What *was* it about Hutch that made all her nerves rise to the surface of her skin and sizzle there, like some kind of invisible fire?

He said nothing as she hurried away, but she would have sworn she felt the heat of his gaze wherever her shorts and tank top left her skin bare—on the backs of her arms and calves, on her nape.

Madison, she soon discovered, was still asleep in her "princess bed," or doing a darned good job of playing possum. Daisy, curled up by Madison's feet, raised her downy golden head, yawned and descended back into the realm of doggy dreams.

Since there was no excuse for lingering—and she'd been the one to suggest this rendezvous in the first place—Kendra forced herself to go back to the kitchen and face Hutch.

He was still standing in the center of the room, hat

in hand, and he pulled back a chair at the table for her as adeptly as if they'd been in some fancy restaurant instead of her own modest kitchen.

She sat, interlaced her fingers on the table top and silently wondered why she'd gotten herself into a situation like this—it wasn't like her. The pop-psychology types would probably say she had an unconscious agenda—sex, for instance.

Definitely not true.

Sex was out of the question with Madison in the house.

Thanks to this particular cowboy, though, the small kitchen seemed charged with the stuff, even electrified.

While Kendra's brain was trying to make sense of her own actions, Hutch hung his hat from a peg beside the back door and came to sit down across from her. He watched her in silence for a few moments, his expression solemn, and finally uttered a mildly plaintive, *"What?"*

Kendra, all fired up over his promise to take Madison for a horseback ride earlier, felt silly now. Why hadn't she simply said what she wanted to say while they were on the phone before?

Because she'd wanted to *see* Hutch, that was why. Ever since she'd watched him on Tara's porch, through those binoculars, he'd been on her mind. She *was* trying to prevent Madison from being disappointed over a much wanted horseback ride that didn't ever quite happen—any mother would feel the same—but in retrospect, the requested meeting looked...well... transparent.

God, this was embarrassing.

"This is really no big deal," she began awkwardly. "It's just—"

And then she couldn't force out another word. Her face burned and she wanted to look away from Hutch's face, but pride wouldn't let her take the easy way out.

"I'm listening," he reminded her quietly.

"Madison is really counting on a horseback ride," Kendra blurted, still awkward.

He raised one eyebrow in silent question. *"And?"* his expression prompted.

"I'm getting this all wrong," Kendra fretted. "It seemed like such a good idea before, to get everything out in the open and all that, but now—"

Hutch looked genuinely puzzled, maybe even flummoxed. If Kendra hadn't felt like such an idiot the look on his face would have made her laugh.

"But now?" he urged, his voice low and baffled. "You've decided against letting Madison go for a horseback ride?"

Suddenly, she giggled. It was some kind of nervous reaction, of course, but the release of tension was welcome, even though it did feel a lot like the spring of an old-fashioned watch breaking and spinning itself unwound. "No, that isn't it," she managed, after a moment of recovery. "I just got to thinking that you might forget what you told Madison, about going riding, I mean, and she's—"

"She's counting on it," Hutch confirmed, looking only slightly less confused than before. "Kendra, what the hell are you talking about?"

This time the giggle came out as a half-hysterical little laugh. She put a hand over her mouth and rocked, hoping the mysteries of incontinence would not be revealed to her. *Especially* in front of Hutch Carmody.

Before she could frame an answer, though, Hutch's eyes darkened with realization, reminding her of a sky working up a booming spate of thunder that might last for a while instead of blowing over quickly.

"You just automatically assumed I'd let her down, is that it?" he demanded, leaning in a little. His eyes flashed with indignation.

Kendra straightened her spine. Lifted her chin a notch or two. "Not exactly," she hedged. *"Not exactly"?* mocked a voice in the back of her mind. Come on. He'd just verbalized her precise thoughts on the matter. She'd been afraid he'd hurt and disappoint her little girl, and decided not to let it happen—that was the size of it.

"If you'll remember," Hutch went on, filling her in in case she hadn't noticed the figurative skywriting arching across the firmament overhead, "I told Madison she could ride one of my horses if it was all right with you. *You're* the one who didn't want to commit to a straight-out 'yes' and just barely settled for 'maybe.' And now it's *my* fault for letting her down?"

Kendra swallowed miserably. Looked away.

"Kendra," Hutch insisted. Just that one word, just her name, was all he said, but it carried weight.

"All right," she whispered, meeting his gaze again. "I'm sorry. I was wrong. Can we just get past that, please?"

His mouth smiled, but his eyes were solemn, even sad. "I meant what I said before," he finally replied. "If you're agreeable, we'll put Madison on the gentlest horse I own and she'll have her ride. Or she can ride with me, whatever you think best."

Kendra's throat tightened and she had to look away once more before reconnecting. Those eyes of his seemed to see into the deepest part of her, seeking and finding every secret she'd hidden away over the years, even from herself.

"When?" she asked, still mortified by her own behavior but trying to put a good face on things. "Madison will expect specifics."

He smiled again, this time with his whole face. "Whenever you say," he answered.

Kendra sighed. The ball was in her court and he wasn't going to let her forget that. "Tomorrow?" she threw out tentatively. "After she gets out of preschool?"

"That'll work," Hutch said, watching her. "About what time should I expect you and the munchkin to show up on Whisper Creek?"

"Three-thirty? Is that too early? I know you probably have a lot of work to do and I wouldn't want to impose or anything."

Lame. Of *course* she was imposing—but she was in too deep and there was no other way out.

"Three-thirty," Hutch agreed. Then, unexpectedly, he reached across the table and closed his fingers gently around her hand. "One question, Kendra. Why was it so hard for you to get all this said? We have a history, you and I, and not all of it was bad—not by a long shot."

"I'm—not sure," Kendra admitted softly.

"That's an honest if inadequate answer," he said, but his grin, if slight, was genuine. He got up, walked over to retrieve his hat, held it in one hand as he looked back at Kendra. "Tomorrow, three-thirty, Whisper Creek Ranch?"

"If it's inconvenient for you, another time would be fine, honestly—"

Hutch narrowed his eyes, not in anger, but bewilderment, as though by squinting he might make out some aspect of her nature he hadn't spotted before. "Women," he said with a note of consternation in his voice.

Kendra got to her feet, led the way back through the house toward the front door. *"Men,"* she retorted with a roll of her eyes.

She'd never planned for it to happen, and maybe Hutch hadn't either, but once they'd stepped beyond the cone of light thrown by the porch fixture, into the soft, summery shadows, they found themselves standing close to each other—too close.

Hutch curved a hand under Kendra's chin, lifted her face and kissed her, as naturally as they would have done in the old days.

And Kendra kissed him back, her body coming awake as both new and very familiar sensations took hold, expanding and contracting, soaring and then plummeting.

Kendra gave a silent gasp. It was still there, then, all of it, the passion, the need, the wildness, the things she'd tried so hard to forget over the years since their breakup.

She knew she ought to change directions, put on the brakes before they collided in the train wreck of the century—but she just couldn't.

She was lost in that kiss, lost in the way it felt to have Hutch's arms around her again, strong and sure, holding her close.

Her knees went weak, and she knotted her fists in the fabric of his shirt and held on, and still the kiss continued, seemingly taking on a life of its own, now playful, now deep and commanding.

"Mommy?"

The word, coming from just beyond the screened door, sliced down between them like a knife.

Both of them stepped back.

"You didn't tell me the cowboy man was here," Madison said innocently, rubbing away sleep with one hand even as she pressed her little nose against the worn screen, looking curious but nothing more. Her side-kick, Daisy, did the same.

"I didn't want to wake you up," Hutch said chivalrously. "Your mom and I were deciding on when you ought to take that horseback ride we talked about."

Madison's eyes instantly widened, and she stepped back far enough to open the screen door so she and Daisy could bolt through the gap.

"Really?" the child cried. *"When? Where?"*

Hutch lifted her easily, naturally into his arms, grinned. "Really," he said. "Tomorrow afternoon, at my ranch."

"I told you she'd ask for specifics," Kendra managed to say. Her face was still flaming, her heart was pounding, and she was frantic to know how much Madison had seen, and understood, before interrupting that foolish, *wonderful* kiss.

Madison literally squealed with delight. "Yes!" she cried, punching the air with one small, triumphant fist.

Hutch chuckled and set her back on her bare feet, tousled her tumbling copper curls lightly, though by then his gaze was fixed on Kendra again. She couldn't read his expression very well, since he was standing on the fringes of the glow from the porch light, but she saw the white flash of his teeth as he smiled.

"I guess that's settled, then," he said. He set his hat on his head, tugged at the brim in farewell and added, "Good night, ladies. I'll see you tomorrow."

And he turned to go.

"Wait!" Madison blurted, and Kendra was relieved to realize she hadn't been the one to speak, because that exact same word had swelled in the back of her throat and very nearly tumbled out over her tongue.

Wait.

Wait for what? A second chance? A miracle? Some passage opening between now and the time when everything had been good and right between them?

You're losing it, Kendra thought to herself.

Hutch paused at the top of the steps, turned to look back over one shoulder and waited quietly for the little girl to go on.

Kendra had forgotten that quietness in him. Hutch was still a rowdy cowboy inclined toward the rough-and-tumble and that probably hadn't changed, but he carried a vast silence inside him, too, as though he were somehow anchored to the core of the universe and drew confidence from that.

"Can Daisy come, too?" Madison asked earnestly.

"It's all right with me if it's all right with your mother," Hutch replied almost gruffly.

Kendra didn't dare say anything, so she nodded. She wanted Hutch to stay, though. She wanted more of his kisses, and still more, and she ached to return to the sweet, secret places where she knew they would take her.

But it wasn't going to happen, she told herself. Not tonight, anyway.

Hutch went his way—down the walk, through the gate, around to the driver's door of his truck; and she went to hers—back into the house, with Madison and Daisy.

HEADED HOME TO the ranch through a pale purple summer night, Hutch felt exuberant and scared shitless, both at the same time. The aftereffects of the kiss he and Kendra had shared on her porch still reverberated through his system like bullets ricocheting around inside a cement mixer and every instinct urged him to get far away from the woman, fast.

Except that there was nowhere to go.

He rolled down the window, switched on the radio and sang along with a country-western drinking song at the top of his lungs for the first mile or so, and by the time he was about to round the last bend, some of the adrenaline had ebbed and there was at least a remote possibility that he could think straight.

He wasn't speeding—the ticket Boone had given him was still fresh in his mind—but he nearly hit the critter sitting in the middle of the road anyhow.

He swerved, screeched to a stop, shut off the engine but not the headlights, and shoved open the door. Sprinting around the back of the truck, he was surprised—and relieved—to see that the animal, either a black dog or a very skinny bear, was still in one piece. The creature hadn't moved from the middle of the road, and as he approached, it whimpered low in its throat and cowered a little.

"You hurt?" Hutch asked, mindful that another rig

could come around the bend at any moment and send both him and what turned out to be a dog headlong into the Promised Land. Swiftly, he crouched, ran experienced rancher's hands over the creature's matted back and all four legs. He stood up again. "Come on, then," he said, satisfied that nothing was broken. "Let's see if you can walk."

Hutch started slowly back toward the truck.

The dog got up and limped after him.

Carefully, he hoisted the stray into the passenger's seat of his truck.

"You oughtn't to sit in the road like that," he said, once he was behind the wheel again and turning the key in the ignition. "It's a good way to get killed."

Here he was, talking to a dog.

A strange thing to do, maybe, but it felt good.

The dog turned to look at him with weary, limpid eyes and shivered a little.

Hutch debated turning around, taking the stray back to town, to the veterinary clinic, or at least to Martie Wren's place, so she could take a look at it, maybe check for one of those microchips that served as canine GPS. He'd been around horses and dogs and cattle all his life, though, and he knew instinctively that this one was sound, underneath all that dirt and deprivation.

Pulling in at the top of his driveway, Hutch was relieved to see Opal's station wagon parked up ahead. Evidently Bingo was over for the night, because she probably wouldn't have left the Elks' basement before the last number was called.

He parked, lifted the dog out of the truck and set him on his four thin, shaky legs. "You're going to be all right, fella," he told the animal gruffly. "You've got my word on that."

They went inside.

Opal was at the table, drinking tea and reading from her Bible.

"Land sakes," she said, at the sight of the dog, "what *is* that?"

Hutch gave her a wry look. "Just a wayfarer fallen on hard times," he said.

Opal closed her Bible, stood up, removing her glasses, polishing them with the hem of her apron, and putting them back on again, so she could examine the dog more closely. "Poor critter," she said. "Let's have us a good look at you."

Next she moved her teacup and Bible and draped a large plastic bag over the table.

"Heft him on up here," she said.

Hutch complied.

The dog stood uncertainly in the middle of the table, convinced, no doubt, that he was breaking some obscure human law and would be punished for it. He took to shivering again.

"Nobody's going to hurt you now," Opal told him, with gentle good humor, as she began to examine and prod. "Just look at that rib cage," she remarked, finally stepping back. "When's the last time you had anything to eat, dog?"

Hutch put the critter back on the floor, went to the cupboard for a bowl, filled it with water at the sink, and set it down in front of the newcomer.

The animal drank every drop and looked up at Hutch, asking for more as surely as if he'd spoken aloud.

Hutch refilled the bowl.

Opal, meanwhile, washed her hands and proceeded to ferret around in the fridge, finally emerging with two pieces of chicken and a carton of cottage cheese.

Deftly, like she cared for starving strays every day of her life, she peeled the meat off the bones and broke the chicken into smaller chunks. She mixed in some of the cottage cheese and set the works down on the floor on a plate.

The dog, lapping up water until then, fell on that food like he was afraid it would vanish before his eyes. He made short work of the meal, and Hutch would have given him another helping, but Opal nixed the idea.

"His poor stomach has all it can do to deal with what's already in there," she said.

After that, Hutch bathed the dog in the laundry room sink, helped himself to a couple of towels fresh from the dryer and rubbed that bony mutt down until his hide gleamed and his fur stuck out in every direction.

When he and the dog got back to the kitchen, Opal had cleared the table and resumed her Bible reading and her tea drinking. She tapped at the Good Book with one index finger and said, "Leviticus. That's the perfect name for our friend here."

"How so?" Hutch asked, washing up at the kitchen sink. The whole front of his good shirt was muddy and wet from giving the dog a bath, but he didn't care.

"Because that's what I was reading when you brought him in."

Hutch smiled to himself. He remembered when he was a kid and his mom would read through the whole Bible every year, a day at a time. She always said if a person could get through the book of Leviticus, they could get through anything.

"I take it Bingo was a bust?" he ventured, watching as Leviticus ambled over to the pile of old blankets Opal must have put out for him, settled himself, gave a sigh and closed his eyes.

"I won the blackout," Opal informed Hutch proudly with a smile and a shake of her head. "Five hundred dollars. So I'm pretty flush."

Hutch looked at the now sleeping dog and felt a space open wide in his heart to accommodate him. "Speaking of money," he said, "I owe you some for all you've done around here, and over at Boone's place today, too."

Opal executed another dismissive wave of one hand. "I don't want your money, Hutch," she said. "And didn't I just now tell you I've got five hundred beautiful dollars in my wallet at this very moment?"

He chuckled, shook his head. "You," he said, "are one hardheaded woman."

"All the more reason not to argue with me," Opal replied. She arched both eyebrows and Hutch saw the question coming before the words left her mouth. "How did things go over at Kendra's?"

Hutch folded his arms, leaned back against the counter alongside the sink. "Well enough that she and Madison will be coming out here tomorrow afternoon for a horseback ride," he said. It was more than he would have told most people, but he owed Opal, and besides, talking to her was easy.

Opal beamed. "They'll stay for supper," she announced. "I'll make my famous tamale pie. Kendra always loved it and so will that sweet little girl of hers."

Hutch spread his hands. "You'd better be the one to offer the invitation," he said, remembering the kiss. By now the regret would be setting in, Kendra would be wishing she'd slapped him instead of kissing him right back. "If it comes from me, she's more likely to say no than yes."

"Now why do you suppose that is?" Opal pretended to ponder, but her gaze found the dog again and she smiled. "You mean to keep Leviticus, don't you?" she asked.

"Unless somebody's looking for him," Hutch replied. "I'll check with Martie tomorrow."

"Nobody's looking for Leviticus," Opal said with sad certainty. "He'd have a collar and tags if he belonged to someone."

Hutch felt a peculiar mixture of sympathy and possessiveness where Leviticus was concerned. The dog was bound to be nothing but trouble—he'd chew things up and he probably wasn't housebroken—but Hutch wanted to keep him, wanted that more than anything except to find some common ground with Kendra, so they wouldn't be so jumpy around each other.

Tomorrow couldn't come soon enough to suit him.

CHAPTER ELEVEN

"I'LL NEED BOOTS," Madison announced the next morning at breakfast. "Can we buy some, please? Today?"

Practically from the moment she'd opened her eyes, Madison had been fixating on the upcoming horseback ride out at Whisper Creek Ranch. Even as she spooned her way diligently through a bowlful of her favorite cereal, her feet were swinging back and forth under the table as though already carrying her toward the magic hour of three-thirty in the afternoon.

"Let's wait and see," Kendra said, sipping coffee. She didn't normally skip breakfast, but that day she couldn't face even a bite of toast. She had orchestrated this whole horseback riding thing, set herself up for yet another skirmish with Hutch and now the reality was almost upon her—and Madison.

What had she done?

More importantly, why *had she put herself and her daughter in this position?*

"Everybody at preschool has boots," Madison persisted. Daisy, having finished her kibble, crossed the room to lay her muzzle on the child's lap and gaze up at her with the pure, selfless love of a saint at worship.

"Most of those children have been riding since they were babies," Kendra reasoned, making a face as she set her coffee cup down. Usually a mainstay, the stuff tasted like acid this morning. "Suppose you get on that horse today and find out you hate riding and you never want to do it again?"

"That won't happen," Madison said with absolute conviction. Where did all that certainty come from? Was it genetic—some vestige of all those English ancestors riding to the hunt, soaring over hedges and streams?

Kendra shook off the thought. She hadn't slept all that well the night before, imagining all the things that might go wrong today, and now she was paying the price. Her thoughts were as muddled as her emotions.

"What makes you so sure of yourself, young lady?" she challenged with a small smile.

Madison grinned back at her. "You're always saying it's good to try new things," she said with a note of triumph that underscored Kendra's impression that the child was only *posing* as a four-year-old—she was really an old soul.

Busted, Kendra thought. She *was* always telling Madison that she shouldn't be afraid—of preschool, for instance, or speaking up in class, or making friends on the playground—and now here she was, projecting her own misgivings onto her daughter. Speaking to the frightened little girl she herself had once been, instead of the bold one sitting across from her on a sunny, blue-skied morning full of promise.

"I'll make a deal with you," Kendra said, brightening. "If you still want boots after this first ride, we'll get you a pair." She wondered if the child had visions of racing across the open countryside on the back of some gigantic steed, when she'd most likely wind up on a pony or an arthritic mare.

"Okay," Madison capitulated, not particularly pleased but willing to negotiate. "But I'm still going to want those boots."

Kendra laughed. "Hurry up and finish your breakfast," she said. "Then go and brush your teeth while I let Daisy out for a quick run in the backyard. You need to be on time for preschool and I have to get to the office."

The spiffing-up process over at the mansion was winding down, according to reports from the painting and cleaning crews, and she already had two appointments to show the place, one at noon and one the following morning.

Things were moving along.

Why did it suddenly seem so difficult to keep up?

Madison set her spoon down, wriggled off her chair, and carried her mostly empty cereal bowl over to the sink. She stood on tiptoe to set it on the drainboard, humming under her breath as she headed back toward the bathroom.

Daisy started to follow her small mistress, but when Kendra opened the back door, the dog rushed through it, wagging her tail. Kendra followed.

The morning was glorious—the grass green, with that fresh-cut smell, and lawn sprinklers sang their rhythmic songs in the surrounding yards. Birds whistled in the branches of trees and a few perched on Kendra's clothesline, regarding Daisy's progress with placid nonchalance.

Madison returned to the kitchen just as Daisy and Kendra were coming in from outside. She opened her lips wide to show Kendra her clean teeth.

Kendra pretended to be dazzled, going so far as to

raise both hands against the sudden glare, as if blinded by it.

Madison giggled, this being one of their many small games. "You're silly, Mommy," she said.

Kendra tugged lightly at one of Madison's coppery curls and bent to kiss the top of her head. "Have I mentioned that I love you to the moon and back?" she countered, taking Daisy's leash from its hook and snapping it to the dog's collar.

"I love you *ten* times that much," Madison responded on cue.

"I love you a hundred times that much," Kendra pronounced, juggling her purse, car keys and a leash with an excited puppy at the other end.

"I love you *the last number in the world* times that much," Madison said.

"I love you ten thousand times that much," Kendra told her as they trooped outside and headed for the driveway, where the trusty Mom-mobile was parked.

"That isn't fair," Madison argued. "I said the last number in the world."

"Okay," Kendra answered, smiling. "You win."

HUTCH MOVED FROM one stall to the next, assessing every horse he owned.

They were ordinary beasts, most of them, but they all looked too big and too powerful for a four-year-old to ride.

Was it too late to buy a pony?

He chuckled at the idea and shook his head. Whisper Creek was a working ranch and the horses pulled their weight, just as the men did. He'd be laughed right out of the Cattleman's Association if he ran a Shetland on

the same range as all these brush cutters and ropers.
The sweet old mare he'd reserved for greenhorns had
passed away peacefully one night last winter and much
as he'd loved the animal, it hadn't occurred to him to
replace her. It was a matter of attrition.

Opal stepped into the barn just as he turned from the
last stall, dressed for going to town. She wore a jersey
dress, as usual, but a hat, too, and shiny shoes, and she
carried a huge purse with a jeweled catch.

"I've got a meeting at the church," she informed him.
"After that, I thought I'd look in on Joslyn's bunch, see
how they're doing."

Hutch smiled, walked slowly in her direction. He'd
already sent the ranch hands out onto the range for the
day, assigning them to the usual tasks, which left him
with nothing much to do other than look himself up on
the internet and see how he was faring in the court of
public opinion.

Not that he couldn't have guessed. Team Brylee was
probably still on the warpath, and so far a Team Hutch
hadn't come together.

"You don't work for me," he reminded Opal affably,
as she had recently reminded him. "No need to explain
your comings and goings."

Opal stood stalwartly in his path, clutching her purse
to her chest with both hands as though she expected
some stranger to swoop in and grab it if she relaxed her
vigilance for a fraction of a second. "I'm living under
your roof," she said matter-of-factly, "so it's just common courtesy to tell you my plans."

Hutch stopped, cleared his throat, smiled again. "All
right," he agreed. "You've told me. It was unnecessary,
but I appreciate it just the same."

Opal didn't move, though she might have loosened her grip on her handbag just a little; he couldn't be sure. "You and Boone," she mused, sounding almost weary, even though it hadn't been an hour since breakfast. "I declare, the two of you will worry me right into an early grave."

Hutch's chuckle sounded hoarse. He shoved a hand through his hair. "That would be a shame, Opal," he said. "Boone will be fine and so will I."

"Just the same," Opal replied, "I sometimes wonder if I'm *ever* going to be able to cross you off my active prayer list."

Hutch felt his mouth quirk at one corner. "We're on your prayer list?" he responded. "Why, Opal, I'm both touched and flattered."

"Don't be," she told him gruffly. "It means you're a hard case, and so is Boone."

"I see," Hutch said, though he didn't really. He wanted to laugh, but some instinct warned him that Opal was dead serious about this prayer list business. "Well, then, maybe I'm not flattered after all," he went on presently. "But I'm still touched."

She smiled that slow, warm smile of hers, the one that seemed to take in everybody and everything for miles around, like a sunrise. "There may be hope for you yet," she said, her tone mischievously cryptic. "I'll be back in plenty of time to make supper for you and Kendra and that sweet little child of hers. Try not to say the wrong thing and drive them off before I get back."

Hutch merely nodded and Opal turned, her purse still pressed to her bosom, to leave the barn.

He'd fed the horses earlier; now he began the process of turning them out of their stalls and into the pasture—

all except Remington, that is. He heard Opal's station wagon start up with a gas-guzzling roar, listened as she drove away, tires spitting gravel.

Opal did everything with verve.

He smiled as he fetched his gear from the tack room, carried it back to where the gelding waited, patiently chewing on the last of his grain ration.

Hutch opened the stall gate, and Remington stepped out into the breezeway—he knew the drill, and suddenly he was eager to be saddled, to leave the confines of that barn for the wide-open spaces.

Five minutes later, Hutch was mounted up, and the two of them were moving over the range at a graceful lope, headed for Big Sky Mountain.

Reaching the base of the trail Hutch favored, the horse slowed for the climb, rocks scrabbling under his hooves as he started up the incline.

Hutch bent low over the animal's neck as they passed through a stand of oak and maple trees, the branches grabbing at both man and horse as they went.

The mountain was many things to Hutch Carmody— for as long as he could remember, he'd gone there when he had something to mourn or something to celebrate, or when he simply wanted to think.

From a certain vantage point, he could see the world that mattered most to him—the sprawling ranch lands, the cattle and horses, the streams and the river and, in the distance, the town of Parable.

After about fifteen minutes of fairly hard travel, he and Remington reached the small clearing that was, for him, the heart of Whisper Creek Ranch.

It was here that, as a boy of twelve, he'd cried for his lost mother.

It was here that he'd raged against his father, those times when he was too pissed off or too hurt or both to stay put in school or in his room or out in the hay-scented sanctuary of the barn.

And it was here that he and Kendra had made love for the first time—and the last.

He sighed, swinging down from the saddle and leaving Remington to graze on the tender grass.

The pile of rocks was still there, of course—waist-high and around six feet long, resembling a tomb, he thought wryly, or maybe an altar for Old Testament–style offerings to a God he didn't begin to understand and, frankly, didn't much like.

Opal definitely would not approve of such an attitude, he thought with a smile. She'd keep him on her hard-case prayer list for the duration.

No doubt, he belonged there.

After taking a moment to center himself, he walked over to the improvised monument, laid his hands on the cool, dusty stones on top and remembered. Every one of those rocks represented something he'd needed to say to John Carmody and never could, or something he *had* said and wished he hadn't.

High over his head, a breeze whispered through the needles of the Ponderosa pines and the leaves of those stray maples and oaks that had taken root in this place long before he was born. Remington nickered contentedly, his bridle fittings jingling softly.

A kind of peace settled over Hutch.

"You were hard to love, old man," he said very quietly.

John Carmody wasn't actually buried under those rocks—he'd been laid to rest in the Pioneer Cemetery—

but this was where Hutch came when he felt the need to make some connection with his father, whether in anger or in sorrow.

The anger had mostly passed, worn away by intermittent rock-stacking sessions following the old man's death, but the sorrow remained, more manageable now, but still as much a part of Hutch as the land and the fabled big sky.

And that, he decided, was all right, because life was all of a piece, when you got right down to it, a jumbled mixture of good and bad and everything in between.

He turned his back to the rock pile then, folded his arms and drew the vast view into himself like a breath to the soul.

In the distance he could see the spires of Parable's several small churches, the modest dome of the courthouse, with the flag rippling proudly at its peak. There was the river, and the streams breaking off from it, the spreading fingers of a great, shimmering hand.

His gaze wandered, finally snagged on the water tower.

Like the high meadow where he stood, that rickety old structure had meaning to him. He'd ridden bulls and broncos, ranging from mediocre to devil-mean, over the years, breaking a bone or two in the process. He'd floated some of the wildest rivers in the West, raced cars and skydived and bungee jumped, you name it, all without a flicker of fear.

And then there was the water tower.

Like most kids growing up in or around Parable, he'd climbed it once, made his way up the ancient ladder, rung by weathered rung, with his heart pounding in his ears and his throat so thick with terror that he could hardly breathe.

Reaching the flimsy walkway, some fifty feet above the ground, he'd suddenly frozen, gripping the rail while the whole structure seemed to sway like some carnival ride gone crazy. A cold sweat broke out all over him, clammy despite the heat of a summer afternoon and, just to complete his humiliation, Slade Barlow had been there.

Slade, his half brother, and at the time, sworn enemy, had dared him to make the climb in the first place. Ironically, Slade had been the one to come up that ladder and talk him down, too, since there was nobody else around just then.

Thank God.

Even now, after all his time, the memory settled into the pit of Hutch's stomach and soured there, like something he shouldn't have eaten.

He forced his attention away from the tower—most folks agreed that, being obsolete anyhow, the thing ought to be torn down before some darn-fool kid was seriously hurt or even killed, but nobody ever actually *did* anything about the idea. Maybe it was nostalgia for lost youth, maybe it was plain old inertia, but talking seemed to be as good as doing where that particular demolition project was concerned.

Hutch sighed, a little deflated, wondering what he'd expected to achieve by coming up here, approached Remington and gathered his reins before climbing back into the saddle.

He stood in the stirrups for a moment or two, stretching his legs, and then he headed for home, where no one was waiting for him.

AT NOON, KENDRA showed the mansion to the first potential client, a busy executive from San Francisco who was looking, he said, for investment opportunities. His wife, he told Kendra, had always wanted to start and run a bed-and-breakfast in a quaint little town exactly like Parable.

She'd smiled throughout, listening attentively, asking and answering questions, and finally telling the man straight out that there were already three bed-and-breakfasts in town, and they were barely staying afloat financially.

The man had nodded ruefully, thanked Kendra for her time and driven away in his rented SUV. Most likely he'd promised his wife he'd take a look, and now he'd done that and could dismiss the plan in good conscience. Instinctively she knew no offer would be forthcoming, but she wasn't discouraged.

Kendra had returned to the office afterward, where she'd left Daisy snoozing contentedly in a corner, and eaten lunch—a carton of yogurt and an apple—at her desk.

Taking a client through the mansion, although almost certainly a fruitless enterprise, had served as a welcome distraction from her mixed-up thoughts about Hutch and that afternoon's horseback ride, but now she was alone in her quiet office, except for Daisy, and her imagination threatened to run wild.

The phones were silent.

The computer monitor yawned before her like the maw of a dragon, ready to suck her in and devour her whole.

She was ridiculously grateful when the mailman

dropped in with a handful of flyers and bills, thrilled when the meter reader put in a brief appearance.

"I'm losing my mind," she confided to Daisy, when the two of them were alone in the silent office again. "You've been adopted by a crazy woman."

Daisy yawned broadly, closed her lovely brown eyes, and went back to sleep.

"Sorry if I'm boring you," she told the dog.

Daisy gave a soft snore.

By the time three o'clock rolled around, Kendra was practically climbing the walls. She attached Daisy's leash to her collar, shut off the lights, locked the front door and all but raced out the back way to her car.

When she arrived at the community center, Madison was waiting for her, along with her teacher, Miss Abbington.

Miss Abbington did not look like a happy camper.

"What's wrong?" Kendra asked as soon as she'd parked the car and gotten out.

"I think Madison should answer that," Miss Abbington said. She was a small, earnest woman with pointy features that made her look hypervigilant—a quality Kendra appreciated, especially in a person who spent hours with her daughter every day.

Madison flushed, but her chin was set at an obstinate angle. "I was incordiable," she told Kendra.

"Incorrigible," Miss Abbington corrected stiffly.

"What happened?" Kendra asked the little girl, at once alarmed and defensive. How could a four-year-old child be described as "incorrigible?" Wasn't that word usually reserved for hard-core criminals?

"I misrupted the whole class," Madison said, warming to the subject.

"*Dis*rupted," Miss Abbington said.

Kendra gave the woman a look, then refocused her attention on her daughter. "That isn't good, Madison," she said. "What, specifically, did you do?"

Madison squared her small shoulders and tugged her hand free from Miss Abbington's. "I borrowed Becky Marston's cowgirl boots," she admitted without a hint of shame. "When she took them off to put on her sneakers for gym class."

"Without permission," Miss Abbington embellished, looking down her long nose at Madison. "And then, when Becky asked for her boots back, you told her you weren't through wearing them yet."

"Madison." Kendra sighed. "We talked about the boot thing, remember? This morning at breakfast?"

"I just wanted to see what they felt like," Madison said, but her lower lip was starting to wobble and she didn't look quite as sure of her position as before. "I would have given them back tomorrow."

Kendra looked at Miss Abbington again. Miss Abbington's gaze connected with hers, then skittered away.

"I'll take it from here," Kendra told the other woman.

"Fine," Miss Abbington said crisply.

"It's wrong to take someone else's things, Madison," Kendra told her daughter. "You know that."

From the car, Daisy poked her muzzle through a partly open window and whimpered.

Madison's eyes filled with tears, real ones. She was a precocious child, but she didn't cry to get her way. "Are you mad at me, Mommy?"

"No," Kendra said quickly, trying not to smile at the image of her little girl clomping around the schoolroom in a pair of purloined boots. *This isn't funny,* she scolded herself silently, but it didn't help much.

"Do I still get to go to the cowboy man's house and ride a horse?"

Canceling the outing would have made sense, giving Madison reason to think about her behavior at preschool, but Kendra privately nixed the idea on two counts. One, she knew Madison's disappointment would be out of all proportion to the misdemeanor she'd committed and, two, she'd have to reschedule the ride and she didn't think her nerves could take the strain.

She was a wreck as it was.

"Yes," she said, leading Madison to the car and helping her into the safety seat in back. Daisy was on hand to lick the little girl's face in welcome. "You can still ride Mr. Carmody's horse. But tomorrow, as soon as you get to school, you will apologize to Miss Abbington *and* to Becky for acting the way you did." A pause. "Fair enough?"

Madison considered the proposition as though it *were* a proposition and not an order. "Okay," she agreed. "But I still think Becky is a big crybaby."

"Don't push your luck, kiddo," Kendra warned.

She got behind the wheel, fastened her seat belt, started the engine.

"None of this would have happened," Madison offered reasonably, "if I had my own cowgirl boots."

Kendra closed her eyes for a moment, swallowed a laugh. She wanted Madison to be spirited and proactive, yes. But a demanding brat? No way.

"One more word about those boots," she said, glancing at the rearview mirror to read her daughter's face, "and there will be no visit to Mr. Carmody's ranch, no horseback ride and definitely no day at the rodeo."

Madison's jaw clamped down tight. She obviously had plenty more to say, but she was too smart to say it.

She wanted that ride.

Half an hour later, after a quick stop at home, where Kendra and Madison both changed into jeans and T-shirts and gave Daisy a chance to lap up some water and squat in the backyard, the three of them set out for Whisper Creek Ranch.

On the way, Kendra told herself silently that she was making too big a deal out of this. Nothing earthshaking was going to happen; Hutch would lead a horse out of the barn, Madison would sit in the saddle for a few minutes and that would be it.

She and Madison could turn right around and come home, none the worse for the experience.

Big Sky Mountain loomed in the near distance as they drove on toward the ranch, towering and ancient. If there was one thing in or around Parable that made Kendra think of Hutch Carmody, it was that mountain.

How many times had they gone there, on horseback and sometimes on foot, to be alone in that hidden meadow he loved so much, to talk and laugh and, often, to make love in the warmth of the sun or the silvery glow of starlight?

A blush climbed her neck and pulsed in her cheeks.

Too many times, she thought glumly.

It had been wonderful.

Her grandmother had found out about the trysts eventually—probably by reading Kendra's diary—and said, "You're just like your mother. I can't trust you out of my sight any more than I could trust her. You turn up pregnant, girl, and I'll wash my hands of you."

Kendra had taken great care *not* to get pregnant, but not because of her grandmother's threat—the old woman had long since washed her hands of her daughter's child. No, it was because she hadn't wanted to trap Hutch, force him into marriage because she was having his baby. A few of the other girls in school had gone that route with their boyfriends, and the consequences were sobering, to say the least.

Though she'd loved Hutch, and sometimes feared that she still did, Kendra had wanted to go to college. Yes, she'd wanted children, but at the right time and in the right way. Knowing what it felt like to be a living, breathing burden, she'd been determined to wait, to start her family when she and Hutch were both ready.

Instead she'd gotten involved with Jeffrey Chamberlain. It had been an innocent friendship at first—she'd been fascinated by Jeffrey's accent, his dry British sense of humor, his style and manners.

Still, she hadn't married him out of love, not really. She'd *wanted* to love him, wanted the fairy-tale life he offered, wanted things to be *settled,* once and for all, so she could get on with her life.

But right up until the moment she'd said, "I do," she'd expected Hutch to step in, to reclaim her, to be willing to slay dragons to keep her.

He'd done none of those things, of course. And she'd been a dreamy-eyed fool to expect him to.

Now nearing the gate at the base of Hutch's long driveway, Kendra put the past firmly out of her mind.

That was then. This is now.

Hutch was in front of the barn, and he'd saddled

three horses—two regular-size ones and a little gray pony with black-and-white spots.

Daisy began to bark, noticing the shy black dog lurking nearby, and Madison, spotting the pony, gave a delighted squeal.

But Kendra was still counting the horses.

By her calculations, there was one too many.

She barely got the car stopped before Madison was freeing herself from the restraint of her safety seat, pushing open the rear door, scrambling out.

Daisy leaped out after her, and Hutch laughed as both the dog and the little girl bounded toward him and the horses. He introduced his own dog, Leviticus, who stayed a little apart, looking on cautiously.

"That's the *littlest* horse in the whole world!" Madison raved, having barely noticed the dog, stopping finally to stare at the pony in wonder.

"Maybe," Hutch agreed, grinning. His gaze rose slowly to Kendra's face and locked on with an impact she actually felt.

"I'm little, too," Madison chattered on eagerly.

Hutch looked serious, thoughtful. "Now, isn't that a coincidence?" he asked. "You and the pony being so suited to each other, I mean?"

Kendra tightened her fists at her sides, forcibly relaxed them. She knew next to nothing about the day-to-day operation of Whisper Creek Ranch, but she was ninety-nine percent sure there was no job here for such a tiny horse.

Everything about the animal was miniature, even by pony standards, including the Lilliputian saddle and bridle.

"Simmer down," Hutch said to Kendra in a near

whisper, though he was still grinning. "I borrowed the horse from a neighbor. She's as gentle as they come."

Kendra swallowed. "Oh," she said.

Hutch's attention shifted back to Madison. The little girl basked in the glow of his quiet approval. "Want to give this thing a try?" he asked her.

Madison nodded wildly. Daisy had lost interest by then, and gone off to sniff the surrounding area for heaven only knew what. Leviticus followed her, as if to make sure she behaved throughout the visit.

Once again, Hutch's eyes rested on Kendra's face. He was waiting for her permission.

"You're sure this animal is tame?" she asked him.

"Sure as can be," Hutch assured her.

"Well—" She stopped, bit her lower lip. "All right, then."

Hutch chuckled, put his hands to Madison's waist and swung her easily into the saddle. He put the reins in her small hands, told her how to hold them, explaining quietly that she shouldn't pull on them too hard, because that was hard on the pony's mouth.

Madison, for her part, looked not just overjoyed, but transported.

"Look, Mommy!" she cried. "I'm on a horse! I'm on a *real* horse!"

Kendra had to smile. "Yes," she agreed. "You certainly are."

Hutch led the pony around in slow but ever widening circles, there in the barnyard, letting Madison get the feel of riding. The child seemed spangled in light, she was so happy.

I'm on a horse! I'm on a real horse!

Inwardly, Kendra sighed.

Madison was hooked.

And that meant she was, too.

CHAPTER TWELVE

HUTCH WATCHED KENDRA watching her daughter ride, on her own now, and he was glad he'd "borrowed" Ruffles from a family up the road, even though he was sure to get a joshing from the ranch hands, among others. The plain truth of the matter was that he'd bought the pony outright—the Hendrix kids were grown and gone and the little mare had been "mighty lonely these last few years," according to Paula Hendrix.

He moved to stand alongside Kendra, close enough but not too close.

Her eyes brimmed with happy tears, and she fairly glowed with motherly pride. "She's loving this," she murmured so softly that Hutch wasn't sure if she was talking to him at all.

"Madison's a natural, all right," he agreed quietly. "A born rider."

"You went to a lot of trouble," Kendra went on, still not looking his way. "Borrowing a pony and everything, I mean." She was pleased, he knew, but there was a tension in her, too—she was ready to spring into action if anything went wrong, rush in to save her baby. And there was something else, too—a kind of wariness that probably didn't have much to do with either Madison or the horse.

Just then, Hutch felt a strange ache in a far corner

of his heart. In a perfect world, Madison would have been their child, his and Kendra's. Her last name would be Carmody, not Shepherd or Chamberlain or whatever it was, and riding a horse wouldn't be a rare adventure, it would be part of her daily life, like it was of any ranch kid's.

But then, this *wasn't* a perfect world, now was it? It was the real deal, and that meant things would go wrong, and people could get sidetracked, screw up their whole lives because of things they should or shouldn't have said or done.

"Ready to ride?" he asked, to get the conversation rolling again.

"I haven't been on horseback in years," Kendra confessed. "Not since—"

Her words fell away into an awkward silence, and she blushed.

She was obviously remembering what *he* was remembering—all those wild rides they'd taken, back in the day, in and out of the saddle.

"It's like riding a bike," he said mildly, throwing her a lifeline. "Once you learn how to sit a horse, you never forget."

She turned her gaze back to Madison, who was riding in their direction now, beaming. The pup had fallen into step with Ruffles—Leviticus watched from the shade of the barn—and they sure made a picture, all of them, an image straight off the front of a Western greeting card.

When Kendra spoke, she jarred him a little. "How do we get past this, Hutch?" she asked very softly.

"This what?" Hutch asked just as quietly.

Her shoulders moved in a semblance of a shrug.

"The awkwardness, I guess," she said, and there was the smallest quaver in her voice. She paused, shook her head slightly, as if to clear her brain. "I can't pretend that nothing happened between us," she went on as Madison and Ruffles and the dogs drew nearer. "But I keep trying to do just that and it makes me crazy."

Hutch chuckled. "Well, then," he reasoned, "why don't you stop trying and just let things be what they are? It's not as if any of us have much of a choice in the matter, anyhow."

She sighed and kept her eyes on Madison, but she seemed a little less edgy than before. "You're right," she said. "Much as we might want to change the past, we can't."

He wanted to ask what she would change, if she could, but Opal's station wagon pulled through the gate just then and came barreling up the driveway.

"Look!" Madison called, as Opal got out of her car. "I'm riding a horse!"

"You sure enough are," Opal agreed, her smile wide. Her gaze swept over Hutch and Kendra, and the two other horses waiting to be ridden. "You about done with riding now?" she asked the child. "Because I've got supper to start and I could sure use a hand with the job."

Madison, Hutch suspected, could have stayed right there on Ruffles' back for days on end, given the opportunity, but she turned out to be the helpful sort.

"I guess I'm done," she said. "For right now, anyway."

Hutch approached and lifted her down off Ruffles's back. "You go on ahead with Opal," he told the little girl when she looked up at him in concern. He could guess what she was thinking. "I'll tend to Ruffles, and show you how to do that another time."

Madison nodded solemnly and patted the pony's nose. "I wish you were my very own," she told Ruffles. Then she smiled up at Kendra, waiting for a nod.

Kendra did nod, a little reluctantly, Hutch thought.

Opal put out a hand to Madison, Madison took it without hesitation, and they headed toward the house, chatting amicably, the dogs ambling along behind them.

"That was slick," Kendra observed with wry amusement, watching as the four disappeared through the kitchen doorway.

Hutch took Ruffles's reins and led the pony toward the barn door. "I didn't put Opal up to anything, if that's what you mean," he said, grinning back at her. "Make sure those horses don't take off. I'll be right back."

I'll be right back.

Kendra sighed. Now she'd have to go riding—alone with Hutch Carmody, no less—and she had nobody to blame but herself. She'd put herself in this position, sealed her own fate.

She *was* crazy.

Gingerly, she gathered the reins of the two horses and waited for Hutch to unsaddle Ruffles and tuck her away in a stall. And she waited.

She recognized the big gelding as Remington, Hutch's favorite mount, but the long-legged mare was a stranger.

"I have a child to raise and a business to run," she told the mare in a hurried undertone. "I cannot afford to break any bones, so don't try anything fancy."

The mare nickered companionably, as if promising to behave herself.

Hutch came back before Kendra was ready for him to, taking Remington's reins from her hands. "That's Coco," he said, nodding at the mare. "She's a roper, so she's lively and fast, but she's fairly kindhearted, too."

"Fairly?" Kendra echoed, waiting for muscle memory to kick in so she could mount up without making an even bigger fool of herself than she already had.

Hutch laughed, steadied the mare for her by taking a light hold on the bridle strap. "This isn't a dude ranch," he pointed out, clearly enjoying her trepidation. "Except for Ruffles, all these horses earn their keep, one way or another."

Having nothing to say to that—nothing civil, that is—Kendra reached up, gripped the saddle horn with damp palms, shoved her left foot in the stirrup and hoisted.

Hutch gave her a startling boost by splaying one hand across her backside and pushing.

She gasped, surged skyward and landed in the saddle with a thump.

He laughed again, mounted Remington and reined in alongside Kendra. "Ready?" he asked.

Her face was on fire, and she refused to look at him on the ridiculous premise that if she couldn't see him, he couldn't see her, either. "Ready," she confirmed, stubborn to the end.

"Good," he said, and he and Remington were off, leading the way, heading for the open range at a slow trot.

Kendra's horse followed immediately, her rider bouncing hard in the saddle with every step. Kendra concentrated on syncing herself with Coco and, when they'd traveled a hundred yards or so, she found her stride.

Hutch's gelding clearly wanted to run—*please, God, no*—but he held the horse in check with an ease that was both admirable and galling. Everything seemed to come easily to this man, and it wasn't fair.

"Where to?" he asked, grinning over at her as Coco matched her pace to Remington's.

"Anywhere but the high meadow," Kendra answered and was immediately embarrassed all over again. Talk about your Freudian slip—Hutch hadn't suggested riding to their secret, special place, now had he? *She'd* been the one to bring it up.

He chuckled at her miserable expression. "Tell me, Kendra," he began easily, "who are you more afraid of—me or yourself?"

"Don't be ridiculous," she sputtered. "It's just that I haven't ridden in a long time and the meadow is halfway up the mountain and—"

"Easy," Hutch admonished good-naturedly. Was he addressing her or his horse?

It had damned well *better* be the horse.

Alas it turned out to be her, instead. "Kendra," he went on, "I'm not fixing to jump your bones the second we're alone. We're two old friends out for a horseback ride, and that's all there is to it."

Maybe for you, Kendra thought peevishly. The answer to his earlier question was thrumming in her head by now, all too obvious. She was afraid of herself, not him. Afraid of her own desires and the way her intelligence seemed to take a dive whenever he turned on the charm.

Not that he'd been obvious about it.

Still the damage was done.

Whether he knew it or not—and it would be naive to think he didn't—Hutch had been in the process of seducing her almost from the moment she and Madison had arrived at the ranch. All he'd had to do to melt her resolve was to act like what Madison wanted most right now—a daddy.

They rode in silence for a while, the horses choosing their direction, or so it seemed to Kendra, the animals pausing alongside a stream to lower their huge heads and drink.

Hutch's expression had turned solemn; he seemed far away, somehow, even though he was right beside her. Sunlight danced on the surface of the creek as the water whispered by.

"Why did you come here, Kendra?" he finally asked, narrowing his eyes against the brightness of the late-afternoon sun as he studied her face.

"To the ranch?"

"To Parable," Hutch said.

She bristled. "Because it's home," she said tightly. "Because I want to raise Madison in a place where people know and care about each other."

Hutch dismounted, stood beside Remington, looking up at her. "And you were so happy here as a child that you figured Madison would be, too?" he asked. It wasn't a gibe, exactly, but he knew all about Kendra's life with her grandmother, so the remark hadn't been entirely innocent, either.

"Not always," she admitted, her tone a little distant. She was tempted to get down off the horse and stand facing him, but that would mean getting back *on* again and her legs felt too unsteady to manage it. "Nobody's happy all the time, are they?"

He gave a raspy chuckle, gazing out over the rippling water that gave his ranch its name—Whisper Creek. "That's for sure," he said.

She shifted uncomfortably in the saddle. No way around it, she was going to be sore after this ride, unaccustomed as she was.

Oh, well. Better achy body parts she could soak in a hot bathtub with Epsom salts, she figured, than an achy heart.

"I lied about the pony," Hutch said out of the blue. He bent as he spoke, picked up a pebble and skipped it across the busy water with an expert motion of one hand.

Kendra frowned, confused. Everything about this man confused her, in fact. "What?" she asked.

"I didn't borrow Ruffles," he replied, meeting her gaze again. "I bought her. The kids she used to belong to grew up and went away, and she's been lonely."

Something softened inside Kendra. Finally she began to relax a little. "Well, then," she said. "Why didn't you just say so in the first place?"

He cleared his throat. "Because I figured you'd think I was trying to get to you through Madison," he told her.

Some reckless Kendra took over, pushed the day-to-day Kendra aside. "Were you?" she asked. "Trying to get to me through my daughter, that is?"

She saw his jaw tighten, release again.

"That would be wrong on so many levels," he said. He was clearly angry, which was rich, considering he'd been the one to raise the topic in the first place. "Madison's not a pawn. She's a person in her own right."

"I quite agree," Kendra said, sounding prim even in her own ears.

That was when Hutch reached up, looped an arm around Kendra's waist and lifted her down off Coco's back. She came up against him, hard.

"If I want to 'get to' you, Kendra," he informed her, "I *can*—and without using an innocent little kid or anybody else."

She stared up at him, startled, breathless and without a thought in her head.

And that was when he kissed her, not gently, not tentatively, but with all the hunger a man can feel for a woman, all the need and the strength and the hardness and the heat.

Instantly she turned to a pillar of fire. Her arms slipped around Hutch's neck and tightened there, and she stood on tiptoe, pouring herself into that kiss without reservation.

This was what she had feared, some vague part of her knew that.

This was what she had *longed for*.

It was Hutch who broke away first. His breath was ragged, and he thrust the fingers of his right hand through his hair in a gesture that might have been frustration. "*Damn* it," he cursed.

Kendra, all molten passion just moments before, went ice-cold. "Don't you *dare* blame me for that, Hutch," she warned, in a furious whisper. "*You* started it."

He didn't answer, didn't even look at her.

No, he turned away, gave her his back.

"I'm sorry," he said, after a long time, his voice rough as dry gravel.

He was *sorry?* He'd rocked her to the core, thrown the planet off its axis, changed the direction of the tides with that kiss. And he was *sorry?*

"So much for two old friends just out for a simple horseback ride," she heard herself say. Humiliation and anger combined gave her the impetus to get back on Coco with no help from Hutch Carmody, thank you very much.

Hutch turned then, glowering up at her. "Don't," he warned. "Don't be flippant about this, Kendra. Something just happened here, something important."

"Yes," Kendra said lightly. He was standing and she was mounted and that gave her a completely false sense of power, which she permitted herself to enjoy for the briefest of moments. "You *kissed* me, remember?"

"I'm not talking about that," Hutch told her.

"Then what *are* you talking about?"

"We're not finished, you and I," Hutch said. "*That's* what I'm talking about."

"That's where you're wrong," Kendra retorted, coming to a slow simmer. "We are *so* finished. So over. So done. So through. We have been for years, in case you haven't noticed."

"The way you just kissed me says different," he replied, mounting up at last, reining the gelding around so that he and Kendra were facing each other.

"You kissed *me,"* she reiterated, almost frantic.

"You're damn right, I did," Hutch answered. "And you kissed me right back. If we'd been up at the meadow where it's private, instead of down here on the open range, we'd be making love right now, hot and heavy. Just like in the old days."

"Your ego," she snapped, "is exceeded only by your

ego. I'm not one of—one of *those* women, the kind you
can have whenever you want!"

He laughed, but it was a tight sound, a challenge, a
promise. "Prove it," he said.

Kendra was practically beside herself by then. She
wanted to get back to the barn, get off this damnable
horse, collect her daughter and her dog, and race for
home, where she could reasonably pretend none of this
had ever happened. "What do you mean, 'prove it'?"
she practically spat.

"Opal is looking after Madison," he said. "Let's ride
up the mountain, Kendra—just you and me. Right now."

"Absolutely *not,*" Kendra shot back loftily, amazed
at how badly she wanted to take him up on what would
surely be, for her, a losing bet.

"Scared?" he asked, leaning in, almost breathing the
word. His mouth rested lightly, briefly, against hers,
setting her ablaze all over again.

"Yes," she said in a burst of honesty.

"Of me?"

Kendra swallowed hard, shook her head from side to
side. He'd been right before—she was afraid of herself,
not him—but she wasn't going to admit that out loud.

"It's probably inevitable," Hutch said, sounding gleefully resigned. "Our making love, I mean."

"Think what you like," Kendra bluffed, her tone
deliberately tart. "But I've been down that road before, Hutch, and I'm not going back. I'm not a gullible
young girl anymore. I'm a responsible woman with a
daughter."

"And that means you can't have a sex life?"

"I will *not* discuss this with you," she bit out, turning Coco around and heading back toward the house

and the barn and Madison. Back toward sanity and good sense.

Of course Hutch had no difficulty catching up. He looked cocky, riding beside her, all cowboy, all *man*.

She was in big trouble here.

Big, *big* trouble.

SHE AND MADISON had to stay for supper—Opal wouldn't hear of anything else, and besides, Kendra knew that leaving in a huff would reveal too much.

So she stayed.

She left Hutch to put the horses away by himself, except for his devoted shadow, Leviticus, then went into the house and washed her hands at the kitchen sink while Madison, swaddled in an oversize apron and elbow-deep in floury dough, regaled her with her new knowledge of cooking.

"She's ready for her own show on the Food Channel," Opal put in proudly, standing next to Madison at the center island and supervising every move.

"I don't doubt that for a moment," Kendra agreed, hoping her coloring had returned to normal by now.

"I'm making *biscuits*," Madison said.

"Impressive," Kendra replied. "Will you teach me how to make them, too?"

Madison giggled at that. "Silly Mommy," she said. "You just need to look in a cookbook and you'll *know* how."

Kendra kissed her daughter's flour-smudged cheek. "You've got me there," she said, with a little sigh.

"Coffee's fresh," Opal said with a nod in the direction of the machine. "Mugs are in the cupboard above it."

"Thanks." Kendra needed something to do with her

hands, so she got out a cup, poured herself some coffee and took a slow sip, hoping it wouldn't keep her awake half the night, thinking about the most recent go-round with Hutch. She was jangly enough as it was.

"How was the ride?" Opal asked, and her attempt to put the question casually was a total flop.

"Fine," Kendra replied noncommittally.

"Where's Mr. Hutch?" Madison wanted to know.

So, Kendra thought. He'd graduated from cowboy man to Mr. Hutch. What was next—Daddy?

"He's looking after the horses," Kendra answered, leaning against the counter and taking another sip of coffee. Oddly the caffeine seemed to be settling her down rather than riling her already frayed nerves, and she was grateful for this small, counterintuitive blessing.

"When can we get my boots?" Madison chimed in.

Kendra laughed. "Does that mean you want to go riding again?" she hedged.

Madison nodded eagerly, still working away at the dough she'd been kneading in the big crockery bowl in front of her. "I want to ride *far*," she said. "Not just around and around in the yard, like a little kid."

"You *are* a little kid," Kendra teased.

"I reckon that biscuit dough is about ready to be rolled out and cut," Opal put in. Without missing a beat, she gently removed Madison's hands from the bowl, wiped them clean with a damp dish towel and lifted the child down off the chair she'd been standing on.

"I can help," Madison offered.

"Sure you can," Opal agreed.

The woman was the soul of patience. Kendra smiled at her, mouthing the words "Thank you."

"But first I need to say good-night to Ruffles," Madison said.

"After supper," Kendra answered.

Hutch came in then, rolling up the sleeves of his shirt as he stepped over the threshold in stocking feet, having left his dirty boots outside on the step. His hair was rumpled, and there were bits of hay on his clothes. Kendra was struck by how impossibly good he looked, even coming straight from the barn.

He nodded a greeting to Opal and Kendra in turn, then spared a wink for Madison as he used an elbow to turn on the hot water in the sink. He lathered his hands and forearms with a bar of pungently scented orange soap, rinsed and lathered up again.

To look at him, nobody would have guessed that less than an hour before he'd kissed Kendra as she'd never been kissed before—even by him—and thrown her entire being into sweet turmoil in the space of a few heartbeats. He'd plundered her mouth with his tongue and she'd not only allowed it, she'd *responded,* no question about it.

He'd said it was inevitable that they'd make love. Dared her to ride up the mountain with him, to that cursed, enchanted meadow where heaven and earth seemed to converge as their bodies converged.

Stop it, she told herself sternly.

"I made the biscuits," Madison was saying to Hutch as he turned away from the sink, drying his hands on a towel. "Well, I *helped,* anyway."

Opal chuckled. She'd gotten out a rolling pin and a biscuit cutter. "Get back up on this chair, young lady, and I'll show you what to do next."

Madison scrambled to obey.

Opal gave the child's hands another going over with a damp cloth.

Together they rolled the dough out flat, used the cutter to make circles, placed these on a baking sheet lined with parchment paper.

Hutch crossed to the oven and reached for the handle on the door.

"Don't you open that oven," Opal immediately commanded. "You'll let out all that good steam."

For a moment Hutch looked more like a curious little boy than a man. "Whatever it is, it sure smells good," he said.

"It's my special tamale pie, like I said I'd make," Opal replied briskly, "and I'll thank you not to go messing with it before we've even sat down to say grace."

Hutch grinned, spread his hands in a conciliatory gesture. "Yes, ma'am," he said. "Far be it from me to mess with supper."

"And don't you forget it," Opal said, evidently determined to have the last word.

It was a mundane exchange, but Kendra enjoyed the hominess of good-natured banter between people who cared for each other as if they were family. When she was growing up, meals had been catch-as-catch-can affairs, and if her grandmother did bother to cook, she slammed the pots and pans around in the process, letting Kendra know it was an imposition. That *she* was an imposition.

Those days were long gone, she reminded herself. She'd come through okay, hadn't she? And she was a good mother to Madison, at least partly because she wanted things to be different for her.

"I'd sure like to know what's going on in that head

of yours right about now," Hutch said, surprising her. When had he crossed the room, come to stand next to her, close enough to touch? And why did he have to be so darned observant?

"I was just thinking how lucky I am," she said.

He grinned, watching as Madison "helped" slide the biscuits into the extra oven built into the wall beside the stove. "You definitely are," he said, and there was something in his voice that took a lot of the sting out of things he'd said earlier.

That was the thing she had to watch when it came to Hutch.

He could be kind one moment and issuing a challenge the next.

Most of the time, he was impossible to read.

Soon enough, they all sat down to supper, Opal and Madison, Kendra and Hutch, and it felt a little too *right* for comfort. After struggling so hard to regain her emotional equilibrium, Kendra was back on shaky ground.

She was hungry, though, despite her jumpy nerves, and she put away two biscuits as well as an ample portion of Opal's delectable tamale pie.

Madison had had a big day, and by the time supper was over, she was fighting to stay awake. "Mommy said I could say good-night to Ruffles," she insisted, yawning, when the table had been cleared and the plates and silverware loaded into the dishwasher.

Hutch lifted the child into his arms, though he was looking at Kendra when he spoke. "And your mommy," he said, "is a woman of her word. Let's go."

What was *that* supposed to mean? Was there a barb hidden somewhere in that statement?

Kendra decided not to invest any more of her rapidly

waning energy wondering. She thanked Opal for supper and for letting Madison help with the preparations, and followed Hutch, Madison and the ever-alert Daisy out the back door. They crossed the yard, headed for the barn, and Madison, half-asleep by then, rested her head on Hutch's shoulder.

Hutch flipped on the light as they entered, and carried Madison to Ruffles's stall.

Kendra watched, stricken with a tangle of bittersweet emotions, as Madison leaned over the stall door to pat the pony's head.

"Good night, Ruffles," she said, keeping her other arm firmly around Hutch's neck. Solemnly, she instructed the little horse to sleep well and have sweet dreams.

Kendra's heart turned over in her chest and her throat tightened.

Too late, she realized that Hutch was watching her and, as usual, seeing more than she wanted him to see.

"We'd better go now," she said, forcing the words out.

Hutch nodded. Still carrying Madison, he led the way back outside, setting the child in her car seat as deftly as if he'd done it a thousand times before, chuckling when the dog joined them in a single bound.

Kendra resisted the urge to double-check the fastenings on the car seat, just to make sure he'd gotten it right.

Of *course* he'd gotten it right. He was Hutch Carmody, and he got just about everything right—when he chose to, that is.

"Thanks," Kendra said, standing beside the car, hugging herself even though the night was warm. Since she didn't want him jumping to the conclusion that her thank-you included that soul-sundering kiss beside Whisper Creek, she added, too quickly, "For letting Madison ride Ruffles, I mean."

A slow grin spread across Hutch's face as he watched her. Overhead, a million gazillion silvery stars splashed across the black velvet sky and the moon glowed translucent, nearly full.

"Anytime," he said easily, Leviticus waiting quietly at his side.

"Right," Kendra said, at a loss.

Hutch opened the driver's door for her, waited politely for her to slip behind the wheel, fumble in her bag for the keys, fasten her seat belt and start the engine.

Madison was already asleep—if she hadn't been, Kendra knew, she would have been asking when she could come back and ride Ruffles again.

When Hutch remained where he was, Kendra rolled down her window. She had her issues with the man, but she didn't want to run over his feet backing out. "Was there something else?" she asked, hoping she sounded casual.

He leaned over to look in at her. "Yeah," he said. "You planning on coming to the rodeo? You and Madison?"

She nodded, smiled. "There's no way I could get out of it even if I wanted to," she said. "Madison's never been and she's looking forward to the whole weekend, rodeo, fireworks and all."

Speaking of fireworks, she thought, as the memory of that kiss coursed through her, hot and fierce, causing her heart to kick into overdrive.

"I'm entered in the bull-riding on Saturday afternoon," Hutch said, "but I'd sure like to buy the two of you supper and maybe take Madison on a few of the carnival rides before taking in the fireworks."

All she had to do was say no, take time to step back and regain her perspective.

Instead she said, "Okay." Immediately.

Hutch grinned. "Great," he said. "I'll be in touch, and we'll work out the details."

She nodded, as though nothing out of the ordinary had happened that day.

Maybe for *him* nothing had.

Dismal thought.

Kendra murmured good-night, Hutch stepped away from the car and she put the Volvo in motion.

At home, she unbuckled Madison, awake but sleepy, and carried her into the house. She helped the child into her pajamas, oversaw the brushing of teeth and the saying of prayers, tucked her daughter in and kissed her forehead.

"Good night, Annie Oakley," she said.

Daisy, probably needing to go outside, fidgeted in the doorway.

"Who's that?" Madison asked, yawning big again, but she was asleep before Kendra had a chance to answer.

Leaving Madison's bedroom, she followed Daisy back to the kitchen and stood on the porch while the dog did what had to be done.

As soon as she was back inside the house, Daisy headed straight for Madison's room.

Kendra, a little too wired to sleep, tidied up the already tidy house, watered a few plants and finally retreated to her home office and logged on to the computer. She'd check her email, both business and personal, she decided, and then soak in a nice hot bath, a sort of preemptive strike against the saddle soreness she was bound to be feeling by morning.

She weeded out the junk mail—somehow some of it always got past the filter—and that left her with two messages, one from Tara and one from Joslyn. Both had attachments—forwards, no doubt.

She clicked on Joslyn's, expecting a cute picture of the new baby.

Instead she was confronted with a page from a major social-media site, a photo someone had snapped of her and Hutch running the three-legged race at the cemetery picnic the previous weekend. Both of them were laughing, pitching forward into the fall that sent them tumbling into the grass.

The caption was short and to the point. "Up to his old tricks," it read. "Already."

CHAPTER THIRTEEN

KENDRA STIFFENED IN her chair, staring at the computer monitor and the picture of her and Hutch, feeling as though she'd been slapped across the face. She clicked back to the main body of Joslyn's email and read, "Now they've gone too far. This means war."

The second message, from Tara, was similar.

The anti-Hutch campaign was one thing, as far as Kendra's two closest friends were concerned, but dragging her into it was one step over the line. Clearly they were prepared to do battle.

She sat back, drew a few long, deep breaths, releasing them slowly, and reminded herself that this wasn't such a big deal—the page was a petty outlet for people who apparently had too much free time on their hands, not a cross blazing on her front lawn or a brick hurled through her living room window.

She answered both Tara's and Joslyn's emails with a single response. "I'll handle it." Then, calmer but no less indignant at some stranger's invasion of her privacy, she printed out a copy of the webpage, folded it carefully into quarters and took it back to the kitchen, where she'd left her purse. She tucked the sheet of paper away in the very bottom, under her wallet and cosmetic case, looked in on her daughter once more and retreated to the bathroom for that long soak she'd promised herself.

The warm water soothed her, as did the two over-the-counter pain relievers she took before crawling into bed. She hadn't expected to sleep, but she did, deeply and dreamlessly, and the next thing she knew, sunlight was seeping, pink-orange, through her eyelids.

Her thighs and backside were sore from the horseback ride, but not sore enough to matter.

She threw herself into the morning routine—getting Madison up and dressed and fed, making sure Daisy went outside and then had fresh water and kibble. She skipped her usual coffee, though, and sipped herbal tea instead.

"You look pretty, Mommy," Madison said, taking in Kendra's crisp linen pantsuit. Lately, she'd been wearing jeans.

"Thank you," Kendra replied lightly, pausing to bend over Madison's chair at the breakfast table and kiss the top of her head. "I have an appointment this morning—a client is coming to see the other house—so hurry it up a little, will you?"

"About my boots," Madison began.

So, Kendra thought wryly, she'd been right to suspect that, while genuine, the compliment on her outfit had its purposes.

"There will be all sorts of vendors—people who sell things—at the rodeo this weekend. We'll check out the boots then."

Madison beamed, but then her face clouded over. "But I still have to say sorry to Miss Abbington and Becky," she recalled.

"Absolutely," Kendra said firmly. "Suppose Becky

had taken *your* boots, without permission, and then refused to give them back. How would you feel?"

"Bad," Madison admitted.

"And so?" Kendra prompted.

"Becky felt bad," Madison said. Then something flashed in her eyes. "But I didn't wear Miss *Abbington's* shoes. Why do I have to say sorry to her?"

"Enough," Kendra said, softening the word with a smile. "You know darn well why you need to apologize to Miss Abbington."

"I do?" Madison echoed innocently.

Kendra simply waited.

"Because I was misruptive in class," Madison finally conceded.

"Bingo," Kendra said.

AN HOUR LATER, with Madison at preschool and Daisy minding the office, Kendra showed the mansion to the second client, a representative of a large investment group with an eye to turning the place into an apartment complex.

Kendra knew right away that there would be no actual sale, but that didn't matter. The real estate business was all about showing places again and again, until the right buyer came along. Generally, she had to bait a lot of hooks before she caught a fish.

Work was the furthest thing from her mind anyway, with that printout of the webpage burning a hole in the bottom of her purse.

At lunchtime, she locked up the office, loaded the always adventuresome Daisy into the Volvo and headed for the neighboring town, Three Trees.

She didn't know Brylee Parrish well—the two of

them were barely acquainted, with a five-year gap in age, and they'd grown up in separate if closely linked communities—but she knew exactly where to find her. Brylee, with her flourishing party-planning business, was the original Local Girl Makes Good—she had a large warehouse and offices just outside Three Trees.

During the drive, Kendra didn't rehearse what she was going to say, because she didn't know, exactly. She doubted that Brylee personally was behind the webpage photo and the remark about Hutch being up to his old tricks, but she'd know who was.

Arriving at Brylee's company, Décor Galore, Kendra rolled down one of the car windows a little way, so Daisy would have air, and promised the dog she'd be back soon.

A receptionist greeted her with a stiff smile and several furtive glances stolen while she was buzzing the boss to let her know that Kendra Shepherd wanted to see her.

"She'll be here in a couple of minutes," the receptionist said, hanging up. Now, for all those sneak peeks, the young woman wouldn't look directly at Kendra. She nodded toward a small and tastefully decorated waiting area. "Have a seat."

"I'll stand, thank you," Kendra said politely.

When Brylee appeared, opening a side door and poking out her head, Kendra was immediately and oddly struck by how beautiful she was, with those huge hazel eyes and that glorious mane of chestnut-brown hair worn in a ponytail today.

"Come in," Brylee said, and her cheeks flared with color, then immediately went pale.

Kendra followed Brylee through a long corridor,

through the busy, noisy warehouse and into a surprisingly plain office. The furniture—a desk, two chairs, some mismatched file cabinets and a single bookcase—looked as though it had come from an army surplus store. There were no pictures or other decorations on the walls, no knickknacks to be seen.

"Sit down—please," Brylee said, taking the chair behind her desk.

Kendra sat, opened her purse, dug out the folded sheet of paper and slid it across to Brylee.

Brylee swallowed visibly, and her unmanicured hands trembled ever so slightly as she unfolded the paper and smoothed it flat.

Kendra felt a brief stab of sympathy for her. After all, losing Hutch Carmody was a trauma she well understood, and it had probably been worse for Brylee, all dressed up in the wedding gown of her dreams, with all her friends and family there to witness the event.

Brylee, meanwhile, gave a deep sigh, closed her eyes and squeezed the bridge of her nose between one thumb and forefinger. Then, rallying, she squared her slender shoulders and looked directly at Kendra.

"I don't expect you to believe me," she said with dignity, "but I didn't know about this."

"I have no reason not to believe you," Kendra replied moderately. She drew in another deep breath, let it out and went on, feeling her way through her sentence word by word. "Some people—maybe a lot of them—would say it's just a harmless photograph and I ought to let it go at that. If this is as far as it goes—fine. I can deal with it. But I have a four-year-old daughter to think about, Ms. Parrish, and—"

Brylee put up a hand. She still looked wan, but a

friendly sparkle flickered in her eyes. "Please," she interrupted. "Call me Brylee. We're not enemies, you and I—or, at least, I hope we're not—and I totally get why this bothers you." She paused, bit her lip, studying Kendra's face with a kind of broken curiosity. "Really, I do."

"Then we don't have a problem," Kendra said, wanting to be kind and at the same time picking up on just how much Brylee wanted to ask if she and Hutch had some kind of "thing" going. "Just ask whoever put this up on the web to take it down, please, and leave me alone."

Brylee arched one perfect eyebrow. "What about Hutch?"

"What about him?" Kendra countered mildly.

"Never mind," Brylee said miserably, looking away for a long moment.

Kendra was relieved when Brylee didn't press the point. *What about Hutch?* Indeed. She had no idea what, if anything, was happening between her and Hutch Carmody. Sure, he'd kissed her, and made her want him in the process, but he was on the rebound, after all. He must have cared for Brylee at some point or he'd never have asked her to marry him.

The realization struck her like a face full of cold water; she grew a little flustered and fumbled with her purse as she rose from her chair. "I'd better go—my dog is in the car and—"

Brylee stood, too, her smile sad but real. "I'm sorry, Kendra. About the webpage, I mean. It seemed pretty innocent at first—all my friends were mad at Hutch and so was I—but enough is enough. I'll see that they take the page down."

To Kendra's mind, Hutch was a big boy and he could

fight his own battles; her only concern was that she'd been featured. "Thank you," she said.

Brylee walked her back along the corridor, through the reception area and out into the parking lot. She smiled when she saw Daisy poking her snout through the crack in the window, eager to join in any game that might be played, but Kendra felt edgy. She knew there was something else Brylee wanted to say to her.

Sure enough, there was.

"I don't think Hutch ever really got over you," Brylee said quietly, and without malice. "I should have paid more attention to the signs—he called me by your name once or twice, for instance—but I guess I was just too crazy about him to see what was happening."

Kendra felt another tug of sympathy, even as all the old defenses rose up inside her. "Thanks again," she said, and climbed into her car.

Daisy whimpered in the backseat, either because she needed to squat in the grass or because she'd taken a liking to Brylee, or both, but the dog was going to have to wait. No way was Kendra going to let Daisy christen Brylee's parking lot right in front of the woman—it might seem, well, like a symbolic gesture.

Brylee waved, watching as Kendra drove away and Kendra waved back.

Thoughts assailed her as she pulled onto the highway leading home to Parable; she heard Brylee's words, over and over again. *I don't think Hutch ever really got over you—he called me by your name once or twice—*

"Stop it," Kendra told herself, right out loud.

Daisy whimpered again, more urgently this time.

Kendra pulled over when she came to a wide spot in the road, got out of the car, leaned into the backseat to hook Daisy's leash to her collar and took the dog for a short walk in the grass.

By the time they were on their way again, she was starting to feel foolish for confronting Brylee with that printout at all. She'd probably overreacted.

Before pulling back onto the highway, Kendra got out her cell phone and called Joslyn.

"Were you asleep?" she asked, first thing.

Joslyn laughed. "I'm a new mother," she said. "We don't sleep."

Kendra laughed, too. "Is your mom still visiting?"

"She left this morning," Joslyn answered. "Mom was a lot of help—Callie has been, too—but it's time things got back to normal around here. Besides, Slade and Shea are great with the baby."

"Good," Kendra said.

"You called to find out if I was sleeping?" Joslyn teased. "Is this about that stupid webpage? Five minutes after I hit Send, I wished I hadn't just sprung the thing on you like that. Tara feels the same way."

"It's all right," Kendra said, watching as cars and trucks zipped by on the highway. "But, yeah, that's the reason I called. I've just been to see Brylee."

"Come right over," Joslyn commanded cheerfully. "Immediately, if not sooner. I want to hear all about it."

"Nothing happened," Kendra put in lamely. It wasn't as if she and Brylee had gotten into a hair-pulling match or anything; they weren't a pair of junior high schoolers fighting over a boy.

"Be that as it may," Joslyn replied, "you obviously need some BFF time or you wouldn't have called. *Come over.*"

"I'll be there in twenty minutes," Kendra capitulated, grateful.

"Good," Joslyn answered.

When Kendra and Daisy arrived at Windfall Ranch, Tara's sports car was parked alongside the main house, next to Joslyn's nondescript compact. Slade's truck was nowhere in sight—maybe he'd driven his mother-in-law to the airport.

Joslyn and Tara both appeared on the back porch as Kendra got out of the car and freed Daisy from the confines of the backseat. Lucy, Tara's dog, was on hand to greet her and the pair frolicked, overjoyed at their reunion.

Joslyn smiled and waved, but Tara looked worried.

"Have I just made a world-class fool of myself or what?" Kendra fretted as she approached the porch. By now, of course, Joslyn would have told Tara about the visit to Brylee's office.

Tara finally smiled. "I'm not sure," she joked. "Come inside, and we'll figure it out over coffee and pastry."

They all trooped into Joslyn's recently remodeled kitchen, including Lucy and Daisy, who greeted Jasper, Slade's dog, and were roundly snubbed by Joslyn's cat.

Baby Trace lay in his bassinet, gurgling, his feet and hands busy as he tried to grab hold of a beam of sunlight coming in through a nearby window.

Joslyn smiled, tucked his blanket in around him, and bent to plant a smacking kiss on his downy head. "I love you, little cowboy," she said softly.

The backs of Kendra's eyes scalded a little, in the wake of a rush of happiness for her friend. Joslyn had built a successful software company on her own, sold it for a fortune and righted an old wrong that wasn't even hers in the first place. But *this*—Slade, his step-daughter, Shea, the baby, the ranch, all of it—was her dream come true.

And it had been by no means a sure thing.

Now, though, she absolutely shone with fulfillment.

Tara, following Kendra's gaze, smiled and said quietly, "There she is, the world's happiest woman."

Kendra nodded and blinked a couple of times, and they all sat down to enjoy the tea Joslyn must have brewed in advance. There were doughnuts with sprinkles waiting, too.

"Do you miss your mom, now that's she's gone home to Santa Fe?" Kendra asked Joslyn, deciding to skip the doughnuts because her stomach was still a little touchy.

"Of course I do," Joslyn said. "It was lovely, having her here, but she has a life to get back to and, besides, we're sure to see her again soon."

"We shouldn't have forwarded that webpage to you," Tara interjected, looking fretful again. "I don't know what we were thinking."

"It's all right," Kendra said truthfully. "I would have seen it sooner or later anyway, and it was better that it came from the two of you."

"You really went to see Brylee Parrish?" Joslyn asked, wide-eyed.

"No," Kendra joked. "I just said that to get a rise out of you. *Yes,* I went to see Brylee, and I feel like an idiot. One of those people who are always on the lookout for something to raise a fuss about."

"I'd say you had reason to raise a fuss," Tara said, loyal to the end. "Sometimes things like that picture of you and Hutch being posted with a snarky comment start out small and then mushroom into a major hassle."

"Well, anyway, it's done," Kendra went on with a little shrug. "Brylee is actually a very nice person, you know. She's going to make sure the page gets taken down—so no harm done."

"Did she ask if you and Hutch are involved?" Joslyn asked. No sense in pulling any punches; cut right to the chase—that was Joslyn's way.

"She wanted to," Kendra said, "but she didn't."

"Are you?" Tara prodded.

"Am I what?" Kendra stalled.

"Involved. With. Hutch. Carmody," Tara said with exaggerated patience.

"No," Kendra said, thinking, *not if you don't count that hot kiss by Whisper Creek yesterday afternoon.*

"I heard he bought a pony for Madison," Tara persisted.

"Who told you that?" Kendra wanted to know.

"Word gets around," Tara said.

"Opal," Kendra guessed, and knew she was right by the looks of fond chagrin on her friends' faces.

"Don't be mad at Opal," Joslyn was quick to say. "We were talking on the phone and it just slipped out that Hutch bought a pony for Madison to ride and, well, it's only natural to draw some conclusions."

"Which, of course, you did," Kendra pointed out sweetly. "It just so happens that you're wrong, though. Hutch bought the pony because the people who owned it before said it was lonely, with their kids grown up and gone from home."

Tara and Joslyn exchanged knowing looks.

"Every hardworking cattle rancher needs a pony named Ruffles," Joslyn observed dryly and with a twinkle.

"It means nothing," Kendra insisted.

"Whatever you say," Tara agreed, grinning.

"You two are impossible."

"At least we're objective," Joslyn said. "Unlike some people I could mention."

Kendra picked up her teacup and took a measured sip. "You are *so* not objective," she said at some length.

"We want you to be happy," Tara said.

"Well, I want you to be happy, too," Kendra immediately replied. "So why aren't we trying to throw *you* together with somebody—like Boone Taylor, for instance?"

Tara turned a fetching shade of apricot-pink. "Oh, *please,*" she said.

Joslyn, comfortably ensconced in her own marriage and family life, grinned at both of them. Happy people could be downright insufferable, Kendra reflected, especially when they were trying to make a point. "There was a time," she reminded them, "when I couldn't *stand* Slade Barlow. And look how that turned out."

"Oh, right," Tara said grumpily. Her teacup made a clinking sound as she set it back in her saucer. "We'll just go out and find men we absolutely cannot abide, won't we, Kendra, and live happily ever after. Why didn't *we* think of that?"

Joslyn's eyes shimmered with mischievous amusement. "You might be surprised if you gave Boone even the slightest encouragement," she said before turning her gaze on Kendra. "And as for *you,* Ms. Shepherd, we all know that Hutch Carmody makes your little heart go pitty-pat, so why try to pretend otherwise?"

Kendra sighed a long, sad sigh. "Maybe he does," she confessed, almost in a whisper. "But that doesn't mean things will work out between us. They didn't before, remember."

"You do feel something for him, then," Joslyn pointed out kindly, patting Kendra's hand.

"I don't know *what* I feel," Kendra said. "Except that he scares me half to death."

"Why?" Tara asked. Her tone was gentle.

"Once burned, twice shy, I guess," Kendra answered. She glanced down at her watch, partly as a signal that she didn't want to talk about Hutch anymore. "I'd better get back to the office," she added, "before people decide I've gone out of business because I'm never there."

Nobody argued. Both Tara and Joslyn rose to hug their friend goodbye.

Kendra called to Daisy and within minutes the two of them were on the road again.

When she reached the office and checked her voice mail, Kendra learned that three prospective new listings were in the works. She called back each of the people who'd decided to sell their property, arranging meetings for the afternoon, glad to be busy.

The first of the three was a modest ranch-style house with a big yard, a detached garage and plenty of space for flower beds and gardens. The owner, an aging widower named John Gerard, had decided to share a condo in Great Falls with his brother. The place had been impeccably maintained, but it needed some upgrading, too—it would make a good starter home for a young couple, with or without a family.

Kendra and Mr. Gerard agreed on an asking price and other details, and papers were signed.

The second property was commercial—a spooky old motel that would be difficult to sell, given the dilapidated state it was in, but Kendra liked challenges, so she took that listing on, too, mainly because it was in a good location, almost in the middle of town.

By the time she visited the third offering, a double-wide trailer in her grandmother's old neighborhood, she was getting anxious. She had to be at the preschool by three o'clock to pick up Madison, that being the present arrangement, and she couldn't be late.

The owner—in her distracted state Kendra hadn't connected the dots—was Deputy Treat McQuillan. His face was still colorfully bruised from the set-to with Walker Parrish the other night at the Boot Scoot Tavern. By now the incident had assumed almost legendary proportions in and around Parable and she wondered, a little nervously, if Deputy McQuillan had followed through on his threat to press charges against Walker for assault.

In uniform, McQuillan was waiting on his add-on porch when Kendra pulled up in her car. She'd dropped Daisy off at home on her way over and, at the moment, she was glad. There was something about this man that made her feel slightly overprotective, of Madison *and* her dog.

"Hello," she sang out pleasantly, a businesswoman through and through, leaving her purse in the car and unlatching the creaky wooden gate that opened onto the rather hardscrabble front yard. "I hope I haven't kept you waiting."

"Some things," McQuillan drawled, letting his gaze drag over her in a way that was at once leisurely and sleazy, "are worth waiting for."

Kendra felt profoundly uncomfortable and not just because her last encounter with this man, when he'd warned her about Hutch at the Butter Biscuit Café, still irritated her. Her grandmother's old place was just two doors down, on the other side of the unpaved road, and the old sense of futility and sorrow settled over her as surely as if she'd stepped back in time and turned into her childhood self, abandoned and scared.

"You're planning to move?" she asked sunnily, pretending this was business as usual. McQuillan was, after all, a sheriff's deputy and, even if he *had* stepped over the line with Brylee over at the cowboy bar, there was no reason to paint him as a rapist on the prowl for his next victim.

"I'm not sure yet," the deputy replied, keeping his eyes on her face now, instead of her breasts. "Maybe I'll buy a patch of land and build a house, if I can get the right price for this double-wide."

Kendra approached confidently, with her shoulders back and her spine straight. "I see," she said. "What if it sells right away, though? Where would you live in the interim?"

He favored her with a slow grin that made her skin crawl a little and stepped down off the porch to put out a hand to her. "I haven't thought that far ahead," he admitted, gesturing toward the trailer behind him. "I'm just taking things as they come." He glanced at his watch. "I'm on duty in a few minutes," he went on, handing her a ring with two keys dangling from it. "You go on in and take a look around and, if you wouldn't mind, lock up on your way out. I'll pick up the keys later on and we'll work out the details."

Kendra was used to being alone in houses and apartments with people who made her uneasy—that was part of being in the real estate business—but she was wildly relieved that McQuillan meant to leave her to explore on her own. The idea of being confined in a small space with this man made her more than edgy.

She smiled, though, and nodded. "I'll be back at the office around three-thirty," she said. "You could stop by any time after that."

"Fine," he said, and walked on toward the gate. With a jaunty wave of farewell, he left the yard, crossed the sidewalk and got into his personal vehicle, a small green truck, clearly old but polished to a high shine.

Kendra waited until he'd driven away with a merry toot of his horn, before starting up the porch steps.

The front door stood open, but there was a sliding screen, so she moved that aside to step into a living room exactly like her grandmother's.

Her stomach curled around what was left of her quick lunch, a fruit cup and some yogurt hastily consumed at home while she was getting Daisy settled, and she instructed herself, silently and sternly, to get over it.

She wasn't a little girl anymore and this wasn't her grandmother's mobile home.

Deputy McQuillan's living room was shabby—the carpet, drapes and furniture had all seen better days—but every surface was immaculately clean, like the outside of his truck.

She made a hasty circuit, checking out the kitchenette, the fanatically neat bathroom, the three bedrooms, two of which were desperately small. The master bedroom boasted a water bed with a huge, mirrored headboard, and the coverlet was made of crimson velvet.

Cringing a little, Kendra backed out of that room. It was a silly reaction, she knew, but she had to force herself to walk—not run—through the kitchenette and the living room to the front door.

Outside, she sucked in several deep breaths and resolutely took a tour of the yard. There was a tool shed, a detached garage and a small rose garden encircled by chicken-wire that was painted white. The blossoms inside seemed timid, somehow, like prisoners waiting to be rescued.

Now she was really being silly, she decided.

It was a relief, just the same, to get into her car, shut and lock the doors and drive away.

"I 'POLOGIZED!" MADISON announced when Kendra picked her up at preschool. "Becky and me are friends now! She invited me to sleep over sometime—and she has *horses* at her house—"

Kendra bit back the correction—*Becky and* I— and smiled as she strapped Madison into her car seat. "That's wonderful," she said. "Did you apologize to Miss Abbington, too?"

Madison nodded vigorously, but a frown creased her forehead. "Where's Daisy? You didn't give her back to that lady at the shelter, did you?"

Slightly stunned, Kendra straightened. "Daisy's at home," she said gently. "And of course I didn't give her back, sweetheart. Why would I do that?"

"Sometimes people give kids back," Madison ventured.

Kendra swallowed hard, worked up another smile. Madison had been shunted from one foster home to the next during her short life, so it wasn't difficult to figure out the source of the child's concern, for Daisy *and* for herself.

"You're staying with me," Kendra said carefully, "until you're all grown up and ready to go off to college. And even then, you'll always have a home to come back to, and a mommy, too."

"You won't give me back? Not ever?"

"Not ever," Kendra vowed, fighting tears. "And the same goes for Daisy. We're in this for the long haul, all three of us. We're a family, forever and ever."

"It would still be nice if there was a daddy," Madison mused, though she looked appeased by Kendra's promise never to leave. It was one she'd made a thousand times before, and would probably make a thousand more times in the future.

"I guess," Kendra allowed, getting quickly behind the wheel and starting up the car so they could head for home.

"If I could pick out a daddy, I'd choose Mr. Carmody," Madison went on.

By then, Kendra was beginning to wonder if she was being played, but she didn't hesitate to give her daughter the benefit of a doubt. Carefully, she put the car in gear and drove away from the community center, waving to other mothers and fathers coming to collect their children. "Unfortunately," she explained, "it doesn't work that way."

"How *does* getting a daddy work, then?"

Kendra suppressed a sigh. "It's not like baking cookies, honey," she said. "There's no recipe to follow. No formula."

"Oh," Madison said, and the note of sadness in her voice made Kendra ache.

They drove in silence for a minute or two.

Then Madison spoke up again. "It's not fair," she said.

"What's not fair?" Kendra asked patiently, concentrating on the road ahead.

"That *my* daddy's in heaven instead of right here in Parable with us," Madison replied succinctly. "I want a daddy I can see and talk to."

Kendra didn't trust herself to answer without bursting into tears, so she held her tongue.

CHAPTER FOURTEEN

THAT EVENING, AFTER supper and a story and going-to-sleep prayers—Madison asked God for a daddy and suggested Hutch Carmody as a promising candidate for the job—Kendra sat alone at her kitchen table for a while, a little dazed by all that had been going on lately.

She'd had a heck of a time keeping back the tears while Madison was putting in her request for a father; now, as she sat there with a cup of herbal tea before her, they ran freely.

Daisy, who had been snuggled up at the foot of Madison's new bed only a few minutes before, meandered into the kitchen, came straight over to Kendra's chair and stood on her hind legs to plant her forepaws on Kendra's thigh. Her brown eyes shone with canine sympathy and she made a low, whimpering sound in her throat.

Kendra gave a raw chuckle, sniffled and laid a gentle hand on the dog's golden head. "You're a good dog, Daisy," she said, thick-throated with all the complicated emotions swamping her just then.

Daisy rested her muzzle on Kendra's leg and sighed sweetly.

Kendra continued to stroke the dog, used her free hand to raise her teacup to her mouth.

"I'm so confused," she confided after several sips and swallows.

Daisy sighed again, lowered herself to all fours and looked up at Kendra with those glowing eyes, tail wagging slowly back and forth.

"Listen to me," Kendra muttered, sniffling again. "I'm talking to a dog."

Daisy sat now, watching Kendra alertly, as if waiting for her to go on. *Yes, you're talking to a dog. That's a problem?*

Kendra laughed and brushed away her tears with the backs of her hands. "I'll be *all right*," she assured the animal quietly. "So please stop worrying about me." Then she got up, took Daisy out into the backyard just once more and returned to the kitchen.

Apparently satisfied that her second-favorite mistress would indeed remain in one piece without her, at least for now, Daisy ambled back to Madison's room, retiring for the night.

Kendra finished her rapidly cooling tea, went into her home office and logged on to the computer. She'd waited this long to see if Brylee had kept her word and had the web picture taken down, but she couldn't wait any longer.

She was too jittery and frazzled to read or take a luxurious bath by candlelight or simply go to bed early, her usual remedies for everything from wrenching trauma to minor frustrations. That was what she did when she *felt* too much—when it all became overwhelming—she read, or bathed, or slept.

While those things were all perfectly okay, in and of themselves, Kendra was beginning to see them as forms of running away now, time-honored methods of avoidance or denial, metaphorical hiding places where she could take shelter from thoughts and emotions that chafed against the bruised and tender parts of who she really and truly was, deep down inside.

She was a woman now, a mother, and while she figured she functioned pretty well in the latter role, the former was beginning to issue some pretty powerful complaints. *That* Kendra was tired of doing everything alone, including sleeping in an otherwise empty bed. *She* wanted a man to hold her when she needed holding, to love her in every way, on every level—emotionally, mentally and, oh, yes, physically.

The problem, she admitted silently, as she clicked her way over to the Down-With-Hutch webpage, was her complete lack of confidence in her own ability to choose the right man.

First, there had been Hutch, not caring enough to fight for her, even after all the dreams and hopes they'd shared, trampling her heart to dust, leaving her self-esteem in shreds. Then along came Jeffrey, the knight in tarnished armor. Had he ever really loved her or had he simply *wanted* her sexually? She'd never thought of herself as anything more than moderately attractive, but she'd had her share of admirers—too many of them shallow and inherently noncommittal.

Sure enough, the picture of her and Hutch in the three-legged race had been taken down, along with the bitchy remark that had accompanied it, but the smear campaign against the errant groom continued, unabated.

That troubled Kendra—made her feel defensive on Hutch's behalf—which was probably just more proof that she was teetering on the edge of the same old dark abyss as before, when he'd essentially handed her over to Jeffrey like a book he'd already read and hadn't found all that interesting in the first place.

She sighed, clicked over to her email.

There were friendly notes from both Tara and Joslyn, along with one from Treat McQuillan. Kendra had, of course, given him the address she used for business, after he'd stopped by the office late that afternoon to pick up his keys. He had seemed pleased about putting his double-wide up for sale and moving on to whatever it was he meant to move on to; they'd come to terms quickly and the contract was signed.

But this was her personal email account—supposedly, only friends knew it.

Hi, Kendra, the deputy had written, as though they were pals from way back. The rodeo is coming up this weekend, as you know, and I was wondering if you'd like to go with me. If you got a sitter, we could have some dinner and stay up late to watch the fireworks. Maybe even make a few of our own.

Instinctively, Kendra lifted her fingertips off the keyboard, as if it had suddenly turned slimy. *Maybe even make a few of our own.*

Was he kidding?

She recalled McQuillan's tirade in the Butter Biscuit Café that morning, when he'd practically ordered her to stay away from Hutch Carmody—as if he had the right to dictate *anything* to her.

And now he had the nerve to suggest *fireworks?* Where did he get off, making a remark like that?

She breathed in, breathed out. Lowered her fingers back to the keyboard, and replied, Thanks for the invitation, but I've already made other plans. Also, I normally try to keep my business and social lives separate. Best, Kendra Shepherd.

The message was short, to the point and only partially true. She *did* have other plans, heaven help her, to go the rodeo, the carnival and the fireworks display with Hutch, bringing Madison along. And socializing was a big part of her business; she did a lot of lunches and dinners, sometimes threw parties for clients, and before Madison entered her life, she'd dated the occasional business contact, too, though only casually.

Seeing Deputy McQuillan on a potentially romantic basis, however, was certainly not in her game plan. She didn't find him attractive, but that was the least of it. She disliked him; it was that simple. He went around with the proverbial chip on his shoulder and the way he'd treated Brylee at the bar that night didn't do him any credit, either.

The male ego being what it was, Kendra fully expected McQuillan to respond to her refusal, however politely it had been offered, by firing her and finding someone else to sell his home for him. There were two or three other real estate brokers in the county, each with a few sales agents on staff, but hers was the only firm in Parable.

A competent businesswoman, through and through, Kendra hated to miss out on a commission, even the relatively modest one she could expect if she found a buyer for the deputy's mobile home, but if things went down that way, so be it. Even at best, real estate was a catch-as-catch-can affair—you showed a lot of houses, the more the better, and if you worked hard and had decent luck, you eventually sold a few.

McQuillan's response popped up in her online mailbox just as she was about to shut down the computer, push back her chair and brew another cup of herbal tea.

You think you're too good for me? was all he'd written, in a line of lowercase letters, oddly spaced and with no punctuation.

A chill slithered down her spine, but anger immediately quelled it. *Please see the first email,* she responded tersely, and hit Send.

He replied within seconds, but Kendra didn't open the new message. She blocked any further communications from Deputy McQuillan's email address and logged off with an irritated flourish.

Was the man merely obnoxious, she wondered, storming back to the kitchen, or did he present an actual threat of some sort?

She considered calling Boone, not as a citizen of Parable County, but as a friend, but she quickly disregarded the impulse. The sheriff had a wide area to police and, besides, sending rude emails wasn't a crime. If it were, she thought, with a tight little smile, she'd probably be in the slammer herself, with Brylee and her posse for company.

Kendra brewed that second cup of tea she'd promised herself earlier and sat down to drink it, silently reminding herself that she didn't have to make all her life decisions that very night, or the next day, or even next year.

She would stop pushing the river, as the saying went, and just let things unfold at their own pace—even if it killed her.

BOONE AND HUTCH met at the Butter Biscuit Café for breakfast the next morning, both ordering the special, as they did whenever they had a free morning, their joking excuse being that they shouldn't be expected to eat their own cooking day in and day out just because they weren't married.

"Did McQuillan go ahead and file charges against Walker Parrish?" Hutch asked, looking across the table at Boone while they waited for the first round of coffee.

"Hell, yes," Boone said, looking as weary as he sounded. His kids were due to arrive soon, probably on an afternoon bus, and while he seemed anxious to see them, it was obvious that he was already dreading the whole thing, too. "I would have had to arrest Walker, except I called Judge Renson ahead of time and she went ahead and set bail before the fact. Walker paid it, of course, so he didn't wind up in my jail, but he still has to go to court in six weeks or so and answer to an assault charge."

Hutch sighed, swore under his breath. "I've always wondered why Slade didn't fire McQuillan when he was sheriff. Now I'm wondering the same thing about you, old buddy. The man's a hothead—the original loose cannon—not to mention a pain in the ass."

"It's not that simple," Boone answered, "and you damn well know it. We're all civil service, remember, and while my recommendation carries some weight, the powers that be aren't going to let Treat go on the grounds that nobody likes him."

The pancakes arrived, stacks of them, teetering on two plates, and Essie herself did the honors, setting the meals down in front of Hutch and Boone with a deft swoop of each arm.

"On the house," she said, with a sidelong glance at Boone. "Even if you *did* give my favorite niece a speeding ticket last week. Now her insurance premium will go up."

Boone chuckled hoarsely, distractedly. "It's Carmody's turn to pick up the check anyhow," he said, then added, "Tell Laurie to keep her foot out of the carburetor of that little car of hers and *poof,* the problem's solved. No more tickets."

Essie shook her head as though she wouldn't have expected any other reaction from the boneheaded likes of Boone Taylor, and walked away.

"Looking forward to seeing your boys again?" Hutch asked after they'd both drenched their buttery pancakes in thick syrup.

"Of course I am," Boone snapped, downright peckish now. "I just wish I had a better place to put them up, that's all."

"There's no better place than home, Boone, and as far as those little boys are concerned, home is wherever you are."

Boone glowered at him over the towering pancakes. "Excuse me for saying so," he growled, "but you don't know F-all about raising kids, now do you?"

Hutch slanted the side of his fork through the syrupy stack on his plate. "You're already moderating your language," he observed lightly. "That's good. Can't have the munchkins picking up all kinds of dirty words from dear old Dad."

"Shut up," Boone said without much conviction.

Hutch chuckled and took a big bite of his food. While he was still chewing, Slade wandered into the café, taking off his hat as he crossed the threshold.

Hutch waved him over and Slade joined them, drawing back a chair and sinking into it.

"Ever since you stole Opal out from under us," Slade told Hutch, probably only half kidding, "I've been having cold cereal for breakfast."

"What a pity." Hutch grinned with mock sympathy. "Poor you."

"How're Joslyn and the baby doing?" Boone asked between bites.

At the mere mention of his wife and child, a light seemed to go on inside Slade. His eyes twinkled and he grinned. "They're good," he said. Then the grin faded. "I'm a little worried about Shea, though," he added, lowering his voice, since the place was doing a brisk trade, as always.

Essie appeared table-side, wielded the coffeepot she carried and took Slade's order for a pancake special like the ones his friends had.

When she was gone again, bustling off to the kitchen to confer with the fry cook, Boone said, "Shea? She's a good kid—never gets in any trouble as far as I know."

Slade sighed, ran a hand through his dark hair in a gesture of suppressed agitation. "She *is* a good kid," he agreed. "But she's normal, too."

"I don't follow," Boone said, still scarfing up pancakes like there was no tomorrow. To look at him, a person would think he hadn't eaten in a week.

Hutch wondered idly if Shea had gotten herself a boyfriend, thereby rousing her stepfather's famously protective instincts, but it wasn't his business either way, so he didn't ask outright. He just went right on putting away his breakfast and swilling his coffee.

"The Fourth is coming up in a few days," Slade reminded Boone unnecessarily. "You know how it is. During the fireworks, a few kids always climb the water tower to get a better look. Joslyn overheard Shea saying something about it to a friend on her cell phone."

Hutch felt a mild twinge at the mere mention of the water tower, but neither Boone nor Slade would have noticed, being intent on their own concerns, and that was fine with him.

"And you think she's planning to scale the tower with some of her high school pals?" Boone prompted, sounding mildly amused now.

"We've both asked her, Joslyn and I, I mean, and she says she wouldn't do anything that stupid," Slade said. "But—"

"Climbing the water tower is dangerous," Boone agreed, making a gruff attempt at reassurance, "but it isn't illegal, as you know."

"Couldn't you station a deputy out there on Saturday night," Slade pressed, "just to keep an eye on things?"

Boone was clearly regretful as he spread his hands in a gesture meant to convey helplessness. "You ought to know better than anybody, Slade, that I don't have that kind of manpower. And I need the few deputies I have to keep the celebrating down to a dull roar. Folks get all riled up after the rodeo and a few spins on the Tilt-a-Whirl over at the carnival, not to mention the beer and the dancing at the Boot Scoot and then the fireworks to top it all off."

"Damn it, Boone," Slade argued, just as Essie returned to set his plate down in front of him with a thump, "some kid could fall and break their neck. Whatever happened to 'serve and protect'?"

"I can't be everywhere at once," Boone pointed out reasonably. "Neither can my deputies. The best I can promise is that somebody will drive by the water tower once in a while to make sure everything's all right."

Slade seemed to deflate a little. "Then I'll watch the place myself," he said. "During the fireworks, anyhow."

Boone held up his fork, like a teacher about to point to something written on a blackboard. "You're not sheriff anymore," he said. "And you're not a deputy, either. Keep an eye on Shea if you're concerned and leave it to the other parents to do the same for their own kids. That tower is a menace, I grant you, but kids have been climbing it since right after the turn of the last century and nobody's ever actually taken a header off it in all those years, now have they?"

"There's always a first time," Slade grumbled, but he began to eat his pancakes.

Hutch didn't bring up the obvious solution—which was to just pull the water tower down, once and for all, and haul off the debris—because better people than he had lobbied for that for a couple of decades now and gotten nowhere. Besides, he wasn't inclined to remind Slade of that humiliating afternoon when they were kids and he'd gotten stuck up there himself, scared shitless and unable to move until his half brother alternately goaded and cajoled him down.

Now mercifully—at least for Hutch—the conversation took a different turn. Slade asked how long Boone's boys would be staying with him and Boone said only until Sunday night because they were both attending summer school this year.

"Summer school?" Hutch echoed. "Damn, Boone, that's harsh. Summers are for goofing off—for swimming and playing baseball and riding horses until all hours, not beating the books. And, anyway, those kids are what, six and seven years old?"

Boone favored his friend with a reproving glance. "Thank you for your profound wisdom, Professor Carmody," he drawled. "I guess if I wanted to raise a couple of cowboys, that approach would suit me just fine. It just so happens that I don't."

"What's wrong with cowboys?" Slade interjected, being one.

"If you wanted to *raise* Griff and Fletch," Hutch retorted, leaning forward to show Boone he wasn't cowed by his tone *or* his badge, "they'd be living with you, like they should."

Boone flushed from the base of his neck to the underside of his jaw. "Opinions are like assholes," he told Hutch, in a terse undertone. "Everybody has one."

Hutch grinned, picked up his coffee cup and raised it to Boone in a sort of mocking toast. "Good thing you went to college, Boone," he said. "You might not have such a good grasp on human anatomy if you were, say, *just a cowboy.*"

Slade chuckled, but offered no comment. By and large, he wasn't much for chitchat. He'd said his piece, about Shea and the water tower, and now he was probably done talking, for the most part.

Boone huffed out a breath, plainly exasperated. "Tell me this," he demanded in a hoarse whisper. "Why does everybody in this blasted county feel obliged to tell me what's best for *my* kids?"

Slade and Hutch exchanged glances, but it was Essie, back to refill their coffee cups from the carafe in her right hand, who actually answered.

"Maybe," she said crisply, "it's because you can't seem to figure it out on your own, Boone Taylor. Those boys need their daddy."

KENDRA, MADISON AND Daisy passed the fairgrounds on their way to the community center and preschool, and Madison could barely contain her excitement. The carnival was setting up for business; banners flew in the warm breeze and a Ferris wheel towered against the sky. Carousel horses, giraffes, elephants and swans waited to take their places on the merry-go-round, hoisted there by teams of men in work clothes, and cars, trucks and vans were parked, helter-skelter, outside the exhibition hall where vendors and artisans from all over the state were getting ready to display their wares. The Fourth of July weekend was a big moneymaker for practically every business in town and it was coming up fast.

"Look, Mommy!" Madison called out as though Kendra could possibly have missed the colorful spectacle taking shape on the fairgrounds. "It's a circus!"

Kendra smiled. "Actually, it's a carnival. And we're going there on Saturday, remember?"

"Couldn't we go *now?* Just to look?"

"No, sweetie," Kendra responded, signaling for a turn onto the street that led to the community center. "It's time for preschool. Besides, the carnival isn't open for business yet."

"When does it open?"

"Not until Friday afternoon," she said. "That's two days from now, so it's three days until Saturday, when we'll go to the rodeo, and then the carnival, and then the fireworks."

"Mr. Carmody is going to ride a bull in the rodeo part," Madison said, mollified enough to move on to the next topic. "We get to watch."

Kendra swallowed. She didn't know which scared her more, the prospect of letting Hutch slip past her inner barriers again—he was bound to score, eventually—or the thought of him riding two thousand pounds of crazy bull, risking life and limb.

And for what? A fancy belt buckle and prize money that probably didn't amount to the cash he routinely carried in his wallet—*if* he won?

He was wild and reckless, a kid in a man's body. Mentally, she added bull-riding to the long list of reasons why Hutch Carmody was her own personal Mr. Wrong.

She made the turn, headed toward the community center.

Glancing into the rearview mirror, she saw Daisy standing with her paws on the back of the seat, gazing out the rear window as the fairgrounds disappeared from view.

"Does Daisy get to go to the rodeo, too?" Madison queried, from her safety seat.

"That wouldn't be a good place for her, sweetheart," Kendra explained. "She could get lost or hurt somehow and, besides, all that noise would probably scare her."

"Won't she be scared if she's all alone at home?" Madison fretted.

"She'll be just fine," Kendra said gently.

They'd reached the community center by then, and a little girl immediately broke away from the crowd of children on the grassy playground, running to greet them.

"That's Becky," Madison said, delighted. "She's my best friend in the whole world!"

Kendra smiled, watching as Becky, a small dynamo with blond pigtails, dashed in their direction. The little girl wore jeans, a ruffled cotton blouse and a pair of neon pink cowgirl boots—possibly the same pair Madison had appropriated—along with a broad grin.

Evidently, all was forgiven.

Madison wriggled out of her car seat and jumped to the ground while Daisy, excited, barked and scrambled around inside the Volvo.

"This is my mommy," Madison told Becky, indicating Kendra, who stood beside the driver's door in her working-mother outfit, a trim beige pantsuit, expensively tailored. "Mommy, this is Becky. She's six already, but she likes me anyway, even though I'm only four."

Becky stopped, looked up into Kendra's face, squinting a little against the bright sunshine and said, "My mom is going to call you on the phone. She says both of you have to get to know each other a little before there can be any sleepovers for Madison and me."

"I'll look forward to hearing from your mom," Kendra said, offering a hand. Privately, she thought Madison was still too young for sleepovers, but she didn't want to cast a pall over the girls' day by saying so now.

The child shook Kendra's hand without hesitation. "Mom says," she went on cheerfully, "that for all you know, we could be a family of ax-murderers."

Kendra chuckled. "I doubt that," she said, though she was a little taken aback by the graphic visual that came to mind. Becky's family must have moved to Parable recently, because she couldn't place them.

Madison waved at Daisy, who had wriggled into the front passenger seat at some point and was pressing her nose against the inside of the windshield, and waited politely while Kendra bent to give her a see-you-later kiss on the forehead.

"Be a good girl," Kendra said.

Madison, young as she was, actually rolled her eyes in what appeared to be comical disdain. "I will," she replied. "Mostly."

"Try to do a little better than 'mostly,' please," Kendra instructed, folding her arms and tilting her head to one side, letting her eyes do the smiling while her mouth pretended sternness.

Madison and Becky clasped hands, giggling, and ran toward the throng of children and playground attendants up ahead.

Kendra watched until they were safely enfolded in the group, then got back into her car, told a fretful Daisy that everything would be all right and drove off.

Deputy McQuillan was waiting on the sidewalk in front of her office, once again in full uniform.

Daisy growled at him, at the same time cowering a little.

"Good morning," Kendra said with a businesslike smile.

McQuillan looked down at the little dog—for the briefest moment Kendra thought he might try to kick Daisy, there was so much distaste in his expression— then turned his attention back to her. "I've decided to get another real estate agent," he announced bluntly. His eyes fairly snapped with suppressed fury.

Kendra shifted her keys from her left hand to her right and unlocked the office door, gently urging Daisy inside. The pup took refuge under the desk Joslyn used when she came in.

"That's certainly your prerogative," Kendra said with cool dignity, setting down her purse and keys. She took their listing agreement from her in-box and handed it across to Deputy McQuillan.

He tore the document into two pieces and threw them at her, before stalking out of the office and slamming the door behind him.

"That certainly went well," Kendra told Daisy ruefully as the dog low-crawled out from under Joslyn's desk, now that the coast was clear.

For the next hour, Kendra busied herself with routine tasks—reading and replying to emails, initiating and returning phone calls, and surfing the web for for-sale-by-owner listings in the surrounding area.

She came up dry that morning, though, and was thinking about locking up the office and playing hooky for the rest of the day when Walker Parrish came in again.

Daisy went right over to him, and he laughed as he bent to ruffle the dog's ears in greeting.

"My friend's decided she'd like to take a firsthand look at your house," Walker told Kendra. Once again she thought how attractive he was, and marveled that he didn't do a thing for her. "Casey's on the road with her band until after the Fourth, but she says she could stop in for a quick look at the place late next week."

"Not Casey Elder?" Kendra asked, surprised to find herself holding her breath for the answer. She'd dealt with a number of celebrities in the course of her job, and she wasn't the type to be starstruck, but Ms. Elder just happened to be one of the biggest names in country music and Kendra was most definitely a fan.

"Well," Walker said sheepishly, "yeah. But I wasn't supposed to mention her name."

Kendra smiled to reassure him. "Your secret is safe with me," she said lightly, "but the minute Ms. Elder sets foot in Parable, everybody is going to know it. She is, after all, a superstar."

Walker chuckled. "She considered wearing a disguise," he admitted.

"A pair of horn-rimmed glasses with a big plastic nose and a mustache attached?" Kendra joked. Then, more seriously, she added, "It must be difficult, being so recognizable."

"Casey copes with her fame pretty well," Walker said, while Daisy sat gazing up at him in her usual adoring way. "And I assured her that while she has a big following around here, nobody's likely to mob her or anything."

That was true enough. People would be curious about her, especially at first, but if Casey Elder decided to become a permanent part of the community, she'd be welcomed with casseroles and supper invitations, like any other newcomer.

"I take it she liked the pictures you took when we went through the house the other day?" Kendra prompted, wondering about the connection between Walker and Casey and immediately deciding it was none of her business. She certainly wasn't about to ask.

"She liked them, all right," Walker answered, looking as though he wanted to say more but wasn't sure he should.

"You told her the asking price?"

"She didn't bat an eye," Walker said with a nod.

He still had that peculiar look on his face.

"Walker," Kendra nudged, "what is it?"

"Casey's from Dallas," he said uneasily. "I'm not sure she understands what it means to live in a small town, even though she writes and sings songs about it all the time."

Kendra folded her arms, tilted her head to one side and waited. What on earth was going on here?

"Casey and I—" Walker began, stopping to clear his throat. "We have a—complicated relationship."

So, Kendra thought, *my hunch was right. They're more than just friends.*

"No need to explain," Kendra said briskly.

Walker looked miserably determined to go on. "We were never married—never even involved, really, but—" He paused, swallowed visibly. "But Casey's kids are both mine."

Kendra barely kept her mouth from dropping open. What he'd said didn't surprise her as much as the fact that he'd said it at all. "I don't—" she began, and then gave up on completing the sentence.

"The thing is, they don't know it yet," Walker went on. "The kids, I mean. Casey and I want to break it to them gently, once they've gotten settled and everything."

"It's a secret, then," Kendra said quietly.

Walker nodded, shoved a hand through his hair, slapped his hat against his thigh once, lightly. "Nobody else knows," he said. "Not even Brylee."

"Then why tell me?"

"I'm not sure," Walker said, looking flustered. It

was odd, seeing him like this, when he was usually so self-possessed.

Kendra made a lip-zipping motion with one hand. "I won't breathe a word," she promised.

Walker's grin was appreciative and she could tell he was relieved. "Thanks," he said. "Casey will be calling you one day soon. To make an appointment to see the house, I mean."

"Great," Kendra said. "I hope she likes it."

"Me, too," Walker said very quietly. Almost, Kendra thought, wistfully.

She shook off the romantic notion. Ever since Hutch had kissed her down by Whisper Creek, she'd been prone to overthink the whole concept of love.

Walker started for the door, and Kendra returned to her chair behind her desk, smiled a goodbye when he looked back at her over one broad shoulder.

"Interesting," she told Daisy, once he'd gone.

Daisy went back under Joslyn's desk and was soon snoring.

Kendra fidgeted. The urge to call Joslyn or Tara or both of them at once to find out if either of them knew anything about Walker and Casey Elder was strong, but she never really considered giving in to it. After all, she'd promised not to tell what she knew, and if there was one thing Kendra Shepherd believed in, it was keeping promises.

CHAPTER FIFTEEN

SATURDAY MORNING ARRIVED right on schedule, although Madison had seemed certain it would somehow be postponed, if not canceled entirely.

The weather was warm and brilliantly sunny, the sky an achy blue that left sweetly tender bruises on Kendra's heart as she stood at the kitchen sink, her arms plunged into hot, soapy water, gazing out the window as she finished washing the breakfast dishes. By her calculations, two bowls, a couple of spoons and the pot she'd cooked the oatmeal in didn't justify running the machine and, besides, she needed to keep her hands busy.

It had been a couple of days since she'd last seen Hutch, but he'd called once, said he'd pick her and Madison up for the rodeo and the other festivities around eleven-thirty, if that was okay with her. He'd sounded almost shy, but that was probably some kind of ruse.

Hutch Carmody didn't have a shy bone in his red-hot cowboy body.

She'd replied in a blasé tone that eleven-thirty would probably be fine and been jittery every waking minute since, much to her private chagrin, wondering if this get-together qualified as an actual *date* or, since Madison was going along, just a friendly outing. Deciding what to wear wasn't a problem: a long-sleeved T-shirt, jeans and sneakers—she didn't own boots—would fill the bill just fine, for both her and Madison. *But what about my hair?* she dithered. What about makeup? She wanted to look her best, of course, but not as though she was hoping she and Hutch could slip away alone at some point and make their way up the mountainside to the magic meadow.

Was she a bad mother for even *thinking* such a thought? Madison had separation issues, though she seemed more secure every day, settling in well at pre-school and in the new house and, anyway, there were only a few people Kendra would feel comfortable leaving her daughter with—Joslyn and Tara, certainly, and of course Opal. But they would all be busy with their own plans, wouldn't they? And, besides, any one of them, if asked to babysit, would instantly guess why Kendra wanted to disappear for a while.

Behind her, Madison and Daisy scuffled on the lino-leum floor, Madison laughing with delight, Daisy barking exuberantly, as she always did when they played.

Kendra emptied the sink of water, rinsed her hands under the tap, dried them on her flowered apron, and turned to smile at the pair of them, girl and dog, raising her voice just enough to be heard over all that happi-ness. "We'd better get going," she said, "if we're going to drive Daisy out to Tara's place and get back in time to meet Mr. Carmody."

Tara had suggested the canine sleepover, reminding Kendra that it would be quieter out there in the country, far from the Fourth of July fireworks, and thus not so frightening for Daisy. Plus, Lucy would be there and the pups could keep each other company. In the morn-ing, Tara could bring Daisy home or Kendra could pick her up on the chicken farm, whichever worked out best.

Madison, fairly bursting with excitement—new boots *and* a day with Hutch Carmody, would wonders never cease?—nodded hard enough to give herself whiplash. She'd been making a ruckus ever since they'd finished breakfast, trying to keep busy until it was time to go.

It was hard to say which event Madison was most excited about: choosing the promised cowgirl boots, watching Hutch ride a bull in the rodeo, going on rides at the carnival, or taking in the fireworks, which weren't even scheduled to begin until ten o'clock, when the sky would finally be dark enough to launch the first sprays of multicolored light against a black velvet background.

This would be a long day for Madison, Kendra thought not for the first time, when they were all in the Volvo, seat belts fastened. She bit her lower lip as she backed the car down the short driveway and eased carefully onto the street. It would be a long day for *her,* too, given that Hutch would be at her side for most of it.

What did they really have to talk about, she and Hutch, once they got past hello? Not the old days, certainly—*how about all that steamy sex we used to have?*—and the present didn't offer a lot of topics, either.

And what if she just kept reliving that sizzling kiss by the creek the whole day and night? She'd be in a perpetual state of arousal, with nothing left of her but smoldering embers by the time it was all over.

"Can we buy Daisy a present at the rodeo?" Madison asked from her safety seat when they were well on their way to Tara's. "And for Leviticus and Lucy, too?"

Kendra knew the little girl was fretting about the dogs being left alone, thinking they might be lonely or scared, even with each other for company. "I think that's a fine idea," she said, smiling. "Tell you what— while we're looking for those boots of yours, we'll keep an eye out for something they'd like."

Madison cheered at that, and Daisy started barking all over again, sharing in the headiness of the moment.

Tara came out of the main chicken coop when they drove up, wearing work clothes and scattering indignant hens in all directions as she came toward the car.

"You're not going to the rodeo like that, are you?" Madison asked with great concern as soon as they'd come to a stop and Tara had opened the back door of the car to help her out of the seat. "You have chicken poop on your shoes."

Tara laughed and shook her head, but before she could reply, Lucy came bounding down the front steps from the shady porch, barking gleefully. This, of course, got Daisy all worked up again and the canine chorus began.

"I'm not much for rodeos," Tara explained when the din subsided a little and Madison was out of the car seat. "But I'll be in town later for the fireworks." A pause. "Without the poopy shoes, of course."

By then, Daisy and Lucy were playing a merry game of chase, and Madison ran right along with them, transcendence in motion, the sunlight catching in her coppery curls.

Watching, Kendra felt literally swamped with love and gratitude. She was so blessed, she thought. She had everything a woman could want.

Then the memory of Hutch's kiss sneaked up on her, as it had a way of doing, and heat swept through her in a fiery flood.

Okay, she clarified to herself. She had *almost* everything.

Tara, meanwhile, took in Kendra's French braid, small gold earrings and carefully applied makeup, and looked fondly sly. "Don't *you* look nice today?" she drawled. Then, in a lower voice, though Madison couldn't possibly have heard her over all that racket she and the dogs were making, "Why, if I didn't know better, I'd think you were looking for a little Hutch-action."

"Oh, please," Kendra said, averting her eyes for a moment.

Hutch-action, she thought. *Oh, Lord.*

Tara merely folded her arms and raised her perfect eyebrows. She might have been wearing dirty coveralls and manure-caked shoes, but she still managed to look like the class act she was, right down to the double helix of her DNA.

"Madison will be with us the whole time," Kendra pointed out when her friend didn't say anything more, probably because she didn't have to, having made her point. "What could happen?"

"Nothing," Tara admitted, pleased. "But that doesn't mean all that time together isn't going to crank up the dials. I don't know why you and Hutch don't just—" she leaned in now, and dropped her voice to a whisper "—*do it*. It's going to happen, you know. It's inevitable, fated, meant to be."

"No," Kendra argued too fiercely, "it *isn't* going to happen, because I won't let it!" Deep down, though, she wasn't so sure, because some part of her had been hankering to head for the meadow ever since Hutch had reminded her of the things they'd done there, back in the day. "This is just an outing, nothing more." She counted off the events on her fingers. "Rodeo. Carnival. Fireworks. Over."

"Right," Tara said. She wasn't actually smirking, but she was close to it.

That was when Kendra blurted it out, the thing she hadn't meant to say at all, to anyone. Ever. "What are we going to *talk about* for a whole day?"

Tara's smile turned gentle and she touched Kendra's arm. "You and Hutch don't need a script, honey," she said. "Just let things *happen*. Roll with it, so to speak."

"Easy for you to say," Kendra pointed out. "You'll be here, shoveling chicken poop all day!"

"Some people have all the luck," Tara confirmed wryly as Madison left the dogs and came toward them. Daisy and Lucy were settling down in the shade of a nearby tree for an impromptu nap.

"Let's *go,* Mommy," Madison said eagerly, clasping Kendra's hand. "It's almost time for Mr. Carmody to come and get us, isn't it?"

"We have a little while yet, sweetheart," Kendra assured her child after a glance at her watch.

"Come inside and have some lemonade, then," Tara said. "I just made it fresh this morning, before I went out to do the chores."

Madison looked doubtful. Like most children and all too many grown-ups, she probably thought she could make the minutes pass faster just by force of will, and she was a nervous wreck from the effort.

"I also have cookies," Tara bargained with an understanding smile.

"What kind?" Madison wanted to know.

"Madison." Kendra sighed.

Tara chuckled. "Chocolate chip," she said.

"Just one then," Madison agreed.

"Madison Shepherd," Kendra said. "What do you say when someone very kindly offers you lemonade and cookies?"

"If it's somebody I know, you mean?" Madison asked. "Because I'm not supposed to talk to strangers, am I?"

Kendra suppressed a sigh. "No," she answered patiently. "You most certainly aren't. But Tara isn't a stranger."

Madison beamed, remembering her manners at last, or maybe just willing to use them. "Yes, please," she told Tara triumphantly, like a quiz show contestant coming up with the right answer and thus taking home the prize.

They all went inside, Tara leaving her dirty shoes behind on the step, followed by the sleepy dogs, who both curled up on Lucy's fluffy dog bed in a corner of Tara's kitchen, Daisy's head resting companionably on the scruff of Lucy's neck, both of them awash in the summer sunlight pouring in through a nearby window. They shimmered.

Tara, as charmed by the scene as Kendra was, quietly got out her cell phone and snapped a picture of the pair.

"I'll send you a copy," she said, setting the phone aside.

Kendra nodded, and she and Madison went off to the powder room to wash their hands.

When they got back to the kitchen a couple of minutes later, Tara was pouring lemonade into cut-crystal glasses, and chocolate chip cookies beckoned from an exquisite china plate.

Kendra smiled at the contrast between the old farmhouse and Tara's elegant possessions, vestiges of her other life back in New York. Close as they were, Tara had been fairly tight-lipped about her pre-Parable life— she'd admitted to a bitter divorce and a passion to reinvent herself completely, but that was about all.

Both Joslyn and Kendra figured Tara would open up to them when she was ready and, in the meantime, they were content with things as they were.

Tara, Kendra and Madison chatted amiably while they enjoyed the refreshments, and then it was finally time to go back to town, much to Madison's delight.

The little girl said goodbye to Daisy, who barely opened her eyes in response, and Kendra thanked Tara for everything, offered up a see-you-later.

Madison and Kendra had been home for fifteen minutes or so when Kendra heard the sound of a vehicle rolling into the driveway.

"He's here!" Madison shouted from the living room. She'd been keeping watch at the window from the moment they got back from Tara's. "And he's in a shiny truck!"

Kendra had never known Hutch to drive anything but one of the battered old pickups used on the ranch— he seemed content to take whichever one wasn't in use at the moment. She, like most people, tended to forget that he had money, and plenty of it, because he lived simply and never flaunted his wealth.

She went out onto the back porch, her heart hammering under her sensible shirt, and watched as Hutch climbed out of a red, extended-cab pickup, the rig gleaming in the sunlight.

"New truck?" she asked. Her heartbeat thundered in her ears, but she probably looked calm on the outside.

Or so she hoped.

"I'm taking it for a test drive," Hutch said. His hair was a little too long and slightly tousled, and he wore a black hat, jeans, a colorful shirt and clean but serviceable boots. He was, Kendra was reminded, planning to ride in the rodeo later that day. "Like it?"

"It's…nice…" she said, rattled. If she asked him not to enter the bull-riding, would he agree?

She'd never know, because asking was out of the question.

Madison, meanwhile, dashed past Kendra, lingering on the porch, and fairly catapulted her small body into Hutch's arms.

He caught her deftly and plunked his hat on her head with a laugh. Her whole face disappeared under the crown. "Hey, short-stuff," he said. "Ready for a big day?"

Madison peeked out from under the hat, transfigured by the sheer magic of Hutch Carmody. "We're buying boots!" she crowed.

Hutch chuckled again, shifting her easily to his left hip. "So I hear," he said. "You look mighty good in that hat, cowgirl. Maybe we ought to get you one of those, too."

Kendra opened her mouth to protest—she worked hard not to spoil Madison, and it wasn't easy because her tendency was to grant every whim—but closed it again in the next instant.

It's no big deal, she told herself.

Hutch's gaze swung back to her then, and he let it roam over her briefly. Appreciation sparked in his eyes.

"Pretty as a mountain meadow," he commented smoothly.

Kendra felt that now-familiar surge of heat go through her. Such an innocent-sounding reference and, at the same time, a bold invitation.

Or was it more of a promise?

"Thanks," she said, hurrying back into the house in an effort to hide her pink face. Once there, she dragged in several deep breaths, struggling to regain her composure, and took her time getting her handbag, making sure all the stove burners were turned off and the doors were locked.

When she came outside again, Hutch had installed Madison and her car seat in the spiffy truck.

With a laugh, Madison plopped his hat back on his head, and it landed askew, pushing down the tops of his ears. He made a goofy face for the child's benefit before straightening it, and Madison found that uproariously funny.

"Ready?" he asked almost gruffly when he turned his attention on Kendra.

It was a loaded question. He was asking about more than the rodeo and the carnival and a fireworks display, and she couldn't pretend not to know it.

She said nothing, because "no" would have been a lie and "yes" would lead to all sorts of problems.

He grinned, reading her well, and held open the passenger door for her. He did give her a brief boost when she stepped up onto the high running board, the way he'd done when they went riding.

She blushed hotly and refused to look at him, staring straight through the windshield when he chuckled again, shut the truck door and came around to the driver's side.

During the short ride to the fairgrounds, Madison

made conversation between the adults unnecessary, if not impossible, chattering away about Ruffles—she couldn't wait to ride again, would they be doing that soon?—and her new boots and whether she should get a pink cowgirl hat or a red one.

The parking lot at the fairgrounds was already bursting with rigs of various kinds, but Hutch found a spot for the truck and had Madison out of her safety seat and standing in the gravel before Kendra had alighted and walked around to their side.

Hutch gave her a sidelong look, grinned and set his hat down on her head. "Relax," he said. "You've got a pint-size chaperone here, and that means I'll have to behave myself, now doesn't it?"

The hat smelled pleasantly of Hutch—sun-dried cotton, fresh country air and the faintest tinge of new-mown grass—and, for just a moment, Kendra allowed herself to revel in the moment, as happy as Madison had been when she wore Hutch's hat back at the house.

Her hands shook a little as she lifted it off and handed it back, and the question she'd promised herself she wouldn't ask tumbled out of her mouth with no prompting from her addled brain.

"You're dead-set on this bull-riding thing?"

Hutch regarded her for a long moment, his expression unreadable. "Does it matter?" he asked.

Madison, by that time, had taken his hand and was trying to drag him toward the ticket booth, some fifty yards away.

Kendra sighed. "Yes," she admitted as he took her hand and Madison pulled them across the lot like a little tugboat. "It matters."

"That's interesting," Hutch said. "Why?"

"Why, what?" Kendra was stalling now. She was between a rock and a hard place, and there was no way to extricate herself. If she asked Hutch not to ride, she'd seem controlling, and he'd probably refuse to skip the event just because he was stubborn. If she *didn't* ask, on the other hand, she'd have lost her one chance to make sure he didn't break his damn fool neck in front of her, half the county and, worst of all, Madison.

"Why does it matter?" Hutch pressed quietly.

"I'd hate to see you get hurt, that's all," Kendra said in a light tone that didn't match the urgency she felt. Madison, the human tugboat, was within earshot, after all.

"I'd hate to see that, too," Hutch said, one side of his mouth tilting up in a classic Hutch Carmody grin. "But I don't believe in sitting on the sidelines, Kendra, just to be safe. I *love* the rodeo, especially the bull-riding."

She felt frustrated and something was doing the jitterbug in the pit of her stomach, on icy feet, even though it would be a couple of hours before he actually climbed down off the catwalk and into the chute where an angry bull would be waiting for him.

"You're not scared?" she asked against her will.

They'd reached the winding line in front of the ticket booth by then, and Madison let go of Hutch's hand and fidgeted.

"What if all the boots are gone when we get there?" she fretted.

Hutch touched the top of her head lightly and briefly and in a very daddylike way. "No worries, short-stuff," he assured the child, though his gaze was still fastened to Kendra's face. "There will be plenty to choose from when our turn comes."

If *she'd* said something like that, Madison probably would have ratcheted up the angst another notch, but the little dickens settled right down after Hutch spoke to her.

Kendra rested her hands on her hips, waited for him to answer her last question.

He grinned. "Walker Parrish has some famously nasty bulls in his string of rodeo stock, and flinging cowboys three ways from Sunday is what those critters do best, so, yeah, I might be a little nervous. I'd be an idiot if I wasn't."

"Then why do it?"

"Because I want to," Hutch said easily, "and because fear isn't a good enough reason to keep to the sidelines when there's living to do."

They'd reached the booth by then, so Kendra didn't reply. She just bit down hard on her lower lip while Hutch extracted his wallet from the hip pocket of his jeans and paid their admission.

Their hands were stamped, so they could come and go throughout the day, and Madison thought that was the coolest thing ever, especially when Hutch told her the mark would show up even in the dark.

Once they were inside the fairgrounds, Hutch crouched in front of Madison, pushed his hat to the back of his head, and looked the little girl straight in the eye. "You stick close to your mama and me, now," he said very seriously. "Will you do that, munchkin?"

Madison nodded solemnly.

Kendra's heart pinched, watching them together. Some things were so beautiful, they hurt.

Hutch straightened, shifted his hat. "Well, then, that's settled," he said. "Let's take a look around."

They headed for the exhibition hall first, where all the vendors had set up booths to market everything from handcrafted silver and turquoise jewelry, always popular with the rodeo set, to custom-made saddles and other tack. There were hats and boots galore, of course, in every conceivable size, style and color.

Madison zeroed in on a pair with a peacock-feather design sewn into the leather and rhinestone accents.

"These are pretty, aren't they?" she said, looking up at Hutch for his opinion.

A little stung that she hadn't been acknowledged, let alone consulted about the boots, Kendra began, "But they're too—"

Hutch silenced her by taking her hand and giving it a light, quick squeeze. "Mighty showy," he agreed thoughtfully, focused on Madison. "But stalls and barnyards are messy places, and riding horses stirs up a lot of dust. Splashes up some creek water, too."

Madison tilted her head to one side, considering. Kendra might have been invisible, for all the notice the child paid her. Hutch's opinion was apparently all that mattered, at least in this situation.

"Boots aren't supposed to be pretty?" Madison asked, looking mildly disappointed. She was a girly-girl, as well as a sporty type, and she loved tutus, flashy toy jewelry and plastic high heels.

Hutch's grin was like a flash of sunlight on clear water. "Yes," he said. "They can be pretty. But a real cowgirl like you needs to think about how her boots are going to hold up over the long haul."

Madison was clearly puzzled.

"You need boots that will last," Kendra translated,

glad to be of some help even if she was on the fringes of the question.

Madison weighed that. "Okay," she finally agreed. "Let's find some that will last *and* look pretty."

"Good plan," Hutch said with another sideways glance at Kendra, fueled by a grin that made her feel as though her clothes had just dissolved. "We'll keep looking until we find just the right pair."

Eventually, they did find the right pair for Madison. They were dark brown and sturdy, with a tiny pink rose stitched into the side of each shaft.

Kendra smiled as she handed her debit card to the merchant and shook her head at the offer of a box. "She'll wear them," she said. "Thanks anyway, though."

Madison, prancing around in the new boots like a little show pony angling for a blue ribbon, had forgotten all about the sneakers she'd been wearing before.

A cowgirl-Cinderella in boots instead of glass slippers, Madison twinkled like a fully lit Christmas tree, showing off for Hutch.

Prince Charming in jeans, Kendra reflected, taking a good long look at Hutch while he was busy raving over Madison's footwear.

Beware, said the voice of Kendra's rocky childhood, and her once broken, barely mended heart. *Danger ahead.*

But there was another voice in her head now, and it repeated something Hutch had said minutes before. *Fear isn't a good enough reason to keep to the sidelines when there's living to do.*

Madison brought Kendra back to the here and now by tugging at her hand. "You need boots, too, Mommy," she said earnestly. "So you can go riding with Mr. Carmody and me."

"True enough," Hutch said with a twinkle. "Boots are a requirement if you're going to travel farther than the creek."

The creek.

The *kiss*.

There she was again, stuck in the same old dilemma. If Madison was set on learning to ride for real—and she obviously wanted that very much—then Kendra, of course, would need to go along, at least until her daughter was older. Which meant she might as well invest in a pair of boots for herself—and it wasn't as if she couldn't afford the purchase. The rub was, doing that meant a lot more than just selecting the right size and style and paying up. It meant she was agreeing to not just one more horseback ride, but very possibly dozens of them.

With Hutch, it seemed, everything had at least two meanings.

It was maddening.

Half an hour later, Kendra was the owner of a pair of well-made and very practical black boots, with no frills whatsoever.

While she and Madison waited in the shade of an awning near the cluster of food concession booths, Hutch took the box out to the truck.

"I wanted to *wear* my boots," Madison said, turning backward on the bench to stick both feet out so she could admire them. "Mr. Carmody says they have to be broken in right."

Mr. Carmody says this. Mr. Carmody says that.

Madison was obviously in love.

"Let me know if they start pinching your toes or rubbing against your heels," said Kendra, ever practical. "New shoes can do that."

Madison turned around, rolled her eyes once, and reached for one of the French fries from the order they were sharing. She swabbed it in catsup and steered it toward her mouth. "Cowgirls don't mind if their toes are pinched," she announced. "They're *tough*."

Kendra laughed, after reminding herself to lighten up a little. This was Madison's first pair of boots and she might remember this day all her life. And Kendra wanted that memory to be a good one.

"Yes," she agreed, "they are. And you are definitely a born cowgirl."

Madison was pleased, and dragged another French fry through the catsup just as Boone approached the table, flanked by two small, dark-haired boys— miniature versions of him.

They wore jeans and striped T-shirts and brand-new sneakers, and they both had freckles and a cowlick above their foreheads. If one of the little guys hadn't been almost a head taller than the other, they could have been mistaken for twins.

Looking at the children, Kendra saw their mother in them, as well as Boone, and a lump rose in her throat. She'd liked Corrie Taylor, and it still seemed impossible that she was gone.

"Well," Kendra said warmly, blinking a sheen of sudden moisture that blurred her vision. "Griffin and Fletcher. You've grown so much I almost didn't recognize you."

The smaller of the two boys huddled shyly against Boone's side. Like his sons, he was wearing casual clothes; he rarely bothered with a uniform, and today he was probably off duty.

The taller boy put out a manly hand. "I'm Griff," he said. Naturally, he didn't remember her. Most likely she was just another friend of his mom and dad's, faintly familiar but mostly a stranger.

Madison, whose mouth was circled with catsup, regarded the boys with a curious combination of wariness and fascination. To her, they were probably members of an alien species.

Kendra shook the offered hand. "Hi, Griff," she said. "I'm Kendra." She peered around at the other little boy, who was still trying to hide behind Boone's leg. "Hello, there," she added.

"Fletch is sort of shy around the edges," Boone said, sounding pretty shy himself.

"This is my daughter, Madison," Kendra said to all three of them, gesturing.

"I have new boots," Madison said. She got down off the bench, rounded the picnic table, and walked right up to Griff, standing practically toe-to-toe with him. "See?"

Fletch peeked around Boone to take a look. "Girl boots," he scoffed, but there was a certain reluctant interest in his tone.

Boone chuckled and made a ruffling motion atop the boy's head. If the kid's hair hadn't been buzz cut, Boone would have mussed it up. "Of course they're girl boots," he reasoned.

"Because Madison's a *girl,* dumbhead," Griff told his brother.

Boone let out a long sigh. He looked overwhelmed,

completely out of his depth, this man who, in the course of his job, feared no one.

Kendra took pity on him. "Join us?" she said, moving over to show that there was plenty of room at the table, with just herself and Madison taking up space. "Hutch took something to the truck, but he'll be back in a couple of minutes."

Boone considered the invitation carefully. "You guys hungry?" he asked.

Both boys nodded quickly.

"What'll it be?" Boone said, indicating the row of concession wagons lined up along the side of the fairgrounds, offering everything from hamburgers and hot dogs to chow mein, Indian fry bread and tacos.

They both wanted hot dogs, as it turned out, and orange soda to drink.

Madison, Kendra noticed, squeezed in beside her and left the bench on the other side of the table to the boys. Like them, she was shy but intrigued.

"Is that your dad?" she asked, nodding toward Boone, who was waiting in a nearby line by then.

"Yeah," Griff said, elbowing Fletch, who sat too close to him for his liking.

Fletch ignored his brother's gesture and shook his head. "No, he isn't," he argued stubbornly. "Uncle Bob is our dad."

Uh-oh, Kendra thought.

And then Hutch was back, all easy charm. He sat down on Kendra's bench, lifted Madison onto his lap, and proceeded to win both boys over in two seconds flat.

By the time Boone returned with lunch for himself and the kids, Griff and Fletch were grinning at Hutch and lapping up every word he said.

CHAPTER SIXTEEN

For all Kendra's fears that the day would drag by, the next couple of hours unfolded easily, naturally. She and Hutch and Madison went on most of the rides at the carnival. On the merry-go-round, Hutch made Madison laugh so hard she nearly fell off the pink swan she'd chosen, just by waving his hat around and pretending the blue-and-green tiger he sat upon was sure to buck him off any minute. Kendra, standing protectively beside her daughter while the mechanism turned and the Kaliope played, watched him, her heart full but on the verge of breaking.

Don't, she wanted to say to him. *Don't make Madison love you. She's lost so much already.*

But it was too late for that, of course. The man had won the child over completely, helping her choose just the right cowgirl hat, and bandannas for the canine contingent. He'd even presented Madison with a giant pink-and-white teddy bear—it had been consigned to the truck for the duration, like Kendra's new boots—having acquired it by getting a perfect score at the target-shooting booth.

Madison hadn't wanted to give up that bear, even long enough to have it safely stowed away until it was time to go home. She'd have preferred to lug the thing around all day, showing it to everyone, recounting the glorious legend of how Hutch had won it for her. He'd been the one who'd finally managed to persuade the little girl to give up the huge toy, however temporarily— Kendra had gotten nowhere with her sensible advice.

She was pleased because *Madison* was pleased, of course, but Rupert, her daughter's beloved purple kangaroo, once her constant companion, formed a lonely figure in her mind's eye. Ever since Daisy had landed in their lives like a space capsule falling out of orbit, Rupert had been forgotten, left behind in Madison's room, albeit in a place of honor. Even though she was having a good time and she knew that Madison's reduced dependence on the tattered stuffed animal was a good sign, Kendra felt a pang when she thought of poor Rupert. She could identify with him.

After the merry-go-round rides—Madison had gone from the swan to an elephant to a giraffe to a regular carousel horse—the appointed hour arrived, and the crowd streamed from the midway into the outdoor arena, where the rodeo was about to start. The bleachers filled quickly, and everybody stood up when the giant flag was raised and last year's Miss Parable County Rodeo sang "The Star-Spangled Banner."

Since the bull-riding would be the final event of the one-day rodeo, Hutch took his place in the bleachers next to Kendra, taking Madison easily onto his lap when they sat down.

A colorful opening ceremony followed the national anthem, and Madison watched, wide-eyed, as pretty local girls rode in formation, each one dressed in a fancy cowgirl outfit and carrying a huge banner. They performed a few expert maneuvers and the loving crowd cheered loudly enough to raise the big sky arching over all their heads by at least an inch.

"I want to do that someday," Madison, having watched every move the girls and their horses made, said with more certainty than a four-year-old should have been capable of mustering up. "Can I do that when I'm bigger, Mommy?"

Kendra smiled, touched her daughter's cheek. For all the disposable wipes Kendra had used on that little face today, it was still smudged with the remains of a cotton candy binge. "Sure you can," she said. "When you're older."

"How *much* older?" Madison pressed.

Hutch chuckled and turned Madison's pink cowgirl hat 360 degrees until it came to rest on the bridge of her nose. "Those girls out there," he told her, "have been riding since they were your size, or even smaller. It takes a lot of practice to handle a horse the way they do, so you'll want to be on Ruffles's back as often as possible."

Kendra gave him a look over Madison's head and a light nudge with her elbow, but he just grinned at her.

The rodeo began and Madison was enthralled with every event that followed—except for the calf-roping. That made her cry, and even Hutch couldn't convince her that calves weren't being hurt or frightened. Calves were routinely roped, thrown down and tied on ranches, he'd explained, so they could be inoculated against diseases and treated for sickness or injury. Privately, though Kendra knew Hutch was right, from an intellectual standpoint anyway, she agreed with Madison; the event wasn't her favorite, and she was glad when it was over.

They watched the sequence of competitions. The barrel racing—since all the competitors were female—cheered Madison up considerably. She wanted to know if she and Ruffles could start practicing that right away, along with flag carrying.

All too soon, it was time for the bull-riding. Hutch took his leave from them and headed for the area behind the chutes.

Like the other livestock in the rodeo, the bulls were provided by Walker Parrish's outfit, and they looked mythically large to Kendra, milling around in the big pen on the opposite side of the arena.

Her heartbeat quickened a little as she saw Hutch join the other cowboys waiting to risk their fool necks, and her stomach, containing too much carnival food, did a slow, backward roll. Saliva flooded her mouth and she swallowed, willing herself not to throw up right there in the bleachers.

The first cowboy wore a helmet instead of a Western hat, a choice Kendra considered eminently practical, and he was thrown before the sports clock reached the three-second mark.

The second cowboy made it all the way to six seconds before the bull he was riding went into a dizzying spin, tossed the man to the sawdust and very nearly trampled him.

Madison looked on, spellbound, huddled close against Kendra's side. Once or twice, her thumb crept into her mouth—a habit she'd long since left behind as babyish.

Another helmeted rider followed, and lasted just two and a half seconds before his bull sent him flying.

Then it was Hutch's turn.

The whole universe seemed to recede from Kendra like an outgoing tide. There was only herself, Madison, Hutch and that bull he was already lowering himself onto over there in the chute. He wore his hat, not a helmet, and Kendra saw him laugh as he adjusted it, saw his lips move as he spoke to the gate man.

Then the gate swung open and the bull—the thing was the size of a Volkswagen, Kendra thought anxiously—plunged out into the very center of the arena, putting on a real show.

The announcer said something about Hutch's well-known skills as a bull-rider, but to Kendra the voice seemed to be coming from somewhere far away and through a narrow pipe.

The big red numbers on the arena clock flicked from one to the next.

Hutch remained on the back of that bull through a whole series of violent gyrations, and then, blessedly, the buzzer sounded and one of the pickup men rode up alongside the furious critter. Hutch, triumphant, switched smoothly to the other horse, behind the rider, and got off when they'd put just a few yards of distance between them and the bull.

Eight seconds.

Until today, Kendra had never dreamed how long eight seconds could seem.

The crowd went crazy, clapping and whistling and stomping booted feet on old floorboards in the bleachers, and the announcer prattled happily about how Hutch would be hard to beat.

Madison scrambled onto Kendra's lap. "Is he done now?" she asked, sounding as breathless as Kendra felt.

Kendra hugged her daughter tightly. "Yes," she said. "It's over."

"Good," Madison said. "That boy-cow looks mean."

Kendra chuckled and, to her relief, some of the tension drained away, softening her shoulders and unclenching her stomach. "I think that boy-cow *is* mean," she agreed.

They watched as Hutch climbed deftly over a fence and stood, watching as the next bull and rider came hurtling out of a chute.

For Kendra, the rest of the event passed in a blur of cowboys and bulls and disconnected words booming over the loudspeakers, all of that underpinned by enthusiastic applause. She sat holding Madison a little too tightly, trying not to imagine how Hutch's ride— or that of some other cowboy—*could* have turned out.

The effort was futile, and by the time Hutch and the other winners were announced and the closing ceremony began—the announcer thanked everybody for coming and reminded them to stick around, check out the goods on offer in the exhibition hall, and enjoy the carnival and, later on, the fireworks—Kendra was weak in the knees.

She and Madison met Hutch, as agreed, outside the arena gate.

Seeing him again, up close, all in one piece, Kendra felt a humiliating urge to cry and fling herself into his arms. Fortunately, she didn't give in to that clingy, codependent compulsion.

"Congratulations," she said mildly, stiffening her spine and lifting her chin.

But Madison was much more forthright. She marched over to Hutch, set her little hands on her hips and tipped her head back to look up at him. Her hat tumbled down her back, dangling by the string Kendra meant to snip off with scissors at the first opportunity. "I don't like it when you ride boy-cows," she informed him. "You could get hurt!"

Hutch smiled, crouched down to look into Madison's pleasantly grungy face and gently tugged at one of her curls. "I'm just fine, shortstop," he said quietly. He might have been talking to an adult, from his tone, rather than a child. He spoke firmly to Madison, but addressed her as an equal. "See?"

Madison softened, as he'd intended. "Do you ride boy-cows *a lot?*" she wanted to know.

"No," he replied. "Just once a year when the rodeo rolls around."

Madison mulled that over. Being so young, she probably didn't have any real conception of such an extended length of time. A year, most likely, sounded a lot like forever.

Kendra, on the other hand, knew those twelve months would pass quickly. Would she and Madison be right here when it was rodeo time again, watching this man deliberately take his life in his hands? Or would Hutch have grown tired of them by then, and moved on to some other woman?

She didn't trust herself to say a word in that moment; just stood there, frustrated and scared and wanting Hutch Carmody more than she ever had before.

What was *wrong* with her?

Why couldn't she just stay away from this man, find somebody else—an insurance agent, say, or a schoolteacher, or an electrician, if she had to walk on the wild side?

Anybody but a cowboy.

Hutch rose easily from his haunches, bent and hoisted Madison into his arms.

She yawned and rested her head against his shoulder, her pink cowgirl hat bobbing between her shoulder blades.

Kendra slipped the hat off over Madison's head and carried it for her.

"I think a certain little cowgirl could use some peace and quiet," Hutch said, looking at Kendra over Madison's bright tousle of hair. "What if we head out to my place for a while?" Seeing the protest brewing in Kendra's eyes, he immediately added, "Opal's there and the fireworks won't start for hours."

Kendra sighed, then gave in with a nod.

Madison clearly needed a break from all the hubbub and excitement, and so did she.

They left the fairgrounds, Madison asleep on Hutch's shoulder and barely waking up when he unlocked the truck and set her gently in her safety seat.

"Did I miss the fireworks?" the child asked drowsily.

"Nope," Hutch said, buckling her in. "We're going out to the ranch to spend some time with Opal and Ruffles, but we'll be back in plenty of time to watch the sky light up. And look—here's your teddy bear, sitting right here waiting for you."

Madison nodded and smiled and drifted off, her head resting against the bear's plush pink shoulder.

Kendra, evidently relegated to sidekick status and feeling like a third wheel, went around the truck, opened the passenger door and climbed inside quickly. She didn't want to linger, taking the chance that Hutch might goose her in the backside again, the way he had before they left her place.

A wicked little thrill zapped through her at the memory, though.

The drive to the ranch passed in silence, Madison sleeping in back, Kendra at a loss for anything to say, Hutch easy in his skin, as usual, and thinking his own thoughts.

When they pulled in at Whisper Creek, Opal was outside, taking laundry down off the clothesline. Leviticus supervised from beneath a shady tree.

She smiled and waved when she saw them, picked up her laundry basket, and started for the house.

Hutch was carrying Madison, so Kendra took the basket from Opal, after a brief, good-natured tugging match.

"That's one worn-out little child," Opal observed as Madison snoozed on, her small arms wrapped loosely around Hutch's neck. "You were right to bring her away from all that dirt and noise at the rodeo."

"We'll be going back in a few hours," Hutch replied. "She's dead-set on taking in the fireworks."

Opal chuckled warmly at that, and softly. "You put her in there on my bed," she told Hutch, gesturing toward a doorway leading off the kitchen. "That way she'll be able to hear our voices when she wakes up and won't be startled to find herself in a strange place."

Kendra followed Hutch, watched as he laid the child on Opal's quilted bed, tenderly pulled off her new boots and draped a lightweight comforter over her.

There he goes again, acting like a daddy.

Madison stirred and then succumbed to happy exhaustion.

Back in the kitchen, Opal was pouring coffee for Hutch and Kendra, and brewing tea for herself. The counters were lined with a wide assortment of casseroles and home-baked pies.

"Somebody die?" Hutch asked, reaching toward one of the pies. Leviticus stayed close to him, plainly adoring the man.

Opal stopped what she was doing long enough to slap his hand away. "No," she said with a sharpness that was soft at the center, "nobody *died.* We're getting a new pastor—Lloyd's decided to retire, God bless him—and he'll be introduced to the congregation tomorrow morning."

Kendra, who had missed the last couple of Sunday services, felt mildly chagrined that she hadn't known such a change was in the works. She opened her mouth to comment, couldn't think of a single thing to say and closed it again.

"You can have some of that cherry crumble over there," Opal told Hutch, gesturing toward a pan sitting all alone on top of the stove. "I made that especially for you."

"Yes," Hutch said, homing in on the cherry crumble.

Kendra, meanwhile, sat down to sip from the cup of coffee Opal gave her.

"Want some of this?" Hutch asked from across the room, lifting a plate with a double helping of dessert scooped onto it.

"No, thanks," Kendra said with a weary smile. "It looks delicious, but I've had way too much sugar today as it is."

Hutch came to the table, set his plate down and sat.

"You keep this up, Opal," he teased, admiring the food, "and I might have to put you on my payroll."

Opal laughed and waved a scoffing hand at him. "That'll be the day," she said. "Slade Barlow signs my paychecks. I'm only here to keep you from turning into a seedy old coot who hangs flags and blankets up for window curtains and eats every meal out of a tin can."

Hutch laughed at the image and nearly choked on the bite he'd just taken.

Kendra, on edge since the bull-riding competition, relaxed a little and even smiled.

"Anyhow," Opal went on, taking a place at the table to sip her tea, "I'm beginning to think there's hope for you after all, Hutch Carmody." She glanced at Kendra, smiled. "Yes, sir, I do think there's hope."

Kendra, catching the other woman's meaning, squirmed a little. "So," she said with a little too much spirit, "Pastor Lloyd is retiring. Will there be a party in his honor?"

Opal nodded. "Sure," she said. "We're planning it for tomorrow, right after church." An odd, distant expression came into her dark eyes as she pondered, gazing past Kendra's right shoulder and into deep space. "The new fellow," she went on, "is a dead ringer for Morgan Freeman. Went to Harvard. And he's single, too. A widower, like my Willie was."

Hutch chuckled at that, but he was too busy consuming cherry crumble to make any remarks. Evidently, riding bulls took a lot out of a person, producing a desperate need for simple carbohydrates. Subtly, he slipped a bite or two to the dog.

"You've met him?" Kendra asked, mainly to make

conversation, though she was a little intrigued by Opal's sudden wistful mood.

Opal shook her head, and the gesture seemed to bring her back from wherever mental territory she'd wandered off to. "I saw his picture, though," she said, and Kendra would have sworn the woman was blushing a little, her mahogany cheeks taking on a rosy glow. "I'm on the pastoral selection committee, you know."

Hutch swallowed, drank some coffee and jammed his fork back into what remained of his cherry crumble. "You hired the man because you think he's good-looking?" he asked in a teasing tone. "Why, Opal, a person would almost get the impression that you're on the lookout for another husband."

She swatted at him, trying hard not to laugh. "You hush," she chortled, obviously embarrassed.

"I'll dance at your wedding," Hutch told her, still grinning.

"You and weddings," she said, and then made a dismissive sound, conveying faux disgust, and rose to leave the table. "There's a combination for you." She paused, sighed, and adjusted the knot at the back of her apron. "I've got a lot of cooking to do," she said, "so I'll thank you to let me get on with it."

Hutch finished the cherry crumble and carried his plate to the sink, where he dutifully rinsed it and set it in the dishwasher, along with the fork.

"I wouldn't mind getting some fresh air," he said.

Again, Kendra felt that strange, surging rush of heat. Her heart struggled up into her throat and pounded there. Was he suggesting...

"It's a beautiful day," Opal said, careful not to look in Kendra's direction. "Why don't you two take a walk or a horseback ride? I'll be glad to look after the Little Miss while you're gone, and Leviticus will be my helper."

Kendra might as well have been back on the Tilt-a-Whirl at the carnival, the way that room seemed to spin and dip around her.

A walk would probably be harmless, but she didn't *dare* go riding with Hutch because she knew where they'd end up.

At the same time, she couldn't bring herself to say no.

To say anything at all.

Hutch looked at her, one eyebrow slightly raised in question.

"Go ahead," Opal told her, blissfully unaware that she, a church-going, Bible-believing woman, was propelling Kendra straight into the dark, raging heart of sin. "Madison will be just fine. Fact is, you'll probably be back before she even wakes up from her nap."

Five minutes later, still dazed, Kendra found herself in the barn, watching as Hutch saddled horses for both of them.

Occasionally, he glanced in her direction, but no words passed between them until he'd saddled both horses and led them out into the afternoon sunshine.

There, Hutch turned to look straight into her eyes. His expression was solemn but not sad, calm but not complacent. He'd been clean-shaven that morning, but now his caramel-colored beard was coming in.

"If you want to stay behind," he told her, "now's the time to say so."

Kendra swallowed hard. Nodded.

Hutch had left his hat in the house for whatever reason, though he was still wearing the same dusty rodeo clothes as before, and he ran a hand through his hair. "You do know where we're headed?" he persisted.

Again, Kendra swallowed and nodded. She walked over to her horse, the same one she'd ridden that other time, put a foot in the stirrup and almost sprang up into the saddle. She took the reins in hand and waited for Hutch to lead the way.

He sighed, shook his head once and finally flashed a devastating grin at her. "So be it," he said, and they were off.

Kendra followed. It was as though there were two women sharing her body—one sensible and wary, the other reckless and wild.

At the moment, the latter was winning out.

Neither of them spoke as they crossed the range, though Hutch looked back at her once over his right shoulder, before urging his gelding onto the trail that twisted up the mountainside toward the hidden meadow.

Stop, turn around, go back, Sensible Kendra pleaded.

I want this man, countered Reckless Kendra. *I want him and I need him and I don't care if it's wrong.*

There will be consequences, warned her reasonable side.

She knew that was true, but it didn't stop her, didn't even slow her down.

Her mutinous body had taken over, pushing aside her fretful mind with all its dreads and worries.

The meadow was just as she remembered it, shady and secluded and, at the same time, offering a wide view of Parable and the surrounding land.

They dismounted, still without speaking, and Hutch led the horses into a patch of sweetgrass nearby, draping the reins loosely over their necks so they wouldn't trip over them, leaving them to graze.

Kendra, meanwhile, approached the curious pile of stones.

"What's this?" she asked when Hutch appeared beside her, their arms touching.

"A way of getting things out of my system, I guess," he replied.

Kendra frowned, puzzled.

He turned her to face him, resting his hands lightly beneath her elbows. "Those are my regrets," he explained, inclining his head toward the pile of stones. "Every rock represents something I'd like to change but can't. I figured stacking them in a pile was better than carrying their counterparts around in my head."

The statement made an odd kind of sense to Kendra, though at the moment, little else did.

Was she really here, in the secret meadow, alone with Hutch Carmody?

As if in answer, he cupped her chin in his hand, bent his head and kissed her. At first, it was just a light brush of his lips against hers, but then it deepened, grew hot and moist, and Kendra's arms went around his neck, while his tightened around her torso, holding her close.

For Kendra, that kiss was a fiery balm, not just to her body but to her spirit, as well. She returned it fiercely, letting go of everything but the heady sensations Hutch stirred in her, the wild needs, the treacherous joy, the sweet sorrow of knowing that life is short and precious.

"I guess that's a yes," Hutch said with a raspy chuckle when the kiss finally ended.

Kendra laughed, and they kissed again, even more hungrily this time.

They eased downward into the thick carpet of grass without their mouths parting, did battle with their tongues, pushed and tugged at each other's clothes.

Nearby, the horses grazed peacefully, saddle leather creaking now and then, their bridle fittings jingling as they raised and lowered their heads.

Birds swooped and sang, and tiny creatures scuttled through the grass, and Kendra gave herself up to Hutch, to his hands, his mouth, his husky whispers.

Time slipped away, just as their clothes had. The ground was soft under Kendra's back and their only covering was the sky.

He kissed her until she was so dizzy that the arch of blue over their heads blurred whenever she opened her eyes.

He ran his lips along the side of her neck, across her collarbone, all the while caressing her breasts, one and then the other, with a gentle, calloused hand.

Kendra gasped with pleasure and arched her back, wanting him *now,* not later.

But the excruciatingly delicious foreplay went on— he nibbled at her, everywhere, tongued her nipples until they were pebble-hard, and finally suckled.

It felt so good that she cried out, offering a single, insensible, desperate plea.

Now. Every nerve, every cell in her body seemed to scream the word.

There was, however, no hurrying Hutch Carmody, when it came to lovemaking, anyway—he continued to take his time, stroking her with his hands, exploring every curve and hollow with his lips or the tip of his tongue.

Finally, he came to the core of her femininity, and

touched the soft, moist curls with the heat of his breath, arousing her to an even higher pitch of need.

She begged.

He parted her, took her full into his mouth and sucked.

Glorious heat pounded through her like a drum beat, and her hips rose from the soft ground, seeking, seeking the warmth and wetness of his mouth. She felt his hands, strong, under her buttocks, holding her up so that he could drink from her like some sacred cup.

Passion and pleasure raged inside her, like a lightning storm, clamoring, climbing, driving her ever upward toward…heaven?

She shattered into blazing pieces, splintering across the sky.

Fireworks, she thought, as her body flexed and flexed again, reveling in wave after wave of satisfaction.

When he'd wrung the last throaty cry of release from her, Hutch lowered her gently to the ground. He knelt astraddle of her, breathing hard, and she was aware of him reaching for something nearby, tearing open a packet, putting on a condom.

Without a word, he poised himself to take her, waited the instant it took for her to nod and slide her hands along the muscular length of his back.

He was inside her in a single, powerful stroke, deep inside her, where all her dreams and secrets lived, and the sweet satisfaction she'd felt only moments before turned to fiery need.

She whispered his name, raised herself to him.

Once they'd attained a rhythm, he increased the

pace, then slowed it, now driving into her, now withdrawing almost completely.

His control amazed her, given that she'd lost hers with the first kiss.

Soon, Kendra was flailing in the grasp of an undulating, rippling climax so intense that she thought she might actually die before it ended.

Hutch murmured to her and she saw the muscles tighten along his neck and upper arms as he plunged through the final barrier and let go, giving a low, ragged shout as he spilled himself into her.

Afterward, they lay side by side in the soft grass, still breathing hard, and a soft breeze rippled over them, like a blessing.

The sky and the tree tops, out of focus before, slowly regained their color and shape, but they blurred a little, too, because Kendra's eyes were full of tears she couldn't have explained.

Hutch raised himself on one elbow, looked down at her face, brushed the moisture from one of her cheeks with the side of his thumb. But he didn't ask why she was crying and Kendra was glad, because she couldn't have explained that the things she was feeling were so big, so ferocious and so wonderful that she wasn't sure she could bear them.

He kissed her softly, briefly, this time offering solace, not passion.

They were silent for a long time, recovering, drawing themselves back together like the scattered pieces of a pair of jigsaw puzzles.

Kendra was the first to speak. "You brought a condom," she observed with a little smile.

"Just the one," Hutch replied. "Damn it."

She laughed richly, freely, openly. For the first time in a long while, she felt whole.

Her joy was bittersweet, though, because she knew it couldn't last.

CHAPTER SEVENTEEN

KENDRA'S WELL AND thoroughly loved body thrummed with residual ecstasy as she slowly, carefully put her clothes back on, determined to come away looking as though she'd never taken them off in the first place. Hutch, wearing his jeans again and shrugging into the shirt he'd discarded earlier, grinned at her.

Things like this, she thought, were so much easier for a man.

All men had to do was tuck in their shirt and zip up their jeans and they were good to go, with nobody the wiser. She, on the other hand, probably had grass in her hair, and her French braid was coming undone. And even if she got her clothes and hair right, her eyes surely glowed and her cheeks were flushed, too—both sure signs that she'd just had the best sex of her life.

Fortunately, Madison wouldn't pick up on the signals. But *Opal* might.

Hutch walked over to her, undid the braid completely, and ran splayed fingers through her hair, letting it spill down over her shoulders.

"That's better," he said, quietly grave. "My God, you're beautiful."

Kendra raised her hands, meaning to gather her hair back and replait it, having momentarily forgotten that the rubber band she'd used to secure it was lost somewhere in the grass, but Hutch stilled her, his thumbs moving in small circular caresses against her palms.

"I left the house with a braid," she told him as her normal state of quiet agitation overtook her again, "and I'm going *back* with one."

Hutch chuckled. The way he was touching her made her regret that he'd brought only one condom. With him, once had never been enough; in the old days, they'd often made love for hours at a time, falling asleep in each other's arms and waking up to make love again. And he'd already made her want him again just by touching her and standing so close.

His body was hard and hot and unequivocally male, and she could still feel the weight of it, the power and the thrust, and her own sweet victory found in complete surrender.

"Kendra," he said. His tone was raspy.

"What?" she all but snapped, flustered.

"Your hair looks fine the way it is. In fact, it looks more than fine."

She was looking around for the lost rubber band by then, but in vain. "Opal will guess—"

Hutch rested his hands on either side of her face, so she couldn't turn her head away. "Opal has *already* guessed," he said, amused. "Why do you think she offered to look after Madison so we could leave the house?"

Kendra ached with embarrassment. Of course he was right—Opal was no fool and the ploy had been a pretty obvious one, too—but on the inside, she was still soaring. Besides, for all her jitters, that reckless part of her remained very much in charge. "Awkward," she said, singsong.

Hutch laughed. "What's awkward? Nobody's judging us, Kendra—we're both grown-ups, remember?"

"*One* of us is, anyway," Kendra said, making a rueful face.

He kissed her forehead, then the tip of her nose, before lowering his hands. "Let's go," he said, "before I throw caution to the winds and take you down again, condom or no condom."

"I might have something to say about that, you know," Kendra pointed out, but she couldn't muster up any real annoyance.

"Is that a challenge?" he asked, low and easy. His right index finger traipsed lightly down her cheek, along her neck and once around her breast, in a slow, heated orbit.

Electricity jolted through her, and she jumped back a step, every bit as hot and bothered as she'd been when they first tumbled into the grass. "No," she said quickly. "It *wasn't* a challenge."

He grinned. Then he made a sweeping gesture with one arm toward the placidly waiting horses.

They each mounted up, Kendra moving quickly so he wouldn't "help."

When they got back to the barn, Hutch took care of the horses and sent Kendra inside to see if Madison had awakened from her nap yet.

She hadn't.

Opal remained in the kitchen and a delicious aroma filled the air.

"All three of you need a real supper," the older woman announced firmly. "Not more carnival food." If she'd noticed that Kendra's hair was no longer pulled back in its former tidy braid, she didn't offer a comment or give any indication that she knew anything special had happened while they were out.

Kendra was fiercely grateful for that; she wasn't ready for anyone else to know, not even Joslyn and Tara, and she told them pretty much everything.

She slipped away to the nearest powder room, washed her hands, splashed her face with cool water—her makeup was long gone but the glow made up for it—and inspected her clothes for grass stains in front of a full-length mirror.

When she came out, Madison was in the kitchen, rubbing her eyes sleepily. "Is it tomorrow?" she asked Kendra. "Did I miss the fireworks?"

Kendra swept her up, hugged her, and gave her a smacking kiss on one pudgy cheek. "It's still today," she said. "And we're going back to town for the fireworks after supper."

Madison looked greatly relieved, and wriggled in Kendra's arms, wanting to stand on her own. Even at four, she had a streak of independence running through her as wide as the Big Sky River. "Good," she said looking around the kitchen, nodding a hello at a smiling Opal. "Where's Hutch?"

So it was "Hutch" now, and not "Mr. Carmody."

Kendra wasn't sure how she felt about that—or anything else, really. Her emotions were still in a jumble, impossibly tangled. She knew the regrets would set in eventually—she could feel them circling around her, slowly closing in, like wolves waiting for a campfire to die down to embers—but for now, for tonight, she was going to let things be all right, just the way they were.

"He's in the barn," Kendra answered.

Madison, more and more awake as the moments

passed, tilted her head to one side and studied Kendra quizzically. "What happened to your hair, Mommy?"

Before Kendra could stumble out a reply, Opal came to the rescue. "I could use some help setting the table," she told the little girl, "and I know you're real good at that."

Madison lit up, allowing Opal to take her over to the sink and quickly wash her small hands with a moist paper towel.

Meanwhile, Opal's gaze met Kendra's, full of kind understanding. The woman might as well have said, "Don't worry, everything's going to be all right," her expression conveyed so much tenderness.

Hutch stepped in from outside a moment later, rolled up his shirtsleeves and went through the hand-washing ritual at the kitchen sink. Except for a certain light in his eyes, he looked like innocence personified.

After drying his hands, he took four plates down from the cupboard and set them between the knives, forks and spoons Madison had carefully arranged at each place. He might have been dealing cards, his motions were so deft.

"You ought to come to town with us," he told Opal fifteen minutes later when they were all seated at the table, enjoying her fried chicken, green beans, mashed potatoes and gravy. "Take in the fireworks."

"Thank you very much but no, sir," Opal replied briskly. "I've got a big day tomorrow and I need my beauty sleep."

Kendra sneaked a glance at Hutch and saw that his eyes were twinkling with mischief, as well as recent satisfaction. Still feeling the occasional sweet aftershock herself, Kendra blushed again.

"I knew it," he told Opal. "You've got your cap set for the new preacher."

"I do not," Opal said. "For all I know, he's a rascal. You good-looking types usually are."

He chuckled. "What do we know about this guy?" he asked. "If he comes a-courting, I need to be sure he's on the level."

"Stop it," Opal said, though she was clearly enjoying the exchange. "He's a looker and a widower and he has a divinity degree from one of the best universities in the country, and that's the sum total of my knowledge."

Hutch chewed on that, and a mouthful of chicken, for a few moments, swallowed, and went right on teasing Opal. "A Harvard man," he ruminated. "Makes me wonder why he'd want to live in a place like Parable, Montana. What's this yahoo's name?"

Opal glowered at Hutch, but her eyes were dancing behind the lenses of her old-fashioned glasses. "If you want to know that," she shot back, "just come to church tomorrow and you'll find out."

Hutch huffed out a laugh. "The last time I was there," he said, "all hell broke loose."

"We go to church sometimes," Madison put in, eager to join the banter. "Don't we, Mommy?"

"Yes," Kendra said.

"Are we going tomorrow?" Madison asked. "To see the new preacher from Harvard?"

She smiled. *A little repentance might be in order,* she thought, *for me at least.* "Unless you're too tired," she answered. "It will be very late when the fireworks get over tonight and you might need to sleep in tomorrow morning."

"Can I ride the merry-go-round again?" the child inquired, on to the next thing, like a firefly flitting from bush to branch. "I want to see if the tiger really bucks like a boy-cow."

Hutch grinned, reached out to tousle Madison's hair. "We'll have plenty of time for tiger rides," he told her. "It's still a couple more hours until it gets dark enough out to set off those fireworks."

"I might be awake at *midnight!*" Madison marveled. No doubt there were a few storybook pumpkin-coaches going through her mind, drawn by talking mice. To a small child, Kendra reflected, midnight was a magical hour.

"You might be," Kendra agreed, sure the little girl would be sound asleep on Hutch's shoulder again before the grand finale.

"Wow," Madison breathed. "Midnight is *really late.*"

"Yep," Hutch said affably with only the briefest glance in Kendra's direction, lavishing attention on his dog, instead.

Half an hour later, after Kendra had helped Opal clear the table and set the kitchen to rights—Hutch had taken Madison out to the barn to say hello to Ruffles while the cleanup was going on—the three of them were back in Hutch's truck, headed for town.

There was still plenty of light, though shadows were slowly creeping down the mountainsides to pool in the valley where Parable rested, all lit up in Christmas tree colors for the Fourth.

The man at the entrance gate to the fairgrounds flashed a black light on the backs of their hands, and Madison was thrilled to see the stamp she'd gotten that morning reappear on her skin.

"It's magic," she breathed.

Kendra loved her little girl so much in that moment that she had to restrain herself from grabbing her up and hugging her tight.

They returned to the merry-go-round—like the other rides, it was doing a brisk business because there was still at least an hour to kill before the fireworks began—though Hutch remarked that half the county was probably over at the Boot Scoot Tavern, whooping it up. After waiting in line, Madison rode the tiger, this time with Hutch standing beside her and Kendra taking pictures with her cell phone each time they went by.

It all seemed so normal, though she still had that strange sense of being two people instead of just the usual one. And those two people were definitely at odds with each other.

Are you crazy? one of them demanded from a hiding place somewhere in the back of her brain. *This is the same man who broke your heart. And just a few weeks ago, he abandoned his bride on their wedding day.*

But this second Kendra was having none of it. She wanted to live in the moment, to enjoy the delicious fantasy of being loved and wanted for just a little while longer.

By the time everybody gathered at the edge of the field next to the rodeo grounds to watch the long-awaited fireworks show, Madison could barely keep her eyes open.

She'd had a big day, this very little girl, and despite a nap and a good supper, she was beginning to run down.

Hutch held the child in his arms and they watched as colored light spattered the dark sky, bloomed into a swelling shape of blue or green, red or gold, and gracefully fell away. Even the sparks were beautiful, a rain of shimmering fire.

Kendra realized, with a start, that she was perfectly happy, alternately watching the breathtaking spectacle in the sky and the bright reflections it cast onto the up-turned faces of the people around her.

She was, in that instant, so happy that it terrified her.

It was dangerous to open her heart and her mind and her spirit to life, to a certain man, to the singular joys of being a young, healthy woman, with needs to be satisfied. Loving Madison so completely was all the risk she could bear to take—why was she pushing her luck this way? Was she greedy to want more than motherhood, more than her career?

Long before the fireworks ended and the crowds dispersed and she and Hutch and a soundly sleeping Madison were in the truck on the way to her place, Kendra had begun the lonely and singularly painful process of drawing back into herself, like a sea creature retreating into its shell.

Hutch probably sensed the change, but he didn't say anything.

When they got to her house, he lifted Madison from the car seat and carried her into the house. Subdued, Kendra led the way to the little girl's room, where he laid her gently on the bed and stepped back.

He left the room without a word and Kendra found herself listening hard for the sound of the front door opening and then closing behind him as she quickly undressed Madison, put her into a soft cotton nightgown and tucked her in with a kiss.

That night, it was Kendra who prayed.

"Thank You," she whispered.

Hutch was in the kitchen when she got there, leaning idly against one of the counters with his arms folded. He'd brought the big teddy bear inside while she was looking after Madison, and set it, like a jaunty diner, in one of the chairs at the table, a gesture that touched something deep inside Kendra and left a faint bruise in its wake. Her new boots, still in their box, were there, too, filling the room with the clean scent of leather.

"Want to tell me about it?" Hutch asked quietly without preamble.

Kendra wanted to avoid his gaze, but she couldn't seem to pull hers away. "What's to tell?" she asked with a flippancy she didn't really feel. "It's been a long haul and we're both tired, and tomorrow is another day."

"If you think we're going to pretend that nothing happened up there in the meadow this afternoon," he informed her, quietly blunt, "you're dead wrong."

"We got—carried away," Kendra said, trying to smile and failing.

"*We made love,*" Hutch said gravely. "That changes things, Kendra. At least, it does for me."

"You said it yourself," she said, careful to keep her voice down, in case Madison woke up and overheard things she couldn't be expected to understand. "We're grown-ups, not kids. We lost our heads for a little while, but now that's behind us and—"

He crossed the room in two strides, took her gently but inescapably by her upper arms, and pressed her to the wall, held her there with the intoxicatingly hard length of his body. And then he kissed her.

It was the kind of kiss that conquers a woman, lays claim to her, body and soul.

Knowing she ought to break away, Kendra kissed

him back, instead. She couldn't help it, because the old hunger, the one she'd pushed down all this time, was rushing through her again, and it was stronger than ever.

She was blushing when Hutch drew back, released her, stepped away.

Moments later, he was gone, out the door.

She heard his truck start up, drive away.

Kendra crossed the room, turned the lock and sat down in a chair at the kitchen table across from the ludicrously large pink-and-white teddy bear Hutch had won for Madison at the carnival.

It seemed to be watching her and a bit smugly at that.

"Oh, shut up," she told it. Then she sprang out of her chair again, marched into the bathroom and ran herself a hot bath.

There were too many feelings welling up inside her and they were too complicated to sort out. She felt frantic.

Kendra stripped, stepped into the tub, sank into the scented water.

She closed her eyes and instantly she was back in that mountain meadow, lying in the grass, with Hutch Carmody riding her as confidently as he'd ridden the bull at the rodeo and the tiger on the merry-go-round.

Kendra's eyes popped open in alarm, and just like that, she was at home again, in her own bathtub, up to her chin in billowing bubbles.

Realistic Kendra was back on the scene, with a vengeance, while the one that had gotten her into trouble was conspicuously absent. Wasn't *that* a fine how-do-you-do?

She soaked for a while, even tried to read the paperback she'd left within reach on the back of the toilet, but nothing worked.

She was all a-jangle.

Her grandmother's voice echoed in her head.

Now you've done it. You're nothing but a tramp, just like your mother.

Kendra got out of the tub, dried herself with a towel and pulled a nightgown on over her head. She padded into the kitchen, flipped on the light she'd turned off earlier and brewed herself a cup of raspberry tea.

The drink soothed her a little, but total emotional and physical exhaustion were the only reasons she slept at all that night. Her dreams were full of garish carnival rides, scary clowns dressed like cowboys and her grandmother, following her around, shaking a finger at her and repeating the same words over and over again.

You're nothing but a tramp, just like your mother.

The next morning, Kendra woke with a pounding headache and Madison, wearing her boots and her cowgirl hat with her nightie, jumping up and down on the bed beside her.

"Get up, Mommy," she chanted, beaming with fresh energy. "We have to go to church and look at the new preacher!"

Kendra sighed, arranged her pillows and sat up, resting against them.

"Of course we do," she said. "And stop jumping on the bed, please."

She didn't want to look at what the soles of those little boots might have left behind on her formerly pristine white eyelet bedspread.

Madison leaped, agile as a gazelle, to the floor.

Her hat was askew and her eyes were wide beneath the brim.

"Get up!" she pleaded. *"Please,* Mommy!"

Kendra sighed again, tossed back the covers and got up. She padded into the bathroom, opened the door of the medicine cabinet and shook a couple of aspirin into her palm, swallowing them with a gulp of tap water.

Madison prattled nonstop the whole time, reliving the carnival, the rodeo, the purchase of her boots and hat and the bandannas for the dogs, and finally the fireworks.

The aspirin didn't kick in for a full fifteen minutes, during which Kendra listened patiently to her daughter's continuous chatter, nodded at appropriate intervals and chopped fresh strawberries to sprinkle over cold cereal.

"I'll bet Daisy misses us," Madison said, scrambling into her chair at the table and taking her spoon in hand. "Can we go get her right after church? And then can we go back to the ranch so I can ride Ruffles?"

"Whoa," Kendra pleaded, raising both hands, palms out. "Slow down. We'll go to church, stay after for Pastor Lloyd's retirement party, and then drive out to Tara's and pick up Daisy. That's pretty much a day-full, sweetheart."

"But what about Ruffles?" Madison pressed, on the verge of whining but not quite there. "She'll be *lonesome.*"

"She won't be lonesome," Kendra replied patiently, forcing herself to eat a few bites of cereal. If she didn't, her stomach would start growling in church for sure, probably during prayers. "She has all those other horses to keep her company, not to mention Leviticus."

"But I want—"

"Madison," Kendra broke in, kindly but firmly, "we're coming *home* after we pick Daisy up, and that's the end of it."

Madison's lower lip jutted out, but, being a bright child, she didn't push the issue. Kendra didn't believe in spankings, but she wasn't above decreeing a time-out, and Madison hated those, because it meant sitting still and being quiet.

"You're mean," she said under her breath.

"A regular Simon LeGree," Kendra agreed. "Eat your breakfast."

THE REVEREND DOCTOR Walter G. Beaumont *was* a dead-ringer for Morgan Freeman, Kendra discovered when she and Madison were seated side by side in the pews later that morning, right next to Opal. He sat in a chair just behind and to the left of the main pulpit, while Pastor Lloyd delivered his farewell sermon.

It was a good message, though Kendra only heard part of it because her mind kept wandering. She hadn't really expected Hutch to show up, but her feelings about that were mixed. She was disappointed that he wasn't there, as well as relieved.

Pastor Lloyd seemed happy about his retirement, and after the services everybody gathered in the social hall adjoining the church for the party.

There was a lot of food—Opal wasn't the only member of the congregation who'd been cooking up a storm, obviously—and small gifts were presented to the out-going pastor, who eagerly introduced his replacement and said what an honor it was to have such a learned man in their midst.

Opal barely took her eyes off the Reverend Doctor Beaumont, Kendra noticed with a lot of affection and no little amusement. The man was tall, slender and graceful, beautifully dressed in a dark tailored suit, and his voice was deep and resonant, but not too loud.

He definitely wasn't the hellfire-and-brimstone type, Kendra concluded with relief. She did wonder, though, as Hutch had at supper the night before, what could have attracted this highly educated and obviously sophisticated man to a small, mostly rural community like Parable.

The party was winding down by the time Pastor Lloyd asked Dr. Beaumont to say a few words.

He didn't need a pulpit or a platform; his voice rolled over them like controlled thunder, quiet but forceful, even commanding.

"It's an honor to join this fine community," he said, revealing strikingly white teeth as he smiled, his gaze sweeping, warm, over the assemblage. "I look forward to getting to know all of you, and I look forward to the fishing, too, which I hear is mighty good around these parts."

A twitter of laughter rippled through the friendly crowd. After church, most of the gathering would be heading back to the fairgrounds to shop in the exhibition hall and enjoy some of the carnival rides, but their affection for Pastor Lloyd, and their wish to make the new man feel welcome, kept them there.

Looking around, Kendra felt a rush of affection for these people—*her* people—all of them hardworking, doing their best to lead good and honest lives, glad to live in a place like Parable, where the fishing was good and the Fourth of July was a big, big deal.

This is home, Kendra thought, soothed. *I was right to bring Madison here. No matter what else happens, this is where we belong.*

By then, the children were getting restless—many of them had been to Sunday school and attended the main service afterward, thereby exhausting their limited supply of patience—and the crowd began to thin.

In her turn, Kendra said goodbye to Pastor Lloyd and shook hands with Dr. Beaumont, then rounded up an overexcited Madison and headed for the parking lot.

They drove out to Tara's house, chatted with her for a few minutes, collected Daisy and headed back home.

There, Madison changed out of her Sunday school dress and into shorts, sneakers and a top, and she and Daisy dashed outside to play in the yard. Kendra, still in the simple blue sundress she'd worn to church, kicked off her dressy shoes and went to sit on the porch step, watching them.

She half hoped Hutch would show up, or simply call, and half hoped he wouldn't.

She needed time and space so she could get some perspective, sort through what had happened up on the mountainside the day before. At the same time, she wanted him close again.

The sound of her ringing cell phone interrupted her thoughts; she slipped into the house, retrieved it from the counter where she'd left it before church, and answered, "This is Kendra Shepherd."

"Hello, Kendra Shepherd," said a cheerful female voice that seemed vaguely familiar. "This is Casey Elder. Walker Parrish gave me your number?"

"Yes," Kendra said, surprised to find herself a little

starstruck and right on the verge of gushing. "Hello, Ms. Elder."

"Call me Casey," was the perky response, "and I'll call you Kendra. How's that?"

Kendra smiled. "That's fine," she said, already liking the woman, sight unseen. "Walker tells me you're thinking of moving to Parable."

"That's right," Casey confirmed. She seemed to radiate energy, even over the telephone, which was pretty impressive, since Kendra knew the singer had been on tour with her band and probably performed the day before. "I don't mind telling you, he makes the place sound pretty darn good."

"It's a great town," Kendra said.

"I'd like to come and have a look," Casey replied. "Would Tuesday be all right?"

"Sure," Kendra answered, delighted. They agreed to meet at Kendra's office at ten-thirty Tuesday morning, said their goodbyes and hung up.

She still had the cell phone in her hand when she stepped outside, smiling to find Madison and Daisy both lying side by side in the grass, on their backs. Daisy's four feet were raised, bent at the joints.

"We're remembering the fireworks," Madison explained.

It being early afternoon, the sky was clear and blue and bright with sunlight.

"I see," Kendra said.

"Daisy didn't see them," the little girl clarified, "but I told her all about it."

The phone rang in Kendra's hand just as she took her previous seat on the porch step, and a little trill of excitement went through her.

Let it be Hutch.

Don't *let it be Hutch.*

"Hey," Joslyn said. "It's me."

"Hey," Kendra replied.

"How was the big date?" Joslyn asked.

Kendra bit her lower lip, considering her answer. She wanted to argue that her time with Hutch *hadn't* been a date, but that would be pure denial. After all, she'd wound up making love with the man up there on the side of Big Sky Mountain.

"Fine," she hedged.

Joslyn laughed. "Fine? There's a lot you aren't telling me, I'm guessing."

Kendra sighed, but she was smiling. Even now, hours and hours after the fact, she still felt the lingering effects of several powerful releases. "And I'm not about to tell you, either," she said. "At least, not over the phone."

"Great," Joslyn answered. "Why don't you and Madison come out here for a visit and some supper? Shea and the baby will keep Madison occupied, and you can tell me *everything.*"

"I don't think I'm ready for that," Kendra said.

"Something happened," Joslyn insisted gently.

"Yes," Kendra admitted. "And I'm positive I'm going to regret it."

"Don't be so sure," Joslyn counseled. She sounded delighted. "So you'll come for supper?"

"Not tonight," Kendra said. "Madison had a big day yesterday and she needs time to settle down a little."

"I understand," Joslyn replied. "Still up for being Trace's godmother? Slade and I are thinking of scheduling the christening for next Sunday, after church, if the new pastor agrees."

"Of course I'm still up for it," Kendra said. "I'm honored."

"Slade is asking Hutch to be Trace's godfather," Joslyn ventured. She was stepping lightly now, Kendra could tell. "Is that a problem for you?"

"No," was Kendra's reply. "And even it was, it wouldn't be my call."

"I might come in to the office for a few hours tomorrow," Joslyn went on. "I'd bring Trace along, of course."

"Of course," Kendra agreed.

"You're stonewalling me," Joslyn accused, good-naturedly. "Don't you get it, Kendra? I'm dying for information here!"

Kendra laughed. "Put your curiosity on life support," she said. "Madison is within earshot, and anyway I'm not *about* to fill you in over the phone."

Joslyn gave an exaggerated sigh. "All right, then," she said. "I guess I'll have to wait until tomorrow."

"Guess so," Kendra acknowledged, still smiling. She didn't plan on sharing any of the intimate details, but she was actually eager to discuss what had happened up there in the meadow yesterday, with her best friend anyway. Joslyn was levelheaded, nonjudgmental and totally trustworthy, and talking things over with her sounded like a good idea.

Maybe she, Kendra, could get some perspective on the situation. If indeed it *was* a situation. Men didn't take the same attitude toward sex as women did—there was no implicit commitment.

Still, hadn't Hutch said, just the night before, after that dazzling kiss against her kitchen wall, that making love had changed things?

Time would tell, Kendra thought as she said goodbye to her friend and let the phone rest in her lap while she watched her daughter and Daisy play in shafts of summer sunlight.

CHAPTER EIGHTEEN

GIVE THE WOMAN some space, Hutch counseled himself silently that bright Sunday afternoon, as he kept busy grooming horses in the barn, Leviticus close by. He was restless, despite his own advice, wanting to head straight for town, find Kendra and—what?

Talk to her? Make love to her again?

Instinct, as well as knowing Kendra so long and so well, warned that she might run for the hills if he came on too strong, too soon.

No, he'd contain his impatience, go slowly. He'd lost her once, and he didn't want to risk losing her again.

He loved her—that was the only thing he was really sure of.

He was finishing up, wondering what else he could turn his hand to that would use up some more daylight, as well as personal energy, when he heard a rig pull up outside the barn. Leviticus, not much of a watchdog, gave a halfhearted woof.

Probably Opal, back from church, he thought, headed for the doorway. He was grinning a little, remembering how she'd left the house all spiffed-up that morning, flatly denying that she was out to impress the new preacher.

When he stepped out into the sunlight, though, it was Boone he saw, getting out of his squad car. Both boys tumbled out from behind the grate that separated the front seat of the cruiser from the back, grinning a howdy at Hutch.

He chuckled and gave them each a light squeeze to the shoulder—they were dressed up, and it saddened him a little, because these were probably their traveling clothes. Boone had said they'd be leaving today, but Hutch hadn't given the matter much thought until now.

"They want to say goodbye to you before they catch the bus back to Missoula," Boone said, looking as lame as he sounded. He was wan, and he hadn't shaved, and Hutch would have sworn the man was wearing the same set of clothes he'd had on yesterday at the rodeo.

The taller boy, Griff, looked solemn. "We don't want to leave," he said. "But Dad says we have to."

"Uncle *Bob* is our dad," the smaller one, Fletch, insisted staunchly.

Hutch stole a sidelong glance at Boone's face and saw that his friend looked as though he'd just been sucker-punched, square in the gut. He waited for Boone to correct the boy, to claim him, as it were, but he didn't do that.

"Well," Hutch said, holding on to his grin because it was threatening to slip away, "I hope you'll come back for another visit real soon."

Griff's dark brown eyes were bright with angry sorrow as he looked up at Hutch. Something in his expression begged him to step in, change the direction of things, get Boone to see reason, to understand what he was throwing away just because he was scared.

The backs of Hutch's own eyes stung like fire; he hated the helplessness he felt. Bottom line, it was

Boone's call whether the boys stayed or went, and he had no right to interfere—not in front of them, at least.

He'd have *plenty* to say to Boone in private, when he got the chance.

Boone consulted his watch. "We'd better go," he said without looking at his sons. "You don't want to miss the bus."

"Yes, we do," Griff argued. "We want to stay here with you, Dad."

"No, we *don't,*" Fletch put in, but his lower lip wobbled and his eyes glistened.

Boone sighed, and his gaze met Hutch's. *Help me out, here, will you?* That was what his expression said, as clearly as if he'd spoken aloud.

"You know what I think," Hutch replied carefully, quietly. "And you can be sure we'll discuss it later."

Fletch wasn't through talking, evidently. He tensed, like he was thinking about kicking Boone square in the shin, looked up at him, squinting against the sun and his whole body trembling, blurted, "You don't want us anyway! You can't wait to get rid of us!"

Boone went pale and, after unclenching the hinges of his jaws, he replied, "We've already had this discussion, Fletcher." He paused, shook his head, tossed a grim, thanks-for-nothing look Hutch's way. "Get in the car, both of you."

After one last imploring look at Hutch, Griff put his hand to his little brother's back and shoved him in the direction of the squad car.

"Damn it, Boone, this is *wrong,*" Hutch growled, as soon as the boys were inside the vehicle again, with the doors shut. "Sending those kids away is the same thing as saying straight out that Fletch has it right, you don't want them."

Boone looked at him in stricken silence and for a long time, but in the end, he didn't answer. He just gave a curt nod of farewell, turned his back and walked away.

Hutch watched the retreating squad car until it was clean out of sight.

Then he went inside the house and, with Leviticus close on his heels, wandered uselessly from room to room, too restless to light anywhere and do anything constructive.

When he'd vented some of the steam that had been building up in him since Boone's visit, he took a shower, put on fresh clothes and headed for town in the new truck he'd decided to go ahead and buy.

He still intended to keep his distance from Kendra, much as he wanted to walk right up to her and tell her straight out that he still loved her—had never *stopped* loving her—and meant to marry her if she'd have him.

But he knew all too well what she'd say—that they'd just gotten "carried away," up there on the mountainside. That he was still on the rebound from Brylee and in no position to make any sort of long-term commitment.

He was sure she loved him—her body had told him things she wouldn't or couldn't put into words—but that didn't mean she trusted him. And without trust, without respect, love just wasn't enough, no matter how strong it was.

So he had to wait. Bide his time.

And that was going to be just about the hardest thing he'd ever done.

The carnival was shutting down when he drove by

the fairgrounds a few minutes later, the rodeo arena was dark, the vendors outside the exhibition hall loading up what they hadn't sold over the weekend.

It all made him feel lonely, as though a small, special world had opened, just for that brief time, and was now closing again. Shutting him out.

He might have gone to the Boot Scoot for a beer and maybe a game of pool, just to get his mind off things, but it was always closed on Sundays. Even the Butter Biscuit locked up and went dark once the after-church rush was over.

He turned his thoughts to Boone and the sorry situation he'd gotten himself into by letting go of his kids after Corrie died. Hutch started thinking about fear, and what it did to people. What it cost them.

It was a short leap, of course, from his friend's worries about being able to take proper care of a couple of growing boys to the things, he, Hutch, was afraid of. One of them was commitment—he'd be staking his heart on an uncertain outcome if he got married, and if things went sour, he'd lose half his ranch in the divorce settlement. Whisper Creek was *part* of him, and without the whole of it, he'd be crippled on the inside.

The other thing he was afraid of was the water tower.

So he drove there, parked in the tall grass, twilight gathering around him, and looked up. The ladder dangled, rickety as ever, from the side, but something was different, too.

Shea, Slade's teenage stepdaughter, peered down at him, white-faced, from the heights. She appeared to be alone, and a quick glance around confirmed that she *had* undertaken this rite of passage on her own.

"Hi, Hutch," she called down, her voice a little shaky.

"What the hell are you doing up there, Shea?" he snapped, in no mood for small talk.

"I'm—not sure," she replied. "You won't tell Dad and Joslyn, will you?"

"No promises," Hutch said. "Get down here, damn it."

Shea's voice wavered, and even from that distance, with her face a snow-white oval, he could see that she was crying. "I—can't. I tried, but I'm too scared."

Hutch felt the back of his shirt dampen with sweat, and his gut twisted itself into a hard knot. "Come on, Shea," he went on, more gently now. "You got up there in the first place, didn't you? That means you can get down."

"Climbing up wasn't scary," she told him. "Climbing *down* is a whole other matter."

Hutch swore under his breath, moved closer to the ladder. The rungs were old, some of them missing, others hanging by a single rusty nail.

He knew then what he had to do, but that didn't mean he wanted to do it. He kept his gaze fixed straight ahead, because he knew if he looked from side to side, even though he was still standing flat-footed on the ground, he'd feel like he was trying to walk the perimeter of the Tilt-a-Whirl while it was spinning full-throttle.

"Okay," he heard himself say, as if from a distance. Say, the next county. "Hang on. I'll come up there, and we'll climb down together."

"All—all right," Shea agreed.

Terror aside, the approach didn't make a lot of sense to Hutch—Shea probably didn't weigh more than a hundred and ten pounds, while he tipped the scales at an even one-eighty. Expecting that ladder to hold both of them at the same time was anti-logic, pure and simple.

Still, he'd been where Shea was once. He knew she was frozen with fear, knew she needed another human being within touching distance, someone to be with her, talk her down.

Just as Slade Barlow had once done for him.

He closed his eyes for a moment, sucked in a harsh breath and started up that ladder.

He kept his gaze upward, on Shea's face as she leaned out over the edge of the flimsy catwalk, looking down at him. Her eyes were enormous and awash in tears.

"Easy now," he said, addressing himself as much as Shea. "Just take it real easy, sweetheart. You'll be standing on solid ground again in no time."

"You're going to tell my dad," Shea fretted.

The remark lightened the moment, brought on a slight smile that loosened Hutch's tight lips a little. His palms felt slick where he gripped the splintery side rails of that ladder, and his stomach shinnied up into the back of his throat like it meant to fight its way right out of him.

"No, I'm not going to tell your dad," he replied evenly, still climbing. One rung, then another, and for God's sake, don't look down. "*You* are."

"He'll kill me," Shea said.

Better him than a fifty-foot fall from a water tower, Hutch thought, but what he actually said was, "If I were you, I'd worry about that later."

He was almost at the top now, and there was a certain dizzy triumph in that, but he still couldn't bring himself to look anywhere but at Shea, the closest thing he had to a niece.

"Now what?" Shea asked.

A reasonable question, Hutch reflected. "Come on out onto the ladder," he said. "I'm right here with you."

As if he could catch her if she fell.

The things Slade had said to him, way back when he was in Shea's predicament and scared half out of his wits, shouldered their way into his head and tumbled right out over his tongue.

"You can do this," he said quietly. "It's just one step, and then another, and before you know it, we'll both be off this thing."

Shea hesitated, then swung a blue-jeaned leg out over the edge, found a rung with her foot, pushed on it a little to make sure it was sound.

"Easy," Hutch said. "Slow and easy."

Shea was on the ladder, but she clung there for a moment, looking as though she might not move again. "I'm so scared," she whimpered.

"That's okay," Hutch reasoned. "Just take another step. One more, Shea."

He moved down a few rungs to give her room.

One of them split when he stepped on it, and he almost fell, felt slivers digging into the palms of his hands and the undersides of his fingers as he held on, found his footing.

"Don't put your weight on any one rung until you're sure it will hold," he told her calmly, even though he felt like a lone sock tumbling round and round in a clothes dryer. Tentatively, she took another step.

Sweat ran down over Hutch's forehead and stung

like acid in his eyes. "That's it," he said evenly. "You're doing fine."

The descent was a long one—several more rungs broke along the way, under Shea's feet as well as Hutch's—but they finally made it.

Hutch swayed, feeling an uncanny urge to kiss the ground.

Shea threw her arms around him. "What if you hadn't been here?" she whispered.

He hugged her once, then stepped back to look into her tear-stained, bloodless face, taking an avuncular hold on her shoulders. "You'd have made it down on your own eventually," he said, though he wasn't sure that was true. "Are you all right?"

She nodded, hugging herself now, even though the evening was warm. "Thanks," she murmured. "Thanks for showing up when you did, and for helping me."

"Let's get you home," Hutch said. Since he hadn't seen a car around, he knew the girl must have come on foot.

"Dad and Joslyn are over at Grands' house with the baby," she explained. "For Sunday supper."

"We'll head for Callie's, then," Hutch told her.

"Do I still have to tell them what I did?"

"Yep," Hutch answered, opening the passenger door of the truck so she could scramble inside.

"Why?"

"Because you do," Hutch replied when he was behind the wheel with the engine started. "Otherwise, it's a secret and I can't be part of that, Shea. Your dad and I have our differences of opinion now and again, but he *is* my brother, he loves you, and he has a right to know what you're up to." He made a wide turn and they bumped back out onto the dirt road that led to the water tower. "What were you thinking, anyhow, climbing up there?"

It was a rhetorical question, a conversation-starter, really. There *was* no good reason for pulling a stunt like that, but kids did it, year after year, decade after decade, generation after generation.

"I did it because I didn't want to be afraid of it anymore," Shea said.

"I hope that doesn't mean you plan on a repeat performance," Hutch answered, biting back a grin. Damned if the kid didn't have a point—*he* wasn't scared of it anymore, either.

"That," Shea said with a tremulous smile, "would be overkill. Once was enough."

"More than enough," Hutch confirmed.

A few minutes later, they pulled into the parking lot in front of Callie Barlow's Curly Burly Hair Salon. Slade immediately appeared in the doorway of the add-on where Callie lived.

"Tell him," Hutch reiterated as Slade walked toward them, looking puzzled.

Shea sighed dramatically, opened her door and hopped to the ground. Hutch got out, too.

"I climbed the water tower," Shea confessed in a breathless rush, "and then I got scared and I froze and Hutch came up to get me. Am I grounded?"

"You are *so* grounded," Slade told her, cocking a thumb over his shoulder to indicate that she ought to go into the house. All the while, though, Slade was watching Hutch.

When they were alone in that dusty parking lot, Slade nodded to him. "Obliged," he said. He, of all people, knew what climbing that damned ladder had meant for Hutch. He'd have ridden the devil's own bull first, if that would have gotten him out of it.

They shook hands, and Hutch was reminded of the splinters he'd have to remove when he got home.

"See you," he said, turning to get back in the truck.

"Hold on a second," Slade said. "I've got something to ask you."

Hutch turned his head. Waited.

"Joslyn and I—well—we'd like you to be Trace's godfather, if you're willing. The ceremony's next Sunday, after church."

Hutch was moved by the request, but he didn't want it to show. "I'm willing," he said, his voice a little huskier than usual. "But you know how it is with me and churches. Lightning might strike or the roof could fall in."

Slade chuckled. "I'll chance it if you will," he said.

"I'll be there," Hutch told his half brother. "Just let me know what time—and promise me I won't have to rent another tux."

"Just dress the way you normally would," Slade said, his grin lingering. "And Hutch?"

Hutch had the driver's door open and he was already on the running board. "Yeah?"

"Thanks," Slade told him. "For helping Shea out, I mean."

Hutch wasn't wearing a hat, but he tugged at the imaginary brim just the same. "Somebody did the same for me once," he said and got into the truck.

He headed for home, feeling like a different man from the one who'd left it.

BY TUESDAY MORNING, Kendra had largely recovered her
equilibrium. Discussing the Hutch situation with Joslyn
the day before, here at the office, had helped a lot.

Now the storefront space buzzed with anticipatory
vibes—even Daisy, who had come to work with Kendra as usual, seemed to sense it.

Sure enough, promptly at ten twenty-five, a powder-
blue sports car nosed into a parking space out front and
a small woman, wearing jeans, an oversize T-shirt, a
baseball cap and sunglasses got out and stood waiting
on the sidewalk while Walker parked his truck a few
slots over.

Reaching her side, he kissed Casey lightly on the
cheek, the way he might have kissed his sister, Brylee,
and then held the office door open for her.

Tendrils of Casey's legendary head of red hair were
escaping from beneath the cap as she stepped inside,
and an impish little smile played on her famous mouth.

She enjoyed being in disguise, that was obvious, so
Kendra didn't blurt out the first thought that popped
into her head, which was, *I'd have recognized you anywhere.*

Walker, as if guessing Kendra's thoughts, winked at
her over the top of Casey's head.

Recalling what he'd told her—that Casey's two children were his, as well—Kendra's curiosity ratcheted up
a notch, but of course asking about that was out of the
question. Whatever had gone on between Walker and
Casey was their own business, not hers.

But she still wondered.

A lot.

She smiled and extended a hand to Casey. "Hello,"
she said. "I'm Kendra."

"Casey," the other woman replied, shaking Kendra's hand. Her grip was surprisingly strong for such a small person. "Glad to meet you," came out sounding more like, *Gladta meet ya,* since Casey had a Southern accent.

"She thinks she's fooling everybody," Walker told Kendra, grinning. "This is the Casey version of low-key."

Casey removed her sunglasses, revealing her striking green eyes and long lashes, and made a face at Walker. "Let a person have a little fun, why don't you?" she retorted lightly. Then she spotted Daisy and went straight over to her, patting the dog's head and talking to her as she would any friend.

Daisy was instantly besotted with Casey, as she had been when she first met Walker. Kendra took this as a good sign, since she believed dogs and other domesticated animals were excellent judges of character.

"I sure am ready to have a look at that house," Casey announced. "I've been excited ever since Walker sent me the pictures."

"We'll take my car," Kendra said, picking up her keys. She'd vacuumed the interior thoroughly that morning before taking Madison to preschool, and covered the backseat with an old blanket for the trip over, removing it after she'd unloaded the dog, all to prevent messing it up again.

"That's fine," Casey said agreeably, and they all left by the back way, since Kendra's car was parked behind the building, and besides, she wanted to draw as little attention as possible.

Daisy wasn't happy about being left behind and

whined pitifully, trying to squeeze through the crack when Kendra went to close the door.

"Oh, let her come along with us," Casey urged.

"She sheds," Kendra said.

"I don't mind," Casey replied.

Kendra nodded and brought Daisy along, already liking Casey Elder for her down-to-earth attitude. She'd fit in well here in Parable—if she decided to stay.

Casey rode in back with Daisy, crammed into the middle because of Madison's car seat, while Walker took the front passenger side. Kendra followed side streets to Rodeo Road, but people peered at them curiously as they passed just the same from yards and sidewalks.

Any stranger would have attracted their attention, but they might well recognize this one—even in disguise, it seemed to Kendra, Casey Elder radiated a sort of down-home confidence that marked her as somebody special.

They reached the mansion without incident and, since the work was done, there were no cleaning or painting crews around.

"Holy *smokes,*" Casey said in her trademark drawl, standing at the front gate and looking up. "That is *some* house."

Kendra was already unlocking the front door, Daisy at her side. "You be good," she whispered to the dog.

Inside the massive entryway, Kendra went over the house's best features, but she sensed that Walker and Casey wanted to explore the place on their own, so she left them to it, saying she and Daisy would be on the screened-in porch in back, or in the yard.

Casey smiled and nodded, and then she and Walker set out on their self-guided tour.

Kendra went on through the middle of the sprawling house and out the back door, taking Daisy with her. She let Daisy sniff her way around the yard while she checked the flower beds—the gardeners she'd hired were doing a good job of weeding and watering—and unlocked the door to the guest cottage, so Casey could look it over when she was ready.

She picked a bouquet of zinnias in the garden, planning to put them in the center of her kitchen table over at the rental house later on, and then just stood there, looking around, waiting to feel the sadness of letting go. After all, this had been her dream house once; she'd loved it, lived in it with pride. There were a lot of happy memories, from before and after the break-up with Jeffrey—she'd played here as a child, of course, taken refuge here, and much later, Joslyn had lived in the cottage, when she'd first come back to Parable and found herself falling hard for Slade Barlow—the last man on earth Joss would have chosen. Later still, Kendra had thrown a huge party right there in the backyard, with dancing and caterers and the whole works, to welcome Tara when she'd bought the chicken farm the year before.

No sadness came over her, though.

She knew, standing there with a colorful bouquet of summer flowers in her hands, that Casey would buy this house and make it a home. She would raise her children here.

And that was all well and good.

This house had been Jeffrey's, really—he'd been the one to pay for it, to furnish and maintain it, even after they were divorced. Now it was going to change hands, and the money from the sale would go into a trust fund for Madison, Jeffrey's child, as it should.

Kendra felt a lot of peace in those moments, thinking about all the changes that had taken place in her life since she'd first seen this house, as a lost little girl, hungry to belong somewhere, to be wanted and welcome.

And she *had* been welcome here, with Opal and Joslyn and Joslyn's laughing, generous mother.

But she wasn't that unwanted child anymore. She was a grown woman, whole and strong, with a daughter of her own to love and bring up to the best of her ability. She liked her life, liked who she'd become, knew for sure and at long last that she'd be happy from now on, with or without Hutch Carmody, because she'd *decided* to be.

It was time to leave her fears and doubts behind and go forward, expecting good things to happen, knowing she could cope with the bad ones.

After half an hour or so, Casey and Walker joined her in the yard.

Casey was beaming. "It's perfect," she told Kendra, bending to stroke Daisy's gleaming golden head when the dog approached, wagging her tail. "Where do I sign?"

Kendra glanced at Walker, then looked at Casey again. "Don't you want to think about it for a while?" she asked. As many houses as she'd sold over the course of her career, she'd never had an instant offer like this one.

"Heck, no," Casey replied exuberantly. "It's just what I want. Why wait?"

That was it.

There was no haggling, no having the place inspected, no anything.

Casey signed a contract when they got back to the office, wrote an enormous deposit check to show good faith and announced that the sooner the deal closed, the better, because she wanted to get her children settled in Parable before school started.

Kendra promised to speed things along in every way she could.

After Walker and Casey were gone, she jumped up and down in the middle of the office and whooped for joy, causing Daisy to slink under a desk and peer out at her with wary eyes.

That made her laugh, and she spoke soothingly to the dog until she came out of her hiding place.

Presently, Kendra gave up on the whole idea of working—there wasn't much to do, anyway—and, after locking Casey's mongo check away in a desk drawer, she summoned Daisy, locked up and returned to her car.

The zinnias she'd picked at the mansion rested on the passenger seat, a damp paper towel wrapped around their stems, reminding Kendra of the fireworks on Saturday night, colorful flowers blooming in the sky and melting away in dancing sparks.

She drove to the Pioneer Cemetery, parked, picked up the zinnias and, leaving Daisy in the car with a window rolled down so she'd have plenty of air, walked along the rows of graves until she came to her grandmother's final resting place.

Eudora Shepherd, the simple stone read, and the dates of her birth and death were inscribed beneath it. No husband was buried nearby, no family members at all.

Her grandmother had been alone in the world, for all intents and purposes.

Kendra crouched and laid the zinnias gently at the base of the dusty headstone.

"You did the best you could," she said very softly, as the breeze played in her hair. "It must have been hard, taking in a child at your age, with money always running short and trouble coming at you from every direction, but you let me stay with you when Mom left, and that was what was important. You fed and clothed me and kept a roof over my head, and I'm grateful for that, Grandma. I'm really, truly grateful."

Kendra stood up straight again, her eyes dry, her heart quiet.

At long last, she'd truly let go, stopped wishing the past could be different. All that really mattered, she realized, was now, what she did, what she thought, what she felt *now*.

She said goodbye to her grandmother, to all the things that had been and shouldn't have, and all the things that should have been, but weren't. She said goodbye to Jeffrey, and goodbye to the reckless boy Hutch had been when she first fell in love with him.

And "hello" to the man he had become.

She was in no rush, though. Things would unfold as they were supposed to, and she was open to that.

HUTCH SADDLED REMINGTON and rode up to the mountainside alone that morning after assigning the ranch crew to various tasks for the day.

He dismounted, left the horse to graze and walked toward the rock pile, pausing briefly in the place where he and Kendra had made love the previous Saturday afternoon.

He smiled. It had been good—their lovemaking—because it had been right. Not to mention, long overdue, from his viewpoint, anyway.

He went on to the stone monument he'd built in fury, in pain, in frustration, lifted up one of the heavier stones, and set it on the ground.

"It's over, old man," he told his dead father, though only the birds and the breeze and his favorite horse were around to hear. "I'm through hating you for not being who I needed you to be. You were who you were. I don't mind saying, though, that I want to be a different kind of man. If Kendra agrees, I mean to make her my wife. I'll love her until the day I die, and maybe after that, too, and I'll love that little girl of hers like she's my own."

Hutch began to feel a little foolish then, talking to a dead man, and anyway he'd said what he wanted to say.

One by one, he tossed aside the rocks that made up that pile and finally stood on level ground.

CHAPTER NINETEEN

HUTCH DIDN'T SEE Kendra again until the day of little Trace Carmody Barlow's christening, when he showed up at the church in a pair of slacks, a white shirt and a lightweight sports jacket with a secret tucked into one pocket for later.

Most of the congregation had stayed on after the regular service for the special ceremony, and Hutch was mildly uncomfortable, stealing the occasional anxious glance at the ceiling, willing it to hold.

The new pastor, Dr. Beaumont, opened with a prayer.

Hutch bowed his head, like everybody else, but his eyes were partway open the whole time, drinking in the sight of Kendra standing next to him and wearing a green dress made of some soft fabric that looked supple to the touch.

When the prayer was over, Kendra opened her eyes, caught him looking at her and smiled slightly.

Dr. Beaumont took the baby boy gently from Joslyn's arms, holding him securely and baptizing him with a sprinkle of water, in the name of the Father, and the Son, and the Holy Spirit.

Promises were made all around.

There was another prayer; Slade was holding the infant now, looking as though he might just bust open with love and pride. His resemblance to the old man was stronger than ever, except, Hutch noticed with a slight jolt, for the quiet self-assurance in his eyes. That was the difference—Slade was fine with being Slade, taking life as it came, but their father had seen it as a battle instead, something to survive and overcome, and the effort of doing all that had used up all he had to give.

The formal part of the christening ended and the small but enthusiastic crowd was dispersing. Now, there would be a celebration picnic on the grounds of the Pioneer Cemetery.

Hutch went over there ahead of time and wound up standing at the foot of his dad's grave.

There was nothing to resolve, really; he'd made peace with John Carmody, once and for all, by taking down that monument up at the meadow, rock by rock.

Resentment by resentment, hurt by hurt.

All that was gone now, scattered, just like the stones.

Still, it seemed right to pause and silently pay his respects, because in spite of it all, he'd loved his father, known all along on some level that the old man had given what he had in him to give.

Folks started arriving right away, filling the picnic tables with food, kids running around, playing, adults talking and laughing in the shade of the trees.

Out of the corner of his eye, Hutch saw Slade heading in his direction. He'd taken off his suit jacket, Slade had, and the sleeves of his white shirt were rolled up.

He came to stand beside Hutch.

"You doing all right?" he asked, his voice husky.

"I'm just fine," Hutch answered honestly. "How about you?"

"Never better," Slade replied. "I've got everything a man could ask for and more."

Hutch looked down at the fancy headstone, bearing their father's name, along with the dates of his birth and death. It was hard to believe that a man's whole life could fit between two sets of words and numbers like that, symbolically or not, but there it was.

John Carmody had been born, lived his life and died.

And behind a single dash, chiseled in stone, was the whole story, much of which they'd never know.

"He should have acknowledged you sooner, Slade," Hutch said without looking at his brother. "Treated you better."

Slade considered that for a few moments. "He gave me life. Maybe that was all he could manage. And he knew Callie would raise me right."

Hutch merely sighed.

Slade rested a hand on his shoulder. "There's a party going on over there under the trees," he reminded Hutch. "How about joining in?"

Hutch lifted his head, grinned when he saw Madison running toward him in a polka-dot dress, her arms open wide.

He scooped her up when she reached him, carried her as he walked alongside Slade. She chattered in his ear the whole way, going on about how she'd missed him and Mommy had, too, and saying she wanted to ride Ruffles again so she'd be ready to carry a flag at the rodeo and compete in the barrel racing when she was bigger.

Kendra, seeing them, broke away from the gathering.

Madison, spotting Shea nearby, squirmed in Hutch's arms and he set her down. She ran toward the older girl with barely a glance at Kendra, and Shea greeted the little girl with a bright smile and a giggle.

Hutch and Kendra, meanwhile, stood a few feet apart, the grass rippling all around them like a low tide, just looking at each other.

Figuring that he'd put this conversation off long enough already, Hutch cleared his throat and moved in closer, cupping her elbows in his hands. She smelled of lavender soap and sunshine, and her eyes were as clear and green as sea glass.

"I love you, Kendra," he said, on a swell of emotion that made the words come out sounding hoarse. "Maybe it's too soon to say it—hell, maybe it's too *late,* I don't know—but it's true." He reached into his coat pocket, brought out the small velvet box, opened it with a motion of his thumb. His great-grandmother's engagement ring was inside—a simple but elegant concoction of diamonds and rubies. After Joslyn had done a little detective work so it would fit Kendra, he'd had it sized, cleaned and polished at the jeweler's. Now, it caught fire in the sunlight.

Kendra's eyes widened as she looked at the ring, but she didn't say anything right away, and the next few moments were some of the longest of Hutch's life. They'd traveled a rocky road, the two of them, and while he knew she loved him, he wasn't sure she'd be willing to throw in with him for the long haul.

"Are you asking me to marry you?" she finally asked very softly.

Hutch was only vaguely aware of the nearby crowd. For him, time had stopped and Kendra was all there was to the universe.

"Yes," he managed at last. "If you feel the same as I do, that is."

She smiled. "I've loved you since we were kids, Hutch," she told him. "That hasn't changed."

"Then you'll marry me?"

She stepped in close, put her arms around his neck, and looked up into his eyes. "I'll marry you," she agreed quietly. "When we're both ready."

"I'm ready *now,*" Hutch told her. God knew *that* was the truth in its entirety.

She laughed. "There are things we have to work out first," she reasoned. "Plans and decisions to make. We have to consider Madison, for a start."

He wanted to adopt Madison, raise her as a Carmody, but this wasn't the place to talk about that. He'd already jumped the gun by declaring himself and shoving a ring at Kendra, in a graveyard of all places, with half the town looking on. This time around, he wasn't going to botch everything, like he had before.

She stepped back and offered him her left hand, and he took the ring out of the box and slid it onto her finger.

He kissed her then, and the town of Parable applauded from the picnic tables under the trees.

One month later...

Opal Dennison sat up straight in her new favorite pew, one that afforded her the best possible view of the pastor, Dr. Walter Beaumont. She'd taken it over the first time he preached and laid claim to it every Sunday since.

Today, on this bright August afternoon, Hutch Carmody was up front, in exactly the same place he'd stood at his *last* wedding, with Boone beside him as best man, just like before.

The church was packed with guests once again and, since the organ music hadn't started up yet, folks were buzzing with excitement and speculation, most of them wondering, unless Opal missed her guess, if history would repeat itself.

She settled in, Joslyn's baby safe in the infant carrier beside her, since Joslyn and Tara, being bridesmaids, were at the rear of the church, waiting for the ceremony to begin. Slade was back there, too, fixing to give Kendra away, though she was still out of sight, except for a spill of shimmering lace, part of her magnificent dress.

Turning a little, Opal saw Slade's gaze connect with Joslyn's, and it seemed to her that their two souls glowed right through their skin, lighting up their faces and surrounding them with a shared aura.

She smiled to herself, turned her attention back to the groom, waiting up there by the altar with Walter, who looked resplendent in his pastoral robes. Oh, he was a handsome one all right, with his full head of white hair and his dignified manner, but this was Hutch's day, and Kendra's, and Opal meant to focus on them.

Settling in contentedly, Opal exchanged a mental high-five with the Lord. *We do good work, You and me,* she told Him silently. She looked over at the best man, Boone, standing beside Hutch and looking solemn. *Course we've still got* him *to straighten out, don't we, and sweet Tara, too, but we can cross Hutch and Kendra off our list, just like we did Slade and Joslyn. Another mission accomplished.*

Just then Walter caught Opal's eye. A small, mischievous smile tilted his mouth up at one side, and darned if that man didn't *wink* at her, right there in church, with him right up front in full view and holding the Holy Book in his hands.

Or did he?

After a moment, she wasn't sure whether he had or not. Had she imagined it?

The idea warmed her all over just the same, clear to the center of her being, but she didn't wink back, of course.

There was a proper way to go about things, after all, and anyway she was in no big hurry to reel Walter in and marry up with him. She liked him a lot and they'd even gone out fishing together a couple of times and talked and laughed so much they'd scared away all the trout. The Sunday after little Trace Barlow was christened, with Kendra and Hutch standing up as godparents, they'd gone to the Butter Biscuit for brunch together after church, she and Walter, and stayed until Ellie practically kicked them out so she could close the place promptly at two o'clock, as she always did on the Sabbath.

Yes, sir, things were looking real promising on the romance front, not just for Kendra and Hutch, but for her and Walter, too.

All she had to do now was wait and trust and let the Good Lord have His way, since He always knew best.

RAISING HER VEIL, Kendra bent, her eyes brimming with happy tears, and kissed Madison, her flower girl, soundly on the cheek. "Nervous?" she whispered. When the organist struck up the prelude, Madison would be the first member of the wedding party to walk up the aisle.

"No," Madison answered in a stage whisper, looking earnest in her blue silk dress with the ruffled skirt. "I'm getting a *daddy* today!"

The comment carried far enough to raise a gentle twitter of laughter from the pews nearby.

Then the organist sounded the first reverberating note and, on cue, Madison strolled down the aisle, a job she'd practiced tirelessly for several weeks by then, scattering pink and white rose petals as she went.

People crooned and smiled as she passed.

When she reached the front, she went right over to Hutch and tugged at his sleeve with her free hand, holding the now-empty flower basket in the other.

He leaned down and she whispered something in his ear, and he grinned at her and pointed out the place where she was supposed to stand.

The prelude continued, picking up speed, and Tara followed Madison's trail of rose petals, looking fabulous in the soft yellow dress she'd chosen herself. Joslyn, like Madison, wore blue—Kendra hadn't wanted to impose any specific fashion statement on her friends.

Joslyn reached back, gave Kendra's hand a quick squeeze, exchanged glances with Slade and moved gracefully between the two rows of pews, coming to stand next to Tara.

"This is it," Slade whispered to Kendra as she took her arm. "Ready?"

"Ready," she replied, clutching her bouquet of zinnias and daisies and drawing a deep breath.

The wedding march began, but before Slade and Kendra could take the first step, Hutch left the platform and started toward her.

A hush fell over the guests and the music dropped away, one jumbled note on top of another, into silence.

Kendra held her breath as she watched Hutch approach. He looked impossibly handsome in the tux he'd reluctantly agreed to wear, just for today, and love welled up inside her.

Reaching her, he smiled and offered her his arm.

"I'll take it from here," he told Slade, who grinned and shook his head as he stepped aside.

The congregation let out their collective breath, and the music started again, faltering at first and then filling the little sanctuary to its walls in a joyous flood of sound.

Hutch and Kendra walked arm in arm to the front of the church and stood together before the pastor.

They'd written their own vows, though they hadn't shared them with each other, and Kendra was so overcome with joy and with love for the man standing beside her that she was sure the carefully prepared words had slipped her mind forever. She'd have to wing it, she supposed, but that was all right.

Hutch spoke first, turning to Kendra, taking her hands in his, holding her gaze through the billowing softness of her bridal veil.

"Sometimes," he began, his voice husky but strong, "a man is lucky enough to get a second chance, whether he deserves one or not, and that's what's happened to me. I love you, Kendra. I always have and I always will. I'll be faithful to you and I'll listen to you. I'll protect you and provide for you, and—"

"You'll be my daddy!" Madison piped up, beaming.

That brought on more laughter and a smattering of applause.

Hutch slanted a look at the little girl, grinned and confirmed in a clear voice, "And I'll be your daddy." He paused, asked amicably, "Do you have anything else to say, shortstop, or can we get on with this?"

Madison considered for a moment, finally shook her head, curls flying, and chimed, "No, that's everything!"

The whole congregation chuckled.

Hutch turned back to Kendra and finished his vows.

Kendra swallowed, looking up at his face, loving him with all she had and all she was and would ever be. "I love you, Hutch Carmody," she began, never taking her eyes from his. "I'll be your friend and your partner, as well as your wife, from this day forward, in good times and bad and everything in between. I'll be the best mother I can to Madison and to all the other children I hope we'll have together, and I promise to trust you, always, and to be worthy of your trust in return."

When she'd finished, there was a short silence, during which she and Hutch simply looked at each other, exchanging further vows, silent ones, deeper ones, ones that went far beyond words.

Dr. Beaumont asked them the usual questions then, and they answered with "I do," and slipped wedding bands onto each other's ring fingers.

Finally, in a booming voice of jubilant authority, the minister pronounced them man and wife.

"You may kiss the bride," he added, pretending it was an afterthought, though by then Hutch had already raised Kendra's veil, smoothed it back away from her face and covered her mouth with his own.

The organ soared back to life.

The congregation rose as one, cheering and clapping.

Madison dropped her flower basket, rushed over and

wriggled in between Kendra and Hutch, and they each took her by the hand, walking back down the aisle together, a family.

THE RECEPTION, HELD IN the community center, took the better part of forever to go by, as far as Hutch was concerned. There were endless pictures to pose for, hands to shake, a big, fancy cake to cut into. There was food and music and enough presents to fill the back of a semitruck.

Hutch enjoyed the festivities, but he was ready for the honeymoon to start, and he knew Kendra was, too. For various reasons, they'd decided to not have sex again until after the wedding, and they'd stuck to the plan—not an easy matter and now that the finish line was in sight, he wanted to cross it.

They'd be staying on the ranch instead of going on a trip, with Madison spending the first night at the Barlows' place with Opal, who'd just moved back there, and of course, Shea, Madison's own personal teen idol.

The time passed like molasses in January, as the old saying went.

They danced, he and Kendra, and holding her close was sweet torment.

"I can't wait to get you alone, Mrs. Carmody," he whispered in her ear.

"You'll *have* to wait, Mr. Carmody," she teased.

Another hour went by before Kendra agreed to slip away. They said goodbye to Madison, who was on the piano bench beside Shea, learning to play the bass part of "Heart and Soul," and dismissed them with a happy grin and "See you tomorrow!"

The new truck was waiting outside, decorated from

front to back with streamers, streaks of shaving cream, and all manner of other stuff, including a big, hand-lettered sign that read Just Married.

He hoisted Kendra into the passenger seat, taking what seemed like an extra five minutes to stuff the skirts of that big dress in behind her. She laughed the whole time.

What a sight they must make, Hutch thought, getting in on the driver's side, him in a tux, and Kendra in all that lace and silk, leaving their wedding in a pickup truck.

Eager as he was to get home to the ranch house and be alone with his bride, to unwrap her from that fancy gown and everything underneath it, he was struck dumb for a long moment, just to look at her.

She was so unbelievably, impossibly beautiful.

And she was his.

Peering out of the billows of white surrounding her, she laughed again, maybe at his expression and maybe for sheer joy.

"I feel like a giant cupcake," she said.

He cocked a grin at her before starting up the truck. "Good enough to eat," he replied, driving away from the church.

When they got home, the house was lit up, even though the afternoon was still bright with sunshine. The night before, he and Slade and Boone had spent hours putting up strings of white Christmas lights, and the whole place twinkled.

Hutch parked the truck near the front gate, got out and came around to lift Kendra off the passenger seat.

He didn't set her down, but looked straight into her eyes and said, "Welcome home, Mrs. Carmody."

Her eyes filled with tears, causing her mascara to run a little. "I love you," she said. "So, so much."

He replied in kind and kissed her to seal the bargain.

Getting the gate open with an armload of woman and wedding dress was tricky, but Hutch managed it, carried Kendra up the walk and the porch steps and over the threshold to boot. Leviticus was right there to greet them, though he soon lost interest and wandered off into some other part of the house.

In the foyer, he set her on her feet, pretending to be winded by the effort of lugging her that far.

She smiled, picked up her voluminous skirts and started up the stairs, looking back at him over one shoulder. She knew where the master bedroom was—he'd shown it to her, along with the rest of that big and formerly empty house—but today was different. Today, and tonight, and every night that followed, they could make use of it.

"Aren't you going to help me out of this dress?" she asked coyly.

"It's the least I can do," Hutch answered, then he bolted up the stairs after her, undoing his tie as he went, shrugging out of his tuxedo jacket and leaving it behind on the rail of the landing.

His cummerbund went next and, by the time he caught up with Kendra inside the bedroom, he was undoing his cuff links.

Kendra, a vision in white, stood looking around, taking in the antique four-poster bed, the old-fashioned fireplace, the built-in bookshelves, bare at the moment because Hutch had been sleeping in a room down the hall since he was younger than Madison was now.

She moved to the mantel, ran her hand along the

face of it, turned to him. "Our room," she said very softly, almost reverently. "The place where our babies will be conceived."

Hutch watched her, etching her image into his mind so he could remember, years and years from now, when they were an old married couple, how she'd looked at this moment. "Some of them," he agreed. "I plan on making love to you in plenty of other places, too."

Kendra came to him, stood on tiptoe, and kissed him lightly on the mouth. "This will do for a start, though," she said with mischief in her eyes. Then she turned, indicating the long row of tiny buttons on the back of her dress with a gesture of one hand.

Hutch began the slow, delicious process of unbuttoning Kendra's wedding gown. He fumbled a little, now and then—what was the point of making buttons that small when a man had big fingers?—but he finally got the thing open, and she stepped out of it, draped it carefully over the chair in front of the fireplace. It looked like a fallen cloud, resting there.

"Madison will wear this dress someday," Kendra said. "And maybe other daughters, too."

The thought warmed Hutch's heart, but it was soon gone. At the moment, he wasn't thinking long-term, he was thinking right now.

Even without the gown, Kendra was still wearing a lot of gear—a big, lacy petticoat-type thing, and a camisole with a bra underneath it. She kicked off her satin shoes and shed the petticoat, unfastened her stockings from the sexy garters that held them up, bared her legs and stood there in panties and the camisole, looking like an angel trying to pass as a pinup girl.

For a moment, he couldn't speak.

She walked over to him, unbuttoned his shirt, pulled it out of his pants. "Do I have to do all the undressing around here?" she asked.

He shook his head, pulled her close and kissed her again, deeply this time, thoroughly, holding nothing back. She wrapped her arms around his neck, pressed her warm softness against him and kissed him back.

He groaned, consuming her, unable to get enough.

At some point, they both got naked, though Hutch was too far gone by that point to say when it happened. He lifted Kendra in his arms, carried her to the bed and laid her down.

"No foreplay this time," she whispered, gazing up at him with sultry eyes and a wicked little smile. "I want you inside me, Hutch. It's been too long since we were together—like this—"

"No rush," he ground out. "We've got all the time in the world." He kissed her mouth, her neck, found her nipple and took it into his mouth. "All the time in the world," he repeated, using his tongue.

Fire shot through Kendra as Hutch took his sweet time at her breast, caressing her all the while running a hand over her other breast, down her side, across her belly to the place where her passions lived.

She whimpered, giving herself up to pleasure. There would be no hurrying this husband of hers—he believed in taking her by inches, by *millimeters,* a touch, a kiss, a teasing brush of his fingertips at a time.

Her voice was ragged when she said his name, rose to a low shout when he put his head between her legs and took her into his mouth.

He suckled until she was near the breaking point

and then withdrew to nibble at the insides of her thighs, even the backs of her knees.

Her breath came deep and fast, and she commanded him to *take her,* damn it, but he only took her into his mouth again, and alternately sucked on her and teased her with his tongue.

Kendra's hips began to rise and fall, faster and faster, and she plunged her fingers into Hutch's hair, holding him to her even as she pleaded to be taken.

She was on the verge, whispering, "Don't stop—oh, God, don't stop—" when the eruption finally came. She exploded against an inner sky, like fireworks, and dissolved into flaming sparks that took a long time to fall.

By the time she'd settled back into herself, Hutch was poised above her on the bed, his forearms braced against the mattress on either side of her still-quivering, exquisitely sated body.

He moved inside her, slowly that first time, throwing his head back as he reached her depths.

Instantly, she needed him again and more desperately than before. This time, however, he didn't hold back, but gave her all of himself, one long, hard thrust following another.

Kendra found the ever-rising ecstasy almost more than she could bear. She tossed her head from side to side on the pillow, and their bodies collided, again and again, until they reached the same pinnacle at the same moment. Hutch went still, deep inside her, and she felt the surging warmth of him.

This time, there was no condom.

They'd wasted enough time and both of them wanted a baby.

When it was over, he collapsed beside her, one leg sprawled across her thighs, his breathing ragged.

A long time passed before either of them spoke.

"What is it with you and foreplay?" Kendra asked, her head resting on his shoulder.

He chuckled. "Get used to it," he said, kissing her temple. "Some things shouldn't be hurried, and making love to you is one of them."

She made a slow circle on the taut, washboard flesh of his belly with the fingertips of her right hand. "Really?" she purred. Then she closed her fingers around him, and he groaned, instantly hard again.

"Woman," he gasped, "you are playing with fire."

She worked him harder, faster, but gently, too. "Am I?"

He pulsed against her palm, huge and hot, and gave a raspy moan.

Then, in a heartbeat, he was on top of her.

She looked up into his eyes, batted her lashes, and said, "But what about the foreplay?"

"You win," he rasped, and then he possessed her in one hard, driving thrust.

HOURS LATER, DOWNSTAIRS in the dimly lit kitchen—Hutch wearing jeans and nothing else, Kendra in one of his T-shirts, happier than she'd ever imagined it was possible to be—they nibbled at the lasagna Opal had thoughtfully prepared and left in the refrigerator. Leviticus, recently fed, snoozed nearby on his dog bed.

"I guess this isn't much of a honeymoon," Hutch fretted, sitting across from her, his hair love-rumpled and his golden beard coming in with the twilight.

"Maybe we should have gone to Vegas or Hawaii or something."

Kendra grinned at him. "No complaints here, cowboy," she said. "We can take trips later. Right now, we've got a lot of settling in to do."

Hutch looked relieved, and the expression in his eyes made Kendra wonder how she'd ever doubted that they belonged together, for always.

They ate what they could, both of them starved and at the same time too riled up to eat much. They'd showered together and made love under the spray, and while Kendra's body still throbbed with aftershocks from the powerful releases he'd brought her to, she wanted more, and she knew Hutch did, too.

"Think we made a baby today?" he asked.

Kendra moved her shoulders in a little shrug. "All we can do is keep trying," she said.

He laughed, reached out, closed his hand briefly over hers. "I have something for you," he told her, turning serious all of a sudden.

"I hope so," she vamped, making eyes at him.

"Besides that," he said, after a raspy chuckle. He stood up, disappeared into his office off the kitchen and returned with a thick packet in one hand.

Kendra frowned, a little unnerved. They hadn't signed, or even discussed, a prenuptial agreement but now, it seemed, he'd reconsidered the idea. Did he really think she'd demand half of Whisper Creek Ranch if, God forbid, they parted ways before one of them died?

"What's this?" she asked warily.

He smiled, reading her trepidation accurately, the way he so often did. "It's a deed," he said. "Maggie Landers drew it up."

Kendra's hands trembled as she opened the document, scanned the legalese and made the startling discovery that she was *already* half owner of the ranch. All that was required was a notarized signature.

"I don't understand," she confessed. "This ranch means everything to you—"

"And so do you," Hutch finished huskily when her words fell away. "This ranch is *me,* Kendra—as much a part of me as my arms and legs and my heart. I'd do just about anything to keep it. But if you divorced me tomorrow, well, so be it, you'd still be half owner of Whisper Creek."

Kendra was overcome, touched to the tenderest part of her soul. Hutch wasn't just giving her his love, but his complete trust. He was staking everything he held dear on their marriage, their commitment to each other and to a lifetime as man and wife.

She held the document to her heart for a moment, not because of what it offered but because of what it *meant,* and then she set it down on the table between them.

"I'm going back upstairs, now," she announced. "Coming?"

Hutch laughed and scooted back his chair to rise. "Definitely," he said.

* * * * *

Look for Linda Lael Miller's next original novel,
AN OUTLAW'S CHRISTMAS,
on sale from Harlequin HQN Books
in October 2012 at your favorite retail outlet.